Spider

SHADOWLAND

Spider World

SHADOWLAND

Colin Wilson

HAMPTON ROADS
PUBLISHING COMPANY, INC.

Cover design by Grace Pedalino
Cover photograph by Grace Pedalino

Hampton Roads Publishing Company, Inc.
1125 Stoney Ridge Road
Charlottesville, VA 22902

434-296-2772
fax: 434-296-5096
e-mail: hrpc@hrpub.com
www.hrpub.com

Library of Congress Cataloging-in-Publication Data

Wilson, Colin, 1931-
  Spider world--Shadowland / Colin Wilson.
    p. cm. -- (Spider world ; v. 4)
  ISBN 1-57174-399-5 (acid-free paper)
  1. Spiders--Fiction. 2. Telepathy--Fiction. I. Title: Shadowland.
  II. Title.
  PR6073.I44 S625 2002
  823'.914--dc21
                                                      2002005688

If you are unable to order this book from your local bookseller, you may order
directly from the publisher.
Call 1-800-766-8009, toll-free.

ISBN 1-57174-399-5
10 9 8 7 6 5 4 3 2 1
Printed on acid-free paper in the United States

To Frank

Contents

Acknowledgments

My friend and editor, Frank DeMarco, should certainly be at the head of these acknowledgments.

Spider World was started in the early 1980s, and its first part, consisting of *The Tower* and *The Delta,* was published in two volumes. The publisher suggested a sequel, and I began *The Magician,* which was published in 1992. But I must admit that I felt myself beginning to flag, and decided to take a break before I launched myself on the conclusion of *The Magician, Shadowland.* I felt like someone who has just returned from a trip to the North Pole, and that I needed to recharge my batteries.

In fact, I became absorbed in the question of the age of the Sphinx, and found it a relief to write nonfiction. *From Atlantis to the Sphinx* was followed by *Alien Dawn,* a book on the problem of UFOs, followed by another study of the age of ancient civilization, *The Atlantis Blueprint.* When people asked me when I intended to finish *The Magician* I said: "Perhaps never." I was afraid the book had gone cold on me.

Then Frank DeMarco, who had published my *Rogue Messiahs* and *Books in My Life,* asked me if I felt like writing a fantasy novel in a new series he planned. I asked him if he had ever read *Spider World* and he said no. So I sent him the three volumes I had published so far. To my delight he liked it, and gave me the go-ahead.

After a decade, I felt a little nervous about returning to the world of the giant spiders, recalling my sense of flagging imagination. But I found that the well had refilled itself in the ten years since I had finished *The Magician,* and I was soon writing with all the old sense of not knowing what was going to happen next.

So in a very real sense, this is Frank DeMarco's book as much as mine. He has even encouraged me to brood actively on its sequel, *New Earth*.

This book also owes a great deal to my son-in-law Dr. Mike Dyer, an expert on wildlife conservation, to whom I turned whenever I wanted to know something about birds, animals, or fish.

I also feel I should again express my gratitude to Roald Dahl, who in 1975 said to me casually over dinner: "You ought to try writing a children's book."

Cornwall, March 2002

Introduction

Niall is born into a world dominated by gigantic telepathic spiders, who breed human beings for food. His family belongs to the small number of humans who are still free; they live in an underground cave in a waterless desert, continually on the alert for spiders who float overhead in silken balloons, probing the desert landscape with beams of willpower. Other humans live in an underground city called Dira on the shores of a dead sea. While visiting relatives there, Niall is captivated by the charms of the ruler's daughter Merlew. But when he overhears her referring to him as "that skinny boy" he decides not to accept her father's invitation to remain in Dira.

On the way home, Niall and his father take shelter from a sandstorm, and Niall finds a telescopic metal rod, a relic of the remote days when men ruled the Earth. By accident rather than skill or choice he uses it to kill a spider whose balloon has crashed in the storm. In doing so, he has committed an offense for which he and all his family could die a horrible death.

Soon after their return to the desert, while Niall is absent, their cave is discovered by spiders. Niall's father is killed and his family taken captive. Niall finds his father's body when he returns to the cave. In trying to follow the trail of his family, he also is captured and taken to the spider city. Upon his arrival he learns that all the inhabitants of Dira are also prisoners. Merlew's father, King Kazak, a natural survivor, has now entered the service of the spiders, and urges Niall to do the same. Rejecting the thought of betraying his fellow men, Niall flees to the white tower in the center of the city, and enters it with the aid of the telescopic rod. There he learns that it is a time capsule left by former men, and through a supercomputer called the Steegmaster, he learns the history of humanity on Earth. He also is presented with a device called the thought mirror, through which he can achieve a high degree of concentration.

On leaving the tower, Niall takes refuge in the slave quarter of the city, and is appointed overseer of a contingent of slaves, whom he leads to the nearby city of the bombardier beetles. The beetles, as intelligent as the spiders, love explosions, and Niall has arrived in time for one of their great annual celebrations, Boomday, organized by their chief explosives expert, Bill Doggins. But the festival culminates in disaster, destroying the complete stock of explosives. Niall agrees to lead Doggins to a disused barracks in the slave quarter, where they expect to find gunpowder.

They find more than that: Reapers, the deadliest weapon ever invented by man, which fire a beam of atomic energy. They use these to shoot their way out of an ambush by the spiders, and escape back to the city of the bombardier beetles in stolen spider balloons.

The ruler of the beetles, the Master, is furious that they have broken an ancient peace treaty, and is inclined to hand over Niall and Doggins to the spiders for punishment. Only the treachery of the Spider Lord, who decides to preempt the decision by trying to strangle Niall, leads the Master to decide to allow Niall to stay after all.

Nevertheless, Niall is dismayed by the Master's decision that all the Reapers should be destroyed—dashing all hopes of using them to free his fellow men. So Niall, Doggins, and a group of young men decide to travel to the Delta, perhaps the most dangerous place on Earth, because Niall has concluded that the Delta is the source of a powerful living vibration that is responsible for the abnormal growth of simple life-forms, including the spiders. His aim is to destroy this source, known to the spiders as the goddess Nuada.

The Delta proves to be even more dangerous than they expected; its perils include octopus-like plants that lurk just below the surface of the ground, and humanoid frogs that can spit a stream of poison. Niall and Doggins are the only ones to reach the heart of the Delta, and there they discover that the "goddess" is actually a gigantic plant that forms the summit of a mountain.

Since Doggins has been blinded, Niall is forced to press on alone. In the night that follows, in telepathic communion with the goddess, he learns that she is indeed the source of the giant life-forms. She came from a distant galaxy, transported to our solar system in the tail of the comet Opik, which came close to destroying the Earth.

Another long and dangerous journey brings Niall and Doggins back to the city of the beetles. There the Master agrees to the Death Lord's demand to hand him over. In a final confrontation, only the direct intervention of the goddess saves Niall from an appalling fate. But the "miracle" also convinces the Spider Council that Niall is the emissary of the goddess, and to his own bewilderment, he finds himself exalted to the rank of ruler of the spider city.

The Spider Lord agrees that there should henceforth be peace between human beings and spiders, and that they should regard one another as equals. However, many spiders secretly regard this treaty as a betrayal. Among these is Skorbo, a captain of the Spider Lord's guard, who—with six accomplices—continues to trap and eat human beings.

One snowy morning, Niall finds the dying Skorbo in a corner of the main square; he has been struck down by some tremendous blow. Following the trail of blood to the garden of a deserted house, Niall discovers that Skorbo has been the victim of an ingenious booby trap: a young palm tree had been bent to the ground and then released by cutting the rope that held it. Human footprints indicate that three men were involved in Skorbo's murder.

Concealed nearby, Niall finds the swollen corpse of a man who has died from spider venom; Skorbo apparently had succeeded in killing one of the "assassins."

In the roots of the palm tree, Niall has found a heavy metal disk, engraved with a birdlike symbol. When he returns to the garden, this disk has vanished. Niall deduces that it has been taken by one of the "assassins," and that they have been able to remain undetected in the spider city by masquerading as slaves. Niall is able to track one of the bogus slaves to a building used as a hospital. The man is subdued with the aid of a glue spider, but immediately kills himself.

The pale skin of the dead man suggests that he originated in some place where he has been deprived of light. With the aid of a "mind machine" in the white tower, Niall learns that Skorbo's killers came from some region beneath the Earth, and that its ruler, whom Niall calls "the Magician," is driven by a deep hatred of the spiders.

The third assassin also is tracked down, but proves to be already dead—an animated corpse.

After witnessing the execution of five of Skorbo's accomplices, and the banishment of one of them who refuses to submit, Niall discovers the whereabouts of Skorbo's "larder," where his paralyzed victims are hung like carcasses in a butcher's shop, awaiting their turn to be eaten. One of these is a girl, Charis, whose pale skin indicates that she is also from the underground realm of the Magician. Recognizing that Charis is his last clue to the whereabouts of the Magician, Niall decides to keep her in his palace until she can be restored to consciousness.

In the house that had been occupied by Skorbo's killers, Niall finds froglike talismans carved from green stone, and realizes that they emanate a malevolent force. A mat of some kind of seaweed proves to be the means by which the assassins were able to draw vital energy from the girl who accompanied them.

Niall learns that Skorbo had once been lost in the mountains to the north of the Great Wall, after a crash landing in his spider balloon. Niall begins to entertain the suspicion that there may have been some connection between Skorbo and the Magician, and that Skorbo's death may have been in revenge for some kind of treachery.

Niall's attempt to learn more about the Great Wall, and the Gray Mountains, is frustrated by the fact that the spiders are almost totally ignorant of their own history. Then he learns that the greatest of all spider warriors, Cheb the Mighty, is kept in a state of suspended animation by the vital energy of young spiders, and that Niall, as the ruler of the spider city, will be allowed to question Cheb.

A journey beneath the city leads him to the sacred cave; there young acolytes bring back the great spider warrior from the land of the dead. Cheb describes how the spiders first learned to make use of human servants, who regarded themselves as spiders rather than human beings, and how these psychological hybrids helped Cheb to enslave all the remaining humans. Niall then speaks with the spirit of Cheb's famous adviser, Qisib the Wise, and learns of the events that led to the building of the Great Wall.

Qisib tells of how Cheb's successor sent his human servant Madig to select a site for a new city in the Gray Mountains of the north. Madig, alone of all his party, returned with a message for the Spider Lord that the Gray Mountains were the territory of the Magician, who would destroy any invaders.

The Spider Lord was incensed—particularly when Madig died, apparently of a slow poison that had been administered by the Magician. An immense army of spiders and human foot soldiers marched north, but were destroyed by a gale and a flood in the deep valley known as the Valley of the Great Lake. The Spider Lord and his councilor Qisib alone survived. After this catastrophe Qisib supervised the building of a Great Wall in what is now known as the Valley of the Dead.

Niall has no doubt that the storm was caused by the powers of the Magician.

Qisib recounts Madig's own story of how his party was overwhelmed in the dark, blindfolded, and taken to some strange city, where the streets are silent and nobody speaks above a whisper. There, still blindfolded, Madig was ordered to carry a message to the Spider Lord, threatening him with destruction if he ventured into the Gray Mountains. Madig was told that if he did not return within thirty days, he would die and the other prisoners would suffer horrible deaths. Madig, of course, did not return, and died—as the Magician foretold—after thirty days.

When Niall returns from the sacred cave to his palace, he learns that his brother Veig, who has cut himself on the ax used to kill Skorbo, is dangerously ill. Grel, a young spider, detects the presence of some evil force in the palace. Niall tracks it down to his bedroom, where he has left one of the toadlike figurines that he found in the house of the assassins.

Niall destroys the force by cutting the figurine in two with an ax. But when the physician Simeon unites the two halves for a moment, the unknown force is able to destroy Charis, who was still lying unconscious in the next room.

After the destruction of the figurine, Veig seems to be recovering. But Grel points out that, like Madig, Veig has been touched by the evil power of the Magician, and will almost certainly die within thirty days.

Niall realizes that there is only one chance of saving his brother's life: he himself must make the dangerous journey to the underground city of the Magician.

PART ONE

Niall stood on the balcony that overlooked the main square, and stared out over the darkened city. The stars in the black sky looked very cold and bright. At this hour, everyone, including the spider population, was asleep. Following the habit of a lifetime, most of his fellow citizens fell asleep soon after dark, and the same force of habit made those who wandered abroad at night glance nervously over their shoulders, as if afraid of being caught and punished. It would take at least another generation for human beings to behave as if they were free and could go where they liked.

He also, he realized, had become a creature of habit. Although he had been in this city for less than six months, he already regarded it as his home, and the thought of having to set out on a long journey made his heart contract with anxiety.

There was a tap at the door, so light that he wondered if he had imagined it. Simeon peeped into the room.

"I wondered if you were asleep."

"No. I don't feel tired."

"Your mother doesn't want you to go alone."

"I know. I have told her it would be too dangerous to have companions."

"Even me?"

"Even you. I feel I have just about enough luck to last me for the journey. It might not be enough for two."

Simeon nodded. "I understand. Then why don't you allow a spider balloon to carry you to the Gray Mountains?"

"Again, it would be too dangerous. There are eyes watching this city, and a spider balloon would be too obvious."

Simeon said: "Then how do you propose to leave the city without being noticed?"

"By traveling underground."

"Underground?" Simeon looked at him as if he doubted his sanity.

"There are underground tunnels beneath this city. They may have been made by men in the days before they were conquered by the spiders—perhaps as an escape route in case they were invaded."

"You learned this in the white tower?"

"No. From the spiders themselves."

But as he was about to tell Simeon about his journey beneath the city, he experienced a sudden sense of caution. It would involve telling Simeon about the sacred cave, and he knew intuitively that this was the most precious secret of the spiders, and should not be discussed with another human being—even as intimate a friend as Simeon.

Instead, he said: "I learned something else. Did you know that there is a river beneath this city?"

Simeon shook his head in bewilderment.

"Are you sure?"

"I have seen it."

"Where does it come out?"

"I don't know. Probably somewhere to the east."

Simeon digested this in silence, then said: "And do you know where to find the kingdom of the Magician?"

"I know only one thing—that it is to the north of the Great Wall, in the Gray Mountains."

"It could be a thousand miles to the north."

"No. Have you heard of Madig, the servant of Kasib the Warrior?"

Simeon shook his head.

"Madig led an expedition to the Gray Mountains, and was captured by servants of the Magician. He was taken to some underground city where people spoke in whispers. . . ."

Simeon said: "It is called Shadowland."

Niall said eagerly: "You know about it?"

"It is a legend among the beetles."

"What do they say?"

"Only that it is an underground kingdom in the north. They believe it is far away—hundreds of miles."

Niall shook his head. "No, that cannot be so. For when the Magician released Madig, he told him to return in a month, or his companions would forfeit their lives. If Madig could make the journey there and back in a month, Shadowland cannot be a thousand miles away. A man on foot can only travel twenty or thirty miles a day—not much more than three hundred miles in two weeks. You agree?"

Before Simeon could reply, there was a knock at the door. It was Nephtys, the commander of Niall's personal guard. She said: "Captain Sidonia is here, highness."

"Thank you. Take her in to my brother—I will come in a moment."

Simeon asked: "Sidonia? The captain of the Spider Lord's guard?"

"I sent for her. I think she might be able to help Veig."

Simeon frowned. "How?"

"Sidonia is fond of Veig."

Simeon smiled. "So are a lot of other ladies around here."

"Good. The more the better."

Simeon was puzzled. "I don't follow you."

Niall said: "Sidonia has plenty of courage and energy."

"Yes." Simeon had seen her risk her life by driving her shortsword into the stomach of a bull spider that was threatening Niall.

"Then don't you think she might be able to convey some of it to Veig?"

"How?"

"Simply by wanting to—perhaps laying her hands on him."

Simeon's wrinkled brow revealed he was unable to understand what Niall was talking about.

"Don't you believe that people can give energy to those they love?"

"I've heard my daughter say so. But I think that's only a manner of speaking."

Niall was disappointed. Simeon obviously found the idea absurd. As a physician he was pragmatic and skeptical. But Niall had seen the young spiders transferring their vital energy to Cheb the Mighty and Qisib the Wise, and knew that it could be done.

"Where is your daughter?"

"She's at home."

"Here, in the spider city?"

"Yes."

Since he had become a member of the Council of Free Men, Simeon had taken over the ground floor of an empty building not far from the square; it saved the daily journey back to the city of the bombardier beetles.

"Could you bring her here? Will she still be awake?"

"Probably. She often waits up for me."

As Simeon was leaving, Niall realized that Sidonia was waiting outside the door. Niall was surprised to see her; he had assumed she would wait down in the hall. As usual, she was standing to attention, her eyes in front of her so she looked like a statue.

He said: "At ease." She allowed her eyes to focus on him. "You know my brother is sick?"

"No, sire." He was probing her mind, and felt her concern. Like most of the women with whom his brother had been involved, she obviously continued to feel a certain affection for him.

He said: "He is suffering from some illness that is draining his energy. Come with me."

He led her downstairs and across the courtyard to his brother's quarters. The room was empty except for Veig, who was asleep, his arm outflung, and his maid Crestia, a slight, blond girl who was sitting by the bed, looking pale and tense. She jumped to her feet, for both Niall and Sidonia were her superiors. Niall gestured for her to sit down.

There was no need to probe Sidonia's mind to sense her anxiety as she looked down at Veig. It struck Niall as odd that a girl with such a high level of self-discipline that she seemed little more than a robot should feel so deeply about his brother.

He asked: "Is he hot?"

She sat on the bed and placed her hand on Veig's forehead.

"Yes."

"Do you know how to take away his fever?"

"No."

"Put your other hand on his solar plexus."

She looked puzzled; her education had not encompassed such anatomical terms. Niall pulled back the bedclothes; his brother was naked. The chest and belly were covered with curly hair that was damp with sweat. Niall took Sidonia's right hand and placed it on Veig's solar plexus. As she sat there, unsure of what he wanted, Niall placed his own hands on hers, then breathed deeply, and allowed himself to sink into a state of deep relaxation. When he was calm enough, his feelings and sensations blended with those of his brother, and he began to feel heat and discomfort. He was interested to observe that Sidonia also followed him into deep relaxation, obeying his thought impulses as if they shared the same body.

Now he began to try to soothe Veig's fever as though it were his own. To begin with, this seemed to have no effect; on the contrary, the fever seemed to burn more fiercely. Then, slowly, he began to respond, as if Niall—and Sidonia—were whispering words that relieved his anxiety, and he was listening to them.

Suddenly, Crestia reached out and laid her hands on Veig. Although unconscious, Veig responded to her, as if his attention had been drawn to someone else who had walked into the room. Then he seemed to recognize her and relax.

What was happening to Niall was what had happened when he had given energy to the girl in the hospital, and to Charis, the girl who had accompanied the assassins from Shadowland. He was giving energy exactly as he might have given a blood transfusion. Veig absorbed this energy as naturally as he absorbed the vitality that flowed from Sidonia and Crestia. As he did so, his fever disappeared, and he sank into a normal sleep.

For a few minutes more, the three of them sat there, suddenly aware of one another. Niall was interested to observe that they seemed to be sharing the same body, or rather that he was as aware of the women's bodies as he was of his own. In that moment, he realized why Veig found the opposite sex so appealing. Holding them in his arms was simply a first step toward this mutual exchange of energy.

This was also the reason that the energies that flowed from Sidonia and Crestia were more satisfying to Veig than Niall's; it had the opposite polarity.

A light tap on the door made them all start. It was Simeon, followed by a woman whose yellow hair flowed over her shoulders. Niall judged her age to be about thirty.

Simeon said: "This is my daughter Leda."

She had an oval face with firm lips, and serene gray eyes. Unlike the women of the spider city, her profile was not perfect, and on this account was more interesting. Niall felt immediately that he had known her for many years. He was glad that she made no move to curtsy or otherwise show respect to him as the ruler.

She asked: "How is the invalid?"

"Feeling a little better."

She sat down on the far side of the bed. As he watched her capable brown fingers taking Veig's pulse, Niall felt his brother was in good hands. He noticed that, even after taking Veig's pulse, she continued to hold his wrist, as if tuning in to his physical state. She finally laid his wrist on the coverlet.

"He is still very ill."

"But he was worse before you came. He was in a fever."

She seemed to understand immediately. "And you took it away?"

"All three of us."

"Then your brother is in good hands."

Niall said: "Can you answer me a question?"

"I'll try."

"If we can take away his fever, why can we not cure him completely?"

Simeon interrupted: "Because his blood is full of tiny parasites like leeches." All this talk about healing evidently made him uncomfortable.

Leda said: "But that is not the only reason. I sense that there is more to it than that."

"What?"

"I don't know. Some kind of hostile force. But it may be possible to neutralize it."

Niall felt a tingle of hope. "How?"

"In this house you have a room with trees in it?"

Niall stared at her in bewilderment.

"Trees? You mean real trees?" For a moment he thought she must be talking of a painting or mural.

"Yes."

He shook his head. "There is no such room."

The maid Crestia said: "Yes there is." They all stared at her.

She said: "It is part of the cellar. I can show you."

She took a pressure lamp and pumped it until it glowed fiercely; Niall took another. The others took oil lamps from their wall niches.

As they followed Crestia across the upper courtyard and into the palace, Niall tried to guess what she had in mind. He was sure he knew every room in the building, from attic to cellar. In any case, how could trees grow in a room?

Crestia led the way across the hall and down the cellar steps. The great stone-flagged room had a pleasant smell of stored food: apples, hams, spices, as well as fermenting mead and cider. Game hung from hooks on the beam. Crestia went on through a small door in the corner, which led into a lumber room full of broken furniture and moldering curtains. Niall had glanced into it on several occasions, but since there seemed to be no exit, had not bothered to explore it. Now Crestia picked her way among broken wardrobes, cracked mirrors, and armchairs with springs sticking out, stirring the dust so it made them sneeze. In the far corner of the room, behind a rickety wardrobe, was a small door, held by two drawn bolts. When Crestia pulled these back and tugged open the creaking door—with some help from Simeon—a smell of fresh air blew in.

Crestia raised her lamp to reveal a chamber that obviously had been a stable at some remote time in its history, and still had horse stalls; harnesses of old, cracked leather hung on the walls, which were built of unplaned wood. The single window was broken, and the floor was made of trampled earth. The stable obviously had been added to the outer wall of the building, and from its floor, roughly six feet apart, grew two trees, each about two feet thick, whose upper halves vanished through holes in the ceiling.

The door was made of rough planks, and when Niall raised the wooden latch, he found himself looking into a small courtyard of whose existence he had been unaware.

Leda was caressing the rough gray bark of one of the trees. She said: "These are abolia trees, whose wood is as hard as oak or mahogany. They grow in the Delta. I would advise you to move your brother's bed between them."

Niall accepted her advice without question. Sidonia was dispatched to the hospital to commandeer two porters with a stretcher, and Veig was transferred to it. Niall directed two of the house servants to dismantle Veig's bed, which was held together by wooden pegs, and it was carried down to the stable and reassembled. Veig was sleeping so deeply that even the hammering when the pegs were loosened failed to wake him.

Niall's mother, Siris, had been awakened by all the activity, and she watched as Veig was replaced in his bed between the two trees. She bent over her son and placed her hands on his forehead. Like Niall, she possessed certain telepathic abilities, particularly where her children were concerned. Her face broke into a smile of relief.

"His fever is almost gone."

As Niall sat on a stool on the other side of the bed and placed his hands on Veig's forehead, he was immediately aware that his mother's diagnosis was too optimistic. Veig's blood still burned with a fever that was like poison. But at least his condition now seemed stable. And as he focused his attention to a deeper level, he became aware that the trees at either end of the bed were, in fact, exercising a soothing influence. They were like a cool breeze blowing through a window. This breeze was a form of vitality, the distinctive vibration of the goddess. On a spider, the effect would have been a slow trickle of energy that would have cured sickness. The flesh of humans was on too high a level to be recharged by this vitality, yet its effect was nevertheless restorative, like soft music. When the dawn came, with its surge of energy, the effect would be even stronger.

At least it was a relief that Veig was in good hands. It meant that Niall could set out on his journey without the same burden of tension and anxiety.

He looked at Sidonia and Crestia, who were standing side by side.

"You must take special care of my brother. And if you become over-tired, then try to find others who can help."

They understood what he meant—that there must be at least half a dozen other young women who had shared Veig's favors.

Crestia asked timidly: "Does my lord intend to . . ."

Before she could finish, Niall raised his finger to his lips. It was impor-tant that as few as possible knew about his intended journey. Crestia blushed as she realized how close she had come to committing an indis-cretion—the servants and stretcher bearers were still in the room—and Niall observed with interest that Sidonia also blushed. This meant that they had established a community of sensation that could only benefit their patient.

Niall turned to the serving men.

"Thank you for your help. You can go." The men shuffled off awk-wardly, unaccustomed to being treated with courtesy. Niall beckoned to Simeon as he followed them.

"I need your advice."

"Gladly."

Niall was silent until they were crossing the main hallway. When he was sure they could not be overheard he said: "You see the problem? As soon as I leave the city, the news will spread, until it is overheard by the spies of the Magician. What can we do?"

Simeon shrugged. "If you think it's all that dangerous, then don't go alone."

"We've been through all that." Niall made an effort to keep the impa-tience out of his voice. "I have to travel alone." Earlier in the evening, Simeon had tried hard to persuade Niall to allow him to go with him. "But how do you think I can I make people think I'm still in the city?"

"We could say that you have to stay in your apartments. You could be suffering from some fever that you caught in the Delta."

Niall thought about it. "Yes, I suppose that might work." He shook his head. "But I'd need to be seen now and then. Suppose we could find someone who looked like me, and who could wear my clothes . . ."

They had arrived outside Niall's apartment. The door opened; Jarita, his personal servant, had heard them coming.

Niall said: "I told you to go to bed."

"I thought you might need something."

"No thank you, Jarita." From the main room, he could see through his open bedroom door, and that a gray pack lay on his bed. "What is that?"

"Your mother brought it. It is for your journey."

Niall exchanged glances with Simeon.

"How did you know I was going on a journey?"

"Your mother said so."

Simeon took her chin between his forefinger and thumb and looked into her eyes.

"No one else must know about this. It is a secret."

She nodded. Niall was glad Simeon had spoken; she regarded him with a kind of awe—since his injections had revived the paralyzed victims of spider venom, word had spread around the city that he was a sorcerer.

Niall examined the pack on his bed. It was made of a thick cloth that was surprisingly stiff to the fingers, and had shoulder straps and a leather drawstring; it contained food in a waterproof cloth coated with spider silk, and a flask of drink, as well as a folding knife and matches. In a side pocket there was a small wooden box, which he recognized; it contained food tablets, which had been given to him on his first visit to the white tower, in the days when he had been a fugitive. There was also a silvery metal tube, about six inches long and an inch wide; this, he knew, held a lightweight garment, developed by men of the twenty-first century for space travelers. His mother evidently had kept these relics of former days. A waterproof pouch with a drawstring contained a watch manufactured in the city of the bombardier beetles, and a smaller pouch contained a compass.

On the back of his bedside chair was a gray cloak of a silky, waterproof material, lined with the soft wool of dwarf mountain sheep.

Simeon stood beside him.

"So your mother knew you were going on a journey?"

Niall nodded. "She can read my thoughts—Veig's too. If we want to communicate with her when we are traveling, we think of her at sunset or sunrise, and it is as if she is there with us."

"Have you ever tried to see her?"

"No. What would be the point? It is enough know she can hear us."

Simeon led the way into the dining room; Jarita had left out food and drink on the table, and Simeon helped himself to a glass of a light golden mead that sparkled in the lamplight.

"When my daughter is away from me, she can make me see her."

"How?"

"Have you ever heard of making the spirit walk?"

"No."

"It is the power to appear to someone when you are not present."

"Ah, yes." Niall suddenly understood. "I have done that."

Simeon looked at him in surprise. "You've done it?"

"It was when I first went into the white tower." Simeon was one of the few people to whom Niall had described his experiences in the white tower. "I had run away from Kazak's palace. The old man told me to close my eyes, and suddenly I was back in the palace with Kazak and my mother."

"And what happened?"

"I tried to speak, and suddenly I was back in the white tower."

"So you wouldn't know how to do it again?"

He shook his head. "I didn't do it. The old man did it. But I don't know how."

Simeon said: "My daughter knows how."

"Has she told you how to do it?"

"No. But she can explain it to you. I have sent Jarita to fetch her."

Niall poured himself some of the mead, then changed his mind; it would only make him sleepy.

"Can you do it?"

"No."

"Then I certainly can't."

"You may be wrong. Speaking to your mother when she is not present is already a way of making the spirit walk."

"Yes, I suppose it is. . . ." But he was not convinced.

When Leda joined them, she refused the mead that Simeon offered her, and poured herself water. She seemed to read the question in Niall's mind.

"Your brother is asleep, and your mother is watching beside him."

"Good." He asked something else that had been puzzling him. "Why do you think that room was built around the two trees?"

"Probably to heal the sick. It would also be good for horses kept in the stable."

Simeon said: "He wants to know about making the spirit walk."

She asked Niall: "You want to learn how to do it?"

Niall was about to disclaim the idea; but something in the gaze of her calm gray eyes made him change his mind.

"Yes."

She took his hands, turned the palms upward, and stared at them.

"You should be able to. You have a strong line of imagination."

"Imagination?"

"It depends on the visual imagination."

He found this baffling, so said nothing.

"Where do you want to send your spirit?"

"I'll show you." He stood up and led her into the next room, with the balcony that overlooked the square. He pointed to the balcony. "There."

"You want to be seen there?" She had a pleasingly quick intelligence. Niall was glad that he did not have to explain his motives at length.

"Yes. But what do I have to do?"

She said: "Let me explain how it first happened to me. I was away from home, attending to my sister, who was sick. I had left my father alone, and after a few weeks I became very homesick. And one night, I was sitting in my room, wondering what they were doing, and I began to think about the room at home, and suddenly I felt that I could actually see it, with children sitting around the table, and my father carrying a dish of yams. Then he looked straight at me, and looked startled. . . ."

Simeon laughed. "I almost dropped the yams."

Leda said: "Then I was back in my sister's home. But I knew something had happened. And when I got back home, my father and the children all said they had seen me. Then I knew I could do it."

Niall asked Simeon: "You could see her clearly?"

"As clear as I can see her now. I thought she had come home. Then she disappeared."

Niall asked: "Can anyone do it?"

"If they really want to."

"But how?" Although Niall believed her, he doubted his own ability to learn it.

She said: "Close your eyes." He did as she asked. "Now try to imagine this room you are sitting in. You know it well. Can you tell me the color of the walls? Keep your eyes closed."

Niall said hesitantly: "A kind of yellow?"

"Open your eyes and look at them." Niall saw immediately that they were blue. "Close your eyes again. There is a table with a plant pot. Point to it." Niall pointed across the room. "Now open your eyes." Niall saw that his pointing finger was missing the table by six feet.

Leda said: "How can you visualize the room if you can't remember it? If you want to make the spirit walk, you must look at it until you can remember every detail."

"That is difficult when I am tired. . . ." But as he spoke, he was struck by a sudden thought. "But I think I may have the answer."

He went into his bedroom and opened a drawer. Hidden underneath his clothes there was a gold-colored disk, nearly circular in shape, on a fine metal chain. He showed it to Leda on the palm of his hand.

"This is the thought mirror. I was given it in the white tower."

She made no attempt to touch it.

"What does it do?"

"It focuses the mind. The first time I used it, I memorized a map in a few minutes."

He placed it around his neck, inside the open neck of his tunic, so it was just above the solar plexus. The convex side rested against his flesh.

He said: "Now I will use it to memorize the room." He reached into his tunic and turned it over.

He had forgotten how painful it could be when the mind was tired. His heart seemed to contract, and began to beat faster, as if he had been suddenly plunged into cold water.

"Does it hurt?"

He nodded. "A little."

After a few moments he adjusted to the sensation. Everything in the room looked more sharp and clear. The lamplight seemed to be reflected off more surfaces than before, although he was aware that it was simply his senses that had intensified.

He looked carefully around the room, registering everything in it. It was unnecessary to make an effort. This was far easier than memorizing the map of the city; he had merely to memorize a few objects and their relation to one another. It took only a few seconds.

He said: "I have done it. What now?"

"Now go to another room, and try to visualize this room. Turn off the light if it makes it easier."

But in his bedroom it was unnecessary to turn off the light. As soon as he closed his eyes, and conjured up the other room, it was as if he was there. Every detail was present in his mind. Yet he was aware that he was still in his bedroom, simply visualizing the room he just left. It was oddly frustrating. He was aware he was doing something wrong.

Then he recalled the previous occasion when this had happened, in the white tower. The old man had told him to close his eyes. And a moment later, he had found himself in a room in Kazak's palace. The old man had somehow transported him there.

Yet the old man was merely a computer simulation. Therefore it followed that Niall had somehow transported himself. The power lay in his own mind.

As soon as he recognized this, it happened. Suddenly he was standing in the room with Simeon and Leda, close enough to touch them. He could actually feel the night breeze blowing from the balcony. His body seemed normal and solid, and he felt that if he wanted to, he could pull back the curtains that led to the balcony, or open the doors.

Leda and Simeon were talking, and had not yet seen him. Leda was the first to realize he was in the room. She stared at him quizzically for a moment, then reached out to touch him. Her hand went through his arm. She said: "You did it."

Niall smiled and nodded, but decided not to try to speak. Last time he had done that, he had found himself back in his body. Even now, he could feel an odd sensation, as if his body was trying to tug him back. He was about to give way to this when Leda said: "Wait." She obviously was aware of what he was feeling. She walked past him, and pulled back the half-open curtains of the balcony. Beyond them, the doors were open.

She said: "Since you are not in your body, you are not bound by gravity. Why don't you walk in the air?"

Although she was speaking the words, it seemed to Niall that she was conveying them directly into his mind, as the spiders did. He knew immediately that what she said was possible. Without hesitation he stepped onto the balustrade of the balcony, then took another step forward. Instead of falling, he found himself standing in the air, looking down at the pavement below. Then he allowed himself to obey the tug of his body. A moment later, he was sitting on his bed.

He reached inside his shirt and turned the thought mirror the other way; the relief was immediate. Then he went out of his bedroom and into the other room. All his tiredness had vanished.

Niall took Leda's hand: "Thank you."

She smiled. "You see, all human beings can make the soul walk."

Simeon grunted. "I'd rather keep mine in my body."

Leda said: "If you intend to set out tomorrow, you should rest now."

Niall shook his head. "Not tomorrow. I must leave immediately. In two hours it will be dawn, and I must leave without being seen."

She said: "But you'll be seen anyway when the Sun comes up."

Niall shook his head. "Not the way I'm going."

T he last time Niall had been in this underground tunnel, he had been accompanied by Asmak, the director of the aerial survey, and the spider had assisted him by transmitting telepathically its own intimate knowledge of the passages. And because spider memory is virtually photographic, the tunnel had appeared to be bathed in a kind of soft luminescence that had enabled Niall to "see" the rock walls, and the irregular stone of the floor beneath his feet. Now his only lighting was a small but powerful flashlight that had been found in a crate of hospital equipment dating from the last age of human rule. The beam, which looked like a bar of white metal, was adjustable, and the atomic storage cells were virtually inexhaustible; yet it seemed inadequate for these caverns of cold blackness.

Niall already had passed beyond the part of the tunnel that had been built by humans, in which great blocks had been held together by a cement that set like marble, and was now walking on natural rock, which had been carved millions of years ago by an underground river. There were fossilized ammonites on its twisted gray surface. Underfoot, there were signs that the rock had been leveled by tools.

It was far colder than he remembered—on his previous visit he had been kept warm by his contact with the spider's powerful mind. And the distances seemed much greater. He seemed to have been walking for at least an hour, and there was still no hint of the rumble of the underground river that he knew to be ahead of him. When he yawned, he realized that a long day without sleep was catching up with him. As the flashlight beam caught a shallow depression in the ground, about the length of a human body, he decided it was time to rest.

He removed his cloak, with its soft lining made of the wool of mountain sheep, and laid it down in the hollow. The air was suddenly cold against his flesh, but he knew he would have to endure it only for a moment. From his backpack he took the silver tube and pressed the end with his thumb. The garment inside—in effect a sleeping bag—elongated itself to twice its length, then unfolded. He allowed it to unroll in the hollow, and as he felt the thin cloth, experienced a momentary misgiving that it might not be warm enough. But as he pulled down the slide fastener and slipped inside, he knew his misgivings were unnecessary; devised for space exploration, the cloth seemed to become warm as he slipped inside it. Its silvery material possessed some remarkable qualities; for example, it was waterproof, so that rain could not penetrate, yet would allow the body's perspiration to escape, so the inside would not become moist when he slept.

Niall adjusted his pack on the floor against the wall, and laid his head on it. He was hungry, but too tired to eat. He switched off the flashlight, and as soon as he closed his eyes, the total silence sucked him into sleep.

Vague discomfort woke him; his shoulder was aching from the pressure of the hard floor. He turned onto his back, wondering if some slight sound had penetrated his sleep, but the silence was unbroken. Nevertheless, he reached cautiously into the pocket of his smock, then withdrew the flashlight and switched it on. It caught the yellow gleam of eyes, and half a dozen shapes scurried into the darkness; he recognized them as rats—the black, long-nosed rats that were found in the drains of the city. About the size of a small dog, these creatures seldom appeared aboveground, for they were a favorite delicacy of the wolf spiders, which could paralyze them with a blast of willpower at a distance of hundreds of yards. Their bite was said to be poisonous; but Niall was reasonably certain that they would keep their distance.

He groped in the bottom of his pack, and pulled out the waterproof bag that contained a watch that had been presented to him by Simeon; it was huge and clumsy, but had phosphorescent numerals, and would run for seven days without winding. He was astonished to realize that it was already two in the afternoon, and that he had slept for about eight hours. He wound it, and was amused to see that even this faint sound made the rats scurry farther into the shadows.

He propped his back against the wall—although its inward slope made it uncomfortable—and felt inside his pack for food. But as he felt a bundle that seemed to contain quails, he noticed the rats' eyes gleaming in the beam of light, and decided against eating. Instead he took one of the brown tablets from its wooden box, and allowed it to dissolve on his tongue. It had a flavor of honey, and as it dissolved, it created a warm glow, as if he had taken a mouthful of brandy. He washed it down with a long draft from a flask of water. Within a few minutes, his limbs were also glowing, and he felt as if he had drunk a bowl of hot soup.

Once the sleeping bag had been refolded, he was glad to slip into the wool-lined cloak; the chilly air made him sneeze. He heaved the pack onto his back, and tramped on into the darkness, resisting the temptation to think about the comfort of his palace.

Within a quarter of an hour he heard the low rumble that he knew to be the underground river. Soon the rushing sound filled the air, and he experienced again the instinctive sense of dread at a force that could destroy him so easily, fear of the unknown.

In fact, he had been to the white tower the previous evening, and memorized a map of these tunnels. There he had learned that they were partly natural and partly made by men during the long war with the spiders. The river flowed from the northwest to the southeast of the city; once, at the end of the last Ice Age, all these tunnels had been full of rushing water. But the map showed an accessible route out of the river tunnel. The roaring sound came from a thirty-foot waterfall farther downriver, and there was a path which led, about five miles farther on, to the outside world. The Steegmaster's maps were out of date—by more than four centuries—but assuming the stream had not changed its course, they should still be accurate.

The river, which was about forty feet wide, was spanned by a metal bridge, but it was unnecessary for Niall to cross this, since the path ran along the near bank. What the map had not shown was that the path entered a kind of low cavern, whose entrance was shaped like a Gothic arch. Niall had to stoop so as not to bang his head. The rock under his feet was rougher than that he had been treading, and it became necessary to scan the ground carefully. Even the rats, whose gleaming eyes had followed him in the dark, decided not to go any farther. Perhaps they found the thunderous roar of water as disturbing as he did.

It was fortunate that the irregular floor made him inch forward slowly; suddenly he found himself slipping, and had to clutch the wall for support. He dropped the flashlight, and for a moment of panic, was afraid he had lost it. When he found it again, he realized that there was a hole a few inches in front of his feet, and that about six feet below, the fast-flowing water looked like black ink. He pulled himself back, and sat down on the ground.

What had happened, he could now see, was that the water had undercut the bank, which had collapsed above it. The hole, about five feet wide, made it impossible to go any farther. But on the far side of it, the path continued.

With enough caution, it might have been possible to edge his way around the side of the hole, on a ledge about two or three inches wide. But there would have been the danger of the rock crumbling, or of his feet slipping for lack of sufficient purchase. He sat there for perhaps ten minutes, his mind oddly static, trying to decide what to do. One possibility was simply to return home. But this would mean leaving the city by a route aboveground, and risking being seen by emissaries of the Magician.

Alternatively, he could cross the bridge and proceed straight on to the sacred cave. But the only way out of it was a long, steep climb up a sheer rock wall, and the thought made his heart sink.

Another possibility was crossing the river by the bridge, to see if any other path ran along the opposite side. But none had been shown on the map.

The safest alternative, he could see, would be to jump across the hole. The distance would be no problem, but the roof was only a few inches above his head, and a blow on the top of his skull would almost certainly plunge him into the water. How high, he wondered, is it necessary to rise off the ground to jump a gap of five feet?

It seemed pointless to sit there any longer; his muscles were becoming stiff with cold. But the first thing he had to do was to make sure he did not lose the flashlight. In the side pocket of his backpack there was a ball of strong twine; he severed some with a knife, and tied it tightly around the flashlight with a double knot; then he made a loop for his wrist. As a final precaution, he tied another length of twine around the flashlight, then fastened the other end to his leather belt.

Now that he was ready, he threw his backpack across the gap, and had the satisfaction of seeing it come to rest within ten feet of the far edge. Now he retreated back a dozen paces, and ran, hurling himself into the air from the edge of the hole, keeping his head as low as he could. Some of the rock on the edge of the gap crumbled beneath his feet, but not enough to slow down the leap. He landed comfortably within two feet of the far side. The flashlight fell out of his hand and the loop slipped from his wrist, but the length of string tied to his belt prevented it from hitting the ground. Simeon's nephew Boyd had warned him that the bulb was the most vulnerable part of the flashlight.

He sat down for a moment to allow his heart to stop pounding. He also decided to chew another food tablet—not because he was hungry, but because the glow would restore his circulation. A few minutes later, with a pleasant warmth inside him, he pulled on his pack and walked on.

Within a few hundred yards, the roar of water became louder, and he realized that the rock wall to his left had been reduced to water-worn fragments. Clearly, there were times when the river was far higher than at present. His memory of the map—etched into his mind by the thought mirror—showed that the path beside the water continued for another five hundred yards or so to the waterfall, although it continued to narrow until it became little more than a ribbon.

Within another fifty feet, he encountered another problem. The path descended toward the water, and its smooth, hard surface became a dangerous slope toward the river. He removed the backpack and carried it by its strap, so that he could lean back against the rock behind him. But a point came when he realized it was too dangerous to go on. The path was now only a foot above the water, whose speed became obvious when it encountered projections of rock, and hissed into a foam of angry streamers. If he lost his footing, nothing could save him from being swept downstream and over the waterfall, whose roar was now deafening. The beam of light showed him that the path narrowed to about three inches, and that at this point it was only just above the water level. Then, a dozen yards further on, it widened again to more than a foot. Without the backpack, he might have edged along it, taking advantage of handholds in the rock. But however he held the backpack, it undoubtedly would be too dangerous. He turned and reluctantly began to make his way back.

His heart was heavy, for he knew he was faced with the prospect of defeat. He had studied the map closely enough to know there was no other way out of this underground cave system except via the river or the sacred cave. Other tunnels, according to the map, were dead ends. The route through the sacred cave—even if he felt like repeating that terrifying climb up the wall—would only lead him to a more distant part of the spider city, which would be no advantage. So if there was no way out along the banks of the river, he would be forced to return the way he came. He thought of asking Asmak or Dravig for help, and dismissed the idea; spiders were terrified of water.

He reached the gap in the rock, threw his pack across it, then jumped once more. This time he landed gracefully on his feet, without even dropping the flashlight. Within a few minutes, he was back at the bridge across the water. Even though he knew it was safe, he trod cautiously, aware of that swift-flowing blackness under his feet. But curiosity made him shine his flashlight down into the black water, and he was surprised to catch a glimpse of a fish, and then another. They must have been carried down from the mountains.

On the far side of the bridge, where the white rock gave way to granite that was almost black, he saw that the prospect was less hopeless than he had feared. The limestone on the far side of the river had been eroded by the torrent, so the path had almost been destroyed. But the harder granite had hardly changed over the centuries. And although the men who had cut the limestone path had left the granite untouched, its waterworn surface was less difficult than it looked from the other side of the river. The granite had, of course, worn less than the limestone, so the bank was higher above the water, in some places with a drop of a dozen feet or more. In one place he had to pick his way through a mass of rock that had fallen from the ceiling, and in another, to squeeze his way along a crevice that looked as if it had been made by an earthquake. But at least his main fear—that the walls would drive him too close to the edge of the water—proved groundless.

Although it was necessary to walk very slowly, remaining vigilant for irregularities and cracks in the surface, he made good progress, and was soon able to look across the river to the point at which he had been forced to turn back. His only fear now was that the waterfall had undermined the rock, for its roar shook the earth and made him unpleasantly aware of its immense force.

And now suddenly the rock underfoot was wet with spray, and dangerously slippery. He was paying so much attention to his feet that he was startled when he turned the flashlight sideways and saw a wall of water hurtling down only a few yards away. It made him feel giddy. Nevertheless, he forced himself to halt, and turn the beam down into the depths. Twenty feet below, the foot of the waterfall was hidden by spray, and the water looked as if it was boiling. Further along, the river turned into a creamy foam, with rocks that broke it into smaller cascades.

The descent was difficult, since it was covered with jagged fragments of rock torn from the walls. Evidently the whole face of the rock had crumbled at some point, turning a vertical drop into a rock-strewn slope, that could be negotiated with extreme care. By now the spray had soaked him from head to foot, and he was beginning to feel an underlying exhaustion.

Close to the foot of the waterfall, he sat down on a flat rock to rest his aching legs. As he narrowed the beam of the flashlight and shone it into the spray, he was surprised to see that there was now a gap of about ten feet between the waterfall and the rock face behind it. This had not been shown on the map. An almost flat ledge ran behind the roaring cascade to the far bank. For a moment he considered crossing the river, then remembered the crumbling limestone on the other side, and decided that he was probably safer on this more difficult but at least solid terrain.

When his teeth began to chatter, he decided it was time to move on. He was tempted to use the thought mirror, which would have raised his body temperature; but he knew this would also drain his energies, and that he needed all his energy if he was to get out of this place within the next few hours.

At least the ground immediately ahead of him was less rocky and twisted; at some point in the remote past, the water had smoothed it like sandpaper. He had now become so accustomed to the roaring sound that he ignored it, and strode beside the rapids as if taking an afternoon stroll. Slowly, the sound diminished behind him. Half an hour later, the river had widened, and the surface was so smooth that it seemed almost static.

When he came upon a stump of rock with a flat surface and an upright like the back of a chair, he took the opportunity to sit down and rest. Walking had raised his temperature so that he no longer felt cold. For a few moments he closed his eyes, and was tempted to doze. Then, remembering the long-nosed rats, he opened his eyes and scanned his surroundings in the beam of the flashlight. The river flowed smoothly, at about half its former speed, while the walls above rose thirty feet to a curved ceiling that looked almost man-made.

While he was directing the beam of light at the opposite side of the river, about sixty feet away, he was startled into sudden attention. The light was reflected off some shiny surface, and when he looked more closely, it seemed to be a small boat. He narrowed the beam by twisting its reflector, and as the pencil of light stabbed into the darkness, saw that he was looking at a boat that had been turned upside down. At this distance it was impossible to see whether it was some wreck that had been cast ashore by the stream; but when, a few yards from it, he saw another upturned boat, and behind that, three more, he knew that he was not looking at the aftermath of an accident. At some point in the not-too-distant past, human beings had lived in this cave and navigated the river.

His wet clothes felt cold again, and he widened the flashlight beam and walked on. He calculated that there must still be about a mile to go.

For about half that distance he was walking on a smooth red rock like sandstone, and able to make good speed. The water had carved it into impressive shapes that towered above his head, and made the cave look like a kind of cathedral, with columns that resembled red stalagmites. But as the narrowed beam of his flashlight probed the ceiling and walls, he saw something ahead that made his heart sink. The tunnel narrowed once more into a canyon, and the sandstone walls suddenly came together to form a bottleneck.

Niall walked on for another hundred yards, hoping to find some alternative route. A hollow that looked like the entrance to a tunnel seemed to offer some hope, and he scrambled down the slope toward it; but when he stood in front of the entrance, the beam showed that it was only a deep cave that came to an end in a wall of rock debris.

With a heavy heart, he climbed slowly back to the top, and walked along the bank to the point where the walls narrowed. The river flowed six feet below where he stood, into a cleft in the rock that was about twenty feet wide. There was no way to proceed any farther except by swimming.

He sat on a rock and stared gloomily across the river. He felt so tired that he thought of lying down and sleeping. But that would feel like acceptance of defeat. If he was going to return, he had a long way to go. And every wasted day could be a day off his brother's life. He found that idea so depressing that he decided, after all, to make use of the thought mirror.

As soon as he turned it inward, his spirits lifted. And the new concentration made him see the situation objectively. Six months ago, he had been little more than a child, living in an underground burrow in the desert, and surrounded by a family. Suddenly, he had been hurled into adulthood. As the ruler of the spider city, he was alone, with no one to turn to except a few trusted advisers like Simeon. He had, he now realized, been happier in Kazak's underground city of Dira, where at least he was surrounded by young people of his own age. And now he was setting out on a journey that might end in his death. If he failed to return, would the spiders honor their agreement to treat human beings as equals? He had no doubt they intended to behave honorably. But how could they treat humans as equals when they obviously were inferiors? They regarded Niall as their ruler because he was the chosen of the goddess. But what would happen if the chosen of the goddess simply disappeared?

Yet although these thoughts were gloomy in themselves, the thought mirror made him aware that they were, in a sense, illusions. Human beings allowed their thoughts to color their lives and plunge them into self-doubt. But he was not taken in by his negative thoughts. A curious optimism burned inside him that told him that surrender to his emotions would be absurd. What he had to do now was to dismiss his sense of disappointment and self-pity, and force himself once more into action.

He stood up and shone the light around the walls of the cave, to see whether there was any way out that he had overlooked. And when it was clear that there was not, he shrugged his shoulders and began to walk back the way he had come.

As he did so, he tried an interesting mental maneuver. The thought mirror had instantly increased his optimism by kindling a glow of inner power. Now he concentrated on that glow, and carefully and deliberately turned the thought mirror the other way.

It was like plunging into a cold darkness. Yet he refused to accept the darkness. The thought mirror had made him aware that things were not as hopeless as they seemed. He had to recognize that his sense of disappointment and defeat was an illusion. And little by little, with a mental effort of concentration, he forced himself into a sense of purpose and inner warmth.

He was not entirely successful; but even his limited success was an important advance. He was making a conscious effort to outgrow the Niall who wished he was back among the teenagers of Dira. What was so important was that he was learning to trust his conscious mind, rather than his thoughts or feelings.

As the roar of the waterfall increased, and he even felt a few drops of cold spray from the rapids, he remembered the ledge that ran to the other side. Then another thought struck him. The boats he had seen must have been brought somehow to this place. But how? It was impossible for them to have come downriver—they would have been smashed to pieces by the waterfall. But they could not have come upriver either, for surely the current was too strong to row against. So there must be some other means of reaching the outside world—tunnels that led away from the river.

Cheered by this notion, he lengthened his stride, and in another quarter of an hour had reached the waterfall.

Now he was struck by the thought that it might be safer to remove his cloak. If he lost his footing and fell into the river, a wet cloak would only impede him. He unfastened the chain that held it round his neck, folded it, and stowed it in the bottom of his pack.

The ledge behind the curtain of water was about four feet above the rapids. It was three feet wide, and its wet surface was reasonably flat. He clambered onto a large rock fragment, glad to find that it was quite solid, and stepped across a small gap onto the ledge. To his relief it was not slippery. Surprisingly, it was quieter there, since the falling water insulated him from the sound.

He stood there taking his bearings. His flashlight showed a crack about an inch wide at the rear of the ledge, and he suddenly realized why it had not been shown on the map. Periodically, this rock face would crumble and disappear into the torrent, causing the waterfall to retreat slowly upriver. When the map had been made, this ledge did not exist, and within another fifty years or so, it would also be carried away downstream. The thought made him peer down the crack to assure himself that it was not about to widen.

He again took his pack in his right hand, so that he could place his back tight against the wall, and then edged sideways across the ledge. The water roared past within a few feet of his face. But he reached the other side without incident. There he found that the distance between the ledge and the ground was greater than on the far side. He threw his pack down first, then sat on the ledge and launched himself, steadying his fall with one hand. As he landed on all fours and fell flat on the ground, the rough limestone skinned his knee.

He stood up and moved on quickly; the spray from the waterfall was soaking his hair and clothes. The surface underfoot was reasonably smooth, and it was not long before the sound of the waterfall had diminished behind him.

As he walked, he played the flashlight beam on the rock wall to his right, hoping to see another tunnel that would take him away from the river. But although there were hollows in the rock and even a cave that stretched for ten yards, there was no sign of another exit from the main tunnel.

The waterfall was almost inaudible when the beam of light picked out the upturned boat. This sign of civilization raised his spirits. But when he was a dozen feet away, he could see a six-inch hole that had been torn close to the prow. The boat apparently had driven against a rock at full speed. It was made of a smooth, gray substance that showed no sign of age. But when Niall lifted the bottom of the boat and looked inside, he saw that a piece of rope had almost disintegrated.

He went onto the second boat. This was smaller, but again, there was a six-inch hole in its bottom.

He shone the flashlight on the other boats, which were a dozen yards away. Two of them also had holes in them. But a third was intact, and the reason was evident. A rock, split in two, lay close by. Someone had deliberately set out to destroy the boats by smashing holes in them with the rock. Then the rock itself had broken, and they had decided to give up the attempt.

He heaved the undamaged boat over onto its bottom, and saw that a length of rope that had been attached to the prow was rotted away. It obviously had been here for decades, perhaps centuries. But a wooden seat that stretched from side to side in the boat was in good condition, and so were the oars that still rested in the rowlocks; these were also made of the gray, hard substance.

Nearby, in a hollow in the floor, he saw the remains of black ashes. This tunnel, then, had at some time been used by men as a campsite. But surely the only reason to camp in such a lonely, desolate place must be that they were hiding from the spiders?

Who were they, and why had they tried to destroy the boats? Again, there could be only one reason: that they were afraid of pursuit. And that, in turn, must mean that they had escaped by boat.

At this point, the tunnel was wider and higher, and the broad stream flowed quietly. The rock sloped down to the water like a flat beach. Niall walked to the edge. The rock shelved gently into the stream. He removed his sandals and walked into the water. It was so cold it made his feet ache. He inched forward cautiously until the water was halfway up to his knees, and shone the flashlight into the middle of the stream. It certainly looked smooth and placid enough.

If men of the past had been able to row down this stream to the outside world, then surely he could do the same?

The alternative was to turn back and return to the spider city.

Before reaching a decision, he wanted to make sure there was no other way out. If he launched himself onto the river, then passed a tunnel entrance, it might not be possible to row ashore again.

In spite of his weariness, he walked on down the riverbank, scanning the wall for tunnels. When, a quarter of an hour later, he reached the point where the river narrowed, he knew there was no other exit.

This thought made up his mind for him. He walked back to the boats, dragged the sound one into the river, then clambered into it. It stuck on the bottom. He sat on the seat and pushed one of the oars against the rock. The boat turned sideways, then drifted out onto the water.

Only then did he recognize a problem he should have foreseen. It was impossible to row with both hands and hold the flashlight. He was tempted to jump ashore and try to devise some method of controlling the flashlight while he rowed; but already the boat was moving out of his depth.

He felt it was more important to see where he was going than to guide the boat. After all, it could only go in one direction. Niall was too much of a landsman even to realize that the boat would naturally find its way to the center of the stream unless he made determined efforts to keep it closer to the edge. And by the time he realized that the stream was swifter than he had assumed, the boat was sweeping along faster than he could have run.

He tried holding the flashlight in his mouth. It was not wide—about an inch in diameter—but still was uncomfortable. He pulled one of the oars out of its rowlock by turning its end into the boat and pulling it clear. At least he could use it to push himself away if he came too close to the wall.

The boat soon moved into midstream. A few moments later, he had reached the point where the walls narrowed, and vertical walls arose on either side. At least there seemed no sign of obstruction, or of rock projections sticking out of the walls.

He reached inside his tunic and turned the thought mirror toward his chest. He instantly experienced a sense of control, and of insight into this situation. But it made him realize that he was now relying entirely on luck, and that if he had used the thought mirror before he launched the boat, he would have decided against it.

At least his increased sense of vitality made his present position seem exciting. The walls had narrowed, and he was sweeping between them so fast that they seemed a blur. One sudden eddy caused the boat to plunge and turn sideways, but it had straightened itself before he could experience alarm.

As he flew along, he even had time to wonder: why had the map showed some kind of path beside the stream until it reached the open air? Then the solution struck him. This stream had not always been as high as it was now. It was late in the year, and the rains had swollen the river. In midsummer, it probably was many feet lower and flowed more gently. No one could possibly have rowed against the present current.

As this recognition burst upon him, the boat began to move faster, and he realized that the river was flowing downhill. The flowing water was now so fierce that waves hissed over the side as they bounced off the walls; sitting upright on the bench seat was impossible, and he was soon thrown backwards on the floor. He managed to scramble to his knees and fling himself down—at least he was now lying with his head toward the prow. The flashlight rolled against his knee, and he thrust it into the side pocket of his knapsack and buttoned it down. Water came over the sides, making him certain that he was going to sink. But the boat builder had known his craft; even when the prow plunged down into a wave and the boat half filled with water, it remained as buoyant as a cork.

He choked as he breathed in water. But through the blur that filled his eyes, he could see daylight ahead. Relief turned to alarm as he realized that the roof was becoming so low that the exit was little more than a narrow slot that might scrape the boat against the ceiling. But there was no time to feel relief as the boat swept out of the tunnel like a projectile, and he was blinded by sunlight. When his sight cleared, he could see that the stream had widened, and that there was vegetation on the banks.

Since his one desire now was to get back onto dry land, he tried to grab the branch of a tree that trailed into the water, but it tore away, almost pulling him out of the boat.

For another hundred yards the river continued to widen, and became almost placid; but he was now too far from the bank to scramble ashore. Further ahead, the stream narrowed, and he sat up, prepared to grasp at the first tree root that offered itself. He was concentrating so hard on the bank that he realized too late that the current was carrying him toward another waterfall. This one was only a few feet high, and if he had realized in time, he might have grasped at a rock in the middle of the stream. But the boat was already plunging over, and he was suspended head downward. Then something struck him hard on the back of the head, and he felt water gushing into his mouth and nose as he lost consciousness.

He was lying on his face, and his head felt as if someone was hitting it with a hammer. Waves of nausea surged up in him and made him vomit, but all that came out of his mouth was the water he had swallowed.

After that, he felt hands under his arms, dragging him through vegetation, but was so exhausted that he was not even curious. Then the sickness began to drain away, and was succeeded by a cool and pleasant sensation. With an effort of will he forced himself to open his eyes, but quickly concluded that there was something wrong with them. The face above him seemed to be made of glass, or perhaps carved out of ice; then it blurred and seemed to dissolve away.

Although his head was no longer throbbing, he was aware that something had struck it a heavy blow, and that the back was badly bruised. He had a vague notion that he had been rescued by a bombardier beetle, but this idea changed with the fluidity of semiconsciousness into a dream about trees under water.

The next time he opened his eyes he saw leaves arching above him, and realized that he was lying on his back in the shade. The thought mirror was lying outside his tunic, and he hastened to thrust it back inside. In doing so, he accidentally turned it the other way for a moment, and the pain behind his eyes was so sharp that he almost cried aloud.

He caught a movement on his right, but when he turned his head, again concluded that his eyes were playing tricks on him. Whatever he was looking at seemed to be a shape without any definite form, like smoke from a fire. But since he felt no sense of danger, it was easier to close his eyes again. This time, the oblivion was more like normal sleep.

When he was awakened again, it was by the discomfort of his wet clothes; when he moved his head, the pain made him gasp. He reached up and touched the back of his skull; it hurt, and when he looked at his fingers, they were stained with blood. A glance at the sky beyond the overarching branches told him that it was close to dusk. He forced himself into a sitting position, and realized that his head had been propped on a pile of leaves, one of which was still sticking to his bloodsoaked hair. In the distance, perhaps a hundred paces away, he could hear the sound of the river. Clearly, someone had dragged him out of the water, and placed the leaves under his head. That argued some intelligent and well-disposed being. But where had his rescuer gone?

A movement out of the corner of his eye made him turn his head, and what he saw made him cry out with shock. It was so unlike anything he had ever seen or experienced that he had difficulty taking it in. The creature seemed to be a man, or at least a human-shaped figure, but its outlines were so blurred and indeterminate that he felt there was something wrong with his eyes. What he was looking at changed from moment to moment, as if it refused to come into focus. Just as he had decided that it was semitransparent, like a creature made of a clear jelly, the face became solid, and once again seemed to be formed out of ice or glass. This made the rest of the body almost invisible, as if the head was floating in the air.

Then, to his relief, the creature's color darkened to a greeny-blue, and Niall suddenly was able to see the whole body. He realized at once that this was not a man. The forehead was out of all proportion to the rest of the face, being twice as high, and had a hole like a mouth in its center. The features were like those of human beings, but more simian, with enormous nostrils, while the wide, downturned mouth reminded him of a fish. The ears were also enormous, extending the full length of the head; but instead of terminating in lobes, they joined the neck slightly above the shoulders. The eyes were large, like those of a night creature, and pale green, with tiny flecks of brown. The thin body had muscles like whipcords, so that the arms and legs looked almost like illustrations of muscular structure from some book of anatomy. Its color seemed to ebb and flow between green and blue, and Niall had the impression that it was maintaining its color with an effort of will that was like balancing on a wire.

A moment later, he felt a strange and almost painful sensation inside his head, which made him wrinkle his face as if he had been deafened by some high, piercing whistle. This was followed by a kind of crackling that was equally unpleasant. It took Niall some moments to realize that the being was trying to communicate telepathically, but that its thoughts were somehow on the wrong wavelength.

Controlling his discomfort, Niall asked hoarsely: "Can you speak?"

The answer was a sudden change of color, from green to a shimmering brown, which Niall felt instinctively to be an expression of frustration. The hole in the enormous forehead opened, but what came out was a sound so deafening that it made him wince. It was like nothing so much as the thunderous roar of a high wind in the treetops. And because it was impossible that any mouth could have produced such a volume of noise, Niall deduced that it was due partly to telepathy, or was somehow amplified by the creature's mind.

Now Niall became aware that they were no longer alone. A dozen or more of these beings had slipped out of the dusk, and were watching him with obvious interest. Like the first one, they were semitransparent, and often seemed to vanish altogether. Niall realized intuitively that the one who was trying to communicate was showing immense courtesy in remaining visible, and not sinking into his natural condition of transparency.

It was clear that this being was trying to speak to Niall, but in what might have been a kind of foreign language that was totally unlike human communication. Periodically, something happened in Niall's brain that intensified the pain of his bruised head and made his ears buzz with a sensation like static.

He did his best to transmit thought images, as he did when communicating with the spiders. This produced a lengthy silence, as if the transparent beings were trying to understand what he said—he had no doubt that everyone present was in constant communication. Then the "static" began inside his head, but on a slightly different note, as if the beings around him were experimenting in communication.

What puzzled—and slightly disturbed—him was there was no deeper sense of exchange. When human beings communicate with one another, they are aware of a "listening" atmosphere, as if each is awaiting what the other has to say. Only if two people are hostile to each other is this "listening" atmosphere absent, in which case they translate the absence as dislike or suspicion. In this present situation, the "listening" atmosphere was nonexistent; these jellylike beings might have been machines.

Even with the spiders and the bombardier beetles, Niall had soon developed this basic sense of waiting to communicate, which was a kind of listening. Could these semitransparent creatures be so unlike any form of life he had so far encountered?

Another burst of "static" caused such a splitting pain that he gasped, and buried his face in his hands. He felt something wet on the back of his neck, and when he raised his hand, it came away wet with blood.

The creature reacted immediately, making signs for Niall to stand up. Niall did so cautiously, afraid of more pain, and leaned against the tree. He was still tempted to rub his eyes as the shapes around him seemed to shimmer in and out of visibility. But now he became aware that this was partly because they took on the coloration of whatever was behind them—a tree, a shrub, even the fading sky. They were, he realized, a kind of humanoid chameleon.

The leader, whom he could see quite clearly, turned and walked into the shadows of the undergrowth. Niall followed unsteadily, and immediately tripped over a root and fell onto his hands and knees. By the time he stood up, the others had vanished. For a tense moment he was afraid he had been deserted. Then he experienced a rush of relief as he saw that the leader was waiting for him, almost invisible against the dusky green background.

A moment later, as if recognizing his anxiety, the chameleon man began to change color, first to a paler green, then to a yellow that made him clearly visible. As he walked on into the trees, he seemed to change shape like a candle flame. Niall was puzzled. If the chameleon man had read his mind, then why was he unable to understand when Niall tried to communicate telepathically? Then he saw the answer. It was his thoughts that these creatures were unable to understand. Emotions—like fear and relief—were a different matter.

As weak as he was, Niall was finding it hard to keep up. Although his guide was moving at walking pace, the ground underfoot was uneven, and he frequently tripped over roots and broken branches—there evidently had been a storm recently—or had to drag his feet through a carpet of dead leaves. His head was throbbing, and when a rebounding branch caught the back of his head, it made it bleed again.

Just as he was beginning to feel he could go no farther, they came to a large clearing, across the center of which lay a great fallen tree covered with ivy, its massive roots exposed like some tentacled monster. Here they all paused for a while, and Niall was glad to sit on a root until his strength returned.

Beyond the clearing the ground began to rise. They now plodded uphill for about fifty yards, through bushes that were so close together that Niall had to push aside clinging branches. Always the yellow figure like a candle flame continued to flicker ahead, and since it was now almost dark, he was glad of this. Suddenly, the figure halted, turned toward Niall, and made a gesture to come closer. Then he bent double, brushed aside a leafy cluster of branches, and disappeared. Following him cautiously, Niall found himself in a low tunnel where he was plunged into total darkness. Yet there must have been some faint light, for he could still see the chameleon man, still bent double, glimmering in the darkness ahead.

When his guide straightened up, Niall did the same, and found that he could now walk upright. But the tunnel was narrow, and in one place he had to clamber down some rough steps that felt like natural rock. As he slipped down the last one and fell to his knees, Niall found himself wishing he still had the flashlight, and reflected sadly that it was now somewhere at the bottom of the river.

His sense of touch told him that he was in a tunnel whose walls were partly rock and partly earth. The floor underfoot seemed to be made of hard earth.

A few minutes later the tunnel widened, and he was unable to touch both walls at the same time. When he reached up and found he could not reach the ceiling, he suspected that he had entered some kind of cave. This was further confirmed as his feet rustled through dry leaves. A moment later, he was able to see clearly as the chameleon man's dim glow suddenly intensified into a light as bright as a full moon, illuminating the walls of a long, low chamber that terminated in a sloping wall of rock. The yellow light lasted for only a few seconds, then vanished completely, leaving him in total blackness; but Niall had no doubt that its purpose had been to enable him to see where he was.

He sat down in the darkness with his back against the wall, and realized that it was covered with a thick, velvety moss that was damp to the touch. It was pleasant to take his weight off his feet, but he felt weary and cold, and uncomfortable in his wet clothes.

He had been sitting there resignedly for perhaps a quarter of an hour, focusing on the beating of his heart and the gradual easing of the ache in his head, when someone touched him on the shoulder, then pushed something into his hands. It seemed to be a vessel shaped like a handleless jug. His invisible companion raised it and touched it to Niall's lips, indicating that he should drink. He tilted it, and tasted a waterlike liquid with a faint earth flavor. There were fragments floating in it, and Niall's guess was that it was a liquid collected from the dripping moss-like substance on the walls. But since he was thirsty as well as hungry, he took a long, deep draft.

The effect of the drink was not simply to quench his thirst; suddenly, the total blackness became less impenetrable, as if the walls were giving off a faint green light. By this dim glow he could now see his companions clearly. They looked as if they had also become phosphorescent; moreover, they had ceased to be transparent, and looked solid and opaque. (Niall guessed that, since they felt safe on their own territory, their power to become transparent was unnecessary.) The eeriest thing about them, as they moved around the cave, was their silence.

All had the same strange, nonhuman face as his original guide, and the same huge nostrils and ears. Their foreheads varied in size, as did the mouthlike organs in the center, and although their actual mouths never seemed to open except to drink, the supernumerary mouth in the forehead was oddly mobile and full of expression; it frequently opened and closed, so that at times they reminded him of fish.

Most of them were drinking from the juglike vessels, and Niall now observed that the jug from which he had been drinking had been placed beside him on the floor, almost buried in leaves. Reasoning that they would scarcely be drinking so much unless they had some reason besides quenching their thirst, Niall picked it up and took another gulp. Once again, it seemed to have the effect of increasing the light around him. And although he experienced nothing like the intoxication induced by mead or wine, he realized that he was now indifferent to the cold— that, in fact, it seemed somehow agreeable. Warmth would have been oppressive. He touched the skin of his face; it seemed as chilly as a corpse. Yet he was actually enjoying the cold just as he would usually enjoy warmth.

Now he noticed something else: that although they were drinking together, these strange creatures were not convivial. On the contrary, they seemed deeply thoughtful. And this, Niall realized, distinguished them from human beings. Of all the human beings he had ever known, he would scarcely describe any of them as thoughtful except under rare circumstances. On the contrary, humans seemed to feel that happiness was *not* being thoughtful. Yet they admired thought, and regarded their great philosophers among the most remarkable human beings. Why, then, did they go to so much trouble to achieve states of thoughtlessness?

Niall observed another interesting consequence of imbibing the mossy liquid. As strange as it seemed, he was not only enjoying being cold, but also enjoying being hungry. This seemed paradoxical; yet he

35

realized that the normal sense of satisfaction that followed food was a dulling of the senses, which was the opposite of the sense of mental alertness that seemed an essential part of happiness.

About to take another sip of the water, he paused, and set down the vessel. Something was happening to him. Not only was the liquid producing an effect unlike that of wine or mead—it was actually having the opposite effect. Wine caused the heart to beat faster and the convivial glow to increase. This earthy liquid caused the silence to increase and to become deeper. A quarter of an hour ago, he had been tired; now the fatigue had vanished to give way to a deep calm, so that he could no longer feel his heart beating. It was as if he had had a long night's sleep and was now completely refreshed.

He began to understand. Back in the spider city, when he returned to his palace in the evening, tired after a long day's work in organizing repairs in the broken-down buildings, or trying to keep members of the Council from squabbling, he usually flung himself on a heap of cushions and allowed his serving maids to bring food and drink until he felt relaxed. But he never relaxed beyond a certain point. As his energies returned, he enjoyed talking with Veig or Simeon or his mother. Too much relaxation would simply have made him yawn.

Now it was different. This relaxation was like being released from bonds that had been cutting off his circulation; it felt as if the blood was being allowed to flow back into his limbs. The process was almost painful.

He had experienced something of the sort once before, lying in bed in Doggins' house in the city of the bombardier beetles, when the energies of the goddess had awakened the morning flowers and made them vibrate like a thousand tiny bells. But this experience had soon ended in sleep. Now the process filled him with a deeper wakefulness, and an enormous curiosity about what would come next.

While these thoughts had been passing through his mind, he had been aware that there was some activity on the far side of the cave, as chameleon men moved in and out of some kind of entrance or tunnel in the far wall. A moment later he was offered a wooden bowl that seemed to contain chopped roots. He bit into one, and found that it had a pleasant, crunchy consistency, and was easy to chew. It was a flavor that he had never before tasted. In his palace, he had eaten many kinds of vegetables and fruits for the first time in his life—after all, until he arrived in the spider city, he had never even tasted an apple. This was like none of them, but was by no means totally unfamiliar.

As he chewed, he tried to compare the taste with other flavors: celery, fennel, carrot, turnip, potato, cucumber, quince, guava, even coconut. Then he realized that something odd was happening. It was as if he was being absorbed by the flavor, and losing his sense of who he was and what he was doing there. This was not unpleasant, for as soon as he transferred his attention elsewhere, it ceased immediately. But in the meantime his consciousness was floating free, like a balloon, without any feeling of identity.

He noticed something else: that his companions were eating with their mouths, while the lips of the mouthlike opening in the forehead continued to move. Suddenly he understood why the chameleon men had two mouths: the lower one was for eating, the upper one for communicating. No sounds were passing through the lips of this upper mouth, but as he watched the movement of the lips, it was impossible to doubt that they were using them to communicate in a wordless language.

At that moment, something happened that made him stare in amazement. Through the ceiling, a few feet from where he was sitting, a shining creature was descending, like someone floating down through a hole. Yet there was no hole; the unbroken ceiling was clearly visible through the shimmering surface. The creature was yellowish in color and round in shape, about two feet across. There were small, hairy tentacles on its body, which waved like tiny legs. Then it emerged fully from the roof of the cave, and floated gently down, as softly as a bubble. As it hit the dry leaves on the floor it seemed to bounce slightly, then went on sinking into them. A kind of tuft of yellow fiber on its head was the last he saw of it before it vanished into the floor.

At the other end of the cave, the same thing was happening: a bubble of yellow light with hairy protuberances floated down from the roof, hit one of the chameleon men on the head, bounced off him like a balloon, then drifted to the floor and sank into it.

Niall bit into another kind of root, and was surprised to find that once again its taste was impossible to compare with anything he already knew. It was stronger than the other flavor, as an onion is stronger than a potato. But other than that, it was impossible to classify.

Again, as he focused his attention on it, it seemed to absorb his sense of identity. He became the taste of what he was eating. It was not unlike floating out of his body.

As he crunched it, he was startled to see a kind of tentacle emerge from the wall opposite; it was like a furry green cat's tail, and it waved as gently as seaweed in a current. Then it split into a dozen other "tails," which looked like long strands of some kind of waterweed. These also subdivided, then subdivided further, until they turned into a faint haze of green light that swirled for a moment like mist, then vanished.

By now, he was beginning to suspect that these strange entities were a delusion induced by what he was eating, and that he alone could see them. He decided to experiment. Reaching into the bowl, he found a green-colored fragment that was roughly cubic in shape. It was harder to chew than the others, and had an acid, almost fruity flavor. And as he concentrated on it and allowed his sense of identity to dissolve, the air became full of diamond-like purple shapes that drifted down as gently as autumn leaves. They seemed to be soft and alive, and they twisted with a lazy, flamelike motion. One settled on the back of his hand, and he was surprised to find it distinctly cold, like a snowflake.

He concluded that the roots he was tasting were acting upon him like drugs, yet produced their effect only because he was in a state of supersensitivity. It was as if each one was speaking to him, trying to tell him something with its own individual voice.

He actually recognized one root as celeriac. When he chewed this, nothing at first seemed to happen. Then he noticed that a brown tree root sticking through the roof was glowing with a pulsating blue color. When he stood up and peered closely at it, he saw that it seemed to be covered with tiny moving bodies like grubs, each one an electric blue. They seemed to belong to the root, as if they were part of it. But when he tried to focus on them to look more closely, they simply disappeared, leaving him staring at a mud-colored root. As soon as he ceased to try to focus, the colored grubs reappeared.

Now intensely curious, he lifted another piece of root to his mouth, and focused his mind on it as he chewed. There was the dizziness he had come to expect, due to the momentary loss of identity, then he became aware of a pulsating shape of blue-green light that seemed to be turning itself continuously inside out. So long as he maintained the sense of nonidentity, he remained aware of the pulsing shape. Then one of the yellow globes drifted toward it, and made a sudden dart at it, gulping it down like a large fish eating a shrimp.

Toward the bottom of the bowl, he came upon a number of smaller pieces of root, some hardly bigger than a fingertip. It occurred to him to wonder what would happen if he put half a dozen into his mouth at the same time. Would he see a half a dozen different hallucinations all at once?

He immediately regretted his rashness. Even before he began to chew, he was assailed by such a rush of strange sensations that he was overwhelmed, and felt his own identity flung far away from him. His mind had become blank. All sense of who he was and where he was abruptly vanished. It was like being suspended in a white void.

When, after several minutes, normality returned, he found himself surrounded by a dizzying variety of semitransparent floating shapes, shapes of so many forms and colors and sizes that he felt as if he had been plunged into some overcrowded aquarium. These living freaks glowed with such an intensity of reality and color that his suspicion that they were optical illusions disappeared. They were undoubtedly real—part of a reality that his senses usually ignored. The same was true of the cave he was sitting in, and the earth that stretched above him; he now realized that these were full of vibrations: the vibrations of tree roots, of living mold that constantly transformed the soil, of tiny worms and grubs and microorganisms that received their life from the mold, and even of clay and stones.

These vibrations occasionally seemed to reach a pitch of intensity where they were transformed into tiny blue-colored bubbles that floated in the air, and that attached themselves to the nearest material objects. They seemed to have a particular affinity for the brown-colored moss that covered the walls of the cave, and they clung to it like a kind of glittering light-blue frost. But sometimes these bubbles became so crowded that they combined to form larger bubbles, which then drifted gently in the air. These, Niall realized instinctively, were one of the simplest forms of life. When he reached out and touched a particularly large one, it burst and transmitted to his finger end an electrical tingle as sharp as a pinprick.

And this, he suddenly realized, explained why the chameleon men had given him the earthy water to drink and the earthy roots to eat. They were intended to make him aware that he was living in a world of rich life-forms of which he normally was unaware.

Why was he so much less aware than his companions? The answer was obvious. Because his mind was moving too fast. He was like a man on a galloping horse, for whom the passing scenery was just a blur.

A better image, he realized, was his watch, now lying somewhere at the bottom of the river. When Dorion, the best mechanic in the city of the beetles, had first given it to him, he had spent minutes at a time staring at its face, hypnotized by the slow movement of the second hand.

If he then looked closely at the end of the minute hand, he could also see it moving. But if he transferred his attention to the hour hand, it was far more difficult to see its movement. His mind refused to slow down for long enough.

But now that he had passed the point of deep relaxation, it would have been as easy to see the movement of the hour hand as the second hand.

At that point he suddenly realized that, although they were not looking at him, each of the chameleon men was intensely aware of his presence. They had tuned in to his mind, and were aware of everything he had been thinking and feeling since he began eating.

For a moment he felt embarrassed, like someone who had been caught talking to himself. Then he saw there was no cause for embarrassment. They were not eavesdropping. They were simply reading his mind—just as he was able to read theirs. And, as odd as it seemed, they found him as strange and exotic as he found them. They were fascinated by the sheer headlong movement of his consciousness—although they found it hard to understand why he wanted to concentrate so hard and move so fast. For them, he was a being whose normal life was lived at a pace that made them feel dizzy.

Now that they had succeeded in making Niall slow down to their own speed, he recognized that this had been their aim ever since they had rescued him from the river. It had been impossible to communicate with him until his mind reached a certain point of relaxation. And now that he had reached that point of deep relaxation, he could communicate with them because he was sharing the slow, casual movement of their consciousness.

There was another interesting consequence of being on the same wavelength as the chameleon men. Niall could now see in the dark, so that the cave was as clearly visible as if illuminated by daylight. But somehow, everything around him had become more vivid and rich. It was not just that colors were brighter, but that everything seemed more real. He inferred that he was now seeing the world through the eyes of the chameleon men, and that they naturally perceived everything as more intense and interesting than Niall's human senses revealed.

He understood something else: why he had never felt entirely at home in the world. He had always had an obscure feeling that there was something strange and unfamiliar about life as a human being. It was as if somebody had made up the rules arbitrarily, and then forgotten to explain them. Now he understood that this was because half of reality was missing: the part that began below the point of deep relaxation.

As he looked around at their strange, monkeylike faces, Niall understood that they were communicating with him as clearly as if they were speaking. Just as human beings can communicate with a smile or a frown, or even the twitch of an eyebrow, so they could communicate by their expressions. This was language on its most subtle level, the direct level of meaning. It took place far more slowly than human speech, but by comparison, human speech was as crude as throwing lumps of rock.

The first thing Niall understood was how these chameleon men passed their lives. The rhythm of their consciousness was the same as that of the Earth and of the things that grew upon it, trees and grass and moss.

This meant that they experienced very little danger. To begin with, no enemy could see them. Like the spiders, they had enormous patience. But unlike the spiders, they had no need to catch prey. They stood still for pleasure. They found nothing so fascinating as falling rain—it seemed unutterably dramatic as it splashed down from the clouds and helped replenish the earth. As to a waterfall, like the one that had almost drowned Niall, it was like standing in a theater where all life passed in front of their eyes. That was why Niall had been rescued so quickly: they had been indulging in their favorite pastime of watching the water foam over the rocks. They often stood there from dawn till dusk.

But who were they? Where did they come from?

The answer was altogether more difficult to comprehend. They seemed to be saying that they were far older than human beings. They had lived on the Earth before man's first ancestors had appeared. Human beings would probably call them nature spirits.

As they conveyed this insight, Niall experienced what it was like to be a spirit, and was overwhelmed by an ecstatic sense of freedom.

But why had they decided to change into solid, material beings?

This was because of a great change that had taken place. The quality of the Earth's energy had suddenly become heavier and richer.

Niall understood what they were talking about: the Great Change had been brought about by the energies of the Earth goddess. But why should that make them want to be solid?

The answer was conveyed in a split second, and seemed so obvious that he felt stupid for having asked the question. Being a spirit brought freedom. But being solid brought a far keener satisfaction: all the incredible, rich reality of the world of matter—of mountains and rivers, of dawns and sunsets.

Niall absorbed this answer for a long time, allowing himself to taste the richness they were describing. But this led inevitably to another question:

If they had no enemies or predators, why did they prefer to remain invisible?

The answer disturbed his peace of mind. What they seemed to be saying was that the Earth was full of dangerous and evil forces, and that no one was immune.

Because this answer was conveyed to him directly, it made his skin crawl. For a moment he thought they might be referring to the Magician. But his mental image drew no response; it seemed they had never heard of the Magician.

Then what, he wanted to know, were these evil forces?

With a suddenness that startled him, the leader of the chameleon men stood up, and as he conveyed to Niall that he should do the same, Niall understood that he was about to be shown the answer to his question.

S tretching his limbs, Niall discovered that they were less stiff than he expected. He was also surprised to realize that, although the cave seemed as cool as ever, his clothes were now completely dry. When he ran his hand over the back of his head, he could no longer feel the bruise under the mat of blood-soaked hair. The earthy water must have possessed some healing quality.

The leader beckoned, and Niall followed him down the cave, and then through the archway that he had assumed to be a kitchen. It was, in fact, the entrance to another tunnel, which sloped steeply downward. A number of wooden barrels, stored in recesses in the walls, caught Niall's attention, because of the deep, rich color of their wood. Then he realized that, in fact, their color was no different from that of any other wood. It was simply that the consciousness he shared with his companions somehow endowed everything with an extra degree of reality.

In fact, everything had changed—not in his surroundings, but in himself. In the time he had spent in the cave—it seemed about two hours—he felt as if he had ceased to be himself. He was seeing himself through the eyes of the chameleon men. It was almost as if he was floating in the air above his own body, and had become a stranger to himself.

When he had entered this place, he had experienced a sense of uneasiness about going into a tunnel under the earth. Now he felt as relaxed as if he had been a badger or a rabbit, and the sensation of having earth above him was as natural as walking under the sky.

Again, he felt quite different about the tunnel through which they were making their way. It was not man-made, but it had obviously been made by some intelligent creatures, who had carefully embedded rocks into the earth to support its weight. Again and again, he had the impression that faces were looking at him out of the walls—blank, nonhuman faces that were aware of his presence.

The tunnel continued to descend for perhaps half a mile, then flattened out, and became wider and deeper. At this point he experienced a puzzling phenomenon. There was a crack in the ceiling, and water seemed to be dripping through it, as if from a leaking roof. Then, as he noticed its sparkling quality, he realized that it was not water, but the blue-colored vital force that had formed a layer like frost on the brown lichen of the cave. It had accumulated in a hollow of the floor, forming a pool.

The chameleon man in front of him paused as he walked through this pool, allowing the falling liquid to drip on his head. When, a moment later, Niall passed under this strange leak, he understood why his companion had paused. The blue liquid that struck the top of his head and ran down his face caused an almost unbearably delicious tingle of vitality. It was so pleasant that Niall was surprised that the chameleon man had not paused longer.

A moment later, he understood. The glowing force filled his body with a sweet, pure joy, like some unutterably delightful food or drink. But he quickly felt he had taken all he could absorb, and a faint dizziness ensued, not unlike feeling sick after overeating. He walked on feeling lightheaded and absurdly happy, but as if he had drunk too much mead.

He noticed something else: his sense that the walls were alive, and full of blank faces, grew even stronger.

Now they were walking on the level, but the ground underfoot became so rocky and uneven that at one point he tripped and fell onto his hands and knees, and was helped to his feet by the chameleon man who was walking behind him. It was hard to understand why the floor had become so rugged and irregular. It was as if it had been deliberately made to twist the ankles of incautious travelers. He noted the same ruggedness on the walls and on the ceiling overhead. He also observed that the tunnel had become much wider, and that the ceiling was almost twice his own height.

The chameleon men seemed to be finding the going far less difficult, gliding over the irregularities with a kind of natural grace that he had observed in cats.

Now they began to pass other tunnels to the right and left, and these increased in number until he was aware that the ground on either side of them must be honeycombed with them. Many of these tunnels sloped downward at a steep angle. It was suddenly obvious that they were in a completely different kind of terrain, and he sensed, from the minds of his companions, that it was inhabited by creatures quite unlike themselves.

Now a slight breeze was blowing from the cross-tunnels, and the air had become colder. There was a curious, sharp smell in the breeze that he failed to recognize, although it reminded him of the smell he had encountered in the shop of Golo the knife grinder when Golo was sharpening knives on a grinding wheel that made the sparks fly, and at the same time cooling the blade with some white liquid that dripped from a narrow spigot.

A quarter of a mile further on, the smell was so strong that it caught in his throat and made his eyes water. To try to control the desire to cough, he reached inside his shirt and turned the thought mirror. To his relief, it controlled the need to cough without causing the pain he had anticipated. But it also broke the feeling of contact with the chameleon men. This loss of contact also meant that he now found himself in semi-darkness.

Suddenly, they emerged from the tunnel, and the chameleon man in front of him came to a halt. Niall also stopped, then stepped backwards so quickly that he almost bumped into the man behind him. He was standing within a few feet of the edge of an abyss, and although it was too dark to see far, a wind that blew up from its depths suggested that it might be miles deep. The wind was warm, and was evidently the source of the smell that made his eyes sting. Being unacquainted with volcanic eruptions, Niall was unaware that this was the smell of molten lava.

Niall looked above his head; a sheer cliff face stretched above him, so high that it made him feel dizzy. On either side, a ledge about ten feet wide vanished into the darkness. Niall was glad he was wearing the thought mirror. He had never liked heights, and this place filled him with a queasy sense of unease. He stepped backward and braced his shoulders against the rock; that made him feel more secure.

But where did they intend to go next? He felt they were waiting for something; but now he no longer shared their minds, he was unable to visualize what it was.

Then he saw the creature that was advancing along the ledge toward them, and was glad he was leaning against the wall; otherwise his legs might have failed him. It was big—so big that it seemed to fill the ledge, and at first glance appeared to be headless. As it came closer, he saw that the head was sunk so deep into the huge shoulders that it had nothing that resembled a neck. The shape was more or less human, but a glance at the face told him that it was only distantly related to his own kind. The naked body was covered in thick hair, and the features looked as if they had been hacked out of wood, but left unfinished by the sculptor. The eyes were sunk so deep that it was impossible to see them, while the straggly beard under its chin grew in uneven tufts.

The chameleon men raised their hands to shoulder level in a casual gesture of salute; Niall inferred that they often made this journey. The giant made no gesture in return, but uttered a growl, revealing that many of its teeth were missing.

The sleep-learning machine in the white tower had stocked Niall's memory with a great deal of knowledge about the past, but its creator, Torwald Steeg, regarded the supernatural or paranormal with total skepticism, with the consequence that Niall was unable to find any item in his memory that offered him any clues about this hairy giant. He decided, upon no particular evidence, that the creature was probably a troll.

The chameleon men stood back to allow the giant to pass, then followed it along the ledge. The great legs made Niall think of ancient, twisted trees. The skin of the enormous feet might have been made of cracked brown leather. The troll's head was so deeply sunken between its shoulders that from behind it looked headless.

The wind from below came in warm gusts, sometimes so strong that they blew him back against the cliff face. Yet the chameleon men did not even stagger.

They walked for a mile or more, the ledge sometimes dipping, sometimes rising, sometimes twisting in or out, but always maintaining roughly the same width, so that the suspicion grew on him that it had been hacked out of the face of the cliff by living hands. This was confirmed when, after a sharp turn to the right, he found himself facing a vast flight of irregular steps. They varied in height between six inches and two feet, and although the troll continued to plod forward without breaking his stride, Niall and the chameleon men found the going far harder, often having to use their hands to pull themselves up.

The light around them was dim—about the equivalent of a starlit night. Niall kept his eyes fixed on the step ahead; but when, at some point, half a dozen steps in a row were shallow, he raised his eyes to peer upward, and felt his heart miss a beat as he realized that the ascent was almost over and that an immense bridge stretched out from the face of the cliff over the gulf from which the wind continued to roar upward.

Moments later they halted on a flat platform of rock, perhaps a hundred yards across. On the far side, the ledge disappeared, probably plunging downward again. Niall suddenly found himself suspecting that they were inside a mountain.

At close quarters he could see that the "bridge" ahead was an outgrowth of natural rock, perhaps fifteen feet in width, whose upper surface was curved like a giant tree trunk. The thought of trying to walk on this in the roaring gale made his heart sink, and he was tempted to crawl on all fours. Then, as the troll led the way, he was relieved to discover that, since the gale was blowing from directly underneath, they were protected from it by the bridge itself. Only a few flurries of wind blew around them.

Although the surface of the rock was irregular, and pitted with holes and cracks, it was not difficult to maintain his balance. And since the thought mirror was now beginning to fatigue his attention, and he anticipated no problems crossing the bridge, he reached inside his tunic and turned it the other way. It took a few minutes to reestablish the mental contact with the chameleon men, but as he did so, the light seemed to increase, and he was able to see that the bridge rose in a curve toward its center, and then descended toward a flat, rocky terrain on the far side, about a quarter of a mile ahead.

Now that he was again sharing the consciousness of the chameleon men, he found he knew the answer to all kinds of questions that had been troubling him. To begin with, he was suddenly aware that the troll was the guardian of this bridge; without his permission, no one was allowed to pass. It seemed that the local trolls lived in caves that were a part of a network of passageways, such as those he had already noticed branching off the main tunnel. Generally antisocial (they particularly disliked human beings), they made an exception in the case of the chameleon men, who were able to do them some kind of favor—whose nature Niall was unable to grasp. The exception fortunately extended to guests of the chameleon men.

What puzzled Niall was that, in spite of their giant protector, the chameleon men seemed oddly tense and nervous, and as they approached the center of the bridge, were pressing forward at a pace he found exhausting. Niall could see nothing to justify their alarm, although the wind seemed to be carrying a smell that aroused unpleasant memories. A moment later he recognized it: rotting flesh, which he associated with his father's corpse, and with bodies left to decay in the slave quarter. (When Niall first came to the city of the Death Lord, the slaves were kept in ignorance of their true purpose as spider food, and a few slave corpses were allowed to rot to allay suspicion.)

Niall blinked. The chameleon men walking ahead of him had simply disappeared. He could still sense their presence, but they had become invisible. While he was still staring in bewilderment, the smell of rotting flesh intensified, and something cold and wet struck the back of his neck, causing him to stumble onto his hands and knees. A hand jerked at his hair, frustrating his attempt to turn his head. But the hand that went on to grip the back of his neck felt more like the claw of a bird. When he reached behind him, his hands closed on a bony wrist that was icy cold. And as he twisted his head around, he found himself looking at a face that was little more than a skull, with eyes sunk deep in the sockets.

Something grasped his ankle from behind. Inspired by panic, he kicked out, yelling with alarm; whatever it was let go. He managed to turn round, and his fist struck the bony face; the grip on his hair was released. Then, to his relief and surprise, his attacker collapsed to the ground, and for the first time Niall could see it clearly. What lay at his feet seemed merely a heap of foul-smelling bones, like the refuse of a graveyard.

Around him, invisible chameleon men were grappling with strange and foul-smelling creatures who were plunging up from below the bridge like birds. The creature immediately in front of him, which had a mass of woolly gray hair, was obviously alive, clinging to its invisible prey like a jockey on a horse. Niall grabbed the hair and pulled, then gave a cry of revulsion as the hair came away in his hand, still attached to rotting flesh. White grubs were crawling on its lower surface.

Terrified that he would be dragged off the bridge and into the gulf, he stared at the giant figure of the troll to see whether it was also being attacked. As he did so, there was a blinding flash, and the ozone smell filled the air. The troll was standing with its legs apart and its right arm outstretched; there was a crackling sound, and another thread of lightning leapt from the end of its finger and struck a flying creature that had just landed on the rock. It seemed to explode and vanish like a bubble, leaving nothing behind but a kind of steam that smelled of decaying flesh—as if the cooks in Niall's palace kitchen were boiling rotten meat.

The troll looked demonic, the lips drawn back from broken teeth, like some destructive god. Each time it stretched out its fingers, the lightning crackled in a short burst, each lasting a fraction of a second. One of the flying creatures was within a few feet of Niall when it was struck, and Niall felt a shock of electrical energy, while fragments like a sandstorm peppered his face.

Within less than a minute, it was over, and the flying creatures had vanished. Niall was sickened by the stench, and felt he was going to vomit; before this could happen, he remembered the thought mirror, and quickly turned it over inside his tunic; an immediate sense of control dispelled the nausea.

Now that he was able to look more closely at the revolting heaps left behind by their attackers, Niall realized they were not skeletons but corpses—corpses in an advanced state of decomposition. There were a dozen or more, and some even had fragments of garments clinging to them—garments whose coarse gray texture told Niall they were slave uniforms.

Niall felt oddly exhausted as he hurried in the wake of the chameleon men, who were now visible once more. Within a few minutes they were on the far side of the bridge, on solid ground. There, to Niall's surprise, the chameleon men flung themselves on the ground, breathing heavily. At least they seemed confident that the attack was over. No doubt this was because the troll was standing there like a huge black statue.

Niall had never felt so frustrated by his inability to talk to his companions in human language. He wanted to know what had happened and why their attackers seemed to be the decaying corpses of slaves.

As he sat with his forehead pressed against his raised knees, an enormous fatigue swept over him. He hardly had the energy to reach inside his shirt and turn the thought mirror. The stench of death filled the air, but he hardly noticed it anymore. His neck was stinging where the hand had gripped it; so was his ankle. And when he peered at his ankle, he saw that the flesh was swollen with small blisters that seemed to be filled with blood. He reached around to the back of his neck, and felt similar blisters there. He knew instinctively that his exhaustion was connected with these blisters.

It seemed only a moment later that someone touched his shoulder and startled him into crying out. But it was only one of the chameleon men. Niall realized he had been asleep, but had no idea how long. He still felt tired, and the stinging pain at the back of his neck and in his ankle had turned into a throbbing ache. The others were already standing. He staggered to his feet, and followed them as they moved off.

At least the ground was no longer hard beneath his feet; it was covered in a gray, velvety moss. There was a mist hanging over the ground that reminded him of the night he had set out from the city of the beetles with another group of companions, to try to locate the Fortress. It seemed to increase the air of unreality that was due to the fatigue. But from the fact that the chameleon men were stepping out with a new vigor, he guessed they were not far from their goal.

For perhaps a quarter of an hour he walked on like an automaton, following the chameleon man in front. Then the ground sloped upward, and they entered a narrow valley where the rock was bare of moss and the ground underfoot was as smooth as a road, although it was so narrow that there was only room for them to walk in single file. The troll in front had some difficulty negotiating it with his massive feet, although he towered over the sloping walls. Then, suddenly aware of their anticipation, Niall shook himself into attention and raised his head. They had reached the end of their climb.

The valley had come to an end, and the light seemed to increase, as if dawn was breaking. They were standing on a plateau-like hilltop above a lake, which extended between hills for a distance of perhaps two miles. Even if he had been alone, Niall would have known this lake was sacred, although he would have found it difficult to explain why.

For the whole of its length, except on the slope on which they were standing, the hills plunged steeply into the water, which was black and very still. On the surface up above, it would have reflected the sky, showing every drifting cloud as faithfully as a mirror. Here it seemed to reflect a sense of mystery.

Since leaving his home in the desert of North Khaybad, Niall had seen two great bodies of water: the sea and the salt lake of Thellam. Both had filled him with wonder. But the sacred lake filled him with awe, as if it spoke of some tremendous secret. It was like some deep vibration that caused his whole being to respond with a deep intentness, as if listening.

Even the troll seemed to be affected by it; he stood there like some great black statue, so still that Niall could have believed that he was turned to stone. Niall himself would have been contented to stand there for hours or days; he felt that he was absorbing the stillness as a desert absorbs rain.

It was the leader of the chameleon men who finally led the way down the slope. This was covered with the gray, velvety moss, whose smoothness made it necessary to walk cautiously. He observed that, in the steepest part of the slope, a row of small hollows had been carved, obviously to serve as chairs, with flat seats and straight backs like the seating in an amphitheater. The implication seemed to be that human beings, or creatures of about the same size, came here to contemplate the lake.

In the last fifty feet, the slope became less steep, creating an effect not unlike that of a beach. At the edge of the water, Niall noticed, the gray moss had become green, and in the water itself, it had developed tiny fronds, like seaweed. From a few feet away, the water looked so exceptionally pure and clear that it was almost invisible.

The chameleon men, being naked, walked straight into the water, and—to Niall's surprise—went on walking until it covered their heads. Niall paused only long enough to kick off his sandals and remove his tunic. The green moss had an almost fleshy consistency that seemed to caress his feet, as if he was walking on tiny tongues. Then he stepped into the water, which was cool but far from cold, and experienced a rush of delight that made him gasp. Now he could understand why the chameleon men had walked in until they were entirely immersed.

The sensation was like the trickle of vitality he had experienced when standing under the water that dripped from the tunnel roof. Again, he was filled with a glowing force that filled him with a sense of purity, goodness, and sheer joy. And as he walked deeper into the sacred lake, he felt that the water was cleansing his whole being. Like the chameleon men, he was impelled to go on walking until his head was immersed. Then, with the pleasure he often felt when emerging from a deep sleep, he walked back a few steps until his head was above water. The sensation was so sweet that he was surprised to taste the water on his lips, and find that it was bitter.

He was disappointed when, although they had been in the water only a few minutes, the chameleon men began to wade ashore. Although tempted to remain longer, Niall decided he had better follow them. As he emerged from the water, he noticed something that puzzled him. The water, which had been completely clear and pure when he went in, was now full of tiny white particles, each one the size of a pinhead. He cupped a little water in the palm of his hand and looked closely. It was hard to tell whether the particles were fragments of some white substance like chalk, or of vegetable matter. But when he placed one of them on his tongue, it tasted so bitter that he spat it out.

There was a simple way of finding out—to try to influence them with his will, as he had once influenced a swarm of glue flies in the city of the bombardier beetles. If it was a mineral, it would be far harder to influence than if it was living matter.

Accordingly, he turned the thought mirror on his chest; once again, as before, this had the effect of breaking the sense of communion with the chameleon men, and of plunging him into semitwilight; but by raising his hand, steadied against his rib cage, he could still see the white particles. He now concentrated his full attention on them. The result was a surprise; the particles were suddenly galvanized into the same frantic motion that he had seen in the glue flies.

That could mean only one thing. This was not mineral, or even vegetable, matter; it had to be some simple form of animal, such as a tiny grub.

This was confirmed a moment later when the swarming fragments responded more slowly, then became still. That meant that he had killed them, as Doggins had once killed a swarm of glue flies—by driving them to frenzied activity until they died of stress.

When he stepped onto the soft green moss, he discovered that his body was covered with a thin layer of the white particles, which vanished as he brushed them with his hands. He picked up his tunic and used it as a towel to wipe himself clean, noting, as he dried his chest, that none of the white grubs had settled on his skin where the thought mirror had rested.

Pulling on his tunic and reversing the thought mirror, he followed the chameleon men up the slope. They were now resting on the row of seats cut into the rocky hillside. Like the slope itself, the seats were covered in layer of gray moss; as he sat down, he found it cool and yielding. All the pain and fatigue were gone. He also noticed that the red ring of blisters around his ankle had faded into discolored skin.

He closed his eyes, focusing on the sense of joy that now pervaded his body. It was not unlike the warm glow that he experienced after swallowing the food tablets from the white tower, the difference being that this glow affected his whole body, making the nerves tingle with a kind of faint electrical vibration.

He observed once more that relaxing among the chameleon men was quite unlike normal relaxation, which soon reaches a certain limit of stability, beyond which it may either remain suspended at a certain level of contentment or decay into drowsiness. This shared relaxation floated gently past these limits, creating a sensation like sinking quietly into a deep hole.

Their ability to relax, he realized, sprang from the fact that the chameleon men felt no fear. Human beings feel that they must remain on guard, in case some sudden danger presents itself. Even when there is a sense of total security, force of habit prevents humans from relaxing too deeply. But the chameleon men had never formed the habit; their ability to make themselves invisible meant it was unnecessary. And now that Niall had learned to descend beyond his normal limit of relaxation, he began to suspect another interesting possibility: that their powers were not restricted to making themselves invisible, but that they could also make their bodies disappear completely, so they could not even be touched. It seemed a perfectly logical extension of their powers.

The first effect of the relaxation was to slow down his heart until its beat was hardly perceptible. A point came when it seemed to stop altogether, although he could still feel a faint throbbing in his lips and a high whistling noise in his ears, which he took to be the vibration of his nervous system. Then even this ceased. The immediate effect was like a light becoming brighter, or like the silence that comes when every sound has died away. All thought had ceased, and his consciousness had become completely weightless. The silence was so complete that he could even hear the sound of his eyelids when he blinked his eyes.

In this state he realized what a price human beings pay for their high level of vitality. Their bodies are like factories that vibrate with the roar of machinery. From the moment a child is born, it wants to investigate everything that moves, to touch bright objects and then taste them. It peers out of the side of its push-chair at the immense world of adults and lights that switch on after dark, and crawling and walking become urgent necessities, to explore farther and deeper this world of endless fascination. Energy becomes its constant demand. This world seems to extend to infinity, like some vast railway terminal, with its rails stretching in all directions, and it can only be explored by calling upon more and more energy. So human beings turn themselves into energy factories, in which the roar of machinery is so constant that it ceases to be noticed.

Now, in this deep stillness, he could understand why the chameleon men preferred invisibility. They craved emptiness and silence, so they could taste the flavor of their own existence, and all the million subtle vibrations and flavors of the nature around them.

But that also had its disadvantages. He was looking at one of them now—the sacred lake, polluted by some tiny creature that also craved energy. Invisibility was no answer to this parasite.

Because their feelings were on the same wavelength as Niall's, the chameleon men could understand exactly what he was thinking. They were not affronted by his rejection of their deepest certainties. This was why they had brought him here—because they were aware that their desire for oneness with nature was no answer to this pollution of the lake.

Niall formulated in his mind the question: where did this pollution come from?

They showed him the answer: from some stream that flowed in to the other end of the lake. But no one knew where this stream originated.

It was unnecessary to ask why they didn't know. Niall could see the answer. The territory of the chameleon men stretched between the waterfall, where the river emerged from under the spider city, and the sacred lake. What lay beyond that was none of their concern.

Aware that his questioning was disturbing the repose of his companions, Niall allowed himself to relax once more into the silence. Now he could understand why the chameleon men never slept. This state of deep serenity made it unnecessary.

Yet because he was human, and human beings never cease to feel curious, he found himself wondering whether he had reached the limit of relaxation. It seemed that his heart had stopped and the blood had ceased flowing in his veins. Physically speaking, therefore, he should be dead; yet he had never felt so alive. What lay beyond this state? Was it possible to achieve still deeper levels?

As if in answer to his question, he once more felt himself sinking. It was like swimming effortlessly toward the bottom of a deep lake. He suspected that his soul had left his body and was exploring a new kind of being. There was nothing around him but darkness; but it was a darkness in which he was fully conscious.

At this point he became aware of something that puzzled him. The darkness around him was not empty. It seemed to be full of energy. But this energy was not like the physical energy with which he was familiar, and which was like a continuous current of power. This energy was in some way fragmented and discontinuous. Instead of flowing, it remained passive. Yet it was also infinite.

In the white tower, Niall had learned something about electricity: how it is positive or negative, and how it flows from one pole to the other. Now he was encountering an energy that was neither positive nor negative, because it changed its nature from moment to moment. So although he was floating in a sea of energy, it might have been a sea of darkness.

It was then that he realized that, although this energy was static and passive, there was nothing to prevent him from absorbing it, exactly as a fish absorbs plankton. As soon as he began to do this, the nature of the energy ceased to be neutral, and became active and positive. This filled him with vitality and made it hard to maintain the relaxation. After a few moments, he gave up the unequal struggle, and lost touch with the source of power.

As he sat among the chameleon men, seething with an almost uncomfortable degree of energy, Niall decided to try an experiment. He went down the hill and removed his clothes by the lake. He could feel the astonishment of the chameleon men, who thought he must be mad to want to enter the polluted water.

He waded in slowly, becoming aware that the little white organisms were attracted to the vitality he exuded like sharks to the smell of blood. They soon covered his body in a thick layer, which had a texture like grease. Mastering his revulsion, he stood there, allowing the layer to increase, aware that these parasites were intent on dissolving his flesh away, and that if he did nothing to stop them, they could eat his body in less than a quarter of an hour. Then, at the thought of a million tiny mouths nibbling his flesh, he turned the thought mirror, and concentrated his will.

Suddenly, the layer of grease dissolved into a cloud of frantic activity like a swarm of gnats, or a million piranhas feeding. They were so crowded together that they must have found it virtually impossible to move. As he continued to concentrate, he felt their activity reach a frenzy that quickly culminated in death.

The water around him was the color of milk, and of an almost gluey consistency; it would clear slowly as the dead organisms sank to the bottom. Niall was tempted to wait there until this happened, and more of the parasites moved in to feed off the dead. He felt that he possessed the energy to destroy every parasite in the lake. But it would be pointless, since they came from some other source, and would simply be replaced.

As he waded ashore, he noticed that his skin had turned a red color, like sunburn. This was the effect of millions of parasites trying to eat his flesh and suck his vitality.

He turned the thought mirror as soon as he stepped ashore, sensing that the chameleon men were uncomfortable with it.

The leader stood up as he approached and said: "We must return."

It took Niall several seconds to realize that the leader had not spoken in words. He had simply conveyed the meaning directly from his own mind to Niall's. When he recollected the difficulty of his first attempts to communicate with them, Niall understood that, in a certain sense, he had now become a chameleon himself.

During the time they had been at the lake—Niall estimated about an hour—the troll had been standing at the top of the hill, apparently unmoving; he obviously possessed the same kind of patience as the chameleon men and the spiders. As they approached he turned and led the way back without any form of acknowledgment.

Niall asked the leader what lay above them. If he had been using human language, he would have had to point above his head, and explain that he meant what kind of landscape lay above the ground; as it was, his meaning was communicated instantly and unambiguously. This kind of directness of communication was something that had developed since they had sat in communion by the sacred lake.

In reply, he was shown a green mountain, the highest of a range of hills that lay to the northeast of the spider city. He had noticed it when Asmak, the chief of the aerial survey, had taken him on a mental voyage to the mountains of the north. But since Niall had been seeking information on the land of the Magician, he had paid very little attention.

Niall knew there would be no point in asking what lay to the northwest of the mountain—in the direction of the stream that carried the parasites; this was beyond the territory of the chameleon men, and they knew nothing of it.

This was not, Niall now realized, out of indifference. The chameleon men regarded the Earth in a completely different way from humans. Men move on the surface of the Earth, and are aware of its contours, which have to be followed by roads, which in turn are punctuated by towns and villages. The chameleon men had a completely different kind of awareness. In a sense, they were more like spirits. Their ability to blend into their surroundings meant that they were aware of hidden forces in their surroundings. Men, for example, are aware of the gravity that pulls them toward the center of the Earth. But when chameleon men came close to a hill or mountain, they were aware of other forces that compete with gravity and tugged at them like magnets. When the moon was full, its force affected them just as it affects the tides. And all through the day, the sun exerts different forces that distinguish each passing hour. For the chameleon man, the hour of sunrise was as different from midafternoon as a mountain differs from a valley.

Like trees and plants, the chameleon men were as aware of the forces of the earth below their feet as they were of the seasons. And since these forces also respond to the planets in the sky, the chameleon men were living in an altogether more rich and complex world than the flat world of human beings.

This was why they knew little of the world that lay more than a few miles beyond their home. It would simply have overstrained their powers of memory. As it was, their world was immensely more rich and real than that of humans.

All this Niall learned as he walked back across the land of gray, velvety moss. It was no longer necessary to ask questions; he could simply explore their communal memory.

As they approached the bridge spanning the abyss, his thoughts turned to the disgusting creatures who had attacked them. He learned, as he had suspected, that they were vampire spirits, known in some human mythologies as ghouls, who inhabited the corpses of the dead. Ancient students of occult lore classified them among a group known as the half-dead.

In recent months there had been an increase in their activity, due to the increased availability of corpses. Before some event (which Niall guessed to be his own accession to power) there had been few corpses, for they were all eaten by the spiders. Now corpses were easily available, for the slaves were too lazy to bury their dead, and simply threw them into the river, to be swept out to sea. Many ended on the mudflats of the marshes, and the ghouls, alerted by the cries of hungry birds, quickly took possession of the bodies. Sometimes a dozen birds were pecking at a corpse—they were particularly fond of the eyes—when it came to life, and they flew, squawking indignantly, into the air. To seize a corpse that possessed at least one eye was regarded by the vampires as a remarkable achievement.

How these spirits took possession of a body was not clear. But it seemed certain that they were able to enter it and use it as a kind of glove puppet. Such spirits lived normally in a ghostly world of unreality; but once they were wearing flesh, the world around them became more real. They enjoyed it most as the flesh decayed, for they were truly necrophiles, or lovers of the dead, and to animate a corpse gave them a gruesome and perverse pleasure.

When they could, these entities attacked human beings and sucked their life force; this was easiest if they could render them unconscious, either from terror, which could deprive them of their senses, or with some sinister hypnotic force that paralyzed their victims. From the activities of these unpleasant creatures came legends of vampires.

Oddly enough, the chameleon men regarded them without fear, indeed with contempt. To begin with, they were disgusted with their morbid obsession with death. But the main reason was that the decayed state of the bodies also meant that they had little muscular power—Niall had noticed how easy it was to repel their attack. A newly dead corpse was more formidable, its hands still being capable of strangulation, but it soon putrefied.

The trolls loathed them. This was because, unlike the half-dead, trolls drew their powers from nature, particularly from trees and certain nonsymmetrical crystalline rocks like quartz. In spite of their size, trolls could become virtually invisible in a forest or rocky mountain landscape. Their energy was of the same nature as lightning—a troll who had been struck by lightning was regarded as a kind of god among his own kind. Their contempt for the half-dead arose from their abhorrence of energy-thieves, the lowest kind of vermin.

So Niall was not surprised to learn that what he had witnessed on the bridge had been a deliberately designed trap. He was grimly amused to learn that he had been the bait—but if he had known this, his caution and nervousness would have alerted them. So he had to be kept in ignorance. The vampires, drawn irresistibly by the prospect of a fresh human body, had attacked in force, and had been allowed time to lose all sense of caution before the troll retaliated. It would be a long time before the half-dead of the abyss again dared to approach one of the troll people.

Niall was also glad to learn that the troll had admired his courage during the attack, and that his opinion of humans had risen in consequence.

Predictably, they crossed the bridge without incident. Even the sulfurous wind that blew from the depths seemed less powerful. But he took care not to look down into the abyss.

On the far side of the bridge, they halted on the wide platform of rock, and Niall was surprised when the chameleon men raised their arms to shoulder height in a gesture of salute. The troll again made a sound that was a cross between a grunt and a growl; for a moment, his deep-sunken eyes rested on Niall, and Niall was pleased to recognize in them a glint of friendliness. Then, as the troll turned his enormous back on them and pursued his deliberate way down the flight of steps, the leader of the chameleon men turned his face in the opposite direction.

Niall had been mistaken in assuming the gigantic rock stairway continued downward; in fact, the ledge made a steep right turn, and then continued steeply upward. Here it became clear that whoever had cut the stairway had intended to make a road to the sacred lake, for the path now became rough and irregular, and often narrowed to a few feet. In one place it came to an end altogether where the ledge had collapsed from a rock fall; but someone had cut a low and narrow passage into the cliff, in which it was necessary to walk in a crouching position until, a dozen or so yards along, it reemerged onto the ledge.

This now climbed steadily for half a mile, and a cold wind that blew in their faces blended with the eye-stinging vapor from below. Finally, it was necessary to crawl again, and Niall was glad to recognize the welcome smell of damp earth. A few minutes later, the wind became stronger, and they emerged into the cold air of a starlit night.

T hey were on a mountainside, and the tunnel behind them was so well hidden that Niall could not see it when he looked back. The wind was chilly, and there was snow on the grass at their feet, which was sparse and tough. Yet because he was still seeing everything with a heightened sense of reality, both the grass and the snow were oddly fascinating; they seemed to be beckoning him to look more closely. But that was impossible; his companions were already moving on.

There was no visible track leading down the mountain—but then, Niall reflected, that was hardly surprising, since it would have drawn attention to the route to the sacred lake. As they picked their way down to the plain below, he found himself wishing that he still had his cloak, which now lay in his pack, somewhere at the bottom of the river.

Ten minutes later, he was so breathless from scrambling among boulders and cracks in the ground that he no longer felt the cold. But he noticed, on two occasions, a whiff of the sulfurous smell, and guessed that there must be fissures through which the gas could escape.

He also noticed, for the first time, the disparity between his own human curiosity and the comparative lack of it in the chameleon men. Nothing in the knowledge he had received in the white tower enabled him to understand the strange scenery that he had just left behind. But he knew enough to guess that this mountain, and the surrounding hills, had been formed at some time by volcanic activity. But why was it hollow? This seemed to him totally paradoxical. Yet the chameleon men were not even curious; they simply took it for granted.

The answer to Niall's question was that the giant cave below him had been formed by a plume of hot gas that had risen from deep in the Earth's mantle sixty-five million years ago, and forced its way to the surface in an enormous dome, more than a hundred miles in diameter. This mountain and the surrounding hills were formed from basalt lava, which had been gradually eroded by weather until the underlying dome was separated from the Earth's surface by little more than a thin layer. And unless the volcano again became active, forcing molten magma to the surface, the dome would eventually collapse to form a huge crater, looking like those on the lunar surface.

Observing this grainy weathered rock beneath his feet, Niall knew enough to guess that it was the remains of some great eruption that had once wiped out all life in this region.

Twenty-five miles to the south, invisible in the starlight, lay the towers of the spider city, and they were traveling directly toward them. Niall estimated that it had been just about twenty-four hours ago that he had left home. Most of that time, he reflected, had been spent underground. It was pleasant to breathe the cool night air.

At the foot of the mountain, the going became easier, and they followed a foaming torrent that ran through a deep valley, then into woods of birch and ash. There, although no path was visible, the chameleon men proceeded with an unerring sense of direction which told Niall that they were familiar with every inch of the territory. They were treading silently over a carpet of dead leaves, and then, quite suddenly, they were climbing the slope that led to the tunnel and their cave. To Niall, it was as welcome as returning home.

A band of humans, returning from that difficult journey, would have flung themselves down and slept. The chameleon men sat quietly on the thick layer of dry leaves, some with their backs propped against the mossy walls, others sitting upright, and simply relaxed. Niall resisted the impulse to lie down, and allowed the weariness to drain out of his limbs in a sitting position. Within half an hour, the tiredness had gone, and he was suspended in a state of peaceful calm.

His stomach began to rumble; it had been many hours since he had eaten. He also suspected that he shared this hunger with everyone else, for as soon as the thought entered his head, there was a bustle of activity, and a few minutes later he was presented with the juglike vessel full of water. This time, the earthy flavor gave him as much pleasure as a glass of mead would have done at home, reminding him of his favorite flavoring, the vanilla orchid, which the cooks in the palace kitchen used in their pale yellow pastries. Even the small fragments that floated in it— which he could now see to be grass-green—seemed to make the taste more delicious, like bits of orange floating in orange juice. It had the effect of immediately satisfying both his hunger and thirst. But he noted something else: this liquid brought him closer to his companions, so their minds were as real to him as his own. This drink was literally a form of communion wine.

What struck Niall as most remarkable was that the chameleon men obviously experienced no desire to sleep. This was due not only to their capacity for deep serenity, but also to the fact that their minds were all interconnected, so they were all aware of one another. A sleepy person gradually becomes oblivious of the outside world. To be aware of what is going on around you, Niall realized, is a definition of being awake. Sustained by the activity of other minds, a chameleon man was as unlikely to fall asleep as a child at his own birthday party.

The result was that being among the chameleon men was like sitting around the fire with a group of boon companions, a state of blissful comfort and endless interest.

At this point, Niall's attention was drawn to a sound not unlike human speech heard from some distance away. He soon identified its source as the leader of the chameleon men, who was seated close by. The "mouth" in his forehead was moving, and these speech-sounds were the result. But they were oddly blurred, as if Niall was listening to a noise made by the wind.

He experienced an acute sense of frustration at his inability to understand. And as if responding to this, the sounds became suddenly sharp and clear. Niall was now able to recognize that they were in no human language. The basic sound was a little like the creaking of branches in the wind, except that the "creaks" were not repetitive, but a little like the pattern of notes in a slow piece of music. They were not like notes played on a single instrument, but were richly harmonized, like many musicians playing together. Obviously, the chameleon men were communicating. But about what?

No sooner had this question entered his head than Niall understood. They were not using language as human beings use it, with words laid out in order like a game of dominoes. Their words *were* a kind of music. But unlike human music, whose meanings were indeterminate, the chameleon language was quite precise. It had been developed out of their mutual experience, and it was intended to convey that experience.

As he entered this shared experience, Niall suddenly understood that the chameleon men were in a basic sense rather like human beings, in that they spent their days engaged in various kinds of activity. As guardians of this vast tract of countryside, they had the task to wander around it, either singly or in pairs, communicating with trees, bushes, plants, and with such animals as moles, slow worms, grass snakes, frogs, and lizards. These creatures, being of low intelligence, were inclined to remain isolated from one another in a kind of half-sleep. The task of the chameleon men was to act as mental bridges between them, making them aware of one another, and bringing a sense of unity that extended from tree mites and grubs to mice, water voles, and squirrels.

So the human notion that nature is full of conflict and confrontation was, as Niall could now see, a misconception. The instinct of the chameleon men was to help create harmony as the instinct of a musician is to create beautiful sounds.

Niall found himself wondering what part the trolls played in this harmony. His access to the minds of the chameleon men instantly provided him with the answer. Their task was to convert the raw energies of the Earth—the electrical force of lightning, the piezoelectric energies released by rocks under stress—into a living energy capable of nourishing the microorganisms that live in the soil, and which give the Earth its living aura. Each troll was like a power station, and this is why they needed to be so massive and formidable—the troll who had guided them to the sacred lake weighed as much as if he was made of solid granite. Trolls were to be found wherever quartz was plentiful, in places like the sacred mountain and the Valley of the Dead.

Unlike the task of the trolls, which was unending, the activity of the chameleon men varied with the seasons. Now, with the onset of winter, when nature itself was preparing to sleep, they had less to do. Even so, when they came together at the end of a day, they had a great deal to communicate, like any group of countrymen sitting in the bar of their local pub. Their language was a language of rhythms and images, and behind it all was a continuous awareness of the sound of the wind and rushing water. The actual syllables of this language could be compared to the sounds the wind makes as it encounters obstacles like trees, or a stream as it splashes over rocks and pebbles.

So as he "listened" to two chameleon men describing (at the same time, their words forming a counterpoint like music) a tree-covered hillside and a family of mice that had made their nest in the roots of the same oak tree as an owl, he was like a stranger overhearing a conversation between two friends, feeling curious and detached at the same time.

Then something happened that startled him. He was no longer "listening" to the conversation. Nor was he in the underground cave. He was on the hillside miles away, observing the activities of the mice in their nest among the roots. Everything was completely real: the moon half-covered in clouds, the branches rustling in the wind, the movements of wood lice under a piece of rotten bark. Yet although he was perfectly aware that he was still in the cave of the chameleon men, everything looked so solid and real that it would have been quite easy to persuade him otherwise.

What was happening was obvious. He had now entered the mental world of the chameleon men. And they clearly possessed a far more powerful faculty for remembering the reality of other times and places than human beings.

He had, in fact, experienced something of the sort before. When the great spider lord Cheb the Mighty had described the conflict between men and spiders, which had resulted in the triumph of the spiders, his words had conjured up scenes of slaughter that were painfully real. But Niall had assumed that it was his own imagination that had helped endow them with reality.

Suddenly, Niall was back in the cave. But only for a moment. Another of the chameleon men was speaking, this time about the plight of fishes who lived downstream. Last year, an exceptional volume of floods, due to melting snow, had damaged the backwater where many of them spent the winter, drowsing in the mud and leaves that covered the bottom. Niall witnessed trees torn up by the roots, mud that had lain undisturbed for years swept away by the flood, water rats struggling to escape torrents that often left them battered or drowned. For Niall, it was an unpleasant reminder of his own experience of near-drowning, and was so real that he involuntarily gasped for breath as his head plunged into a foaming eddy.

What happened next puzzled him deeply.

He was struck by the reflection that, with the river flowing so strongly, his backpack must by now have been swept out to sea.

His thought entered the shared stream of awareness, and because Niall was a guest, automatically commanded more attention than it might have done otherwise.

Their immediate response was to show him that the stream he had just seen was not the river that flowed under the spider city, but one that issued from the hills to the northeast. His pack might have found its way to a mud bank on the edge of the marshes, where corpses of slaves were often carried.

Niall saw this country of the marshes, twenty miles from the spider city, looking desolate in the light of a waning moon that was close to the horizon. There was a smell of rotting vegetation, and he wrinkled his nose in disgust at the sight of a decaying carcass whose eyes were being pecked out by a sea bird.

And then, among the reeds just beyond the corpse, Niall was startled to see his own pack, lying in the mud. He was so surprised that he said aloud: "Look, there it is!" before it struck him that they could see it as well as he could.

His words caused the scene to fade, and he was back in the other reality of the cave.

The sight of the westering moon reminded Niall that the night must be almost at an end, and that it would soon be time to leave. But Niall's companions had overheard the thought, and as he started to rise to his feet, the leader indicated that he thought this was not a good idea—that traveling by daylight was dangerous. Niall would be better advised to wait until nightfall.

Niall explained that his time was short. "My brother is ill and I must seek a remedy."

This brought a silence, followed by the reply: "But humans need to sleep. It is safer to sleep here than aboveground."

Niall explained: "But we sleep when we are tired. I am not tired."

"That is because you are among us." They were speaking to Niall as if they were one person. "When you are alone, you will feel tired."

Niall knew this to be true. Nevertheless, he had never felt more wide awake.

The problem, as far as Niall could see, was that the chameleon men never felt sleepy. When they were fatigued, they simply rested, and drank some of their amazing green-colored water. And then their interest in one another, in what each one had to communicate, simply kept them wide awake.

Niall had never realized so clearly that human beings fall asleep because they are cut off from one another.

The chameleon men said: "Show us how you fall asleep."

It seemed a strange request, but Niall attempted to oblige.

He closed his eyes, and sank into himself, like someone turning off the lights before getting into bed.

He was surprised to find that sleepiness came easily. The normal length of the human day is about sixteen hours, and it had been more than that since Niall had slept. So now the physical rhythms of his body took over naturally. It seemed odd to be falling asleep with a dozen other people inside his head.

The result was that although his body sank into a pleasant drowsiness, his consciousness remained wide awake.

When Niall was normally on the point of falling asleep, thoughts and impressions ceased to pursue their own purposes, and began to wander around freely, with no sense of direction. It was as if the director of consciousness went off duty and left them to their own devices, at which point dreams took over. But now, supported by the chameleon men, Niall's consciousness remained on duty and watched his mind falling into disarray. His thoughts ran around like headless ants, and often collided with one another. It was all strange and rather amusing, like watching a slapstick comedy.

This brought a sense of lightheartedness and gaiety. Then he noted a pleasant smell, like the smell that issued from the kitchen in the palace on the day his mother had given a party for his sisters, and invited the friends they had made when they were staying in the nursery on the far side of the river. The cooks had surpassed themselves with sweet cakes, and with a mass of pink, green, and blue candy floss, a substance as light as a tangle of hair, which melted on the tongue with a delicious caramel flavor. They had also made brightly colored drinks with flavors Niall had never tasted before.

At this point, Niall experienced a sensation like hands pressing on either side of his head, and felt himself propelled back toward consciousness. Then he realized that he had allowed himself to become too absorbed in memories of birthday parties, and was on the point of falling truly asleep. Somehow, the chameleon men had sensed this loss of attention, and gently nudged him back toward wakefulness.

He was still hovering on the borderland between sleep and waking. Sleep tugged at him like an impatient child, and once again he felt himself drifting. As soon as this happened, the sweet smell returned.

He was standing in a kind of street made of stripes of green, blue, and yellow, in which there were a number of immense conical buildings, also decorated with the same bright stripes. Around him, a vast striped plane with irregular and broken blue surfaces, like natural rock, stretched in all directions. The sky above was a pale blue, lit occasionally by strange flashes of lightning.

The sweet smell billowed around him in misty clouds, which seemed to be issuing from cracks in the pavement. There were large pools of water, which made it look as if it had been raining, except that the pools were in bright colors—yellow, red, violet—and were obviously not rainwater.

There was nothing dreamlike about this landscape; it looked as firm as the ground under his feet. He knelt and pressed his fingers against it. It was solid, and seemed to be made of a kind of colored rock with many parallel stripes, some an inch wide, some a foot or more. A piece of the stone was loose, and he levered it off with his fingernail and put it in his mouth. It was sweet but would not crumble when he bit it, so he finally spat it out.

What was so amazing was to be conscious that he was dreaming. It brought a marvelous sense of freedom. But what puzzled him most was where, in this strange city, were the people?

He decided to walk toward the nearest "building," which he judged to be about a quarter of a mile away. This was a kind of lopsided tower, with something that looked like a door or gateway in one of its sides. But even when he had been walking for ten minutes, during which time he should have covered at least half the distance, the building seemed to be getting no closer.

Another striped building to his left looked not unlike several circus tents piled one on top of another, rather like a comic hat. This also seemed to have an entrance, like an inverted V with curved sides. This time he strode purposefully toward it. But even after he had taken a dozen strides, it was visibly no nearer.

This was absurd. He walked to one of the cracks in the ground and peered down it. A kind of steam that blew up from it made his face hot and damp, and smelled cloyingly sweet. Then there was a hissing noise that made him jump back. It was followed by a gurgle that was not unlike laughter, after which the steam subsided.

Next he sat down on a projection of rock to rest his legs. The seat was uncomfortable, with sharp edges that soon began to hurt his buttocks. He whistled with pain and stood up, screwing up his face. As he did so, he noticed something interesting: concentrating his attention seemed to make the rock he had been sitting on more brightly colored. As soon as he relaxed his concentration, it returned to normal.

This was encouraging, a sign that he could exercise some control in this strange place. He clenched his teeth and stared at the rock; again, the color deepened, and it became, in some subtle sense, more real. He remained focused for as long as he could; then, as his concentration slackened, watched it become paler and less real.

Another idea occurred to him. He tried concentrating hard, then walking toward the "circus tent." This worked; he could actually see the building coming closer, as it would in normal life.

The engagement of his will in the process of walking felt odd, a little like rowing a boat—a skill he had learned in the harbor of the spider city. This "deliberate walking" brought a sense of effort and strain, but it was oddly satisfying.

He began practicing "deliberate walking" in the direction of the circus tent, and was pleased when each determined step took him closer. When he was finally standing in front of it, he could see that it was made of stone, which looked rougher and less finished than that of the ground under his feet. The entrance he had seen was not a true doorway, but merely a kind of slit in the wall that might have been slashed out with an immense knife or hatchet.

As he approached the doorway, the resistance seemed to increase, as if some force was trying to keep him out. He concentrated harder, and pressed forward through the entrance. Immediately, he found himself in semidarkness, as if he was wrapped around by bands of gray silk. Still encountering resistance, he continued to practice "deliberate walking" forward; it was a little like wading through deep water. Soon he was in total darkness. He turned and looked back toward the entrance, but nothing was visible. Bewildered, he thought of going back. But now he was not even sure of which way *was* back.

In a sense it was worse than being outside on the endless striped plane, for now there was nothing whatsoever. Then he tried concentrating again, and ceased to feel lost. He reflected that it did not matter which way he walked. Since he was inside a building, he was bound to encounter the other side sooner or later. So he devoted all his attention to concentrating, and simply strode forward. The darkness went on for a long time, but while he continued to practice "deliberate walking," he was not troubled. Then the light turned gray, and he was passing through another door, and out once more onto the pavement.

But this time it was different. The buildings were smaller and closer together—it was evidently some kind of residential quarter—and the road was not striped, but made of gray cobbles. When he turned round, he saw that the conical buildings had disappeared. It seemed clear that he was in another place—or another dream.

Now he noticed that there were living beings wandering in a haphazard way across the pavement. It would have been inaccurate to call them people. They were white, and had faces that were old and wrinkled, with white hair that had been allowed to grow totally out of control, and which virtually concealed most of their faces. The eyes that peered out from this foliage of hair were round and too big for the face.

These creatures seemed at first to have four legs, but a closer look convinced Niall that they had two long legs and two long arms, at least twice as long as human arms, with enormous, long hands at the end of them. They walked naturally on all fours, and it was hard to see how they could have done otherwise, since even if they had stood erect, the hands would have been close to their feet. Niall thought they looked like ghosts with four legs. And although he was glad that he was no longer alone, something about them worried him slightly; he was not at all sure that he liked them.

The sky was also different. Whereas it had formerly been blue, it was now covered in silvery clouds. But ordinary clouds lie more or less parallel to the Earth. These clouds were vertical, and were small and shiny, so they looked rather like a vast curtain of beads, or some giant crystal chandelier. They imparted to the light a curious silvery quality.

Some of the four-legged creatures looked at him curiously, and a few advanced to peer more closely. Niall was equally curious about them—he suspected that they were some type of nature spirit, like the chameleon men. Soon there were a dozen or more gathered around him. One of them who seemed smaller—and younger—than the others reached out to touch him with one of its absurdly long hands. There was a hiss of warning from some of the others, and the creature snatched its hand away. But a moment later, another reached out and tentatively prodded Niall with a long, crooked forefinger, the back of which was covered with white hairs. When Niall showed no reaction, smiling to indicate that he was not alarmed, several more reached out and touched him.

They seemed mainly interested in his face, his bare arms, and his legs—with their immense long arms, it was as easy to touch his feet as his head. He noted that their hands were very cool, and there was some curiously soothing quality about their touch.

Soon they all were stroking him as if he were a dog, their hands caressing his arms, shoulders, back, and even his thighs. He began to find it surprisingly pleasant, not unlike being massaged by his female attendants after he had taken a bath. A warm, drowsy feeling began to spread through him, which—oddly enough—reminded him of the pleasure he had once experienced holding Princess Merlew in his arms.

Suddenly he was startled by an angry shout, and the white creatures shrank back guiltily. Striding toward them came a human he knew instinctively to be female. Long, dark brown hair fell below her waist, and she wore a brown garment that almost reached the ground. But the face had neither eyes nor a nose—simply a mouth in its center, with long, sensual-looking red lips.

She said, in a strained, throaty voice: "What are you doing here?"

Being addressed in his own language was the last thing Niall expected—it was the first time he had heard it since he left the palace.

He said nervously: "I . . . I don't know."

This, of course, was true. But she evidently found it preposterous.

"You don't know?"

She leaned forward until her face almost touched Niall's. Her breath was as sweet as the breeze that blew around them. Even so, it was bewildering to look at this blank face, with only smooth skin where the nose and eyes should have been, and at the angrily contemptuous mouth. Her next question startled him.

"Can you fly?"

He said hesitantly: "I don't think so."

"In that case, you deserve to be eaten."

Niall switched his gaze to the faces around him, and suddenly realized she was serious. Most of the white creatures had now brushed back their hair from around their mouths, and their pointed yellowish teeth were unmistakably those of carnivores. They were eyeing him hungrily, and some were licking their lips—one was even dribbling. With a sudden shock, Niall realized that those gentle caresses had been intended to soothe him into a state of hypnotic acquiescence and surrender before they sank in their teeth. What was even more worrying was that he suspected he might have let them do it.

The woman said impatiently: "Get him out of here."

She seemed to be addressing someone over Niall's shoulder. Before he could turn round to see who it was, he was seized by the waist and jerked into the air with such speed that he had no time to feel alarmed. Great wings flapped above him, and his waist was held in the grip of immense claws that bore an odd resemblance to human fingers. He looked up—which was not easy, since his body was almost horizontal—but instead of the feathered breast he expected, he saw gray, scaly flesh like a reptile's, and a blunt face that resembled a tortoise. The leathery wings were those of a bat rather than a bird.

As he shot away from the ground at breathtaking speed, he saw the city dwindling below him until it was blotted out by the silvery clouds.

A moment later, he woke up in the cave of the chameleon men. No one seemed to notice that he was awake—or, if they did, no one paid any attention. Several minutes passed before he realized that this was a form of courtesy. They were giving him time to reflect on what had happened.

It was quite different from waking from normal sleep, which was like returning from unreality to reality. This was like returning from one reality to another. The dream seemed as real as the world around him.

But what did it mean? What was the significance of that city of striped cones? When he was a child, his grandfather Jomar had often spoken about dreams and their meaning—he believed that dreams are full of all kinds of omens. But Niall's dream seemed a medley of absurdities without obvious import.

He experienced a feeling of angry frustration. What was the good of possessing the power of reason if it could not even provide the key to a dream?

Then he felt ashamed of his irritation. The serenity of his companions was like a reproach. He deliberately induced in himself the same spirit of calm and patience, then attempted to relive the dream.

He closed his eyes and tried to visualize the striped plane with its conical buildings. At first it remained nothing more than this—a visualization, like a blurred and unfocused picture. But this, he realized, was because he was using his mind, rather than a faculty that was capable of re-creating reality.

This required relaxing further, as if trying to reactivate a memory. Then it happened, suddenly and instantaneously, and he was on the striped plane, with the sweet smell like candy.

There was one difference; this time he was aware that he was recalling it, and therefore had control over it. As soon as this happened, he understood the source of the dream.

The sweet smell was the smell of cotton candy at the children's party. And the pools of liquid on the pavements were the brightly colored drinks at the same party. As to the green and yellow stripes, he now recalled that they reminded him of the sticks of peppermint-flavored rock that were a favorite of the children in the city of the bombardier beetles. Some dream-artist inside his brain had mingled these elements into a fantasy of the candy-striped city.

So the dream expressed nostalgia for childhood innocence. But why had the buildings come no closer when he had walked toward them?

A moment's reflection told him the answer. Because he knew instinctively that nostalgia for lost innocence was no solution. He had recognized this when he called up an adult faculty—concentration and willpower—to achieve his objective. But all this had done was to plunge him into the interior of the circus tent, where he was lost in darkness. . . .

And what about the next part of the dream—the creatures with white hair and bulging eyes, who had lured him into a sense of security only in order to be able to eat him? And what of the woman with no eyes or nose?

He followed the same procedure as before: conjured up the mental image of the gray pavement with the ghostlike creatures with their long hair, then retreated into deeper relaxation. This, he could see, was the essence of the technique; the relaxation served to activate some refocusing faculty that made it all real. This time he could see that the dream-artist had not even bothered to create the houses in detail; they were simply sketched in, as a painter might sketch in a background he meant to finish later.

Niall even noticed something he had not noticed when dreaming the dream: that there was a high-pitched humming noise somewhere in the background.

The white ghosts began caressing him, stroking his bare flesh until the delicious, drowsy feeling began to spread over him. Just as he was relaxing into a trance of pleasure, there was a shout, and the woman in the brown garment came striding toward them. This time Niall paid attention to the white ghosts, and noticed how they brushed aside their long hair to uncover their mouths with their pointed teeth.

Again, the woman asked him if he could fly; again, Niall raised his hands above his head and rose up like an arrow, experiencing the marvelous sense of freedom. This feeling, he saw, was in a sense the most important thing about the dream. . . .

As he opened his eyes, Niall realized that his companions had been following what had been happening with interest, as well as with admiration. For them, this human ability to use the power of reason seemed almost miraculous. Their admiration spurred Niall to think once again about the dream of the ghosts.

His grandfather Jomar had been very fond of dream interpretation, and loved telling stories of dreams that foretold the future. Jomar certainly would have said that the dream of the "ghost people," who seemed so harmless until he realized they wanted to eat him, was intended as a warning. By appearing to be nervous and apprehensive they had lured him into trusting them. . . .

And what of the woman with the long hair, who had no eyes or nose? Surely the answer must be that if she was sent to warn him of danger, then all she needed was a mouth?

Niall was startled by a curious rattling noise, like a shower of pebbles falling on a roof. He looked at the faces of his companions, and smiled with astonishment as he realized that the sound was inside his head, and that it was their equivalent of applause.

At that moment there was a sudden silence, and a sense of expectation. Niall knew, without being told, what was going to happen. In the world above, the Sun had just appeared over the horizon.

In the desert, Niall's family never saw the dawn—they were all safe inside the shelter of their cave. Niall had witnessed its power for the first time when he was in the spider city, fleeing from Kazak's palace, and had seen the reaction of an elm tree to the vibrations that poured from the goddess, and watched its branches waving like living arms.

And now, even under the earth, Niall could feel the power of the goddess. There was a strange, heavy silence, creating a calm so deep that his soul seemed to contract to a point. Then, in the stillness, there was a tingling sensation, followed by a burst of pure joy. It swept through the cave like a breaking wave, making him feel breathless. Then it subsided, to be followed by the gentler energy of the rising Sun. Aboveground, birds would be bursting into song. Around him, the chameleon men were experiencing a state of bliss that was too intense for Niall's human senses.

He also felt a certain guilt, knowing that the chameleon men normally would be outside to greet the dawn, and that they were now underground solely because of the courtesy they felt toward a guest. But at least there was no need to express his gratitude; they were already aware of it.

Now it was time to try to make contact with his mother. In Niall's family, there had always been an agreement that, when anyone was away on a journey, they should be ready to establish communication at dawn or sunset.

Niall sat upright with a straight back, and again induced the feeling of inner silence. He visualized his mother, then emptied his mind. Five minutes went by, and he felt nothing—like most of the inhabitants of the palace, she probably had slept through the dawn. Then, quite suddenly, he became aware of his mother's presence, as if she was sitting a few feet away. Back in the palace, she would have the same sensation, aware of her son's presence.

Niall conveyed to her, quickly and economically, that he was among friends, and that he would soon continue his journey.

She, in turn, conveyed that all was well at home, that Veig seemed stable, that the women (she meant Sidonia and Crestia) were looking after him, and that he had eaten supper the night before. Then, about to break off the conversation (telepathy was not intended for exchanging gossip), she added: "Watch out for the captain." From the mental image that accompanied the words, Niall knew she was referring to a renegade spider, an intimate of Skorbo, the brutal captain of the guard. The captain had been ordered out of the city because, like Skorbo, he had continued the practice of eating humans.

From the fact that she then ended the communication, Niall inferred that she was merely conveying a cautionary injunction, not a specific warning.

He felt better after speaking with his mother. Niall was still young enough to feel homesick. But he was also young enough to have an underlying sense of indestructibility, and this had now returned.

Like the chameleon men, Niall now rose to his feet. It continued to astonish him that, after sitting on the ground for hours, his legs were not stiff, and he was free of aches and pains. The chameleon men seemed to know the secret of directing a flow of earthforce, which rippled through the cave like a breeze, inducing a sense of well-being and vigor.

As they made their way back through the low tunnel, Niall was glad that he could now see clearly, to avoid bumping his head or stumbling on the flight of steps. Nothing in this tunnel suggested that it was the work of hands; anyone who found it by accident would assume that it was a natural fissure in the rock.

As he pushed past the holly bush that almost blocked the entrance, Niall had to close his eyes to protect them from the sunlight. Because his senses were still attuned to those of the chameleon men, walking into daylight was a breathtaking sensation, a little like wading into chest-high water; it made him gasp. And the sound of the birds, and the rustle of the dawn wind in the branches, were almost deafening.

On the far side of the holly bush, Niall tripped over something that for a moment he thought was a rock; then saw with incredulity that it was his backpack. He laughed aloud as he snatched it up. One side of it was wet and sticky, and it covered his hands in mud. Fortunately, it was the back of the pack, and the heavy canvas had kept the water from leaking inside. He knelt on the grass and wiped off the mud, then unbuckled the strap and untied the leather thongs that closed the neck. These were so tight with moisture that he had difficulty loosening the knot. But when he reached inside, he was delighted to find that the contents were dry. Only the matches were ruined.

The chameleon men waited with their customary patience, glad to see Niall so elated. And Niall knew they were in no hurry. Unlike human beings, they experienced no impatience, no desire to hurry.

Niall asked: "How did it get here?" and received a mental image of a large bird, like an eagle, which had carried it in its claws. And now that he looked more closely, Niall could see the marks of talons on the cloth.

He cleaned off the mud with a handful of grass, then slipped his arms through the straps.

"And which way must I travel to reach the Gray Mountains?"

The chameleon men turned and pointed in a direction that seemed to Niall to be the northwest, then added a simple image that conveyed the message: "But since you are our guest, we shall show you the way to the edge of our domain."

Niall was delighted. He had no idea where their territory came to an end, but he hoped it was a long way.

T raveling with the chameleon men was like no other journey Niall had ever made.

To begin with, nothing in his hours spent underground had prepared him for the riotous pandemonium of color that surrounded him in the forest. He assumed at first that his eyes were simply adjusting to the sunlight, but it was soon apparent that it was far more than that—every color was deeper and richer. The dark green of the leaves and ferns reminded him of the Delta; the yellows of the buttercups, autumn crocus, and toadstool fungus, and the reds and salmon pinks of a wand-shaped flower that grew in thick clusters, were almost painful to the eyes.

His first assumption—that this area of woodland was particularly sensitive to the vibrations of the goddess—had to be abandoned when he observed that the sounds of birdsong and even the rustling of the leaves were almost deafening. And when a frog jumped into a still pool, the sound made him flinch like an explosion. It was then that he realized that his senses were attuned to those of the chameleon men, which were far more sensitive than those of human beings.

The result was that during the first half hour with the chameleon men, Niall felt slightly dizzy and drunk; it was as if his body had become lighter, or as if some force were trying to lift him off the ground. This sensation was strongest before the sun rose above the line of the trees; then, to his relief, the world gradually returned to normal. The bombardment of colors and sounds continued, but his senses were adjusting to it.

It took him some time to notice that his companions had become virtually invisible. His mental contact with them was so close that he could sense their presence as well as if he could see them, and it was only when he noticed how a bank of blue flowers shimmered, as if seen through running water, that he realized that transparent chameleon men were walking in front of it.

He also noticed that birds and animals regarded him with curiosity. They were totally unafraid, and simply stared, one group of rabbits ceasing to nibble grass in order to watch as he went past. Yet when the shadow of a hawk passed over the grass—Niall was aware of its identity without even glancing upward—they all vanished into the undergrowth.

It was as they were walking along the banks of a stream that he became conscious of other varieties of life. In a hollow in the bank, formed by a piece of moss, he saw the movement of something white, which he took to be a fish. He stared hard, and blinked with amazement as he saw that the white blur was actually a white bird like a seagull. Niall had never heard of a bird that could breathe under water. A moment later, it became a white blur again, and as he thought he saw the distinct movement of a fish's tail, he became convinced that his eyes were playing him tricks. Then its upper half emerged above the water, and he was startled to see that it was a small human form, about nine inches high. It was female—he could distinctly see tiny breasts—and had long hair of a dull yellow color. Then it vanished like a wisp of vapor, and he could see only sunlight on the ripples. There was no sign of the white body in the clear water.

During the next ten minutes, he saw several of these "water sprites," and realized that, like the chameleon men, they seemed to be able to make themselves visible or invisible, or change their form at will. If he tried hard, he could see them after they disappeared, but by that time they had become transparent, as if made of glass.

Among the assorted folklore Niall had absorbed in the white tower was a knowledge of fairies and water sprites, but he had been taught that they were curious and quaint superstitions; now it was plain that they really existed.

A moment later an even odder thing happened. They were crossing a stream on a moss-encrusted log, and Niall stumbled forward into the chameleon man who was walking in front of him, and was afraid that he had knocked him into the stream. He was surprised when there was no impact, then astonished as he saw the legs of the chameleon man partly blended with his own. Far from objecting to this superimposition of Niall's body on his own, the chameleon man seemed to enjoy it, and the care required to reach the other end of the log prolonged the contact for about ten seconds more, during which time Niall became aware that they were surrounded by tiny figures, none more than a foot high. There must have been a dozen or so in the stream and on its banks, mostly female, although a few appeared to be male, or of indeterminate sex. Moreover, on a carpet of fallen leaves among the trees on the far bank there were taller beings, perhaps two feet high, and who Niall at first took to be naked children, as well as some creatures resembling small brown animals.

All these vanished as soon as Niall stepped ashore and lost contact with the chameleon man. But now that he knew they were there, he made an effort to see them by staring hard at the shadows among the leaves. This at first had no effect. Then he tripped over a fallen branch, and as he did so, was suddenly able to see them again. Although they instantly vanished, he was now aware that looking too hard was counterproductive, and that he had to relax and use a kind of natural instinct. He later came to refer to it as "looking sideways."

As soon as he did this, the figures reappeared, but he was intrigued to see that they were now fully clothed, wearing gray garments and green headgear that fitted tightly around the skull. This seemed so incongruous that he almost laughed. He was quite certain they had been naked when he first saw them.

Another collision with a chameleon man offered him a clue. Once again, it was his own fault—he was trying to look back over his shoulder when he tripped over a rock. This time he landed on all fours, and several chameleon men walked into him. As their bodies blended with his, the gray-clad figures suddenly became naked, looking like small, overweight men. By the time Niall stood up and wiped the damp earth off his hands on dry leaves, the figures had disappeared altogether. He made them reappear by "looking sideways"; but again they were clothed in gray garments.

But the trick of "looking sideways" had given him the clue. He had made them reappear by using his own mind. They had been there, but were invisible until he made the effort. But when he saw them through the eyes of the chameleon men, they were naked. Was it possible that he was somehow adding the clothes with his imagination?

There was, of course, another possibility—that the clothes were "added" by the little creatures themselves. Perhaps that was how they preferred a human being to see them.

All this had fascinating implications. The trees around him looked solid because he was sure they were really there, and sure they looked exactly as he thought they looked. But suppose his imagination also "added" something to their appearance, just as it seemed to "add" clothes to the little men?

It was a bewildering thought whose implications seemed endless. But Niall was in no condition for such speculations. This was one of the drawbacks of seeing the world in such dazzling colors; his brain was so flooded with impressions that it was difficult to think clearly. He found himself wishing that he had a pair of the dark spectacles that Simeon wore when the Sun was too bright.

Farther downstream, Niall caught a glimpse of the brown, furry creatures, and was amused to see that they looked like a parody of human beings. They walked upright on tiny legs, and carried their short arms—or forelegs—in front of them. Their faces emerged from a fringe of fur, and had bright, intelligent eyes, and a long nose like a hedgehog's, ending in a flat point resembling a pig's snout, which snuffled continuously. But when they saw Niall, then noticed the chameleon men, they hastily vanished among the trees. When Niall inquired why, he was told that they were mischievous and destructive beings, ruining young trees with their sharp teeth—not merely for food, but simply for the pleasure of using their teeth. Niall found it almost unbelievable that some of the creatures in this woodland paradise should be wantonly disruptive.

Soon after this he had an opportunity to observe that they they were not the only ones. Half a mile farther on, the stream widened into a brown pool that covered half an acre. There was obviously a blockage downstream. The chameleon men spread out among the trees, and asked Niall to fall back to their rear; they clearly blamed some living agency for this flood, and wanted to approach unseen.

On the far side of the pool, they found its cause: two dead trees that held back a conglomerate of leaves and black mud. From its far side came a high-pitched, chattering squeak that sounded like excited birds.

Quite suddenly, the chameleon men made themselves visible, and the chattering sounds turned into shrieks of alarm. About a dozen humanoid creatures fled in all directions, some of them diving straight over the dam—these latter rose into the air like enormous silver fish, then, once in the brown water, simply vanished.

For a moment, Niall had a hallucinatory sense of being back in the Delta, for the creatures resembled the frog men he had encountered there. But the similarity was only superficial. The frog men of the Delta were gray, with yellow carnivorous teeth, and they spat jets of venom. These creatures, who were about two feet high, looked almost human, except for their abnormally long arms and legs and their webbed hands and feet. They had pointed, foxlike faces, with a fringe of green hair and large bulbous eyes. They were silvery-green, with black markings. And they ran like humans, covering the ground at enormous speed with their spindly legs. In about ten seconds, all had vanished.

Niall was hypnotized by the sight of the waterfall created by the dead trees, for it flashed and sparkled in a way that could not be attributed entirely to reflected sunlight. After staring intently for several minutes, he had no doubt that the flowing stream released some form of energy, created by the sunlight, which was absorbed by the elementals who shimmered in and out of existence in the green water.

The chameleon men—now quite obviously solid—went on to dismantle the dam; after the logs had been removed, it collapsed with a gurgling roar, and the water thundered down the valley. Within minutes, the pool had been drained.

But why, Niall wanted to know, had these fish creatures wanted to block the stream?

The answer, it seemed, was: to make themselves a kind of swimming pool. These froglike beings never ceased to look around for some kind of mischief that would irritate the chameleon men and undo their work of creating harmony. Like the brown animals, they had a destructive streak. Niall thought of the bombardier beetles, with their love of explosions, and felt he could begin to understand.

Throughout most of the morning they continued to travel through an amazingly varied landscape of woodland, low hills, and winding streams. This was Niall's first opportunity to see an October landscape, with its falling leaves and distinct autumn smell, and he found it almost painfully beautiful. Because of the heightening of his perceptions, it often seemed that the landscape was speaking to him, or that it had some deep significance it was trying to convey. And on at least two occasions he experienced a curious sense of familiarity, of having seen it before.

He also learned from the chameleon men that most trees had their own elemental spirit. One young oak made such an impression of radiant vitality that he stopped to stare at it. The leader of the chameleon men thereupon touched his elbow, causing an instant alteration in his perceptions which revealed that the trunk of the tree was surrounded by a dim green aura that extended about a foot beyond the bark, while the tree itself, which now seemed transparent, was of a deeper and more brilliant green. As he gazed into this core of vibrating energy, he suddenly realized that it contained a living shape, which vibrated at a different rate than the tree, and that he could make out a face. If he changed the focus of his gaze, the face disappeared, so that he was not certain whether it was real, or whether, like faces seen in the fire, it was the result of his imagination.

A moment later, the being inside the tree seemed to become aware that it was being observed, and the wavering outline suddenly became more real. It was a thin face, with high cheekbones, a long chin, and sharp, intelligent eyes. For a few seconds, these gazed back into Niall's. Then the creature seemed to lose interest, and dissolved away again. Once more, Niall could see only the rough brown bark.

As they moved on, Niall asked the chameleon men if the nature spirit ever came out of the tree. The answer was that it did so frequently, taking on a solid shape. In fact, it was essential that it emerge from the tree, for it then absorbed a certain energy from the atmosphere, which was carried back inside the tree and stimulated its growth. It was because this tree spirit (which, Niall seemed to recall, was referred to by humans as a gnome) made a dozen such excursions every day that this tree glowed with vital energy. But the tree elemental never ventured more than a few hundred yards from its home. A familiar place was essential to it. Niall found himself reflecting that human beings are not so very different.

Whenever the chameleon men halted to unblock a stream or clear away dead wood that was stifling the vegetation, Niall tried to help, but soon realized that his clumsiness was only an impediment. The chameleon men worked as a group, yet seemed to respond to one another like a single organism, of which the leader played the part of the head. The result was that they were able to accomplish an amazing amount of work in a short space of time, even to moving dead trees that should have required the strength of a giant to budge them.

But the most memorable event of the day occurred when they found themselves on a hilltop above a valley that looked as if a storm had swept through it, leaving half the trees lying on the ground, or broken, or leaning against one another. These trees were covered in a thick, glossy ivy, and with some other parasite creeper with yellow flowers. There was also a type of bramble that Niall had never seen before, with thorns as big as a man's thumb, and this had covered many of the fallen trees, making an impenetrable mass. There was also a kind of gray grass that reminded Niall of the beard of an old man, which had choked most of the bushes.

In the bottom of the valley lay the remains of a long and narrow lake, also choked with dead wood and gray vegetation, so that its surface looked at once oily and dusty. Yet the trees on the other side of this stagnant water seemed relatively unaffected; most of them had lost their leaves, but at least they looked healthy.

The wind that blew through the valley from the northwest was unpleasantly cold. It seemed to Niall that there was some evil influence in the place.

The chameleon men were obviously surprised by this devastation, and one of them projected a mental picture of the valley as it had been last time they saw it, with green leaves reflected in the clear waters of the lake.

Before they walked down to the lake, Niall took the cloak from his pack; as he fastened the clasp at the throat, a sudden gust of wind almost tore it from his hands. Protected from the chill breeze, which seemed to threaten snow, Niall was glad of its warmth.

The chameleon men were now completely invisible, and anyone looking down from the height above would have taken Niall for a lone traveler.

As they followed the overgrown path beside the lake, Niall observed a smell of rotting vegetation that reminded him of the Delta. Now, in the bottom of the valley, the air was so motionless and stifling that Niall felt breathless, and had to remove the cape. And, as in the Delta, he had a curious feeling of being watched. He felt instinctively that the chameleon men found the place as uncomfortable as he did. Niall assumed that, like himself, they would want to move on as quickly as possible, but in fact they halted to confer among themselves, meanwhile staring intently into the confusion of broken trees and giant brambles. Niall stared too, but could see nothing to explain the chaos.

At that point the leader sent him a clear message: he was to walk on to the top of the next hill. Although puzzled, Niall nevertheless did as he was asked. The leaden atmosphere made his body feel unpleasantly damp and heavy, and he plodded with slow steps, feeling as if his feet had turned into blocks of stone. The path had been almost obliterated, and in one place was blocked by a large uprooted bush, which looked as if it had been torn out by the roots, and which forced him to scramble over a landslide of fallen rocks.

When he reached the far side of the obstacle, he heard the unmistakable crackling of burning wood. He clambered back up the pile of rocks, which immediately began to slide under his feet, and understood why the chameleon men had sent him away. The hillside was turning into a sheet of flame that spread upward like an explosion. The chameleon men, visible now only as vortices of energy that somehow distorted the air around them, were causing this fire by directing crackling bursts of energy at dry leaves and twigs. A blast of acrid smoke blinded him and made him cough. And as a moss-covered tree behind him turned into a blazing torch, he realized with alarm that he had to move quickly. The flames were already setting trees alight a mere twenty yards behind him. As he stumbled uphill, he could feel that heat burning his shoulders.

The hilltop was still fifty yards away when, to his relief, a blast of icy north wind filled his lungs with clean air. It also had the effect of blowing out the flames of burning grass that were threatening to overtake him.

Suddenly seized by anxiety about his companions, he turned and gazed downhill. Billowing smoke was now being blown in the opposite direction, and its white clouds blotted out the lake and the bottom of the valley. The hillside above was a mass of surging flame and rising sparks. Niall found himself reflecting, incongruously, that the bombardier beetles would have appreciated this spectacle; then, as a whirlpool of spiraling smoke surrounded him, he began to run with clumsy steps up to the hilltop.

Once there he experienced an irrational feeling of security; in fact, there were rocks on either side of him, and the path plunged into another patch of woodland where the flames could not follow. When he looked back, the whole northern side of the valley had become an inferno, with the flames racing toward the topmost ridge

The fire was still a hundred yards from this ridge when Niall suddenly understood why the chameleon men had started the blaze. From the burning hilltop, an immense winged creature soared upward— Niall's first confused impression was that it was a giant bird. Then the shape of the purple wings made him aware that it was some kind of bat. With a squawk of rage that echoed down the valley, it flapped into the smoky sky, then, to Niall's horror, changed direction and flew straight toward him. Niall flung himself flat on his face, expecting to feel its talons sinking into his back. A sensation like a wind rushed past him as he clutched the grass, but when he looked up, he found he was alone. The sky above him was empty.

It was then that Niall realized he had seen another "elemental"; no natural creature could have vanished so suddenly and so completely.

Moments later he was joined by the chameleon men, whose presence he could feel although he was still unable to see them. The fire had done them no harm; in their transparent state, they apparently were impervious to the elements.

In answer to Niall's questions, they explained that the elemental was of a kind that preferred solitude, and that liked to make its home on hilltops, where it blended so completely with the earth and rock that it became undetectable. Because it hated to be disturbed, it made itself unapproachable by transforming the hillside into an obstacle course of fallen trees and giant brambles, turning its chosen valley into a wilderness. Such creatures were not actually malevolent, but their determination to be alone made them ruthless and destructive. Given the opportunity, they told Niall, it would undoubtedly take revenge for this indignity.

Niall asked: "But if you cannot be harmed by fire, why should this creature be driven out by it?"

The answer, expressed in images that were more forceful than human language, was that all creatures dislike being regarded with disapproval, and that the flames were a powerful expression of this feeling; in fact, the creature was being expelled by the force of their minds rather than by the fire.

Niall observed that the colors of the woodland through which they were now making their way seemed in some way oddly faded and dim, as if seen on a cloudy day; he tried "looking sideways," but was unable to glimpse any nature spirits. The chameleon men confirmed this; the presence of the unfriendly elemental had driven all other spirits away.

Niall was deeply interested in this insight; it was something he had often sensed intuitively, yet had never consciously grasped: that the life of nature depends on elemental spirits, and that without these spirits, the most beautiful scenery lacks some essence of vitality.

A mile or so farther on, the woodland came to an end, and the stream vanished underground into a cave with a low entrance. The grass here was rich and green, spotted with late buttercups, and the practice of "looking sideways" revealed once again the presence of nature spirits.

The path they had been following continued in a straight line toward a ridge of hills. Here Niall made another interesting observation. It was quite apparent to him that the stream continued to flow under his feet; it produced a distinct tingling sensation. Niall had always possessed this ability to sense underground water; it was part of the essential equipment of the desert dweller. But it had been merely a faint tingle in his legs. Now it was a curious, vibrant sensation that he could sense throughout his body.

Where the path curved to the left toward a gap in the hills, the tingling stopped; obviously, the stream and the path had diverged.

The grass they were walking on now was springy and green, bringing back a memory of the city of conical towers in his dream. The track they were following must at some time have been a road, for they passed large stones that were partly buried in the turf, and a few of these had some kind of writing carved on them, although Niall was unable to decipher it, or even make out the configuration of the letters. The chameleon men were unable to say who had placed the stones in position, or what they were intended for, although they believed they were thousands of years old. But they pointed out, on the moor they were now crossing, other stone monuments. One of these, a hundred yards off the road, was like a gigantic stone mushroom, whose top was at least six feet wide. Glancing sideways at this, Niall was startled to glimpse a figure like a little old man sitting on the top of it. When he turned his head to stare, the figure was no longer there.

Now, quite unexpectedly, a freezing wind blew from behind them, carrying rain. The gust was so powerful that it almost blew Niall onto his knees. He recognized immediately that this was not a natural wind, but that it was somehow connected with the elemental they had driven out of its home. This was the revenge the chameleon men had anticipated. It was not directed against them—since they could not be harmed by natural forces—but against Niall, who was vulnerable to wind and rain.

Niall's companion indicated some kind of monument on the hillside, and they hurried toward it as black clouds turned the sunny afternoon into a kind of dusk and the wind caused Niall to stumble on the uneven turf. As they came closer, Niall saw that it consisted of six large upright megaliths placed close together, with another huge flat stone balanced on top of them. They hurried into this shelter as the storm broke, and the rain came down so hard that it turned the hillside into mist. Niall lost no time in flinging his pack on the ground and taking shelter from the wind against the largest of the great uprights. But although it was at least four feet in width, it seemed inadequate to protect Niall from the wind, which seemed to blow from all sides, or from the driving rain.

As Niall began to shiver, the chameleon men became increasingly concerned. A great crash of thunder sounded so close by that it made the stones vibrate, while lightning that struck the ground ten feet away gave Niall a distinct electric shock.

The chameleon men clearly felt it was time they did something. They made Niall stand up—he had been crouching behind the upright stone—so his head almost touched the triangular granite block that formed the roof, and then made a circle around him. Niall assumed they were trying to protect him from the wind, and that the maneuver was doomed to failure, since the powerful blasts blew straight through them.

In fact, they went on to place their hands on Niall, some on his shoulders, some on his back, some on his head, which immediately induced the deep sense of calm that he had experienced in the underground cave. What they were actually doing was transmitting to Niall the vibrations of their physical being. For a few seconds, he instinctively resisted the force that was attempting to alter his rate of vibration. Then he realized that what they were trying to do could only be achieved with his help. It required a peculiar kind of mental effort, which involved using their energies and somehow blending them together by an act of will.

As soon as he did this, Niall felt himself dissolving, as if his body was turning into air. As the vibrational rate of his being increased, something fell around his feet, and he realized that it was his clothes; but his feet and legs had become invisible. He was standing there naked, and the wind and rain were blowing straight through him.

There was another vibrational change, and a wave of cold energy ran up his spine. As it reached his head, the chameleon men suddenly became visible, looking more solid than he had ever seen them before. And his own body was also clearly visible. But he could no longer feel the wind, which continued to howl past him, and which blew his clothes against the opposite wall. On the other hand, the stones around him seemed to turn into glass, so that he could see straight through them, and see the rain that ran down their sides like a shower down a windowpane.

With a tremendous final blast, the wind and rain suddenly stopped, banishing any notion that this might have been an ordinary storm. Within minutes, the sky was blue. But Niall was in no hurry to leave the rock shelter. In fact, he was in no hurry to do anything—his bodiless state brought a marvelous sense of freedom. He had never realized before how much the human body weighs, and how much effort it costs to carry it around. It suddenly struck him that if he had to carry a burden weighing as much as his own body, he would soon be exhausted. The lightness was intoxicating.

But it also brought a disconcerting sense of timelessness, rather like the relaxation that followed a large glass of wine. Time seemed merely another name for anxiety, and he felt glad to be rid of it. On the other hand, the world around him had never seemed so fascinating. To begin with, this strange building that had sheltered him from the storm was not merely a monument from the dawn of history; it was also a marker, placed upon this spot because it was the most important place for miles around. It was the place where many earth forces joined together. If Niall had chosen to sit there for a few days, he could have learned not only the history of this moor, but all the secrets of nature.

He was also aware that this place had a guardian, an old man who now seemed benevolent, but who once had been a brutal warrior king who had slain many enemies and dismembered others while they were still alive. This area of the moor had once been the site of a great battle, where the king had died of his wounds after putting his enemies to flight. Now he would have also gladly left, but memory of the cruelty he had inflicted bound him to this place.

Niall could have learned the king's life story merely by staying there and absorbing what had been written in the stones. But his own memory told him this was no time to delay. They were close to the edge of the territory of his companions, and soon it would be time for him travel into the unknown.

The chameleon men, who were aware of all Niall's thoughts and feelings, were saddened by his decision; it seemed incredible to them that anyone could want to leave their eternal realm of nature to return to the busy human world. Now that they had shared Niall's thoughts and feelings for so long, they had become aware of the peculiar difficulties of being human, the narrow limits of human consciousness, the mechanicalness of the human body, and its need to struggle against the hard facts of physical reality, and they no longer found it all so fascinating.

Niall felt the same, and if it had not been for the thought of Veig, might well have remained with them until days drifted gently into weeks. But the day had already passed its midpoint, and the autumn dusk would soon be falling.

He knew instinctively how to return to his normal human state; it merely required slowing down his increased vibrational rate. Admittedly, he had to overcome intense reluctance to do it; it was like getting out of a warm bed on a cold winter morning and then jumping into a freezing cold bath. But as he forced himself to do it, the chameleon men faded away, and once more he was aware of them only through the sympathy they had established. The stones became opaque once more, and the presence of their sad warrior guardian grew dim, like a dream.

Yet in the moment of returning to the physical world, Niall felt a surge of happiness, and knew that this was the world in which he had been intended to live out his life. In that brief moment, he seemed to understand why he had been born.

It was time to leave. He bent down and picked up his damp clothes, then dressed quickly because there was a chill in the air. Before pulling on his pack, he took his watch from it and looked at the time; it was within two hours of dusk. But he was not looking at his watch simply to check how late it was, but as an expression of pleasure at returning to the world of time.

Because they knew they would soon be taking leave of their guest, the chameleon men also returned to their physical forms. As they left the stones that had sheltered them, they made a ritual gesture of thanks to its guardian, and Niall, although he was no longer conscious of the presence of the old warrior, did the same. Then they went out again into the pale sun of the autumn afternoon.

The bright green grass sparkled in the sunlight, and it was no longer necessary for Niall to "look sideways" to see nature spirits—his brief transformation to the bodiless state meant that their vibration was no longer slightly beyond his normal range of perception. So as they walked on over the springy grass, with its intersprinkling of gorse and heather, he was able to see clearly the flickering of vital forms that hovered on the edge of physical existence. They appeared like a glimmer of color, not unlike a flame seen in the sunlight; but as soon as he tried to focus his eyes on them, he became aware once more of the curious nature of nonphysical things. A physical form can be seen simply by looking at it, whereas seeing a nonphysical form is like speaking to it and receiving a reply. Before it can be seen, a nonphysical form must decide—so to speak—what to reply, or even whether to reply at all. In other words, a nonphysical form *chooses* to be seen.

Niall was aware of the absurdity of such an idea. Yet it was here, in front of his eyes. A nature spirit seemed to flicker on the edge of a patch of gorse whose flowers had long ago withered away. But when he looked at it, it simply disappeared, and he could see only the prickly green gorse. In order to see it, he had to look at it more gently, less demandingly, as if saying: "Please show yourself to me." Then the form might emerge, looking like a pulsating ball of light, or a will-o'-the-wisp, or a furry small animal, or even a grotesque little human being. But there was always a split second before it appeared when Niall was aware that he himself was making the final choice about what it would look like.

He knew intuitively that these forms did not possess much intelligence—probably less than an animal—or much willpower. But their bodiless existence meant that they hardly needed intelligence.

Instead of following the path toward the ridge, the chameleon men led him into a hollow not far from the track. In the bottom of the hollow there was a construction of flat stones, which covered a well. The water was so clear that Niall felt the need to kneel and gaze into it, as if plunging his soul into the cool depths. It was about three feet deep, and the bottom was of a white substance like sand. The sides of the well were thick with green moss. In a small annex built of flat stones was an earthenware vessel, similar to the one from which Niall had drunk in the cave of the chameleon men, except that it had a handle, and a crooked wooden stick, part of a branch from which the bark had been stripped.

One of the chameleon men took this stick, plunged it into the water, and stirred vigorously. The result was that moss flaked into the water, filling it with floating fragments. Niall was instructed to take the earthenware jug by the handle and fill it with water. He dipped it and filled it to the brim. Then the leader of the chameleon men took it from him, and took the first drink, after which he handed it back to Niall, who also raised it to his lips and drank.

The familiar earthy taste was so startling and invigorating that Niall stared into the water, wondering if it possessed some magical property. He then handed it to the others, and they drank in turn. As they did this, Niall was aware that this was more than a ceremony of leave-taking; it was a ritual whose purpose was to establish a sense of abiding kinship and to offer him protection.

As the jug returned, the leader of the chameleon men handed it to Niall and pointed to the water.

"If you wish to return to us, remember this taste."

As he stared into the green, brown-flecked eyes, Niall experienced a rush of gratitude, mixed with a certain astonishment. He became suddenly aware that he had inspired great affection in his companions. This seemed incomprehensible to him until, with an instinct that sprang from telepathic closeness, it struck him that they were deeply concerned for his safety. This strange being who was a king among his own kind, and who had the courage to launch himself into a river that came from nowhere (for this was how the chameleon men thought of the river that flowed under the spider city), was now about to risk his life seeking out a dangerous enemy.

What impressed them above all was that he was alone. The chameleon men had never been alone for a moment of their lives, and even their leader was more of an elder brother than an authority figure. Niall realized, with a kind of embarrassment, that they saw him as a person of heroic stature. But he was aware that being alone is part of the lot of all human beings, and that there is nothing particularly heroic about it.

He took out the flask of water from his pack, emptied it on the ground, and refilled it with water from the well.

In the annex that had contained the jug, there were also a number of flat stones that he recognized as worked flints; cooks in his kitchen still used them when they ran out of matches. The flints obviously had been left there—like the jug—for the benefit of travelers. Niall took two of these, struck them together to produce a spark, and stowed them in his pack.

They climbed out of the hollow and uphill to the top of the ridge. Looking ahead across moorland that extended as far as the eye could see, Niall understood why this ridge had been chosen as the westward limit of the territory of the chameleon men. The lands behind them were full of a variety of valley and woodland, and of many different kinds of creatures, where the work of the chameleon men was necessary to preserve harmony. But the terrain that lay before him seemed to be lacking in variety. To the north, Niall could see the Gray Mountains, to the south the farmlands that were the territory of the spiders and the bombardier beetles; beyond them lay the sea, and beyond that the Delta.

Of these lands the chameleon men had known nothing before Niall came among them; now his awareness had become part of their own, extending their knowledge to more than ten times that of their own boundaries. But Niall was also the gainer, for he was now as familiar with their territory as they were themselves.

There was no time for a lengthy leave-taking; it was time to move on. The chameleon men would return to their peaceful, timeless world of woods and streams, while Niall would return to the time-obsessed human world.

At this point, human travelers would have shaken hands or embraced. But the chameleon men had no equivalent of the word "good-bye." In any case, they were not saying good-bye; as Niall walked swiftly downhill, he was as aware of their presence as if they had been walking beside him. But when he looked back a few minutes later, they had already vanished.

Something about the bleak moorland ahead of him made Niall feel uncomfortable. It was not simply that these miles of coarse gray grass reminded him of the gray mold that covered the broken trees in the valley of the elemental, but that he had the same disturbing sense of being observed by hostile eyes. But he could see only a few ravens circling overhead.

Since there was no longer the slightest trace of a path in this monotonous wilderness, he decided to make his way to the top of a hill that would afford a view of the way ahead. It was higher than he expected, and as he stood on the weatherworn granite that protruded from the dry turf at the summit, he could look back more than twenty miles to the snow-capped mountain above the sacred lake.

This brought to mind a question he had been intending to explore further: the source of the stream that polluted the sacred lake. The chameleon men had no idea of where it began, which meant that it lay beyond their territory.

Since Niall's contact with the chameleon men had implanted in his mind a clear and detailed image of their domain, he was able to infer that if the stream flowed directly from west to east, its underground course should pass fairly close to the hill he was standing on. And since, sooner or later, Niall had to turn his steps to the north, there seemed no good reason why he should not do so immediately. Pulling his cloak around his shoulders, since the wind was growing chilly, he made his way down the northern slope of the hill.

He had not far to travel; within half a mile he felt under his feet the tingling sensation that told him he was crossing an underground stream. At this point he turned west again, and began to follow its course. What puzzled him was that the stream beneath his feet seemed smaller than he expected—at a guess not more than six feet wide—while his impression from the size of the sacred lake was that it must be fed by a river, or at least more than one tributary.

The countryside that stretched ahead of him was bare and treeless: low hills covered with coarse grass, and valleys full of gorse and brambles. And since the Sun was less than an hour from the horizon, Niall began to think about finding somewhere to sleep. It had been a long day, and he had walked over twenty miles; his legs were beginning to ache. Now that he was no longer with the chameleon men, he had become subject once more to ordinary human tiredness.

But it was not simply this that made him feel oddly depressed. After the domain of the chameleon men, with its trees and streams and autumn flowers, this moorland landscape seemed drearily lifeless. He had not observed a single elemental since he left his companions, and this did not surprise him. Elementals, he had noticed, possessed a certain joyousness; they seemed to love nature, and lived off its vitality. In his present surroundings there was very little vitality.

Following the stream beneath his feet, he found himself walking along a low ridge with a view of the valley below, with a peaty brown lake full of dying sedge. The ridge led to a plateau a few hundred yards wide, in the center of which was a tall stone, perhaps twelve feet high, surrounded by dense, prickly bushes. Niall was tempted to camp at the foot of the stone, where the bushes would protect him from observation. But when he came closer, he observed a kind of yellowish moss on its surface, which seemed to resemble the face of an old man. Suddenly convinced that this was the home of an elemental, he stared at it intently, as if trying to force it to reveal itself. At that point, the rock seemed to turn into a hostile face that glared back at him, angry at this encroachment on its territory. As clearly as if his senses were still attuned to those of the chameleon men, he perceived that the rest of the elemental was sunk up to its shoulders in the turf; moreover, it seemed inclined to emerge and make Niall feel sorry for intruding. He turned and walked on without delay, relieved that the nature-craft he had absorbed from the chameleon men had saved him from choosing this spot to sleep; the elemental certainly would have found some way of making him pay for his blunder, if only by sending him vivid nightmares.

The sun was now close to the horizon, and when, still following the underground stream, he descended into the next valley, it was dark with shadows. Tempted to curl up under the nearest bush, he was discouraged by the unevenness of the ground, on which it was necessary to tread carefully to avoid twisting his ankles on gorse roots. And when he stumbled over a boulder that stuck up like a large egg out of the ground, he decided to sit down and rest his feet. This was such a relief that he was tempted to remove his backpack and close his eyes. But the encroaching darkness made him decide to resist the fatigue and press on.

When he reached the top of the next ridge, he was relieved to find the landscape ahead still bathed in evening sunlight. He was looking down on a basinlike valley that faced toward the west; it was at least a mile wide, and in its center was a lake that looked golden in the sunlight, but which, as he descended the slope toward it, proved to be of a striking pale green, which suggested either that it was stagnant or that its surface was covered with some green vegetation like the algae that covers ponds. A moment later, he noticed a stream that flowed into it from the far side of the valley, disposing of the notion that it might be stagnant.

But could this be the source of pollution of the sacred lake? He found it hard to believe—this lake looked somehow too peaceful and inviting. Even the grass that swept down to its edge was as fresh and green as the lake itself. It looked the ideal place to camp for the night.

By the time he reached the edge of the water a quarter of an hour later, the sun was touching the horizon. At close quarters, he could see that the color was due to tiny green particles. He dipped in his hand and cupped a little of the water in the palm; it was quite clear, and the fragments looked like particles of moss. This, then, was almost certainly not the source of pollution, in which case, he must have been following the wrong underground stream.

Since the ground shelved toward the lake, he decided against sleeping too close to the water. Instead, he began walking back up the southern slope until he found a spot where the ground flattened into a slight hollow. Within minutes the sun had dipped below the horizon, and he was in darkness. He flung his backpack on the ground, then sank down beside it and stretched out on his back, his arms beneath his head. The sense of relief was enormous.

But when the tiredness had drained out of his body, he realized he was hungry. He sat up in the dark and fumbled with his bag. The string that tied the neck was extremely tight, a circumstance to which he owed the fact that the contents were now dry. He switched on the flashlight and took out the flask of drink. As he had hoped, it contained mead— the kind he had drunk on the boat that had brought him to the country of the spiders, which was sweet and smelled of honey. He gave a chuckle of pleasure as it ran down his throat and spread warmth to his stomach. Next he opened the parcel of food. This contained a hard, unsweet pastry biscuit—a crunchy variety of which he was particularly fond—and some goat cheese. He spread the cheese with his knife. His mother had also included a waxed paper box that contained small green cucumbers pickled in vinegar, and even a jar of salt. He ate three of the biscuits and half the cheese before his hunger was satisfied. He also drank about a third of the mead, which he found induced a pleasant light-heartedness. While he was eating, the Moon rose, making the flashlight unnecessary.

The sky was full of stars, and he was able to recognize many his grandfather had taught him to identify—Capella, Epsilon Cassiopeia, and the constellation of Perseus the Hero. He yawned and replaced the food in his pack. The temperature of the air was so agreeably warm—presumably because the ground had soaked up hours of sunlight—that he was tempted to sleep covered only by his cloak. Then it struck him that if he did that, he would have to use his pack for a pillow. It seemed more sensible to use the sleeping bag, which had a kind of pocket intended to accommodate a pillow, and rest his head on the folded cloak.

He fell asleep in the manner that had been taught him by the chameleon men—that is, he concentrated hard and maintained this concentration as he grew sleepy. The result was that he lowered himself into sleep as he might have lowered himself into a warm bath. As he did so, he had a sense of the presence of the chameleon men, and felt dreams swirling around him like a mist blown by a breeze. Even as he sank into sleep, a part of himself remained conscious.

Half an hour or so later, he was awakened by spots of rain on his face, and sleepily pulled the top of the sleeping bag over his head. Then, as the rain became heavier, he pulled up the zipper as far as it would go, to prevent the rain leaking inside. Soothed by the sound of raindrops on the waterproof fabric, he drifted back into sleep.

He was dreaming about the chameleon men. They were in their underground cave, and they were talking about him. That, he realized, was why he was dreaming about them; there was a link between their minds and his. But since he knew he was dreaming, then he must in some sense be awake. Where was he? Where was his sleeping body? He had forgotten where he left it.

Then the leader of the chameleon men spoke to him in their own symbolic language. His meaning was perfectly clear. He was saying: "Lie perfectly still."

Moments later he was wide awake. He could still feel the presence of the chameleon men. He could also sense danger, and an awareness of the importance of not giving the slightest sign that he was awake.

The first thing he noticed was a curious and distinct smell that reminded him of the Delta: a blend of fish and rotting vegetation. Then he noticed that he could no longer feel the hard pressure of the ground underneath him. Instead, he might have been lying on the softest feather mattress in his palace. And both he and the mattress were floating through the air, as if transported on a flying carpet. He knew this because the waterproof flap was no longer covering his eyes, and he could see the lake glimmering in the moonlight, and recognize that he was moving toward it. Something—or someone—was carrying him with infinite gentleness, to prevent him from waking up. And he suddenly knew that his life depended on showing no sign that he was awake.

The curved fingers of his right hand were resting against his chest, and by moving the middle finger slightly, he could feel the slit at the top of his tunic. Since he had fallen asleep on his right side, the thought mirror had fallen down in this direction. With immense caution, he stretched the middle finger until it encountered the fine metal chain that held the mirror. Then he hooked the top of his finger into the chain and bent the joint until he was in contact with the thought mirror. A gentle movement of two fingers turned it over until the concave surface rested against his skin. Instantly, he felt the surge of power and wide-awakeness.

The increased attention induced by the mirror told him that he was being conveyed toward the lake at a speed of a few feet a minute. And the water still lay about a hundred yards ahead.

Now he knew that he would have to call on all his powers of focused attention if he was to escape with his life. But whereas this knowledge would normally have caused a certain nervous tension, it only increased his sense of self-control.

But what was carrying him? He did not dare to move his head, even slightly, to try to see what it was. But whatever it was, it did not possess the same telepathic ability as the spiders. A spider would have known long ago that he was wide awake.

Because the ground was sloping downward toward the lake, the waterproof flap fell open enough to allow Niall to see what was happening. He was about two feet above the ground, and the creature that was carrying him forward shone in the moonlight like a giant slug. But unlike a slug, it was not using the expansion and contraction of muscles to provide locomotive power. It seemed to be rolling forward, like a great mass of jelly.

Niall knew precisely what would happen if his slightest movement betrayed that he was not unconscious. He would instantly be absorbed into this huge cushion of slime and suffocated. This would have happened sooner, except that his body was enclosed in the sleeping bag. The slime-creature was unaccustomed to animals that could not be absorbed, yet could sense that, inside this waterproof cover, Niall was made of living flesh.

A moment later, a faint stir of breeze caused the waterproof flap to fall away from his eyes enough to be able to form an estimate of what was happening. The creature that was carrying him so silently and smoothly was transparent in the moonlight, and he could see the ground through its jellylike body.

Niall ignored what was happening, and the fact that he might be dead within a few minutes. Instead he focused his sense of interest until he felt himself sinking into the relaxation most animals achieve on the point of sleep. Using the trick taught him by the chameleon men, he went beyond this level to the point of deep relaxation, the level accepted by the chameleon men as a natural limit—indeed, which is a natural limit, in the sense that it allows simple organisms to survive temperatures close to absolute zero. Again, Niall felt his metabolic processes become static as his heartbeat sank to a point that no medical instrument could have detected.

There followed the strange sense of swimming down through total darkness. He no longer felt the slightest concern about what was happening to his body as the slime-creature conveyed it toward the lake; this now seemed absurdly unimportant. Instead, his mind was entirely concerned with detecting the first sign of the fragmentary energy that flickered in the darkness. Moments later, he felt it all around him, like a million bubbles. As that happened, he began absorbing it, sucking it into himself, and experiencing a sense of pure joy.

As before, this soon became almost too much to bear. Sheer vitality threatened to destroy the relaxation, and like a swimmer whose lungs are bursting, Niall allowed himself to be drawn back into present awareness.

The slime-creature sensed this increase in his vitality, and began to move faster, probably looking forward to its anticipated meal. But Niall was aware that his own vitality—and therefore his will—was far stronger than that of this absurd mass of semiconscious protoplasm. With deliberate concentration, he took over the instinctive will that organized these cells, and sent out the command to halt. It took several seconds before it responded, and Niall guessed that this was because it possessed no unifying control center, and the order had to be diffused to all its cells. The edge of the water was less than a dozen yards away when it finally came to a stop.

He swung his legs sideways, as if dismounting a horse, and encumbered by the sleeping bag, landed awkwardly on his feet. He unzipped the bag and stepped out of it. The slimy surface of the jelly reflected the moonlight, and seemed to be in continuous motion, like running water.

Niall was deeply curious. How could an organism as simple as this—little more, after all, than animated frog spawn—behave as if it possessed muscles and some kind of central nervous system? Niall sent out a command for it to move in the opposite direction, away from the water. This took a far greater effort of concentration than merely ordering it to halt, since the hunger in its cells, which Niall could actually feel as a discomfort in his own stomach, pulled it toward the lake. But the force of his will finally compelled it to obey.

As it moved, he watched carefully what happened, trying to fathom the secret of its locomotion. The whole transparent mass rolled in the direction he commanded, with no sign of how this was done. He had half expected it to reach out with some kind of pseudopodia, but in fact it seemed to move as a whole, each part touching the ground in turn on the same principle as a wheel.

But in that case, how had it prevented Niall from sliding off? There could be only one logical explanation: that the creature possessed enough control to divide itself into two halves, one of which remained static, like the saddle on a horse, while the lower used its own peculiar mode of locomotion.

Its transparency brought to mind something that had happened in the Delta. After he had communed with the goddess, Niall had experienced a sense that the Earth itself had become transparent, so that he was clearly aware of surging waves of vital force. This had been accompanied by a sensation that he called "double vision," as if he possessed two sets of eyes, one of which saw the solid material world, while the other could see through it to the deeper reality that lay underneath. And since this was related to the trick of "looking sideways" in order to see elementals, he now tried applying it to this pulsing mass of slime that was waiting patiently like a tethered horse.

The result shocked him. The slime-creature began to dissolve, as if it was turning into water. As it did so, its distinctive smell became overpowering. Seeing it dissolve was like watching a block of ice melt very quickly. Within less than a minute it had vanished; all that remained was a clear liquid that soaked the grass as it trickled toward the lake.

Suddenly he felt tired, as if his own energy had drained away. The past ten minutes had involved a tremendous effort of concentration. He wanted to sigh and close his eyes and let his energies return.

He picked up the sleeping bag, whose surface was wet, and climbed the hill toward the place where he had been sleeping. The ground was wet where the creature had passed, but when he bent and touched the grass, the moisture felt like water, without the viscosity he had expected.

His pack was where he had left it, and its surface was dry; apparently the creature had felt no interest in it. Since the ground where he had been sleeping was wet, he moved the pack to a spot a dozen yards away. An instinct told him there was nothing more to fear from the lake, but that it was important to get a good night's rest. Within a few minutes he was asleep.

It was past dawn when he opened his eyes, and although the Sun had still not reached the top of the hill behind him, it already was bathing the moorlands to the west. He climbed out of the sleeping bag—noting, as he did so, that it was covered with a faint layer of whiteness that smelled fishy—and pressed the catch that caused it to fold. His throat felt dry and he was ravenously hungry; he would have appreciated his usual breakfast of newly baked bread with butter and honey. Instead, he took a mouthful from the flask of well water, and once again felt oddly invigorated. It tasted, if anything, even better than when fresh from the well, and had a smell that reminded him of green things—of grass and leaves and young shoots. Moments later he was no longer hungry.

The Sun rose above the hilltop while he was repacking his knapsack, and illuminated the hillside and the green surface of the lake. He was struck by its beauty and by the soothing peacefulness of the landscape. He noticed something else: in the morning sunlight, the dewy grass looked brilliantly green, yet in the slight hollow where he had first fallen asleep the night before, the grass had the same faint chalky tinge that he had noticed on the underside of his sleeping bag—the side that had become damp with slime. Obviously, the whiteness was some deposit that was formed when the slime dried out. What puzzled Niall was that this area of whiteness extended over an area about twenty feet wide. The slime-creature Niall had seen in the moonlight had not been half that size.

Intrigued by the puzzle, Niall followed the trail of chalky grass downhill as far as the lake. It remained about twenty feet wide to the point where it vanished into the clear water.

Niall shook his head. How could a creature that was at most eight feet long leave a trail twenty feet wide?

The solution dawned on him, and made him feel like cursing his obtuseness. The creature must have been capable of reducing itself to a thin layer, so it could insinuate itself under him like a sheet of water.

What had happened, then? It must have wrapped itself around the sleeping bag, since the whole bag showed traces of whiteness. Fortunately, Niall's head was inside the waterproof pouch that was intended for a pillow. The slime-creature might still have covered his face and suffocated him—but then have lost its prey, since Niall might have struggled and escaped. That, he could now see, is why it had decided to carry him back to the lake and drown him before eating him.

And why had he experienced no intuition of danger the night before? Had it exercised some curious hypnotic influence to soothe him into a sense of confidence?

Now suddenly Niall had no doubt that the slime-creature was the origin of the pollution of the sacred lake. Like all living creatures, the slime shed millions of cells over the course of a lifetime. But whereas the skin cells shed by human beings are already dead, the cells of this simple organism remained alive; the only reason the creature abandoned them was that its vitality was not great enough to sustain more than a certain quantity of cells—otherwise it could have gone on spreading until it filled the lake.

But as he stood staring over the lake, Niall was troubled by one more question. Why had the creature suddenly dissolved away? At the time it had happened, Niall had assumed that this was the creature's own way of escaping the domination of his will—a kind of suicide. Now, on reflection, he realized this was unlikely. It was impossible to imagine a slug committing suicide, and this creature was even simpler than a slug.

Therefore, it had been destroyed by some will other than its own. But whose? And why?

This question continued to preoccupy him as he shouldered his pack and set his course for the northwest. When Asmak had taken Niall on a mental "reconnaissance" of the country between the spider city and the Gray Mountains, Niall had carefully memorized the route, and later reinforced the memory with the use of the thought mirror. So now he had at least a clear sense of his direction.

Outside the valley of the green lake, the moorland was uneven, irregular, and unattractive. The ground itself might have been designed as an obstacle course, and Niall frequently stumbled over tussocks of thick grass, twisted roots, and stones that stuck up out of the turf. A few ravens wheeled in the sky, but he could sense no elementals, not even a hostile spirit like the one that had shown so much resentment when he thought of choosing its rock as a campsite. The lack of elementals probably explained the roughness of the terrain and the coarseness of its vegetation.

After an hour of plodding through this uninspiring landscape, with an unseasonably warm October sun playing on the back of his head, his legs were beginning to feel heavy and he was longing to take his weight off them. But the ground was either too wet or too rugged. Finally he saw a flat stone, about three feet across, and flung himself down with relief. As he did so, he caused the stone to tilt, and a small rodent scampered out from under it. Before it reached the safety of a thorn bush, a large raven startled Niall by swooping down on it, killing it with one blow of its beak, and carrying it out of sight.

He took from his pack the parcel of food and ate some of the hard, crunchy pastry. As he was eating, the raven alighted on a gnarled tree a dozen feet away and watched with lively interest. It was a big bird, which stood more than two feet high, with a dangerous-looking ivory-colored beak.

Niall drank some of the well water, and began to feel more relaxed. He had often seen ravens of this size in the desert, and admired their sharpness of vision, which enabled them to see the movement of a mouse from a quarter of a mile in the air. Idly, simply to pass the time, he tried "looking sideways" at it, to see whether his faculty of double vision would reveal anything beyond its physical reality.

Looking with double vision seemed to create a second pair of eyes, which showed the soul of things rather than their appearance—the chameleon men possessed it to a high degree, which was why they could see elementals. On this occasion, it showed him only that this bird was a typical scavenger, always on the lookout for any kind of food. But because of his contact with the minds of the chameleon men, Niall could also catch a glimpse of himself from the bird's point of view—this odd bipedal creature that carried its food on its back, and ate sitting down instead of in the more sensible position of standing upright. The bird's chief preoccupation at the moment was whether he might leave a few crumbs behind. Looking at himself from behind the raven's eyes, Niall even noticed that he had allowed his pack to fall on its side, and that the flask of mead had rolled out.

Glad of company in this solitude, Niall said aloud: "I wish I could fly like you."

Hearing his own words made Niall aware of their meaning. He again transferred himself behind its eyes, and again saw himself from the bird's point of view. But it required an odd kind of effort to do this for more than a few seconds at a time, like being in two places at once. It had to be done sitting down, or would have induced a certain dizziness.

Once achieved, though, this change of viewpoint was extremely interesting—for example, he could see himself far more clearly than with his human eyes. Niall had always regarded himself as having rather good eyesight. But compared to the raven, his normal vision was little better than a myopic blur.

Tired of the staring match, the raven launched itself into flight. It cost Niall an effort to remain behind its eyes and not to return to his own point of view, but he succeeded, and found himself looking back on himself from a tree a hundred yards farther away.

He was beginning to enjoy this strange experience, and all his weariness had gone. Leaving his body behind had recharged it with energy, and he realized how much human tiredness is due to seeing the world through the limited vision of one pair of eyes.

Recognizing that the raven would remain immovably where it was until he moved on and gave it the opportunity to search for crumbs, Niall left a piece of the white pastry on the stone, and swung his pack onto his back. As he walked toward the nearest large bush, he made no attempt to maintain his double vision—he probably would have tripped and fallen. But once out of sight behind the bush, he watched the raven fly down to the stone and gobble down the pastry, after which it spent several minutes examining the ground for crumbs. Finally convinced that none remained, it flew back to the tree. Niall, unable to see anywhere to sit, went back to the stone. Within a few moments he was again looking at himself from behind the raven's eyes.

He now attempted to suggest to the bird that it was time to move on. It resisted the suggestion, hoping that he was going to eat again. It took another ten minutes before it became bored and launched itself into the air. And Niall, who had been waiting patiently, suddenly found the ground receding beneath him. The sensation was so real that he had to reach down and touch the stone to assure himself that he was still sitting on it.

Niall had already experienced the sensation of flying under the guidance of Asmak, chief of the aerial survey. This time it was quite different. The raven's sight was much sharper than Asmak's, and everything appeared more precise and real. From a thousand feet in the air, the green lake looked surprisingly close—although it was at least ten miles away—and he could even see the spires of the spider city to the south. To the east lay the sacred mountain, and it was obvious even from this height that the domain of the chameleon men was far more green and beautiful than the moor below him.

It took Niall some moments to realize that the raven was flying in the opposite direction to the one he was interested in. It was flying southeast, and Niall could even see the silver-gray expanse of the sea in the distance. He tried suggesting that it should fly to the north or west, but to no effect. A hungry bird in search of prey is interested only in food, and everything else seems irrelevant.

At that point, the sight of the sacred mountain reminded him of the chameleon men, and made him aware that he was adopting the wrong approach. They would not have tried to persuade the bird to change direction against its will, but would have blended with its own natural impulses to make it feel that it wanted to change direction. Niall therefore tried implanting the suggestion that it was useless flying over woodland, where the ground—and potential prey—could not be seen. This had the desired effect. Convinced that this was its own idea, the bird curved to the north, giving Niall a glimpse of a distant mountain range, and then continued to the east.

Niall could even see the spot where he was still sitting—since the bird's gaze was oriented toward it, associating it with food—and the terrain to the immediate north. It made him aware that he had been traveling in the wrong direction. A mile or so ahead lay a stretch of country with brown stagnant pools, tracts of black mud, and the yellow-green vegetation that betokened swampland. This extended as far as the bird's eye could see. If Niall had continued in his present direction, he would have been forced to retrace his steps and would have wasted most of a day.

To the northwest, on the other hand, he could see an overgrown track, probably invisible from the ground, but quite distinct from the air, which wandered across an area of high moorland in the direction of the Valley of the Dead and the Gray Mountains.

After carefully noting its direction in relation to the spot where he was sitting, Niall changed the focus of his awareness until he could feel the cold and rough surface of the rock on which he was sitting. With the speed of thought, he ceased to be a quarter of a mile in the air, and was back on the ground, feeling slightly disoriented. Far away in the sky, he could see the raven flying westward with great flaps of its wings.

Niall used his compass to calculate the way toward the track he had seen from the air, then swung his pack onto his back and set out northwest. His years as a desert dweller had instilled in him a strong sense of direction, and this uncompromising moorland was, after all, a kind of desert.

Soon the ground underfoot was dry and hard, indicating that he was, at least, leaving the swamp behind. But as the Sun reached its zenith, he still found the going tiring and rough. When, at one point, he had to wade across a shallow stream, the feeling of cold water on his bare feet was so pleasant that he knelt in the water and drank deeply, then sat down on the bank with his toes in the stream. If there had been some shade, he might have been tempted to stretch out on the bank and doze; as it was, the flowing water soothed him into an almost hypnotic state, so he began to yawn. Then, out of the corner of his eye, he saw a movement that he felt to be a nature spirit. It was not there when he tried to look directly, but after a few attempts at "looking sideways," he was able to see it clearly, a tiny colored whirl of energy that seemed to delight in the rippling surface of the water, and danced up and down on it. After he had been staring at it for a few minutes, its shape changed and it became a tiny female, dressed in a minimal costume of some gauzy white material. But Niall was virtually certain that it was his own mind that had created this shape, by the same mechanism that creates faces in moving clouds.

The thought that he was once again in a domain where elementals held sway raised his spirits. But the track he had seen was still—at a guess—two or three miles distant, and it was time to move on.

At least this moorland was covered in heather instead of tall, prickly gorse bushes, so he could see for several miles around. To his right there was a long, low ridge, and he struck out in this direction, knowing that trackways often followed ridges.

Twice during the next hour he heard the cry of the raven as it flew above him. That it was the raven he had already encountered he had no doubt; its cry seemed as distinctive as a human voice. Was it following him because he had given it food? Or simply because he was the only other living being in this empty landscape?

The ridge proved to be farther than he thought, but an hour later, he was able to stand on top of an escarpment and look south over miles of open country, and north toward distant mountains.

After following the ridge for another half mile, he was relieved to see that his sense of direction had served him well, and that he had stumbled onto an old narrow track that ran from the southeast and cut across the ridge to the northwest. Unless he had been on the ridge, he would not have seen it at all, since heather and rocky moorland extended on either side.

He began to follow the track—which he guessed to be some old trade route—with a new sense of purpose and direction, enjoying the impressive view. But this began to evaporate as he realized that the problem of being able to see so far was that his progress seemed infinitesimal. He seemed to be able to see himself from the air, moving like an ant through this vast landscape. Soon he felt so impatient that he was almost tempted to break into a jogtrot, although fully aware that this would only exhaust him.

Then he had a better idea. He turned the thought mirror on his chest, and felt a surge of power and energy that made him lengthen his stride. His newly focused attention noted the scent of the heather, the feeling of the wind on his bare chest, and the cries of birds, in a wave of pure perception—perception without any taint of thought or emotion.

He was aware of the disadvantages of the thought mirror—that after half an hour or so, it produced a feeling of strain behind the eyes, and then headache. But the sense of freshness and energy seemed worth it. Besides, he noticed that the thought mirror brought a pleasing sensation of control, and reasoned that if he deliberately kept on extending the

105

time he used it, he would become accustomed to longer periods, and gradually cease to find it so tiring.

The sky had clouded over, and a soft rain began to fall. This normally would have weighed upon Niall's spirits. But the effect of the thought mirror was to make him aware that allowing himself to become mildly depressed would have been a purely automatic reaction. He could see that it was entirely his own choice whether to feel depressed or not—that it was as simple as placing a weight on a scale and watching the scale pan sink.

As this thought came into his head, he was struck by a sudden astonishing insight: the recognition that he was *free*. He also realized that this was the first time in his life he had grasped it.

He paused to digest this remarkable insight. He could see clearly that, from childhood on, he had accepted that his choices were limited by physical needs like hunger, thirst, and tiredness. Above all, he had allowed these needs to weigh upon his spirits. They were like invisible masters who stood behind the present moment, issuing orders. Now he could see that obeying these orders was a matter of his own choice. He could deliberately resist them, or even ignore them.

This was an amazing moment, and he was aware of it as a moment of great change. He had seen and recognized a fundamental truth about human life, and nothing would ever be the same. It was as clear and distinct as leaving childhood behind and emerging into puberty.

As if to underline his insight, the rain stopped and the sun was reflected on the wet heather. Niall concentrated his attention, screwing up the muscles of his face and clenching his teeth. The sense of joyous energy made him want to laugh. He held it like this for perhaps half a minute, feeling that he could see as clearly and sharply as the raven. The problems and dangers ahead became unimportant, since he could see that all that mattered was refusing to be defeated by them.

In this sudden state of absurd optimism, it seemed to him that he could see the answer to any question he chose to think about; it was as if he had stumbled on a point of view from which any problem could be solved. And he recognized that a basic part of this feeling was his own natural and inherent optimism. Ever since he was a child, he had somehow taken it for granted that his future would be exciting because he had some important role to fulfill. Even when he had found his father's body in the desert burrow where he had spent most of his life, this basic optimism still remained underneath the sorrow and bewilderment. It was untouched even when he was captured by the spiders and transported to their city as a slave.

And his optimism had proved well founded: his rescue of a spider that had been washed overboard during a storm at sea had established him in a position of privilege, and he had become an ally of King Kazak, who obviously regarded him as his potential son-in-law and successor. It was not until he had realized that remaining in Kazak's palace would involve betraying his fellow human beings that he had decided to risk his life by trying to escape from the spider city.

His deepest and most powerful desire had been to destroy the spiders and free the inhabitants of the spider city. But this had proved unnecessary when his encounter with the empress plant, the goddess of the Delta, had enabled him to free the inhabitants of the spider city without the necessity of making war on the spiders. And now that he had friends among the spiders, like Dravig and Asmak and Asmak's son Grel, he was deeply relieved that war had proved unnecessary.

And so, he reflected, he had powerful reasons for optimism, and did not intend to relinquish that considerable advantage. His decision to set out for the unknown stronghold of the Magician had seemed an act of madness, since he had no idea of where to find it, or what he would do when he found it. Yet, just as when he set out from his home in the desert for the city of the Death Lord, he knew that he had no alternative than to rely on an intuition that safety lay in going forward. The only certain disaster lay in allowing himself to be undermined by doubt.

These were Niall's thoughts as he strode along the old trackway. He had been following it for more than an hour, and calculated that he had covered at least seven miles, when the scenery changed. The terrain due west remained flat, but the track to the northwest was climbing into foothills with outcrops of rock. Then a turn in the road brought a dramatic change as the track wound and twisted through a river valley whose walls of red sandstone had been weathered into columns.

Halfway along the valley, an immense red rock jutted into the sky, marking the point where the road made a forty-five-degree bend. As if to welcome him, the raven was standing on top of it. A dozen feet below road level, at the bottom of a rock-covered slope, ran the river that had carved out this valley. At this late stage in its descent to the plain, it was wide and not too deep—in fact, its edges were relatively shallow, and the sunlit ripples made the water look invitingly cool.

Niall paused to take in the scenery, then stood looking up at the raven. Why was it following him? Was it simply hoping for more food? He once again applied the technique of "looking sideways," and instantly found himself behind its eyes. The raven turned its head sharply, as if aware that something was happening. It was then that Niall understood why it was following him. Its consciousness was far weaker than his own, and so Niall's mind—even at second hand—added a certain intensity to its existence. It was akin to the feeling of "strangeness" that Niall was now experiencing inside a bird's body, with folded wings where his arms should be and powerful claws that could carry a lamb.

Since his own feet at the moment were black with dust, he climbed down to the river and seated himself among the roots of a large willow tree that overhung the water, then slipped off his pack and his sandals, and turned the thought mirror the other way. He was glad to note that he had still not experienced the usual headache caused by wearing it for more than half an hour. That meant that he was becoming accustomed to it. Certainly, he felt at the moment as fresh and full of energy as when he had begun to use it an hour earlier.

The effect of turning its curved side away from his chest was to induce relaxation. He yawned, sighed with relief, and dipped both feet into the water. But it was colder than he had expected, and he had to plunge his feet in and out several times before they became accustomed to the temperature, and he could ease himself into the water and stand with it up to his thighs without discomfort.

After so much walking, it felt delightful to stand there and look at the clouds and the branches reflected in the slow-flowing water. The desert dweller in him never ceased to feel astonished that the Earth was so prodigal with its rivers and streams. He noticed that the steep sides of the red rock looked even more dangerous when seen upside down.

It was as he was looking at the reflection of this rock, and imagining falling from its top into the sky, that Niall was startled to see the mirror image of something moving on the road. For a moment he thought it was the raven, then saw that the bird was clearly visible on top of the rock. When he looked at the moving reflection more closely, he realized it was a spider.

His mood of total relaxation prevented him from reacting with surprise. Instead, he raised his eyes slowly. Less then twenty feet away, a Death Spider was advancing cautiously along the road. Its attention was directed entirely to peering around the corner beyond the rock. If Niall had moved, or if the spider had glanced downward with any of the ring of eyes that circled its head, it would have seen him standing in the water. But it was not interested in the river—only in making sure that it was not seen as it turned the corner.

Niall recognized it immediately: it was Skorbo's friend and ally, the captain of the guard. And the purpose of his caution was to make sure that he was not seen by Niall.

F or five minutes after the captain had vanished around the corner, Niall continued to stand perfectly still. He was deeply puzzled. Why was the spider following him? And how long had it been doing so?

The second question was easier to answer than the first. As he had walked along the ridge, Niall had been visible for miles around against the skyline. So the answer was that he could have been followed for more than an hour.

Could this have been why the raven had flown above him? Was it trying to tell him he was being stalked?

But why should the captain want to follow him? If his intention had been to kill Niall—out of revenge for his own downfall—it would have been easy enough during the past hour: a few of those giant steps, approximately four times as long as a human stride, and the poisonous sting would have dispatched Niall within seconds.

Perhaps it intended to attack him when he was asleep? Again, that seemed unlikely. It would have been just as easy to attack him as he walked unsuspectingly along the road.

If it had been Skorbo, or one of his flesh-eating subordinates, Niall would not have been so puzzled. They were of fairly low intelligence, and might simply have been obeying the instinct that makes a hunting spider stalk its prey. But Niall had observed the captain defying the Death Lord and refusing to accept his sentence of execution, and had sensed that he possessed considerable intelligence and self-discipline. If he was following Niall, it was with some definite purpose.

There was one more possibility. Skorbo had made a forced landing in the territory of the Magician, and may have become his prisoner—and possibly his ally. In that case, the captain might be another ally. Was it possible that his aim was to capture Niall and hand him over to the Magician?

But why bother, when Niall was already making his way in that direction? He might just as well follow Niall, and make sure he arrived at his goal.

This, Niall decided, was the likeliest explanation.

In which case, it could serve no purpose to remain concealed. Since, by a fortunate chance, the captain had lost whatever advantage he might have gained from surprise, there was no point in hiding from him. Niall slipped on his sandals and began to climb the bank up to the road.

Within a few feet of the top, he could see clearly along the road beyond the red rock; it ran straight for at least a quarter of a mile, and he was surprised to see that it was empty. The spider would hardly have had time to disappear out of sight, unless he had been running at top speed toward the next hilltop. That meant he had concealed himself somewhere close by.

As Niall stared up at the raven on top of the rock, he saw a possible solution. He relaxed into the mode that allowed him to share the bird's consciousness, and immediately found himself behind its eyes, staring out over the valley and the plain stretching eastward to the sea. Twenty feet below him, on his right, he could now see the captain, standing poised at the top of a slope that ran down to the road.

What had happened was obvious. The spider had also seen that the road ahead was deserted, and that therefore Niall must still be somewhere nearby. He was waiting to see whether Niall would pass him, and was hoping not to be seen.

Niall braced himself by turning the thought mirror toward his chest, took a few moments to concentrate the surge of energy it created, then stepped out beyond the rock and looked up at the spider.

Its response was—as Niall had expected—instantaneous and automatic; it struck at Niall's central nervous system with its will, immobilizing him as if he had been encased in a block of ice. But Niall felt no fear, for he had already calculated what would happen. As he remained relaxed in the grip of the spider's will, which held him as tightly as if he was embraced by the tentacles of an octopus, he could sense its doubt about what to do next. Its instinct told it to attack a prey it had immobilized and sink in its fangs, while the logical part of its mind opposed this.

Niall seized this moment of indecision to exert the full force of his concentration to break free. He could sense the spider's surprise that a human being should be capable of such will-force. The effort had made the thought mirror warm against Niall's chest, but not—as on the last occasion when he had opposed a spider—painfully hot. Niall and the captain surveyed one another, Niall casually and without alarm, the captain obviously unsure of what to do next.

Niall played his next move in this chess game of dominance, address-ing the captain as if he had no fear of further attack.

"Where are you are going?"

He spoke in a confident tone that implied that he had every right to ask, and he could sense the captain's surprise at being addressed so clearly in the telepathic language of the spiders.

After a silence, the captain answered: "It does not matter where I go. I have no home."

If he had been a human being, the answer would have been accom-panied by a shrug.

Niall knew then that he had won: the spider had accepted his right to ask questions as if Niall was his superior officer. Niall said: "In that case, we may as well travel together."

If he had been speaking to a human being, he would have made a gesture inviting him to join him on the road. But since he was using telepathy, this was unnecessary. The captain negotiated the steep, nar-row slope down to the road with surprising ease.

He was smaller than Niall remembered, being only about a foot taller than Niall. (Most Death Spiders were between seven and eight feet tall.) His coat was very dark brown, instead of black, like most of the Death Spiders, and his glossiness reminded Niall of Grel, the son of Asmak—that is, it carried a suggestion of juvenility, which nevertheless was belied by the spider's obvious strength and agility.

The track that led north was scarcely wide enough for a spider and a human being to walk side by side, and the spider's wide leg span obliged him to walk with his four right feet on the grass verge.

Niall said: "You say you have no home. But surely your home is in the eastern Koresh?"

"That would take two weeks by sea. But by land it is more than a year."

"Then why not return by sea?"

"That is out of the question. The Death Lord has decreed that no ship will be allowed to carry me."

Niall remembered the exact words of the Spider Lord: "No ship will carry a traitor who prefers dishonor to death." He could sense that the spider knew what he was thinking, and that he was experiencing a twinge of humiliation.

Niall asked: "Do you wish to return by sea?"

In human speech that question would have been ambiguous, but the spider immediately understood what Niall meant.

"You could give orders for a ship to take me?"

"Yes."

Niall could sense his surprise.

"And overrule the decision of the Death Lord?"

Niall said: "I am the master of the spider city, which means I can overrule even the Death Lord."

The spider's eyes—which were in the side as well as the front of his head—surveyed Niall with astonishment. Because they were speaking telepathically, he knew that Nial was speaking the truth.

Sensing the unanswered question, Niall added: "Ask me what is in your mind."

"How did you—a human being—become the master of the spider city?"

"By the decree of the goddess."

"You have spoken to the goddess?"

"Yes."

Just as the captain's insight into Niall's mind would have made any dissimulation impossible, so Niall's present contact with the spider's mind meant that he could assess exactly what he was feeling. He recognized that what he had just said aroused a mixture of incredulity and superstitious awe.

This reminded him of something else that he had often noticed in his contact with spiders: that while they could be remarkably intelligent, their intelligence was less subtle than that of human beings. The reason had to do with their evolution. Humans had evolved over more than a million years of conflict with other humans, so they had achieved a high degree of psychological insight into other minds, which served them well in playing games of bluff and double-bluff, such as Niall had just played with the captain. By contrast, spiders had never had to fight for survival against other spiders; their lives had consisted mainly of waiting patiently in the corner of a web for the tug that told them that a fly or an insect had been ensnared.

The captain's attitude toward humans had been simple. They were a conquered people who were good to eat. That is why he and Skorbo had been so angry when told they could no longer eat their favorite food, but had to content themselves with farm animals and the occasional bird. When told that this order came from the Great Goddess, they were inclined to disbelief, for neither Skorbo nor the captain had been present when the goddess had manifested herself through Niall. But now that he had heard it from Niall's own lips, the captain had no alternative than to believe. Besides, had not Niall proved that he was more than an ordinary human when he had broken free from the grip of the captain's will?

Soon the valley along which they were traveling widened enough for them to walk comfortably side by side. Although the captain had to walk at half his usual speed, the pace was still a great deal faster than Niall would have preferred. At least they were covering a great deal of ground. Then they were traveling through foothills whose slopes were covered with woodland. To their west lay a mountain range which, Niall seemed to recall, overlooked the coastal plain and the ruined town of Cibilla, once the summer retreat of Cheb the Mighty, who had conquered the human race.

Niall asked the captain: "Have you traveled this way before?"

"Only once on the ground, but many times with the aerial survey."

"How far is the Valley of the Dead?"

"Perhaps half a day's journey."

Niall found that encouraging, until he reflected that half a day for a spider meant at least a full day for a human being—perhaps forty miles.

He preferred traveling with a companion who knew the road. Traveling with the captain had only one disadvantage: Niall was obliged to wear the thought mirror turned toward his chest. If he turned it the other way, the captain would sense his loss of will-drive. That meant that, whether he liked it or not, he had to live at a higher level of tension and purpose.

In fact, by midafternoon he was beginning to feel the beginning of the headache usually caused by the thought mirror, but he resisted it, and hoped that it would not increase. He also noticed that contact with the spider's vitality increased his own energy. It struck him that maintaining a high level of energy depended upon refusing to entertain the thought of tiredness.

As they walked, there was very little conversation between them. Unlike humans, spiders do not feel the need to maintain contact by speech—even telepathic speech—for their sense of one another's presence is far more palpable than with men. Even walking beside the captain, Niall soon began to know more about him than if they had talked all the time.

The captain had been born in a ruined city that was much like the spider city, except that it was smaller, and was surrounded by desert. In the days when humans had ruled the Earth, it had been a flourishing seaport. After the Great Exodus it had been virtually deserted, and an earthquake had reduced much of it to rubble, killing the few humans who still lived there. But it was still swarming with huge rats, and soon became the home of a colony of intelligent Death Spiders, who found its impressive buildings and tall palm trees ideal for their giant webs. Gray wolf spiders preferred the ruined buildings of its old slum quarter. And so a kind of two-tier society had developed, in which the Death Spiders were the aristocrats.

When contact by sea had been established with the realm of the Death Lord, human servants and slaves had been imported to farm the giant rats, which were particularly prized by the spiders.

The captain's grandfather, then his father, had been members of the ruling council, and his two elder brothers had also been prominent. The captain, because of his smaller size, had always had a sense of inferiority, and had spent much of his time with the wolf spiders in the slum quarter. Regarded with admiration by the young wolf spiders, the captain had led a small group of them in raids on the rat farms. On one occasion they had been opposed by the humans who ran it, and had killed and eaten them, including some babies. They found human meat so superior to rat flesh that they began to make a habit of eating slaves whenever the opportunity presented. This was not against the law, but when they killed a highly regarded overseer, the council of Death Spiders was outraged, and the miscreants were sentenced to death.

Through family influence, the captain escaped, and was sent by ship to the spider city, where intelligent officers were always in demand. Strict discipline brought out his best qualities, and he soon became a member of the Death Lord's entourage. But his small size continued to engender a sense of inferiority. He became friendly with Skorbo, the captain of the Death Lord's guard—strictly speaking, the captain's social inferior—who was feared by humans for his brutality and short temper. Skorbo was impressed by his intelligence and aristocratic background, while the captain was impressed by Skorbo's courage and sheer willpower.

The Great Revolution, when human beings regained their freedom, made no difference to Skorbo—except for depriving him of human meat—or indeed to most of the other spiders. Life in the spider city went on much as usual; men continued to work as before, under the surveyance of female overseers, who in turn were answerable to spiders.

115

But to the captain, this change came as a profound shock, further under-mining his self-esteem. He was intelligent enough to grasp its long-term implications: that when the spiders stopped trying to breed intelligence out of human beings by killing the clever ones while they were still in the nursery, the human race would begin to overtake the spiders. Skorbo and his kind had been too stupid to see human beings as a challenge, but the captain knew better.

The death of Skorbo had come as another enormous shock, partic-ularly with its implication that Skorbo had been a traitor. The captain had never tried to probe Skorbo's mind, any more than Skorbo had tried to probe his; their mutual respect made it unthinkable. But now Skorbo was dead, and the captain had been banished from the realm of the Death Spiders. Overnight, everything he had struggled for had been destroyed.

Now Niall was able to understand why the captain had fought so grimly to stay alive. He must have felt that life had treated him with out-rageous unfairness. For the spiders, his refusal to accept death made him contemptible. But for the captain, it was a gesture of rebellion against fate itself.

And now, for the first time, there was a glimmer of light in the dark-ness. By pure chance, the captain had allied himself to the human being who was the emissary of the goddess. Perhaps the fates had not turned against him after all.

As Niall absorbed this knowledge by a process akin to osmosis, he ceased to feel guilty about making the captain walk at half his usual pace. He understood that this was nothing compared to the sacrifices the captain would be prepared to make to regain his position and self-esteem. Niall represented the possibility of his becoming again a leader among spiders, respected and admired. To gain his support, the captain would cheerfully have walked on his knees.

The captain, for his part, was fascinated by the information he was able to absorb from Niall—his childhood in the desert, his journey to the underground city of Dira, his capture by the spiders, his encounter with the goddess in the Delta, and his confrontation with Skorbo's assassins. The human beings whom the captain had known had all been slaves or servants, so it was a new experience to be in contact with a human whose intelligence was at least equal to his own.

What had impressed the captain most was that although he had treated Niall with hostility and disrespect in their recent encounter, Niall had responded without any show of resentment. This seemed incredible. Because the spiders had achieved their evolutionary superiority through the power of the will, they attached immense importance to dominance. Two spiders who had once faced each other as aggressors could never simply forget it, even if circumstances made them allies. A sense of unresolved rivalry would always remain between them. So Niall's lack of resentment only seemed to confirm the superiority of the chosen of the goddess.

The hard mud road continued to wind among foothills of the mountain range to their left, crossing the occasional path that ran directly up to the heights. The wind here was colder than in the territory of the chameleon men, and in unsheltered places, seemed to Niall cold enough for snow. Although it was only late afternoon, it was already becoming dark, since the sun had dipped behind the mountains.

Niall was thirsty; he excused himself, took his pack from his back, and took a long draft of the spring water. As on the previous day, when he had filled his flask from the well, it brought a sense of exhilaration. Since he was also hungry, he ate some of the hard, crisp cake. When he offered some to the captain—out of politeness rather than any expectation that he would accept—the spider replied: "Thank you, no. I prefer meat." And in answer to Niall's unspoken question: "And I think I know where I can find some."

The road wound up to a hilltop, and below them in the dusk they could see a small lake. On its far side there was a wood that covered a few acres of hillside. Twenty minutes later they were among its trees. The captain stood still, and Niall realized he was using some sixth sense that was natural to a hunter. A few moments later, a plump brown woodcock walked out from the trees, its long beak probing the dead leaves. The spider let it take a few steps more, then paralyzed it with a blast of his will. A few moments later he had snapped its neck with his claw. Then he left it on the ground and once more faded into the shadows.

Niall knew nothing of the behavior of snipe, but was soon aware that this wood was one of their haunts, and that they emerged at dusk looking for food. Within a quarter of an hour, the spider had killed four of them. The birds made a forlorn heap, with their attractive black, brown, and red patterns and blood-spattered feathers.

Niall could sense the captain's satisfaction at the prospect of a meal; he obviously was hungry. Yet when he had finished killing the fourth bird, he stood aside and said: "Please take what you want."

Niall smiled politely. "Thank you. But I cannot eat raw flesh. Please do not let me prevent you from eating."

With a gesture that was oddly like a human shrug of bewilderment, the captain proceeded with his supper, rending the birds with his claws. Remembering that spiders were sensitive about being watched as they ate, Niall wandered toward the lake.

The water looked very peaceful in the evening light, reflecting the darkening sky. A few widening circles on the surface made Niall aware that it contained fish. Then, in the shallows just below the bank on which he was standing, he saw the gentle movement of a large trout. The thought crossed his mind that if he could use his will as effectively as the captain, he could catch it for his supper. Then, reflecting, "Why not?" he stared at the trout and concentrated the force of the thought mirror. He could feel his mind making contact with the fish, and feel its resistance, just as if he had grabbed it with his hand.

A moment later, it gave a jerk and became still. Startled at this unexpected outcome, Niall glanced over his shoulder. The captain was standing behind him, looking down with satisfaction at the stunned fish. He reached into the lake and dropped it at Niall's feet, asking: "Do you like fish?"

"Very much. But humans prefer it cooked."

The spider obviously found this notion puzzling, and for the next half hour, watched with curiosity as Niall gathered dead wood and dry leaves. He was even more intrigued by Niall's attempts to light the fire using flints. Niall had often watched the cook light the kitchen fire, but now had to admit that it looked easier than it was. Finally, after bending over the dead leaves to exclude the faint breeze, and making both thumbs bleed by hitting them with the flint, he succeeded in making a leaf smolder, then blew it into flame.

The captain asked: "But can you not do that with your will?"

"No. Can you?"

The spider's answer amounted to "I think so." He obviously had never tried it. Now he focused on a heap of leaves, and made an obvious effort of concentration—the first time Niall had seen a spider make such a visible effort. After about a minute, a thin plume of smoke rose upward. Niall was impressed; it had never entered his head that an effort of will could light a fire—although, now that he thought about it, he had noticed a sense of warmth behind his eyes when he had been focusing hard on the trout; the feeling reminded him of the warmth he could make by placing his mouth against his sleeve and blowing through it.

Niall's own fire was now crackling, and the occasional gust of windblown smoke made his eyes water. There was plenty of dry wood on the ground, and the blaze was soon uncomfortably hot. The captain watched with what Niall suspected to be wry amusement, wondering why Niall was going to so much trouble to spoil a perfectly good fish. But finally the fire died down, and there were enough red-hot ashes to toss the fish among them, where it made appetizing sizzling noises. While it cooked, Niall provided himself with a long rod cut from a tree, and hacked off all its smaller twigs until only one remained at the wider end, about the size and thickness of his thumb. This, in due course, he used to hook the fish out of the ashes, breaking off the charred tail in the process.

The tree from which he had cut the rod also had thick red leaves that were six inches across; a dozen of these made a makeshift table-cloth, onto which he dragged the burning-hot fish. He sliced open the blackened skin below the gills, revealing pink, well-cooked flesh. He burned his fingers cutting off a large slice, but it was still too hot to taste. Ten minutes later, sprinkled with salt and eaten on a hard biscuit, it was delicious. As he ate, he made a mental note to thank his mother for remembering to include salt, without which the flesh would have been too rich. He washed down the meal with spring water.

The captain had settled himself comfortably on the other side of the fire, his legs folded under him. A cold wind had blown up—Niall suspected it was snowing up in the mountains—and the warmth was welcome. Because the fish had been so large, Niall had left more than half of it; in any case, the heat had failed to reach through to the center, which was still uncooked. When Niall observed the captain eyeing it with interest, he asked if he would care to try it, and was mildly surprised when it was accepted with alacrity. The spider held the trout between two claws, and ate it like a corncob, until he had left nothing but the bones. Then he rolled himself into a ball and relaxed once more, his claws lying contentedly on his distended belly. Evidently Niall was wrong, and not all spiders had an aversion to eating in front of humans. The explanation, Niall decided, was simply that the captain had been brought up in a remote province where manners were different.

Niall's greasy hands were making him uncomfortable, so he went and washed them in the lake. On his way back to the fire, he collected more dry tinder—it was easy to find as it cracked under his feet. Finally, he opened the sleeping bag, noting that it still smelled faintly of the slime-creature, and that a kind of white dust came from it as he shook it to spread it on the grass. He lay down on it, and placed his pack under his head as a pillow.

As he relaxed in the light of the crackling sticks he had tossed into the glowing embers, he was interested to observe that there was a definite sense of contact between himself and the spider, such as is only achieved between humans who have known one another a long time. Yet they had only met a few hours ago. It gave him a sudden insight into what it must be like to be a spider, in continuous contact with the mind of every other spider.

Of course, this was not entirely true—otherwise each individual spider would have been overwhelmed by the input of millions of telepathic signals from his fellows. The fact remained that every spider was aware of a kind of vague, blurred mass that was the group mind of all the spiders in the world. And the strength of the spider will came from the immense power of this collective mind.

By comparison, each human lived alone in a kind of prison cell. The sense of connection with his or her fellows was comparatively weak. This is why the human will was so feeble, and why humans became so easily bored. To maintain a sense of purpose, human beings needed to find the present moment interesting and exciting. And that is because they lacked a deeper sense of their own existence.

What was happening to Niall, he realized, was that he was changing into a different kind of human being, a type that could actually share the minds of other beings, as well as spiders and chameleon men. Every day he became more conscious of the change that was gradually taking place.

As he was beginning to fall asleep, he was aroused by a bird that flew down low over the fire. All he could see as it vanished into the darkness was a blur of two white spots, as if it was being trailed by two smaller birds. Then, as it came back again, he saw that the trailing spots were at the end of immensely long feathers that sprouted from the tip of the wing like feather dusters. Simeon had once pointed out the bird to him as they walked through the darkness to the city of the bombardier beetles; it was called a nightjar.

As it came back for a third time, flying as silently as an owl, the captain knocked it to the ground with a blow of his will. Curious to look more closely at the wing feathers, Niall said: "Excuse me."

As he bent down over the twitching bird, which was about the size of a swallow, he noticed something that made him peer more closely.

Around one of the legs, just above the foot, there was a tiny black circlet made of some glossy material. This was not a wild bird, but one that had been tagged by its owner. For a moment Niall thought that it might have come from the city of the bombardier beetles, where a few of the humans kept pet birds—Doggins' children even had a pigeon loft in the garden. Then he reflected that no one would keep a nocturnal bird as a pet, and that, moreover, the city was more than a hundred miles away.

The bird had stopped moving, and was obviously dead.

Niall asked: "Why did you kill it?"

"I knew there was something wrong with it."

Niall pointed at the black circlet. "I think it is a spy."

The two looked at one another, and since each could read the other's mind, further comment was unnecessary.

Niall said finally: "So he may be expecting us."

"Except," said the captain, "that the bird is dead."

It was a point worth considering. But the Magician probably had many spies.

The captain, who had overheard the thought, said: "Then he *will* be expecting us?"

"Probably."

"But you still intend to go?"

Niall said: "I have no alternative. My brother is infected with a deadly disease. I have to try and save him."

"Do you have any plan?"

"No. I am hoping for help from the goddess."

In using this phrase, Niall had only meant something like the human expression, "I am crossing my fingers." But he saw that the spider had taken him literally, and felt that Niall had answered his question.

Niall realized there was no point in trying to explain. It would have been pointless to tell the captain that he was traveling to Shadowland without knowing how to get there, or what he intended to do when he got there. The truth was that if the Magician was already forewarned of his approach, then he was walking into a trap. Yet he could see no alternative. His brother's life was at stake, and there seemed to be no other way.

Before climbing into the sleeping bag, he picked it up by the bottom corners and shook it vigorously to remove more of the white powder left by the slime-creature. As he did so, his fingers encountered something hard inside the cloth; he used the flashlight to look more closely. There was a tiny retractable tube sealed by a plug, which he quickly recognized as a mouthpiece; when he blew into it, the bottom of the bag inflated into a series of small balloonlike patches which, when he lay down, made him feel he was lying on a soft mattress.

Niall accepted this discovery as a good omen, and allowed it to tranquilize the slight unease he had been feeling about the incident of the nightjar. But as he closed his eyes, he remembered to exercise the discipline taught him by the chameleon men, and to concentrate his consciousness as sleep overtook him. Once again there was a sense of flying into a mist of dream images that blended with the sound of the wind in the trees.

He woke up in the dark, sleepy and relaxed, and lay there contentedly listening to the sounds of waves on the lake shore. A few bright stars showed through the canopy of leaves overhead. A faint breeze from the direction of the lake still caused an occasional red glow among the ashes of the fire, from which Niall deduced that he had been asleep for only about an hour.

At this point he felt the unmistakable signs of someone trying to probe his mind. Whoever this was obviously assumed he was asleep, so he remained totally passive. If it was the captain, Niall would be disappointed, for he thought they had established an element of trust. Then a gust of wind blew a dying fragment into a red glow that became, for a few seconds, a flicker of yellow flame, and he saw that the captain was fast asleep, his legs bunched underneath him.

Unless there was some enemy hidden in the darkness, he was left with only one possible conclusion: that it was the Magician himself. But why? What could he gain by probing Niall's mind when he was asleep?

Still wondering, he sank back into sleep.

When he woke up, it was dawn, and there was no sign of the captain. On the far side of the fire, a woodcock was exploring the dead leaves with its long beak. Moments later it collapsed, and the captain pounced on it from the undergrowth. Perhaps to avoid shocking Niall's sensibility, he carried it out of sight.

Niall sat up, climbed out of the sleeping bag into the cold air, and pulled out the plug to deflate it. He made his way down to the lake through the dew-soaked grass, and found a place where the shore sloped gently into the water. There he knelt down to splash water on his face. He found it so invigorating that he turned the thought mirror toward his chest and then, fortified by a surge of energy, stripped off his clothes and walked up to his armpits in the still water. He knew there was no danger of predators like the slime-creature—otherwise the lake would not have been full of fish. A large brown trout glided past his chest, obviously unafraid, causing Niall to reflect that in this quiet place, with its peaceful sky and autumnal trees reflected in the still water, there must be so few predators that wild creatures had no idea that man is dangerous.

At that point he tripped over a dead branch that was sunk in the mud, and his head plunged below the water, which filled his mouth and nostrils. When he had blinked it out of his eyes, he saw the captain regarding him from the shelter of the trees, and sensed quite clearly his feeling that human beings must be mad to immerse themselves voluntarily in this suffocating liquid. At the same time, Niall had a glimpse of why land spiders disliked water. In the remote past it had soaked their webs and made it more difficult to catch insects, in addition to which, great drops of water from leaves, almost as big as the spider itself, threatened to wash them away.

Back on land, he pulled his tunic over his wet hair and slipped his feet into his sandals. When the captain asked him if he would like to eat another fish, Niall declined politely; there was no time to light a fire. He wanted to reach the Valley of the Dead before nightfall.

He ate his breakfast of crisp-bread with his back propped against a tree and his legs inside the sleeping bag, and washed down the food with spring water. The nightjar, he noticed, was still lying by the ashes of the fire—its scrawny body evidently held no interest for the captain, whose belly now sagged with the weight of half a dozen woodcocks.

Within a quarter of an hour they were back on the road, with the air full of birdsong. Behind them, the Sun was only just above the still surface of the lake. And above them, perhaps a hundred feet in the air, flapped Niall's self-appointed guardian, the raven.

T he clarity of the morning and the sight of the snowcapped mountains against the blue sky caused a rising bubble of happiness
that was like intoxication. Here on the slopes of the mountains,
the leaves were beginning to turn brown, and some had already fallen;
it was Niall's first experience of the beauty of autumn.

The road they were following was so overgrown with grass that it
was no longer clearly visible. But the captain seemed to have no doubt
of his direction, and Niall soon concluded that he possessed some kind
of inner compass. Where there seemed to be a choice of two ways, he
chose one without hesitation.

Niall himself was experiencing that pleasant sense of wide-awakeness
that he often felt in the early morning. Back in his palace, he was usually awake before dawn, and went to the roof to watch the sun rise. On
a clear day he could see the outline of these northern mountains against
the sky. Then he experienced this same feeling of excitement and optimism, as if he was on the brink of some marvelous discovery. Now the
excitement was so strong that it was almost uncomfortable, and he felt
he was beginning to grasp its full import. It was not simply a feeling of
physical or emotional well-being, but a recognition that the world, when
seen with this wide-awakeness, is entirely good.

Another thought caused him deep satisfaction: that he was not only
enjoying wearing the thought mirror with its concave side turned toward
his chest, but was at last becoming accustomed to it. Wearing the
thought mirror was rather like swimming—more difficult than walking
on land, but more exhilarating.

This was evidenced by the fact that, in spite of his increased concentration, he was aware of the presence of nature spirits in the woods.
As they approached one huge, gnarled tree, whose bark was so thick and
knotty that it looked as if it had been carved by a sculptor, he thought
he saw an old man sitting among the roots; but when he looked more
closely, the shape vanished, making it apparent that this must be its res-

ident spirit. And in one place where the trees were spaced widely apart, yet so tall that the air was green and shadowy, he saw several more old men whose faces were so similar that they might have been members of the same family.

It was clear that the captain could not see them, for he never gave them a glance. The reason, Niall realized, was that spider perception is limited by a basic interest in nature as a source of food. Therefore, anything else was ignored.

In one sunny clearing, the air was loud with the buzzing of insects; its source proved to be the bloodstained bones of some dead animal that were covered by large fat bluebottles, many an inch long.

As they approached, the buzzing ceased as the captain paralyzed them with will-force, then paused for a few minutes to eat them one by one, his tarsal claw picking them up as delicately as if they were sugared cakes. He even offered Niall one, but Niall smiled politely and shook his head. "Thank you, but I have only just eaten." Unaware that this was intended as a joke, the spider went on crunching the faintly buzzing flies with gusto.

Niall was puzzled by the state of the bones, which were shattered and fragmented. The only way this could have happened was if the carcass had been dropped from a great height. But this was hard to credit, since the creature was the size of a cow.

The captain read Niall's mind.

"It came from the sky."

"But what dropped it?"

What the captain conveyed to Niall's mind was an image that seemed to be of some kind of bird, but with a face that resembled a turtle.

"Where I was born the slaves called them 'oolus.'"

The word was accompanied by an image like an egg, which confused Niall even more.

The sight of the cracked, broken bones disturbed and disgusted him. He asked: "Is it dangerous?"

The captain's reply, compressed into a terse image, could be translated as: "Not for me."

Ten minutes later, they passed a decaying log covered in twists of orange fungus. Niall was gazing at it, enchanted by its bizarre beauty, when he noticed a tiny round face, as orange as the fungi, peeping at him from under the log. It was yet another tree spirit, and Niall was aware that he would not have noticed it if his senses had been less alert. His concentration made everything more interesting, or rather, made him aware that everything he looked at *was* more interesting then he supposed, and that our human senses are too dull and narrow to see it.

Crossing a stream in the middle of a wood, they stopped to drink, and the spider paused at the side of the running water, enjoying the sunlight that covered the ground in fragmented tree shadows. In a human being, its state of mind would have been called laziness, but in a spider was merely an expression of its lack of sense of time. Niall sat down on a rock, and took the opportunity to transfer his consciousness to the raven, which was perched on a high branch.

Since meeting the captain, Niall had been concerned in case the spider saw the raven as a potential meal. But he seemed to sense that Niall had his reasons for wanting the bird to remain alive.

From behind the raven's eyes, Niall could look down on the gently rolling landscape of the foothills, which became suddenly steeper to the north, forming a clifflike wall. The bird, he noticed, enjoyed playing host to his consciousness, which gave its world an extra dimension, and responded to his suggestions like an extension of his own body. Suddenly, Niall could understand how easily the Magician could control the minds of birds, and use them as spies.

Since the captain seemed to show an inclination to rest in the dappled shade, Niall caused the bird to launch itself from the branch and fly upward. Its powerful wings soon carried it to a height of a quarter of a mile, enabling him to see that a few miles ahead, the apparently unbroken wall of cliffs contained a gap, from which a broad stream flowed. This obviously had been formed by some geological upheaval, and then smoothed and deepened by the river. Running northwest, it might have formed a shortcut to the Valley of the Dead, except that its slope was uncomfortably steep and ended in a jagged pinnacle like a finger pointing at the sky. The top of this pinnacle glittered as if it contained a very bright light.

On the near side of this valley, on a level with the skyline, Niall was interested to observe a ruined town or village with a broken wall, which reminded him of the coastal town of Cibilla. Like Cibilla, this place obviously dated to the days before the spider conquest.

Niall was tempted to get the raven to overfly it, but rejected the idea, since the captain might wonder why they were pausing for so long.

He was right. The spider had moved into the shade of a great conifer, and was waiting patiently for Niall to emerge from his reverie.

The road had now disappeared completely, but the direction they were following led them downhill and into another valley with a lake that was about two miles long. The grassy plain beside the water was easier on the feet than the rough mountainside, and if it had not been for the spider's dislike of water, Niall would have been glad to stop for a bathe. As it was, the uphill road out of the far end of the valley gave Niall his first ground-level sight of the gap in the mountains.

Niall pointed to it, and asked the captain if he had ever explored it.

"No. There would be no point, since it leads nowhere."

Niall persisted. "That is a pity, since it would shorten our road by many miles. Are you sure it leads nowhere?"

He had in mind the notion that the inhabitants of the ruined town might have created some steep and narrow path that led downhill to the Valley of the Dead.

"I cannot be certain, since I have never been that way."

Niall sensed, nevertheless, that the captain found the idea of a shortcut agreeable.

This is why, more than two hours later, when they were close enough to the valley to hear the sound of rushing water, they made no attempt to find a way across the river, but turned left into the valley whose dark cliffs, lined with horizontal veins of dark blue and purple crystal, were more than a thousand feet high.

As Niall had suspected, they soon came upon the remains of a road that led uphill to the ruins of the town. It had been well made of square carved blocks that had survived the centuries, and was still surprisingly smooth to the feet. This road ran beside the stream, which became narrower and faster as they ascended the valley, filling the air with its rushing sound. Farther on, the road turned left and climbed steeply toward the town, while the stream itself descended in a series of waterfalls before it became broader and slower. At this point, the stream was partly blocked by the ruins of a stone bridge that had collapsed into the water. If they were going to cross, this was obviously the best place.

They descended the steep bank, then had to climb the broken blocks. The bridge had once been an archway, and enough of its big, roughly carved stones lay in the stream to afford a way across, although the water foamed alarmingly between some of them, and covered others, so that Niall had to remove his sandals. The spider, who could have crossed the stream in half a dozen huge strides, was obviously nervous, and preferred to allow Niall to lead the way. It was not until they reached the far side, where Niall had to wade in the water up to his thighs, that the captain went past him in a single great bound.

Now the pinnacle of stone was clearly visible ahead of them, rising to a point about a hundred feet above its base. It was twisted and weathered, and a few trees had succeeded in gaining a foothold on its ledges. From a mile away, it looked distinctly man-made, or at least improved by human beings who had appreciated its romantic appeal. The top had the same purple color as the crystal of the cliffs, and reflected the sun.

The track on the other side was narrower than the road that had brought them to the bridge, and less well made. But it was clear that the bridge had been constructed only to reach this track that led up to the pinnacle, for it had no downhill continuation.

The track became so rough and steep that Niall soon had to sit down to drink some springwater. This refreshed him, but did nothing to alleviate the heat of the sun, which beat fiercely on the top of his head and made the sweat stream down his face. There were places where the path had been carved out of solid rock, with V-shaped notches cut into it. He envied the spider for the ease with which he climbed—giving the impression that he easily could have run uphill to the pinnacle. Yet Niall also noted that if he concentrated hard, the tiredness vanished, and his knees and thighs ceased to ache. The thought mirror obviously made available considerable reserves of strength.

Half an hour later, when they reached the base of the pinnacle, it became clear that this was not, as Niall had supposed, the top of a mountain, but only of the immense cliff that formed the southern wall of the Valley of the Dead. Above the ruined town, the mountain continued until its top vanished in mist.

Down below them was a green plain that, as Niall knew, extended to the sea in the west. To the east the plain continued as far as a low range of mountains, less high than those that surrounded them. A long black lake occupied the center of the Valley of the Dead, and from where they stood, Niall could see the river that flowed into it from the east. On the far side of the lake, a battlemented wall stretched the length of the valley and continued about fifty miles to the east. Even from this height it looked impressive, being a hundred feet high and at least twenty feet wide. Every hundred yards or so there were square towers that rose fifty feet above the level of the wall. This was the wall that had been built on the orders of a Spider Lord called Kasib the Warrior, to keep out the unknown enemy from the northern mountains. It had cost the lives of twenty thousand human slaves.

Across the valley, on the far side of the wall, rose the dark cliffs of these forbidding northern mountains—the domain of the Magician. Yet the cliffs were beautiful as well as forbidding, being streaked with the same dark blue and purple veins as the cliffs behind them; where the afternoon sunlight fell on them, these glittered and sparkled as if from some inner fire. In the cliff on the far side of the wall, Niall could make out buildings that looked as if they were carved out of the solid rock.

But below them was a sight that made Niall's heart sink. There was no steep path that ran down the face of the cliff to the Valley of the Dead. In fact, it would have been impossible, since the cliff sloped inward.

So their journey up the "shortcut" had been a waste of time.

It seemed there was nothing for it but to return the way they had come, and take the other route. This was going to take the rest of the day, for their shortcut would have saved them a detour of at least ten miles. Moreover, to the east, the cliff wall came to an end in a mountain prominence that extended a quarter of a mile across the valley.

Niall found a patch of shade and sat down; the captain rested nearby in the shadow of a twisted tree. He could now see that the pinnacle above him, which towered about a hundred feet, was made of volcanic lava, which had weathered into a shape not unlike the twisted conical houses of the city of the bombardier beetles, but far less symmetrical. To the west the base stuck out, forming a kind of table on which a miniature wood of small trees and bushes had taken root. From this small plateau, a path climbed the pinnacle. It obviously had been man-made, and the marks of tools could still be seen on its gray-green surface.

Since it would be a pity to descend without examining the pinnacle more closely, Niall clambered up onto the rock plateau and started up the path. The captain watched him incuriously; for him, the pinnacle obviously held no interest whatever. For Niall, it was an odd puzzle. Why had the natives of the ruined town taken the trouble to build the bridge across the stream, then hack the path up the steep hill? And it must have taken years of labor to chisel this ramp out of the hard, smooth lava, which billowed into cushions, so that in places it looked like intestines.

The ramp followed a corkscrew path up the first third of the monument, sometimes wide, sometimes narrow. On one corner it had become so narrow that the workers had been forced to create more space by hacking a wall at an angle of forty-five degrees into the rock. On the next bend, Niall found himself looking out over the Valley of the Dead, with a sheer drop below him. He had never liked heights, and it made his stomach feel queasy.

Round this bend was another platform whose uneven surface suggested it was natural, and a stunted tree had managed to find a foothold. At this level of the pinnacle, the rock was full of veins of crystal, some blue, some purple, some as clear as glass. There was a hole in the rock face behind the tree, like a cave entrance. Niall took the flashlight from his backpack and shone it inside. There was a squawk, and a bird blundered past him, almost knocking him backwards.

The light showed an oval chamber, about ten feet in diameter, with a stone bench carved around the wall, which seemed to be made entirely of blue quartz crystals; its floor was a shallow bowl. It reminded Niall vaguely of the underground council chamber of the bombardier beetles. Higher around its walls, at a height of about seven feet, were niches, which had probably held oil lamps, since the stone above them was blackened. In one of these niches there was a bird's nest. Niall stood on the bench and peered into it; half a dozen tiny birds raised their heads, their mouths wide open.

Niall sat down on the bench, switching off the flashlight; there was enough light from the doorway to see around the chamber. Something was odd about this place, although it was hard to say what; the blue crystal made Niall feel he was under water. He tried turning the thought mirror away from his chest, causing a drop in the intensity of his concentration. For a few moments he felt nothing—it was like walking out of sunlight into darkness. Then the feeling returned even more strongly. It was as if there was a vibration that made him feel more alert, and it unmistakably came from the crystal. He had experienced a similar sensation in the valley of the sacred lake: the sense of some great secret or mystery. Niall realized that he was in a place that generations of men had regarded as holy, and had left it impressed with their thoughts and feelings.

This, he understood, was a place of worship, and the inhabitants of the small town had regarded it as so important that they had built the bridge across the stream and the road that led to the pinnacle.

He was also clearly aware of the hunger of the tiny birds, and the alarm of their mother, who was waiting until this intruder left her home, anxious in case he harmed her chicks. Feeling guilty, he made his way out into the sunlight. The bird, which was perched on the tree, quickly flew back inside.

At this point, about halfway up the pinnacle, the path became narrower and rose more steeply. Niall gazed up the sixty-degree slope, then glanced into the depth below, and wondered if it was worth going any farther. In the rock to his left, a round hole had been chiseled, and six feet farther on, a second. He guessed that their purpose had been to hold a rope to serve as a handrail; but this probably had rotted away centuries ago. Without such a rope, the path looked slippery and dangerous. But when he turned the thought mirror again, the surge of energy caused his nervousness to evaporate, and he began to mount the slope, keeping his eyes fixed on his feet.

After twenty feet, he was relieved when the path turned left past a cushion of crystal shaped like a lion's face, and continued to mount between two walls that were a mixture of dark, granitelike rock and blue quartz. Where it came to an end above another sheer drop, steps had been carved in the right-hand wall. These were shallow, scarcely three inches deep, but at least he could use the higher steps as handholds. Far above him, the peak of the tower looked as if it was made of blue glass.

He decided to remove his backpack, which obstructed him in this narrow passageway, and also to take off his sandals. He left them on the steps, then continued to climb up the steep face—wondering, at the same time, why he was bothering to risk his life like this.

Twenty feet higher, he no longer had the protection of the other wall; it terminated in its own pinnacle. But a dozen feet above him, he could now see another cavelike opening in the rock, this one no more than three feet high and wide.

He paused to recover his breath—climbing an almost vertical wall was hard work, and he was glad he was unencumbered by his pack—then pressed on up the final dozen steps, taking care not to glance down or even think of the drop below. At last his head reached the ledge that was the entrance. Remembering the bird that had startled him last time, he became cautious and braced himself. And in fact, as he reached over the threshold, and felt a groove that obviously had been created as a handhold, there was a loud flapping of wings, and a few feathers descended on him. But the birds flew away through a window inside the tower.

Finally he was standing upright in a chamber about six feet square, its floor covered with bird droppings. The room had two windows, each about eight feet above his head and reached by three tall, shallow steps carved into the wall. The ceiling was high—perhaps twelve feet—and seemed higher because the walls sloped inward, a consequence of the narrowing of the pinnacle toward its summit. Against the left-hand wall, a bench had been carved out of the rock.

Niall sat down on it, closed his eyes, and rested his head back against the wall. It was such a relief that he was almost tempted to fall asleep. The chamber was cool; a faint breeze blew through the door and windows.

When his breathing had calmed, he turned the thought mirror away from his chest. The result was a feeling of security, and the total disappearance of his subconscious anxiety about his dangerous position and the problems that would face him on the way down. It was almost as if he had walked into a comfortable room with a fire and been given a seat in a deep armchair. It reminded him somehow of his arrival at King Kazak's underground city, and the warmth with which he was greeted by relatives he had never seen.

The vibration that he had sensed in the room downstairs was even stronger here. This place was the center of a vortex of force—the same force that he had sensed in the cave of the chameleon men. But there it had been a kind of background vibration that he tuned into by deep relaxation. Here it was so powerful that the relaxation was unnecessary. He could feel it merely by opening his senses.

At once, he knew that this force made the stone of the pinnacle alive, so that it had somehow recorded everything that had ever happened there. All Niall had to do was to open himself to this knowledge and absorb it. The most powerful presence Niall could sense in the room was that of a man, who had lived here for many years. The name was unusual, and it took Niall a moment to grasp it; it was Jan Sephardus.

Sephardus had discovered this place in the century after the Great Migration of the twenty-second century. And from Sephardus's powerful mind, Niall learned more of the history of the Earth during the last years of human freedom, before the coming of the spiders.

He learned, to begin with, the answer to a question that had struck him when he had absorbed the history of the Earth from the Steegmaster in the white tower: why so many human beings had been left behind during the Great Migration. Was it their own choice, or had they been ruthlessly selected to remain behind and face destruction by the comet Opik?

The answer was that, for huge numbers, it had been their own choice. They simply did not have the imagination to believe that the Earth would be destroyed, and were too lazy to launch themselves on a new adventure. But there were equally large numbers who were deliberately excluded from the Great Migration because its genetic scientists regarded them as subnormal—one notorious official document referred to them as the "dregs." Of course, this process of discrimination was a closely guarded secret—lest the "dregs" start a rebellion—but the precaution proved unnecessary.

So after the departure of the giant space transports for Alpha Centauri, the "dregs" inherited the Earth. And in a sense they were proved correct: Opik missed Earth by a million and a quarter miles. But so much material from its radioactive tail fell into the atmosphere that nine-tenths of animal life was destroyed. There followed a great ice age, and as the warmth slowly returned, most lands reverted to what would once have been regarded as barbarism. The majority of the surviving human beings went back to the kind of life men had always lived in the countryside. As generators broke down, few made any attempt to repair them or build more; instead they returned to the use of fire and oil lamps. Now there were no more giant automobile plants, cars were replaced by horses, and tractors by oxen. Cities became almost deserted, since they were full of robbers. Now that there were no more fire brigades, whole cities burned to the ground.

Monasteries began to flourish, as they had done in the Middle Ages, and in this new Dark Age, they became the guardians of learning. Sephardus, whose parents were farmers, had attended a monastery school, and had become fascinated by geology. This was how he had come to discover this pinnacle above the Valley of the Dead (which was then covered with grazing land, farms, and tilled fields).

Sephardus had built himself a hermit's hut at the foot of the pinnacle. He was attracted to it because he had immediately felt its power. After living there for only a few weeks, he had decided he never wanted to live anywhere else.

The nearest farm was at the bottom of the valley, fifteen miles away. The farmer, in exchange for teaching his children reading and writing, had provided Sephardus with the basic necessities of life. Soon Sephardus was regarded throughout the Valley as a holy man, and many came from remote villages to ask advice and pay homage.

Humans had lost none of their belligerence since the Great Migration, and local warlords fought to establish their authority. One of these, known as Rolf the Vandal, built a stronghold in the mountains to the east and often raided the Valley. That was why men built the town on the heights, choosing a position that was virtually impregnable. The pinnacle was an obvious lookout for raiders, and stonemasons worked for three years carving out this chamber in which Niall was now sitting. Then, at the request of Sephardus, they carved out the chapel below.

But Sephardus himself preferred the lookout room, for it was here that he could feel most strongly the force that waxed and waned at different seasons of the year, but which was always stronger here than anywhere else in the Valley.

What was this force? Sephardus had no idea, except that it was associated with the sun and the moon, and that it could fill him with an ecstatic energy that left him in no doubt that the destiny of man is to become a god.

And what was the force that Niall could now feel in Sephardus's meditation chamber? Was it the spirit of the long-dead Sephardus? Almost certainly not; yet it was a part of Sephardus, which had been imprinted on these surroundings as he might have imprinted his spirit on the words of a manuscript.

Niall stood up and climbed the three steps to the window opening. Handholds had been carved into the walls. He found himself looking out on the way he had come in the past few hours. The eastern plain, with its range of low green mountains, lay straight ahead, while beyond the foothills to the south he could see the wooded country he had crossed with the chameleon men.

Drawing his head in through the window, he noticed an odd thing. When his head was back inside the room, his view of the outside world became notably clearer and sharper than when it was outside. He had failed to notice any difference when he had looked out, but as soon as he drew his head inside, it became obvious. In fact, as he stared at the mountains, they seemed to become much closer, as if he was looking through a magnifying lens.

This, Niall assumed, was due to some peculiarity of the energy vortex that made this place sacred. And its purpose was clear: if this tower was a lookout, then the power to magnify distant objects would be invaluable. Staring at a gap in the eastern mountains that looked like a pass, Niall could see it so clearly that he had no doubt that he would be able to see a solitary traveler as well as if he were only a few hundred yards away.

Niall stared out of the window for a long time, absorbing the knowledge of Sephardus, and of the men who had built the town on the other side of the river. Then, as he was about to climb down, his head full of the violence of Rolf the Vandal, he noticed a movement far across the eastern plain. He shook his head with incredulity; a large band of horsemen, perhaps a hundred strong, was emerging from the pass in the mountains and riding toward him. Incredulously, he stuck his head out of the window; the horsemen immediately vanished. As soon as he pulled his head inside the chamber, they reappeared, looking quite solid and normal. It was hard to believe that they were some kind of mirage.

He noticed something else. When he withdrew his head, and the warriors—probably led by Rolf the Vandal—reappeared, he felt something happen in his brain. It was almost as if there was a click as some mechanism was activated. It was clear suddenly that the horsemen were indeed a product of his brain—an imaginative creation somehow inspired by what he had learned in the meditation chamber. But it was imaginative only in the sense that the horsemen were not there at the present moment. He was looking into the past.

The insight overwhelmed him. It was the recognition that these warriors had once been alive, just as he was now. They had taken it for granted that the present moment was stable and real, just as he did. Were they then wrong?

The answer was obvious. They were not *wrong*; it was simply that their minds were too weak. Sephardus had seen the answer, aided by the strange force that permeated this sacred place. The human mind had to become strong enough to grasp the reality of other times and places.

For no particular reason, he found himself envisaging the wood where he had slept the night before. This was recent enough to be able to conjure it up in some detail. Then he used the trick he had learned a moment ago—causing something to click in his brain. He was immediately standing in the wood, and noticing that the grass was still flattened where he had lain. A linnet, startled by his sudden appearance, flew off in alarm.

The sensation was not unlike that of being behind the eyes of the raven. Although he seemed to be here, in the woodland clearing, he knew that his body was really in the tower overlooking the Valley of the Dead, and that the person who stood here was a simulacrum. When he looked down at his hands, he could see through them. It was not exactly that he was transparent, but that he seemed to be made of some kind of shimmering energy.

This, he realized, was why Sephardus had chosen the pinnacle; it was full of energies that gave him certain magical powers. The Earth was full of such energy vortices.

Because the wall was making his legs cold, Niall climbed down from the window, and went and sat on the bench; it felt safer than standing on a narrow step.

Now he envisaged the cave of the chameleon men, making the kind of mental effort he had just taught himself; immediately he was in the cave, in the strange semidarkness by which things are nevertheless clearly visible. The cave was empty—as it would be at midafternoon, when the chameleon men were "at work." Niall was interested to note that the yellow bubbles of light—with hairy protuberances—were drifting down from the ceiling, and that they seemed more real than last time he had been here—perhaps because he himself was semitransparent.

Inevitably, being so close to the spider city, Niall thought of Veig. After the now-familiar mental effort, he found himself standing in Veig's bedroom. It was empty, and it was only then that he remembered that his brother was in the basement room, between the abolia trees. He transferred himself there, but took care to envisage the far corner of the room; he had no desire to startle or alarm anyone.

His caution proved unnecessary; Veig was asleep and, to Niall's relief, seemed to be sleeping peacefully and breathing normally. A few feet away, the maid Crestia sat with her back to him, sewing by the daylight that came in at the door.

Resisting the temptation to go and see his sisters, Niall transferred his attention back to his body, sitting on the stone bench. It seemed strange to be back in the tower room, like coming back from a long journey, or waking in the morning with the room full of sunlight. All fatigue had vanished, and he felt as fresh as when he set out that morning. It made him realize that fatigue is largely an attitude of mind.

He crossed to the other side of the room, remembering as he did so that the captain was waiting for him down below and that he ought to leave soon. Then, recalling the incredible patience of spiders, he dismissed the thought; it was more important to learn what he could in this magic chamber of Jan Sephardus.

The opposite window, as he expected, looked down on the Valley of the Dead—so called because of the tremendous disaster that had taken place there in the reign of the Death Lord Kasib the Warrior. Qisib the Wise had described to Niall how, when Kasib's vast army had prepared to march into the Gray Mountains to make war on the Magician, a tremendous storm had caused the lake to burst its banks, and within less than a minute, Kasib's army had been destroyed.

Niall had already looked down on the valley from the top of the cliff, but had not expected the view to be so breathtaking. This window, like the other, seemed to have a slightly magnifying effect, and to deepen colors. When he thrust his head out, this effect disappeared; the colors paled, and the view also became less impressive.

Directly below him was the eastern river, which flowed into the lake; this latter looked very deep and black. The Great Wall looked as if it had been built only yesterday—he almost expected to see armed warriors on guard. He leaned out to test how far this was due to the curious properties of the window; as soon as he did so, the rich coloring vanished, and the wall became weatherworn and eroded by the centuries.

He focused on one guard tower with a missing battlement like a broken tooth and fractured brickwork; when he withdrew his head into the room, the battlement was instantly restored and the brickwork became pristine.

It was apparent that this window also had the power to make him see into the past. What could it divulge? Niall focused his attention until he felt the sensation like a click in his brain. Suddenly, the valley below was full of men and spiders, and the wall was incomplete. The workers were all stripped to the waist, except those whose task was to transport great stones; viewed from a thousand feet above, they looked like ants. The workers were commanded by wolf spiders, and Niall was interested to note that they were smaller than the spiders of today, yet obviously tremendously strong, for one of them was carrying a great stone block.

Niall observed that the cave dwellings carved out of the opposite cliff face looked much as they did at present. Curious about those who made them, he made a focused mental effort. The Great Wall disappeared, and the gray-blue rock dwellings became sharper and clearer. Instead of empty doorways, they now had wooden doors, and strongly built ladders were propped against the cliff face. He could also see a few people moving around down below or climbing the ladders, although they were too distant to see clearly. Once more, an effort of focus had the effect of magnifying them, as if through a pair of binoculars, and he was able to see that they were a primitive people dressed in coarse brown garments. The men had rounded yet powerful shoulders and shaven bald heads—he knew they were shaven, for many had beards—and the women were thin, although some had large breasts. The man he was looking at—bald-headed and clean-shaven—reminded him of someone, but Niall had to look more closely before he recalled who it was.

The beaky nose and receding chin were those of the assassin who had killed himself when a glue spider had immobilized him. Other men had this same characteristic face—the face of a servant of the Magician.

But in that case, why were these cliff dwellings now deserted? Was it possible that these original men of the valley, who had built their homes as fortresses, almost certainly drawing up their ladders after nightfall, had been conquered and carried off as captives by the Magician?

Niall's brain was becoming weary with speculation. He dismissed this vision of the past by thrusting his head out of the window and reestablishing the present moment. It was time to leave. For the moment, he had learned as much as he could take in. The next stage of the journey required returning the way he had come.

He put his head out of the window and studied the wall. There were doors at the base of each guard tower, so he could reach the top. But how could they get down the far side?

It was then that Niall remembered something he had absorbed from the mind of Sephardus. This tower had a bell rope, and it descended past the window from which he was now leaning. In fact, it was still there, but was so worn and shabby that it looked as if it was not strong enough to bear Niall's weight. Niall took hold of it and gave it as strong pull, hoping to snap it where it joined the bell. Instead there was a loud clang that rang out across the valley, causing alarmed birds to squawk.

Niall retreated into the room and pulled as hard as he could. The only effect was another clang that echoed off the cliffs.

Suddenly he dropped the rope, and almost tumbled backwards on the floor. There was a noise like a frog's croak magnified many times, and something huge swept past the window. He knew instantly what it was—one of the creatures called oolus birds, for the head was saurian, like a turtle. He retreated across the room as the creature flew with a crash against the window frame; fortunately, its wingspan was too great for it to get in.

Niall looked around for something he could use as a weapon, but could see nothing. Now he regretted leaving his pack, with the expanding rod, down below. On its next attack, the creature succeeded in getting its head into the room, and it glared at Niall with small, red eyes before it fell away. A moment later, a crash from the opposite window revealed that there was more than one of them. Niall looked down with sudden alarm at the doorway below, and was relieved to see that it was scarcely bigger than the windows, and would certainly not admit a creature with a twelve-foot wingspan.

A moment later his certainty vanished as one of the birds gripped the windowsill and made an effort to perch. Its feet looked oddly like human hands, flesh-colored and hairy; they easily spanned the window ledge. Niall made a rush at it, realizing that if it succeeded in perching and folding its wings it might squeeze through the window opening; but his rush made it flap its huge wings against the wall, then let go.

The other bird also tried the door, but again, lacked the intelligence to try perching with closed wings. It clung there, flapping, and again Niall regretted not having the expanding rod, since the bird's breast would have made a perfect target.

They continued trying to gain an entrance for perhaps ten more minutes, thrusting their heads in at the windows and beating their wings against the walls, before they tired and flew away; as the squawking croak retreated, Niall climbed the steps and watched them soar down over the valley.

His next thought was to get down the pinnacle as quickly as possible, in case they decided to return. He was concerned at the possibility that their withdrawal was designed to tempt him out, but he was reassured by the thought of their stupidity.

As he climbed down from the chamber, he noted that he was no longer worried about the height—only about his vulnerability in case the birds came back; he descended the steps to his pack as confidently as clambering down a ladder, spurred on by the memory of the crushed animal with the broken bones that he had seen that morning. At the bottom he decided to put his sandals in his pack; bare feet would give him a better purchase on the rock. Then he hurried on down the sloping path, relieved to arrive at the first platform, where the second chamber would afford shelter in case of attack. But the sky remained empty, and he felt free to slacken his pace for the remainder of the descent.

The captain was waiting patiently in the shade of a bush, as Niall had known he would be. He asked: "Did you see the birds?"

Niall said dryly: "At close quarters." He sat down on the stone ledge, mopping the sweat from his face, then took the water bottle out of his pack and moistened his dry lips and throat. "Have you ever been attacked by them?"

"No. They have learned that spiders are dangerous. But sometimes we make use of them."

"Make use of them? How?"

"Because they are so powerful, they can be used to transport us."

Niall was baffled. "How?"

"They can carry very heavy burdens." He explained himself in a single flash of imagery, most of which went past too quickly for Niall to understand. But he grasped a picture of an oolus bird carrying a net that contained a number of sheep.

The thought that passed through his mind seemed so absurd that, if they had been speaking in human language, he would not have bothered to voice it. But because their minds were in communication, the spider picked it up immediately.

"That is possible, if they could be brought back."

"Could you bring them back?"

"No. They are too far away. And they are afraid of us."

Niall said: "They didn't seem afraid of me."

"No. They are afraid of the spider people."

As the captain said this, Niall suddenly grasped the idea that had occurred to him: that if the bell was rung again, the birds would almost certainly return.

He looked up at the bell tower against the blue sky. But the thought of climbing the pinnacle again made his heart sink.

Then he remembered the way that the bell had echoed out across the valley. He climbed to the point on the cliff top that overlooked the valley. He cupped his hands to his mouth, leaned back his head, and shouted as loud as he could. As the shout died away, it echoed back from the opposite cliffs, then continued down the valley. The two opposing cliff faces made an ideal echo chamber.

But there was no sign of the birds. He shouted again, this time even louder, and then a third time. Echoes coincided with his shouts, making the valley ring.

There was no answering squawk. Niall, rather enjoying making so much noise, prepared to shout again, when he saw the birds. They must have been perching on one of the towers of the Great Wall, and were now flapping upward, with slow and purposeful beats of their wings.

He turned and hurried back to the captain.

"They're coming. Don't let them see you."

The spider immediately pressed himself into one of the twisted hollows at the base of the pinnacle. Niall stared at the cliff top with a certain apprehension, and turned the thought mirror toward his chest. Then the two flapping shapes appeared over the cliff top, and swooped unhesitatingly toward him as if they already knew precisely where he was.

Before they could reach him, both had been gripped by the will-force of the spider. They tried to twist in the air to escape, but it was too late. With a certain reluctant admiration, Niall watched the captain force them to the ground. Their unwillingness was obvious.

Now that he could study them at close quarters, he saw many things that he had failed to observe when they were trying to get in through the windows. The head was that of a snapping turtle, with the upper and lower lips ending in a kind of curved beak. Both were panting, and their open mouths showed a thick, fleshy tongue, in the center of which was a small, pink object about the size of a small finger; Niall knew intuitively that this was for luring prey. Like birds, they had no teeth, but the lips were horny, resembling beaks, and obviously capable of tearing and masticating flesh. The face was scaly, like a snake's, the eyes, red and menacing, surrounded by loose flesh.

The wings of the oolus bird were covered with pale, sandy-colored feathers, and were enormous and powerful. The legs were scaly, but the feet looked oddly incongruous, shaped rather like enormous human hands covered in black hair, with claws that might have been purple-colored nails.

The spider made them stand upright on the edge of the stone platform, and moved close to them, rolling himself into a tight ball with the legs invisible beneath him.

The captain asked: "Can you control yours?"

Niall said: "I think so." In fact, he was by no means sure.

Instantly he felt himself seized in the bird's great hands. He felt its wings stretch above him, blotting out the sun; then suddenly he was airborne. The hands were holding him below his arms, and were so big that they met around his ribs. Up they went, past the top of the pinnacle, so that he could see inside the belfry, with its huge bronze bell. Then the tower was below him, and they were soaring above the valley.

The sight of the ground so far below him caused a certain involuntary nervousness—the knowledge that the creature had only to loose its grip to send him plunging to his death. As this thought passed through his mind, he felt the hands tighten around him, and realized that the bird was responding to his will.

He had a curious sense that this had happened before. Instantly, he remembered the dream in the cave of the chameleon men, in which he had been transported skyward by a bird with human hands.

As soon as he recognized that his mind could control the bird, he ceased to be nervous. He could actually feel his own dominance over the feeble will of the creature, whose small purposes were entirely dominated by its interest in food. And suddenly, Niall understood. This great creature was an evolutionary freak, brought into existence by the vital force of the goddess. When its ancestors were smaller, they had to fight hard for subsistence; but now, with its powerful body and formidable claws and beak, the oolus bird had no real predators. There was an abundance of prey; from this height—they were still above the cliff tops—he could see large animals grazing. So it led a lazy existence, which had sapped its will, and would lead, in due course, to its extinction.

This journey was not unlike being transported by the imagination of Asmak. In the northern distance he could see the Gray Mountains, with their curious, twisted peaks, one of which concealed the entrance to Shadowland. But Niall was more interested in looking directly ahead, anxious to observe where they should go next. The Great Wall, which he had looked forward to seeing more closely, was far below, and although he easily could have made the bird land on top of it, he decided that it would serve no purpose. Besides, he was hungry.

He had already decided that, if possible, they would spend the night in the cliff dwellings, but had been wondering how they could climb up to them without ladders. But now, seeing a path that led up the cliff face from the level of the dwellings, he saw that the answer was to land on top of the cliff and then descend from above.

Therefore, he directed his bird to fly across the valley, to a place on the cliff top near the beginning of the path—which, at close quarters, he saw to be more like a flight of steps. The bird planed down and gently released Niall onto a kind of thick, tough grass whose pure green color belied its coarseness. The bird landed, flapped its wings, then folded them and stood waiting. A moment later, the other bird, carrying the captain, landed a few yards away.

The captain unfolded his legs and stood upright. He asked Niall: "Shall we kill them?"

"Why?"

"Their flesh is good for eating."

But Niall had noticed, about half a mile away, a herd of creatures about the size of sheep, grazing on the thick grass.

"I don't think that will be necessary. After all, they have served us well."

He could feel the captain's surprise; the spider obviously felt that loyalty to these stupid creatures was completely inappropriate. Nevertheless, he conveyed to them the message that they were free to go, and the birds lost no time in launching themselves off the cliff and swooping downward, their hoarse, squawking cries expressing their relief.

In the late afternoon sunlight, the Valley of the Dead was beautiful, with its dark, mirrorlike lake resembling black steel, and immense dark cliffs that sparkled with veins of blue and pink rock crystal. A few hundred yards to the west of where they had landed, the ground rose, and was covered with stunted trees and bushes, among which Niall was glad to observe a dead tree that could provide fuel for a fire. The first thing he did was to take a long drink of the springwater; it was delicious to the throat, but sharpened his hunger.

The captain was eyeing the sheeplike creatures with interest, and Niall could sense that he was also hungry. By mutual consent, and without exchanging a word, they moved toward the herd at a walking pace. On his own, the captain could have covered the ground in less than a minute, but then, speed might have caused the sheep to flee. So, since there was no cover, they approached slowly and casually.

These sheep, Niall observed as they came closer, were bigger than those in the fields around the city of the bombardier beetles. Many among them were black. Niall took out the telescopic rod and lengthened it into a spear; apart from the knife, it was the only weapon that he had.

The sheep saw them when they were about fifty yards away. Niall expected a stampede; in fact, their reaction was totally unexpected. The black sheep moved quickly to the front of the herd, so the white ones were behind them, then stared across at Niall and his companion with unmistakable hostility.

Expecting the captain to select one of them and pin him down with willpower, Niall pointed to the fattest of the black sheep facing them. "That one."

He was startled by the effect of his words. The sheep lowered their heads and began to charge. Within seconds the whole herd was thundering toward them. Ever since moving in the direction of the sheep, he and the captain had established a telepathic link, and Niall now used the whole force of the thought mirror to direct his will toward the animal they had selected. It immediately stumbled and collapsed, causing the sheep behind to tumble headlong over it. But the rest of the sheep simply divided around the fallen ones, and continued to charge. Niall was astonished at the ferocity in their eyes, and at the fact that they were snarling like wolves, with their lips drawn back. The exposed teeth looked as if they could give a dangerous bite.

At the same moment, Niall and the captain made the same decision—to flee. There was no other sensible course. The captain loped away; then, remembering that Niall had shorter legs, turned and picked him up with his forelegs, then carried him, his claws holding Niall by the waist like some huge doll. The thought mirror had prevented Niall from panicking; now he felt like laughing at the thought of running away from a flock of sheep.

They quickly outstripped their pursuers; within a quarter of a mile, the sheep had given up and returned to grazing.

The danger had stilled Niall's hunger, but as they walked back, it soon returned. Moreover, since it would be dark in half an hour, they had to think seriously about finding their supper. Niall would have been quite happy with the crunchy biscuits and goat cheese, or even a food tablet, but would have felt guilty if the captain had been forced to go hungry—which, after all, was the most important problem in a spider's life.

From the bushes and shrubs on the rising ground came the shrill voice of crickets. In the desert of North Khaybad Niall's family had often eaten giant crickets; roasted with herbs they were filling and appetizing. So he and the captain now made their way cautiously toward the bushes. But closer inspection revealed that the crickets here were far smaller than those of North Khaybad, and that they would need dozens to make a meal.

But from their changed position on the higher ground they could see that the sheep were moving away from them, and that the fallen animal was still lying on the ground. They made their way back to it warily, in case they were seen by the sheep, but by the time they reached it, the flock was a mile away. The black sheep was dead, with a broken neck, either as a result of its fall or the spider's will-force.

The captain carried it back to the edge of the bushes, and it was among these that Niall lighted a fire with wood and bark fragments, hoping that no enemy would see the flames, and relieved that the dry wood burned fiercely without smoke.

Meanwhile, the captain used his claws to skin the sheep, which was about the size of a small pony. The black wool was so thick and wiry that it would have defied the teeth of most predators; but it yielded to the spider's razor-sharp pincers, and in twenty minutes the skinless carcass lay on the grass. After Niall had sliced off two large steaks from the back leg, the captain proceeded to eat with relish, his powerful jaws tearing out the flesh in chunks, each of which would have fed several people. Niall looked discreetly the other way, and tried not to hear the grinding of the spider's jaws.

When he had finished his meal, the captain found a comfortable hollow among the bushes and went to sleep, his legs bunched underneath him. Niall had been keeping an eye on the sky, anxious about spies of the Magician, but apart from a distant flock of birds, the heavens were a dusky blue and empty. By now he was so weary that he would willingly have lain down to sleep—tiredness had taken the edge off his hunger—but he forced himself to stay awake, yawning heavily, until the steaks were cooked in the glowing embers of the fire. Then he scraped off the black ashes, cleaned the charred meat with a handful of grass, and ate one of the pieces with a biscuit. While he was eating, the raven reappeared and perched on the stunted tree whose branches stretched above him. Niall gave it some of the biscuit, followed by a piece of the lamb, sliced off with his knife; it ate this with violent shakes of its beak. The meat was undercooked but tender. After eating, he carefully wrapped up the remaining steak in leaves, and stowed it in his pack. Then, somehow reassured by the presence of the bird, he stretched out in his sleeping bag.

He was not entirely happy about the idea of sleeping in the open; he had meant to explore the caves below, but climbing down to them would have been dangerous in the falling dark. As it was, the thick, coarse grass made a soft mattress, and within a few minutes he was asleep.

By the time he woke up, the sky was gray with dawn, and tearing and masticating sounds told him the captain was already enjoying his breakfast. Again, good manners made him turn away; instead, he lay with closed eyes and reflected on the puzzle of how the local sheep had become so aggressive. The vital force of the great goddess explained why they had grown to twice the size of domestic sheep, but not their belligerence. The fact that the black sheep had moved to form a barrier between the black and the white ones indicated that they were the bolder of the two. But that failed to explain how their belligerence had evolved.

Then he saw a possible answer. The creatures had attacked when Niall had pointed at one of them and said: "That one." Was it possible that they were telepathic? And, furthermore, was it conceivable that their usual predators attacked them with will-force, leading them to evolve this tactic of charging? Niall recalled the assassin he had encountered in the hospital, and his formidable will-force, and felt that he might be close to a solution.

The chewing noises had stopped, so Niall sat up and unzipped his sleeping bag. It was covered with dew. By now the sun was up, and the captain was sitting a dozen yards away, digesting his meal. Niall went and sat a few yards away, and after cleaning the burned wood off his hands on the dewy grass, ate a light meal of goat cheese. This time the raven did not join him; it was probably winging over the valley hunting its own breakfast.

He stood up to take stock of their position. To the north, the foothills soon turned into mountains with snow on their summits. There were no obvious passes between them, which meant that the best way forward was probably to go east until they reached the plain, then turn north, up the continuation of the valley that had brought them here.

But first, Niall wanted to look at the cave dwellings below, to learn what he could of the cliff dwellers.

Niall went to the edge of the cliff and looked down the steps. They were very steep—so steep that it would have been folly to try and descend with his back to them. One slip would send him plunging a quarter of a mile down to the valley. But, like the steps up the pinnacle across the valley, these had handholds cut into them.

For safety, Niall decided to leave his pack behind; he hid it among the bushes, in case birds came to investigate. And since it was warm in the morning sun, he decided to leave his cloak behind too. But he slipped the flashlight into the pocket of his tunic. Then he eased himself over the edge of the cliff, and began the long descent. The spider, who was obviously unworried by heights, gave him a ten-foot start and then followed.

Provided Niall faced the cliff and concentrated on the handholds, he was in no danger. The steps were not as precipitous as they looked from above, and he was soon clambering down them at a reasonable speed. Even so, it was twenty minutes before he found himself on the wide ledge that formed a terrace in front of the cliff dwellings. Below him, there was still a drop of a hundred feet or so.

Across the valley, five hundred yards away, rose the Great Wall. Its top was level with the cliff dwellings, but its towers were fifty feet higher. From here it looked a truly formidable and impregnable barrier. At the foot of the wall there was a ditch about twenty feet deep, which could probably be flooded to form a moat. It struck Niall that the spiders must have entertained a deep fear of their enemy to expend so much time and effort on such a vast project.

Having recovered his breath, he now turned his attention to the cliff dwellings. The nearest entrance led into a cave that was probably a store room. Niall's flashlight revealed that it was about fifty feet deep.

The next doorway, which still had a disintegrating wooden door jamb, led into a room with a seven-foot ceiling. Birds flew out through the window as they entered. This room was about eight feet square, and in the far wall, another doorway led into a smaller room, probably a bedroom. Beyond this, there was an even smaller room, which looked like a children's bedroom. When Niall considered the effort entailed in cutting this small dwelling out of solid rock, he felt overawed—it must have taken years.

But why had they gone to so much trouble? Had this land once been so wild and dangerous that the valley floor was unsafe?

They went to the end of the terrace, peering into each of the rooms. In only one of them there were the remains of a bench, whose nail holes held crumbling rust. The others were empty.

At the end of the terrace there was a tall, heavy rock set in a hole in the ground, obviously placed there to prevent children from falling off the end. The raven was standing on it, but flew away as they approached.

They turned and went back the other way. Beyond the stairway were more dwellings, one larger and with four rooms instead of three—probably the home of a chieftain. Next to this there was the largest room so far, with a ceiling ten feet high and at least thirty feet deep. Niall guessed this to be some kind of assembly room, or perhaps even a church.

He turned the thought mirror away from his chest, to increase his sensitivity to the atmosphere; since he knew the kind of people who lived here, he felt he could dimly sense their presence: the strongly built women with big breasts, the bearded men with shaven heads and faces resembling the assassin of the hospital.

The captain obviously found all this uninteresting, and wondered why Niall was wasting his time. So Niall decided against exploring further, and turned back along the terrace.

About to start the reascent, he paused for a moment to glance at the "store room." It was obvious at once that special attention had been devoted to it. The doorway, which was ten feet high and wide, had been carved and smoothed with care, and two feet inside it, a six-inch-deep groove had been chiseled into the wall on either side—Niall guessed that it had once held some thick wooden door that could be lowered like a drawbridge. A long rectangular hole in the ceiling seemed to confirm this assumption.

This place, Niall guessed, had been a cave before the cliff dwellings were carved, for its walls were rough and full of hollows, obviously created by nature, not by human hands. At the rear, against the wall, were a number of large clay jars which had probably held oil or wine, and a large cubic object made of wood. The flashlight beam revealed a skillful carving that showed a man with his feet braced apart, and his arms, spread wide above his head, as though supporting some enormous weight. The wide-open mouth created an appearance of agony.

Niall peered inside; it had been carved out of a piece of solid wood, evidently the trunk of some tree that must have been four feet across; the sides had been cut straight, and the inside carefully hollowed out. But what had it been for? What had it held? Its smooth interior offered no clue.

Niall knelt to study the underside of the vessel. It was below floor level, standing in a square depression in the stone. But why, he wondered, bother to chisel into the floor?

His immediate suspicion was that the vessel covered a hole—or even a descending passage.

He placed both hands against one side, and pushed to test its weight. It was unexpectedly heavy—far heavier than its size warranted; even Niall's full strength could lift it only an inch from the floor. He released it with a gasp and stood back.

The captain watched this effort curiously, then came and stood in Niall's place. He placed his front legs against the wood, braced himself, and pushed. Having six legs to exert pressure, he was in a stronger position than a human being. The vessel tilted, revealing a hole underneath it.

Before Niall could shine his flashlight inside it, there was a violent crash that jarred his teeth, and they were plunged into total darkness. The doorway was blocked with some obstacle, and the light beam showed it to be a door, which obviously had descended from above.

Closer examination revealed that the barrier was made of a single piece of smooth stone, which sealed the entrance tightly; the only daylight that showed through was a few inches at the top. Niall now recalled the six-inch groove carved into the wall on either side of the doorway. He had assumed that it had been made for a wooden door that had long since disintegrated; in fact, this stone door must have been poised above their heads.

Niall realized that it would be pointless to give way to panic. If the door slid down from above, then it must be balanced by some kind of counterweight mechanism. In that case, it ought to be possible to find how it worked. Perhaps the answer lay in the wooden vessel they had moved. If moving it had caused the door to close, then moving it the other way ought to open it.

He now cursed himself for leaving his backpack behind. He might have used the expanding rod to make contact with the white tower, and asked the old man to look up information about counterweights. His own knowledge of them was nonexistent, since he had never before encountered them.

On the other hand, perhaps the mechanism was simple and straightforward. He was relieved, at any rate, that he had the flashlight. Without it, their situation would have been truly alarming.

He tried to push over the wooden vessel, and again had to give up and ask the captain to do it. As the bottom lifted, he shone his light underneath. Just as he suspected, a heavy chain was attached to the bottom, explaining why it had been so hard to move. This must be the mechanism that had lowered the door.

The captain could not support its weight for long. What was needed was something to prop up the bottom. The only thing that suggested itself was one of the clay jars. Niall tried moving the nearest one; it was almost his own height, but by tilting it, he was able to roll it like a wheel on its bottom rim. The spider meanwhile had been forced to release the wooden vessel. But when Niall had positioned the jar next to it, he raised it again, and Niall tilted the jar almost to the floor and pushed it forward. The gap was not quite wide enough, and the captain had to make an additional effort to raise it another few inches. Then Niall pushed the jar forward, and succeeded in wedging its bottom into the gap. When the spider released the weight, there was an ominous cracking sound, but the jar held, and the wooden vessel remained tilted at an angle of thirty degrees. Niall and the captain both relaxed with a gasp.

Next he stretched out on the floor, and shone the flashlight underneath the wooden vessel. Its bottom must have been six inches thick, and the final link of the rusty chain was held by a metal half-ring that was embedded in the wood. The chain was rigid, and disappeared into a hole in the floor.

Niall moved into a sitting position and tried to reason it out. The chain disappeared downward, yet it must be part of a mechanism that somehow ran overhead and lowered the door.

He crossed the cave, turned off the flashlight, and studied the top of the door. The thin sliver of daylight was broken by a small, dark shape that he had not noticed before. When it moved, Niall's intuition told that it was the raven. He focused his attention and performed once more the mental act of identification that allowed him to share the bird's consciousness.

At once he was outside in the sunlight. The raven was perched on top of the stone door, wondering what had happened to the human it regarded as its benefactor. The door itself, he could now see, was six inches thick, and must have weighed many tons.

Niall caused the bird to fly down to the ground; it now obeyed his suggestions without hesitation. From there, Niall could survey the wall beside the doorway. He was hoping to observe some device like a lever that controlled the mechanism. But there was nothing. Next he made the bird fly to the top of the door. From there he was able to see that the door had been lowered into place by two heavy chains on either side, both coated with thick rust, and sunk into the stone. But when he tried to get the bird to fly upward into the dark slot from which the door had descended, it panicked and began to squawk, then flew away. Aware that this experiment had provided no answers, Niall transferred his attention back to his own body, and was once again in darkness.

He next shone the light over the ceiling, then the walls, hoping to find some clue to what controlled the door. Again he found nothing. After that he returned to the hole below the wooden vessel, which was square and about eighteen inches deep. It had been carved out of the solid rock, but again, offered no clue to the door mechanism.

The spider was standing patiently, waiting for Niall to reach some decision. Knowing that Niall was the chosen of the goddess, he did not have the slightest doubt that they would soon be out of this trap.

For trap it undoubtedly was. Niall had seen a rat trap of this design—a door that came down when the mouse nibbled the bait.

151

Presumably the massive stone door had been intended to catch thieves who entered the chamber to steal food. But even that explanation was puzzling. Surely no food thief would bother to move the wooden vessel.

Next, merely as a test, he pulled the clay jar clear of the wooden vessel, his eyes fixed on the door. The jar immediately split in two, and the vessel fell with a crash, but there was not the slightest tremor in the door. This tended to confirm Niall's increasing suspicion that perhaps there was, after all, no connection between the wooden vessel and the door mechanism.

Then how did the men who had engineered this mechanism release those who had been trapped? There surely must be some lever or similar device concealed somewhere. But that might even be in the house next door.

Assuming, then, that there was no mechanism for raising the door, what other possibilities were there? The most obvious solution was to wait till dusk and attempt telepathic contact with his mother. And she in turn would tell Simeon or Doggins, or even Dravig, and some sort of rescue attempt would be organized. By spider balloon, the Valley of the Dead could be reached in less than two hours. But it would be a poor solution. The whole purpose of coming here on foot was to approach the kingdom of the Magician unnoticed, and a full-scale rescue expedition would be an infallible way of attracting attention to themselves.

They had been in the cave for about an hour, and Niall was beginning to feel chilly, and to wish he had not left his cloak with his pack. As soon as he thought about being cold, he shivered. The captain asked him what was troubling him.

"I am cold."

The captain found this hard to understand, since the will-force of spiders could simply increase their blood flow. He immediately shared his own warmth by a simple act of telepathic rapport, which had precisely the same effect as if the temperature of the cave had been raised by a flow of warm air.

It made Niall aware that he could have raised his own temperature by turning the thought mirror and concentrating. But for the moment, he was intrigued to find that he could also see around him, as if a dim light had been turned on. He had noticed the same effect when walking through the underground tunnel with Asmak, but had assumed that this was because Asmak was so familiar with his surroundings that he was transmitting this familiarity to Niall, producing an impression of light.

Now that the cold and the darkness had both been dispelled, Niall felt better. It was as if the spider had also given him some of its enormous patience. He therefore began examining his surroundings with a close attention that was free of anxiety.

It seemed to him logical that the key to escaping from this place probably lay inside the cave itself. After all, suppose someone became accidentally trapped inside?

But where? For the tenth time he played the flashlight inch by inch over the walls and ceiling, but could find no sign of anything that might conceivably activate the mechanism.

One by one, he looked into the jars and, as he expected, found them all empty.

At that point he noticed something that intrigued him about the jar that had split. It had cracked across the bottom, and a large piece had broken away. Spilling from this broken segment was a substance that looked like clay or chalk. When Niall peered more closely, he realized that he had been wrong to assume the jar had a flat bottom; in fact, its inside terminated in a point, presumably to trap wine sediment.

The white substance was hard to the touch, but crumbled when squeezed between his fingers.

With the spider watching him with mild curiosity—obviously wondering what he found so interesting about crumbling chalk—he looked at the other broken half of the jar. There the chalky substance was intact, and its top was flat. In effect, the jar had a kind of false bottom.

He laid the next jar on its side and crawled inside it. A few jabs with the rim of the flashlight revealed that its bottom was also made of chalk, which cracked and then crumbled as he poked at it.

It was the same with the third, fourth, fifth, and sixth jars. Each had a layer of chalk that gave the impression of a flat bottom.

As he crawled into the seventh jar he knew this would be crucial. Either the chalk had an innocent explanation, or it had been introduced to deceive anyone who looked casually into the jars.

This time, the metal rim of the flashlight encountered something hard as it smashed the chalk. He laid down the flashlight—his other hand was trapped against the wall of the jar—and probed with his fingers. They encountered a ball-like object, about three inches in diameter. Niall gave a grunt of self-congratulation.

He wriggled back out of the jar, sat on the floor, and eagerly rubbed away the chalk from the object. He found himself looking at a ball made of glass or crystal—he suspected rock crystal, since it was so heavy. And as he held it between his palms, he felt a faint electrical tingling sensation.

He showed it to the captain. "What do you think this is?"

The spider touched it with his pedipalp. "I have never seen anything like it. What is your opinion?"

"I don't have one yet. But they must have had a good reason for hiding it so carefully."

He closed his eyes, concentrating his attention on his fingertips. The tingling increased, and became stronger when he held the ball against his palms. But even at this stage Niall was aware that the globe was in no sense alive; it was merely a device for communication.

But with what?

The captain had been waiting patiently, observing Niall's total absorption. But now he could see that Niall had returned to the world of the present, he asked: "Have you learned how to raise the door?"

"No. The mechanism is broken."

Noting that Niall seemed unperturbed, the captain asked: "Then how can we escape?"

As he spoke, causing Niall to reflect upon the problem, a bright green spark of light appeared in the center of the crystal, and the globe began to glow with a gentle warmth. This faded after a few moments, leaving behind a tingling sensation in Niall's hands. As he focused on this, Niall seemed to lose his sense of identity, as if he had become part of the crystal. He deliberately focused on this sensation, recognizing that it was somehow an answer to the captain's question.

Fascinated by the crystal, he ceased to be conscious of the passage of time. An hour might have passed when his attention was drawn back to the present as the captain became alert, listening with total concentration. Niall could hear nothing, but the spider's sensitivity to vibrations was greater than his own.

Several minutes later they heard stones that rattled down from above. Someone was descending the stairway with a slow and deliberate tread.

The sounds ceased in front of the door. Then there was a long pause. Whoever was outside was obviously considering how the door could be raised. Then the stone barrier rattled, shaken back and forth in its groove. As Niall peered up at the gap at the top of the door, hoping to catch a glimpse of the visitor's face, two giant hands slid through it, and fingers that were an inch thick gripped the stone. There was a grinding sound as the great door was lifted a few inches. Then one of the hands vanished, and reappeared underneath the door, while the other held its weight suspended. With a rumbling noise that was like thunder, the huge mass of stone was raised, and they saw that the giant who was raising it was kneeling. They were looking at a bearded creature whose size made the troll of the sacred mountain seem small.

He growled something in a guttural voice, which they understood to be an invitation to come out quickly. Niall, being closest, darted under the slab, followed closely by the captain. When they were outside, the troll stood up, grunting, still holding the door, and raised it until it vanished into the stone slot above. But it was obvious that whatever catch had held the door in position was now broken. With a grunt of disgust, the giant released it, standing back, and the door fell down with such force that it split in two, one of the broken halves falling into the cave, while the other hung suspended lopsidedly on its rusty chain.

The leatherlike skin of the giant's feet, and the black toenails that looked as if they were made of some dark rock, showed that it belonged to the same species as the troll Niall had already encountered; otherwise they had little in common. The troll of the sacred mountain looked as if his face had been hacked out of wood by an inexpert sculptor; this giant was far more human, with a bulbous nose and cheekbones, and a friendly face. The other troll had been naked and covered in hair; this one wore leather garments stitched crudely with thongs. The brown hair and beard suggested that he was still young, while a wide gap between his front teeth underlined the impression of good humor. Niall estimated that he was about twelve feet tall.

The giant was obviously dubious about the captain, not certain whether a death spider could be trusted. Niall suspected that he had had some unpleasant experience with one of them in the past.

Niall was still holding the crystal globe. The giant peered at this with interest, then held out a brown, leathery palm that was more than a foot in diameter.

Niall placed the ball in it. He expected the giant to look at it closely; instead, he closed his fist round it, and held it close to his ear as if it were a ticking watch. After perhaps a minute he handed it back. Then suddenly, the giant was communicating with Niall as if speaking in human language.

He was asking where Niall and the captain came from. Taking only a moment to adjust to the wavelength of his thought, Niall transmitted an image of the spider city. The giant considered this, frowning, then asked where they were going. Since this was more difficult to answer, Niall raised his hand and pointed northward. Again the giant frowned, and his thought waves unmistakably conveyed the idea that this troubled him. Then he shook his head, and beckoned them to follow him.

Niall had already been wondering how these huge feet could negotiate the rocky stairway. Now he watched with amazement as the troll climbed as effortlessly as if he weighed no more than Niall. The captain went next, swarming up with an easy motion that made Niall think of an octopus. By comparison, Niall felt slow and clumsy, his limbs distinctly stiff, as he heaved himself painfully upward.

When he reached the top nearly half an hour later, he found the captain relaxing in the afternoon sunlight. To Niall's surprise, the troll was nowhere to be seen. It took Niall several moments to observe a shimmer in the air that told him that, like the chameleon men, the troll had the power to make himself transparent. It had never entered Niall's head that trolls had any such ability.

Niall flung himself down beside the captain, glad to give his aching knees a rest.

The troll asked: "Are you tired?"

Again, as with the chameleon men, it was the meaning of the words rather than words themselves that entered Niall's brain. Niall answered that he was.

He failed to understand the giant's next question, which seemed to be some kind of offer of help. Was he offering to let him stay there and rest? Or pick him up and carry him? But a moment later he understood, as his muscles responded to a rippling, electrical sensation that was as refreshing as plunging into cool water. It seemed to flow upward from the soles of his feet, and left him tingling with energy. He said with astonishment: "Thank you!"

The reply was a good-humored grunt, accompanied by the suggestion that it was time to move on.

As Niall went to retrieve his pack from its hiding place, he noticed that the captain was still relaxing on the grass; it was obvious that he had not received the thought-message. Niall had to ask him: "Are you ready?" before the spider heaved himself to his feet.

They walked due east, following the cliff top for more than a mile before it began to slope down toward the plain. When they walked on soft, springy turf, the ground vibrated, and it was obvious that this troll was immensely heavy. Niall observed that when he stood on a piece of chalky rock, he crushed it flat.

Niall asked the troll: "Do you have a name?"

"I have been known as Mimas. Also as . . ." What followed was simply a meaningless sound.

From this, Niall gathered that, like most of the spiders, trolls did not have any use for names, since identity could be conveyed with a mental picture.

To keep abreast of them, Niall had to walk with a swinging stride that normally would have left him breathless, but which he found himself maintaining like a long-distance runner. He attributed this energy to the stress he had experienced during the past few hours, and the relief of being free again. Then, as they began the descent, his sandal caught on a root and his two companions halted while he retrieved it. As his bare foot touched the grass, the faint tingling sensation made him aware why the pace was not tiring him. He was receiving energy from the ground. So as they set off again, he pushed his sandals into the long pockets of his smock. It was not until they reached the valley, and the ground became hard and stony, that he put them on again.

After that the going became difficult. On this bare ground, the energy had ceased to flow. And compared to the broad southern valley that lay behind them, the narrow way to the north was strewn with boulders that looked as if they had been carried down from the mountains by some immense flood. It made Niall think of the Mighty Cheb's story of the destruction of his army, and reminded him that they had just entered the territory of the Magician.

Now that they were sheltered by overhanging cliffs and the westering sun filled the valley with dark pools of shadow, the troll had allowed himself to become visible again. Even he had to pick his way carefully among rocks weighing a few pounds to boulders of many tons.

As far as Niall could see, the valley stretched bleakly ahead, with no sign of any cavern or hollow that might afford shelter. The cliffs to the east were also steep and flat, giving the impression of having been the bank of a water channel. But within a quarter of a mile of the valley's entrance, the troll stopped and turned toward the western cliff where the quartz had split into a cleft that was full of rubble and debris. It looked as if some earthquake had torn the rock face apart, then closed it again so the halves overlapped. One corner of the dislocated lower slab vanished into a layer of blue clay.

The troll approached the angle where the two joined, then, to Niall's puzzlement, turned sideways as if to squeeze through a narrow gap. He stepped to his left, then vanished. Niall, who had been watching closely, also turned sideways and took a step to his left, experiencing as he did so a curious sense of ease and confidence, as if receiving power from the quartz. A moment later he found himself in a narrow tunnel that sloped gently downwards. The troll was visible because he glowed with a faint blue light.

A moment later, as his eyes adjusted, Niall found he could see perfectly clearly.

Niall heard the captain's voice in his head. "Where are you?"

He turned to the troll. "He can't get in."

The troll pushed past him, turned sideways, and disappeared. Niall imitated his movement, and again found himself outside. It was rather like being caught up in a current of water.

The troll said to the captain: "Do exactly as I do."

But it was quite obvious that the captain could not hear him—either that, or simply could not understand. Niall suspected that he was hearing the same unpleasant crackling noise that caused him such pain when he first met the chameleon men. The troll made a gesture indicating "Follow me," then turned sideways; a moment later he had vanished. The captain understood the gesture and tried to follow. But he found the rock barrier impenetrable.

He asked Niall: "Can you show me?"

Niall said: "Follow me and do exactly as I do." He stepped forward, and found himself standing beside the troll in the tunnel. But the captain evidently had found it impossible to follow. His voice, reflecting his frustration, sounded in Niall's head. "I can't do it."

Niall stepped outside again. As he did so, he could see what was wrong. The captain, like all spiders, had achieved all his higher functions—like speech and reason—through sheer willpower and self-discipline. So when he approached a problem like this, he automatically braced his will, and lost that instinctive relaxation that made it easy. Niall, on the other hand, was making use of an instinct that enabled him to penetrate the barrier as easily as breathing. It was simply a knack.

He held out his hand to the spider. "Give me your claw."

It was furry, not unlike the paw of a dog or cat, but harder and more bony. Niall stepped toward the rock face. But even as he passed through it, he was aware that the spider's sudden fear that he would find himself trapped inside the rock prevented him from following.

The troll saw the problem. He said: "Give me your other claw," and took it in his huge hand. And now, since the spider had two human creatures on either side, his fear of being trapped disappeared, and he slipped into the instinctive attitude that enabled him to pass through the rock. A moment later, as all three of them stood side by side in the tunnel, the captain made an exclamation that in human speech would have been: "That is incredible!"

The troll said: "That is because your mind created a barrier where none existed," and Niall knew, without being told, that the spider was now able to understand the troll's telepathic language. Subjugating his will to the troll's had placed them in sympathy. Niall knew they now trusted one another, and that the troll's misgivings about the spider had vanished.

The tunnel down which they now followed the troll was completely unlike the one that led to the cave of the chameleon men. To begin with, it obviously had not been carved and shaped by hands, but was natural rock. What made it so strange was this rock looked more like the wood of old, gnarled trees, with flowing curves and grooves, and even places where it had twisted into something that looked like knots. Niall could only guess that it was some kind of volcanic formation, or that molten rock had flowed into these treelike forms. There were places where the tunnel widened and where the floor was almost flat. In others, it narrowed into a passage with curved walls that looked like green glass, and a floor that was simply a point where two walls curved down to meet underfoot. The spider, with his eight legs, found these difficult to negotiate. Even Niall, placing one foot before the other, was in continual danger of twisting his ankle. Only the troll seemed perfectly comfortable in these strange surroundings, moving surefooted over the distorted surfaces.

There were places where other tunnels led off to the right or left, and at one intersection there was a deep hole that had to be skirted; from its depth came the roaring sound of running water, and a downdraft indicated that it was flowing fast. He could feel the spider's tension as they edged around its rim. But beyond this, the tunnel became so wide, and the floor so flat, that they might have been walking on one of the pink-colored roads of the spider city.

There came a point where the sloping floor changed into a wide flight of steps, at the bottom of which was a light. They obviously were made for creatures who were taller than humans, since each step was more than two feet deep. The troll strode on down them without a change of pace, while the spider, because of the flexibility of his body, was able to move easily from step to step. But Niall, who found it easier to descend with his face toward the steps, using his hands as well as his feet, soon fell far behind.

When his feet encountered a flat surface, he knew he must be at the bottom. He turned round, sitting on the last step, both knees aching, and stared with astonishment at the great hall that faced him.

His first impression was of light reflected from a thousand crystals, created from angular surfaces whose edges reminded him of a giant saw made up of pyramids. They stretched in all directions, many half as tall as a man, others a mere quarter of an inch high, covering the cave to its far depths. Between the crystals were winding paths that twisted and turned to avoid the larger blocks. Against the wall of the cave were tall columns made of a green crystal that were shaped like tropical vegetation with long, swordlike leaves. There were also crystalline deposits that looked like sleeping birds, or skeletal hands and arms, or even gargoyles. The total effect was overpowering.

There was a sound of running water, and Niall observed a stream that flowed in a channel below the level of the floor, while small bridges that carried the paths across the water made it clear that at least some of this profusion was the work of living hands.

All Niall's tiredness had vanished. There was something about this extraordinary place, and the power of mind that seemed to be reflected in its bright surfaces, that woke him to full alertness.

Since his mouth was dry, he knelt at the side of the stream and dipped up a little water in his hand. The taste startled him. It produced the same kind of shock of pleasure as the well water in his flask, but far stronger. It was as if the water was effervescent with tiny bubbles. Yet when he cupped both hands and filled them with water, it seemed perfectly still. He dipped his tongue into it and it prickled; so did his lips as he immersed them. Moreover, when he reached out to steady himself against a huge crystal, a faint current made him snatch his hand away.

There could be no doubt that this great hall of crystal was alive with some powerful force, the same force that had flowed up through his feet and that now ran through his body as he swallowed the water. The place had been designed as an energy trap.

The sound of footsteps brought him back to the present. The troll had come back to find him. Smiling his broad, good-natured smile, he said: "Come. My wife is preparing food."

N iall followed the giant to the far corner, where the captain was waiting under an archway in the rock. This arch, Niall noticed, seemed to be natural, and traces of seashells and ammonites that roughened the walls revealed that this great hall had once been a sea cave. The crystals, then, were the result of evaporation, although it was hard to imagine how seawater had become so concentrated as to crystallize into this profusion.

Through the doorway, more steps descended steeply to another tall archway. And as the troll reached the bottom, two young trolls ran out and began to jump up and down, and shout so loud that Niall winced. Both had red cheeks and red hair, and a gap between their front teeth; the younger was probably two, and was already bigger than Niall; the elder looked about ten, and was over eight feet tall. Both ran to their father and hugged him. Then the young one noticed the captain, and eyed him with alarm. His father picked him up and said something reassuring in the guttural language in which he had first addressed Niall.

A bright light shone from beyond the archway. This proved to be a lamp in the form of a crystal column, two feet high, that stood on a table, and that made the room as bright as a sunny day. The tabletop was a slab of rock whose legs were six-foot tree trunks covered in thick bark.

Although the roof of the cave was high—at least twenty feet—the room was warm, and Niall realized that the source of the warmth was another rock crystal, this one shaped like a massive rough boulder that stood by a far wall and emitted an orange glow. A few feet from this, seated in an armchair that had been made out of a single piece of dark rock, was another troll who Niall guessed to be the grandfather. He had a beard that was at once bushy and straggly, sprouting from his chin in irregular but thick gray tufts. Like the troll's of the sacred mountain, his face looked as if it had been hacked out of wood, and the nose was broken. And like his son, he conveyed an impression of enormous power.

At his feet sat an animal covered in scales, with a face like a bull-frog. At the sight of the strangers it stood up on four short legs and made a strange booming, bellowing sound that made everything in the room vibrate. The man in the chair silenced it with a roaring noise that sounded like "Groosh!" and it subsided.

A woman came through a door of rough planks on the far side of the cave, wiping her hands on an apron of sackcloth. She had red hair that fell halfway down her back, and wore a red blouse and a wide gray skirt of coarse material. At first sight she struck Niall as ugly, her upturned nose and wide nostrils giving her a piglike appearance, which was not improved by the widely spaced front teeth. But her broad smile was so good-natured that Niall like her immediately.

Conversation being impossible, since the children were playing a noisy game that involved chasing one another in circles, the troll took a wooden cup from a shelf and filled it from a black crystal jug that would have been too heavy for Niall to lift. The liquid foamed over the rim of the cup. The troll filled three more, handing one to his father and one to his wife, and offering the fourth to the captain, who declined it, making a gesture signifying thanks that Niall had often seen Dravig use.

The grandfather and the woman both drank deeply as soon as their cups were placed in their hands, and Niall, who had been hesitating, assuming they would all drink together, realized that trolls have no interest in such niceties as toasting one another's health.

The taste made him gasp. It was as if he was now drinking a concentrated version of the water he had just tasted in the cave above. But this was full of bubbles, and tasted of some citrus fruit that was neither orange nor lemon. This was not water but a kind of wine, and the effect was almost as powerful as that of a certain colorless liquid that the chief wife of Bill Doggins distilled from mead. For a moment Niall was afraid that one mouthful had already made him drunk. But after a few seconds, during which the energy sang in his ears, it subsided and left him feeling only mildly exhilarated.

The children were both clamoring for a drink, and their father let them taste from his cup. This had the immediate effect of making them noisier than ever, until Niall wondered how much of this ear-shattering din their parents could stand.

At that point, the wife beckoned Niall and the captain to follow her. Through the doorway was a room that was obviously a kitchen, since there was a great loaf of bread on the table and a dish of apples the size of small footballs, as well as a bowl with a white mountain of curd that looked like goat cheese, and an assortment of huge sausages.

She led them on through another door, into a larder with animal carcasses hanging from a beam and joints of ham—there was a similar larder in Niall's palace.

Since the children were now two rooms away, and it was possible to speak without shouting, she addressed Niall and the captain in her own language, which her pleasant voice made sound less guttural than her husband's, and gestured toward the carcasses. She was obviously asking them what kind of meat they would like to eat. Niall felt his mouth watering at the sight of a large joint of ham, and pointed at this. But the spider again declined. The lady looked concerned, and asked a question that was obviously whether he was feeling well—she lacked the telepathic abilities of her husband, but her meaning was perfectly clear.

Niall looked inquiringly at the captain, and saw immediately why he had refused. The immense energy that filled this place was making him feel sick—merely tuning in to his vibration made Niall feel sick too.

It was easy to understand what was wrong. Again the problem lay in the immensely powerful will of the death spiders. In most species, evolutionary development takes place over such a long period that qualities like instinct, will, and intelligence develop in parallel. In the spiders, the brutal war against human beings had led to a completely disproportionate development of willpower. This meant that the spider's capacity to absorb and adjust to experience was limited in comparison to its capacity for dominance and self-discipline. The captain could be compared to a person with a small stomach, who finds that anything more than a limited quantity of food makes him feel sick. This, Niall realized, was why spiders were so prone to seasickness—they lacked the ability to adjust to the tossing of waves. And the waves of energy transmitted by the crystal were not unlike a stormy sea.

Niall tried to express this to the troll woman, but it was hard without telepathic contact. Looking up at this magnificent embodiment of womanliness towering five feet above him, with great rounded breasts that could hardly be contained in her blouse, Niall tried to tune in to her mind, while she, like someone leaning forward to hear better, tried to open herself to his thoughts.

The result was unexpected; it was exactly as if she had picked him up and kissed him—he was almost overwhelmed by the sheer power of her femininity. He had not experienced anything like it since the last time he had kissed Merlew.

As she understood what he was trying to convey, her face became serious. She looked down sympathetically at the spider, then reached out her hand and placed it on his head. The captain flinched, then became suddenly still. A moment later, as Niall again probed his mind, he found that the nausea had vanished; the woman had somehow soothed it away.

When once more she gestured to the captain to choose food, he indicated a joint of uncooked beef. She removed this from its metal hook, then with the beef joint in one hand and the ham in the other, smiling her gap-toothed smile, she led them back to the kitchen.

Her husband was standing at the table and contemplating the food with the interest of the famished. His wife placed the joints on the table and spoke in her own language; her husband translated for her.

"Do you prefer it hot or cold?"

"Hot, please," said Niall, wondering at the same time how she proposed to cook it in a kitchen that did not appear to have an oven.

The captain said he would prefer his meat cold. Niall had expected that—he had never seen a spider eat anything hot.

The troll asked Niall: "Where is the . . ." It sounded like "denkuta," but since it was accompanied by an image of the globe, Niall understood what he meant, and went to fetch it. He noticed, as he took it from the pack, that it was making his fingers tingle, obviously responding to the energy that filled the cave.

The woman took it in both hands with admiration, turned it carefully against the light, and placed it close to her ear. She said something in her own language, and her husband translated: "She says it looks like the work of Salgrimas, who was the most famous of our craftsmen."

The woman asked Niall—again it was easy to read her thoughts—"Where did you find it?"

He conveyed to her mind a picture of the cave where they had been trapped.

She said: "Ah, that is what the karvasid was looking for."

"The karvasid?"

The troll said: "It means the Master or the Great One. He has made many attempts to find it."

This casual mention of the Magician made Niall's scalp prickle. He asked: "Do you know anything about the master of Shadowland?"

The troll said: "Yes. But my father knows more."

Niall had to suppress a chuckle of delight.

He was puzzled to see that the woman was slicing open the ham joint, cutting round the bone to make a pocket, and forcing the globe into it. Her husband then placed both hands on the table, leaned over the joint, and stared at it as if looking for something. A moment later, there was a hissing noise, like a sizzling frying pan, and a column of steam rose from the cut in the joint. A few minutes later there was the unmistakable smell of roasting meat.

They returned to the other room. There the children had subsided enough to make conversation possible, although the youngest continued to run back and forth, making roaring and hissing noises.

Niall asked the troll: "What game is he playing?"

"He is being a dragon."

Niall was startled: "Has he seen a dragon?"

"No. But we tell him stories."

It struck Niall that, with the telepathic abilities of the trolls, their children would receive a more realistic and fearsome image of a dragon than any human child could receive from a story book.

The old man in the corner spoke for the first time.

"My grandfather saw a dragon."

His ability to communicate telepathically was as strong as his son's.

Niall asked: "Was that a long time ago?"

The troll nodded, and the glance of his eyes was so powerful that Niall felt like dropping his own gaze. But he sensed that this ancient troll was friendly.

"A long time. Trolls live more than twenty times as long as humans, so this was more than a hundred generations ago."

A quick mental calculation told Niall that he was speaking of about three thousand years.

"Did they breathe fire?"

"No, but their breath was so hot that it felt like fire." His thought conveyed far more than his words said. He meant that just as an adult produces more body heat than a child, so these great creatures produced enough heat in proportion to their vast bulk to make their breath as hot as a furnace.

While they had been speaking, the woman had laid the table. The smallest child was seated on a high chair, while the elder only needed a cushion to raise him to a comfortable level. Seating Niall was obviously going to be a problem, since the tabletop was as high as he was. This was solved with the aid of another high chair, even taller than the younger troll's, and Niall, feeling rather precarious, sat with his feet dangling more than a yard above the ground.

Niall wondered how he could convey tactfully that spiders prefer to eat alone, but the captain saved him the trouble by explaining that, since he was unaccustomed to chairs, he would prefer to eat in the kitchen. The troll handed him the joint of red beef, and the captain disappeared, closing the kitchen door behind him. Soon distant crunching noises indicated that he was enjoying his dinner.

The food was simple, consisting of the steaming ham joint, large enough to feed a dozen guests, a loaf of bread, a pale yellow vegetable that looked like cauliflower, and a dish of cheese. There were also cups of the sparkling water.

The troll sliced the joint, removing the globe, which he laid on the plate, and gave Niall a slab of ham more than half an inch thick. Niall was interested to note that this was fully cooked, although the crystal globe had been placed inside it less than a quarter of an hour ago. But he had become accustomed to wonders in this strange world. The ham was eaten with a green substance called apsa, which Niall assumed to be a kind of mustard, but which had an astringent flavor that he had never tasted before, and was full of a crunchy seed; Niall found it much superior to mustard. The green cauliflower, called titri, was also completely unlike cauliflower—indeed, unlike any vegetable he had ever tasted.

Niall concentrated his full attention on eating, both because he was hungry and because he had some difficulty handling his huge knife and fork. The knife was the size of a carving knife, and the fork had only two prongs, spaced wide apart. He almost lost a slice of ham when the woman noticed his predicament, and found him a much smaller knife and fork, obviously intended for children. The young trolls found this funny and roared with laughter. Niall felt pleased that he was making them laugh.

The sparkling water soon had him feeling drunk, and he was astonished to see the children draining their cups and asking for more. But instead of making them noisier, as Niall expected, it made them drowsy, and within ten minutes, both were yawning and rubbing their eyes. Their mother took the small one and let him sleep in her arms.

The food and drink filled Niall with euphoria, and made him feel that the trolls were the most delightful family he had ever met. The mother seemed to radiate love for them as the great crystal in the hearth radiated heat. And when she spoke to Niall to offer him more titri or apsa, he felt himself showered with a feminine warmth that reminded him of Merlew, Odina, his mother, and every other woman who had given him affection. The sight of her holding her child against her breast made him wish that he was in that fortunate position.

The male troll also aroused in him feelings of warmth and even affection. With his good-tempered red face and his gap-toothed smile, he exuded good nature and strength—the same unfathomable Earth-power that Niall had observed in the troll of the sacred mountain. He struck Niall as the ideal father, and Niall could now understand why the children were allowed to make as much racket as a whole playground full of children in the beetle city. The immense vitality of the parents was impervious to the pandemonium.

The grandfather troll emanated a different kind of strength. When he moved across the room from his chair, Niall had observed that he walked with a limp, and that the right side of his face was stiff, as if he had suffered a stroke. And his son had told Niall with a kind of pride: "My father was struck by lightning." It seemed an odd kind of information to impart, until Niall recalled that he had learned from the chameleon men that a troll who has been struck by lightning is regarded as a kind of god. This obviously accounted for his air of latent power.

Niall was anxious to raise the subject of the Magician, but felt that it might be presumptuous to question a person of such commanding presence. Moreover, the old man devoted himself to his food with a single-minded attention that discouraged conversation. But when the meal was over, and the children had become silent from overeating, he pushed back his chair and said in his troll language: "So you have met Hubrax?" The mental image showed that he was referring to the troll of the sacred mountain.

Niall said: "He led us to the sacred lake." His own accompanying mental image showed he was speaking of himself and the chameleon men.

The grandfather had produced a curved pipe, into which he tamped a rich brown substance. He lit it by inserting a short crystal rod, whose end glowed red as the old man furrowed his brow and stared at it. He blew out a cloud of smoke whose smell was far more fragrant than that of the tobacco smoked by the beetle servants. He said: "Hubrax liked you."

Niall asked: "Have you seen him?"

"Not recently, but we speak occasionally."

Niall did not like to ask him by what means they communicated over such a distance. But the old man read his mind.

"We use a resonating crystal."

The captain had meanwhile returned to the room, and stood quietly by the hearth, obviously enjoying the heat. To Niall's surprise, he accepted a glass of the sparkling water that was offered by his hostess; holding the cup in his chelicera, which was as flexible as a hand, he looked oddly human. Niall sensed that the spider wanted to behave like a human being, and that it gave him pleasure to feel that, rejected by his own kind, he was now accepted on equal terms by humans—for he regarded the trolls as yet another species of human being.

The old man included the captain in his conversation. He continued to speak in troll language, which he obviously found more comfortable, but accompanied with telepathic suggestion whose skill reminded Niall of Dravig.

"Shadowland is a dangerous place."

The spider said dryly: "So I have been told."

"And the karvasid has a particular hatred of spiders."

"Do you know why?"

"Yes, I know why." The old man settled himself comfortably with his pipe, and his daughter-in-law refilled his cup. The children, anticipating a story, leaned forward with their elbows on the table.

"After the exploding star fell from the sky"—he obviously meant the comet Opik—"the land was covered with snow and ice. But it also brought the great goddess. Before her coming, the trolls were a dying race"—his word for trolls was "patara"—"but she gave us new life. We became even bigger and stronger."

He turned to the captain. "As you know, your species also became bigger and stronger." They sensed the spider's puzzlement, and Niall realized that the captain knew nothing of the history of his own kind. "The spiders began to grow, although at first they were less than half the size of Gryllus there"—he gestured at the doglike creature now gnawing the hambone. "But humans, especially women, were afraid of the spiders, although their poison was not dangerous. And then a human warlord called Ivar the Brutal conquered this land. He hated spiders, and drove them to take refuge in the mountains.

"The warlord extended his conquests to the north. He had many wives, but his chief wife was a woman called Huni. And when he heard that a whole valley was full of spiders, she begged her husband to kill them all."

It was the first time that Niall had heard that a woman had instigated the war against the spiders, but now that he knew, he saw that it made sense. His Aunt Ingeld had hated spiders, and if she found one in the desert cave where they lived in North Khaybad, screamed until her husband killed it.

"So the spiders were driven out of their caves with fire and smoke, and thousands were massacred."

Niall knew this part of the story, for he had heard it direct from the mouth of the Mighty Cheb. Nevertheless, so compelling was the troll's narrative power that Niall remained fascinated by every word.

"Yet this was the beginning of the victory of the spiders. As their intelligence increased, so did their desperation and hatred. They began to dream of revenge. Because they had always understood that the world of matter can be influenced by the will, they began to develop the will as their only defense against human aggression. To begin with, they learned how to hunt their prey with their minds. When the spiders were starving in the mountain valleys, certain hunting spiders learned how to paralyze birds as they flew in the air. The greatest hunter was called Cheb, and he became their leader.

"One day, he and his brother saw some shepherds below in the valley. They crept down unseen, and from the shelter of a rock, they paralyzed two of the shepherds so they were unable to move or speak. They intended them no harm—they only wanted to know whether they could immobilize a human being. Cheb thought that humans were far stronger than they are, but on that day he discovered that they can be conquered by will-force.

"For many more years the spiders prepared their assault, determined to win a final victory and give the humans no chance to recover. They knew that if only a few men escaped, they would have to fight the whole battle over again. And at last, led by the grandson of Cheb the Hunter, who was also called Cheb, they surrounded the city of Korsh and locked their wills together like an unbreakable net. And every human being in the city was paralyzed, and Korsh became the capital of the Spider Lord Cheb."

The troll was addressing these words to the captain, sensing that all this was new to him. The spider was still standing, although he had moved from the hearth, which obviously was too hot for him. Like birds, spiders were capable of standing for hours, or even days.

Now the captain asked: "Do you understand why human beings are so warlike?"

The troll turned to Niall. "Perhaps you should answer that question."

It was a matter on which Niall had reflected a great deal, particularly since he had listened to Cheb's account of the war that had led to the enslavement of the human race.

"I think that humans produce far more energy than they can use. Before the great comet, it had made them lords of the Earth. But even then they were becoming aware of the problem it created. Most animals spend their lives trying to get enough to eat. Man solved that problem and became the lord of the Earth. Yet even before the coming of the great comet, he was bored and dissatisfied because he had too much energy, and felt suffocated by leisure and security." Niall was drawing heavily upon what he had learned in the white tower. "Then fate brought them their greatest challenge so far, and they had to seek new worlds. But those who were left behind soon became as violent and warlike as their ancestors of a thousand years earlier. Even though I am a human being, I cannot help feeling that they deserved to become the slaves of the spiders."

As he spoke, he became aware that the trolls were listening to him with astonishment and a certain awe. They had taken it for granted that he was little more than a boy, and now he was speaking with the authority of one who knew the history of the human race. The old man said: "Where did you learn all this?"

The captain saved him the trouble of answering by explaining: "He is the chosen of the goddess."

This caused a silence while they took it in. Then the trollwife said: "And why is the chosen of the goddess traveling without retainers?"

"I am trying to save the life of my brother."

The old man asked: "Is your brother then a prisoner?"

At that moment Niall wished that he possessed the ability of the Mighty Cheb to transmit an enormous amount of information in one short telepathic burst, for he foresaw endless explanations. He said: "No. He has been poisoned." He turned to the trollwife. "He may have only three weeks to live."

The younger troll said: "Then perhaps we can help. My father knows all there is to know about poisons."

Niall felt a sudden gleam of hope. The old man said: "Describe to me the symptoms."

Niall explained how his brother had been feeling the edge of an ax that belonged to the assassins of Skorbo, and how he had cut the ball of his thumb on the blade. As he described the aftermath—the increasing fever, the occasional bouts of delirium—the old man shook his head.

"That is not an ordinary poison. It sounds like uusli, from the roots of the trekuta tree, which contains tiny living organisms that the karvasid can control, even from Shadowland."

Niall said: "Is there no way of killing these organisms?"

"If the karvasid prepared the poison, almost certainly not. But there is a tree that can interfere with his mental vibrations—we call it the nirita tree."

Niall recognized the mental image. "The abolia? We have already placed him in a chamber with two of these trees."

"Then you have done all you can."

The woman asked: "Can you not ask the goddess for guidance?"

Niall shook his head. "She would tell me that this is a problem I must solve myself."

Her husband asked: "What are you hoping to do?"

"I want to speak to the karvasid face-to-face, and see if we can bargain for my brother's life."

"And that is why you are traveling to the northern mountains?"

"Yes."

There was a silence as the husband and wife looked at one another with doubtful expressions, then at the old man. He stared thoughtfully into the bowl of his pipe.

"It might work. But you might find yourself paying a higher price than you expect."

"In what way?"

"He hates the spiders more than anything in the world. If you placed yourself at his mercy, he would ask himself how he could use you against them."

Niall asked: "Why does he hate the spiders so much?"

"Because he was in the city of Korsh when it fell to the army of Cheb. The spiders were allowed to gorge themselves on human flesh, and his wife and children were eaten."

"What was his name?"

"In those days he was known as Sathanas. He was in charge of the guards who patrolled the city walls, and had a reputation as a strict disciplinarian. Soon after the fall of the city, he escaped to the Gray Mountains."

"Have you ever met him?"

"No, but I have seen him. On his journey north, Sathanas camped with a few of his soldiers less than a league from here, and I made myself invisible and watched him. I have never seen anyone so consumed with hatred. And I guessed even then that he had learned the secret of the spiders."

Niall looked at the captain, who was listening intently. It was for his benefit that he asked: "What is the secret of the spiders?"

"Why, the knowledge of the power of the mind. The spiders had seen their own people massacred, first by Ivar the Brutal, then by Skapta the Subtle, who burned the city of Cibilla, and after that by Vaken the Terrible, who drove the spiders to the cold lands of the north, where many froze and starved to death. That was when the spiders learned the power of hatred, and that in turn led them to the secret of the will."

Niall said: "I have never understood how men dared to go on fighting the spiders after the death of Ivar the Brutal. Even then, the spiders had developed the ability to paralyze men with willpower."

"That made men more determined than ever to destroy them. And they learned that if they could ambush the spiders before they were prepared, they had no time to unite their minds into a web of force. Vaken destroyed so many in ambush that he became known as the Spider Killer. He was lucky that he died peacefully before the spiders conquered the city of Korsh; otherwise he would have perished as horribly as Ivar the Brutal."

Niall said: "Why was Sathanas allowed to live when Cheb invaded Korsh?"

"He was not. The spiders were hunting for him when he went into hiding in the caves beneath the city. He and a dozen men escaped in boats that were stored there."

Niall remembered the ruined boats he had seen on the banks of the underground river, and suddenly guessed that they had been destroyed by Sathanas and his followers to prevent pursuit.

The old man said: "When I saw them, they were tired and dispirited—all except Sathanas, who held them together with the force of his will. I could see then that he would survive. But I could also see that he was driven by a hatred that might easily destroy him."

Niall asked: "Did the spiders pursue him?"

"I don't know, but I doubt it. They probably felt that he could do them no harm. That was a mistake, for Sathanas and his warriors discovered the entrance to Shadowland, and there he began to plan his revenge."

Niall asked: "Where is the entrance to Shadowland?"

He felt like holding his breath as he waited for the answer.

"It is seven leagues to the north, on the side of the mountain called Skollen."

His words were accompanied by a mental image of the mountain. Niall immediately recognized the phantasmagoric landscape, with some peaks like needles and others with the flat tops of volcanoes. It was the place where Skorbo had crashed.

Niall asked: "What kind of a place is Shadowland?"

"You have been in the land below the sacred mountain? Shadowland is like that, but far bigger. My people used to call it the Land of Green Twilight. It is more than thirty leagues from end to end."

"Have you been there?"

"Many times. Long before I was born it was the home of creatures called 'Troglas'"—the accompanying mental image was of a kind of black ape—"but many of them were killed by poisonous fumes when the mountain erupted. When I was a child, it was a ghostly wilderness haunted by the half-dead. Then Sathanas and his warriors found refuge there. And gradually their number increased."

Niall asked the obvious question.

"How did their number increase if they had no women?" But even as he asked, he had already guessed the answer.

"They raided the cliff dwellings and carried off everyone who lived there."

So Niall had guessed correctly. Skorbo's assassins were the descendants of the cliff dwellers.

"What happened then?" It was the elder of the two boys who asked the question. He had been listening with fascination ever since he woke up and heard Niall speaking of his brother.

His grandfather replied: "Only Sathanas knows that. But in those early days, I once overheard one of his guards say that he had discovered some old carvings on a tomb, and that it was from these that he began to learn the magic arts."

Niall suddenly remembered his visit to the library in the white tower, and how the old man had told him that anthropologists had concluded that certain primitive tribes were able to perform feats of magic, such as rainmaking. He asked: "Is it true that the karvasid can control the weather?"

"Certainly. But that is not difficult. Even I can control the weather."

Niall asked curiously: "How?"

"One method is through this." He reached out for the crystal globe, and handed it to Niall.

Niall had expected it to be greasy; to his surprise, it was as clear as if it had been newly polished. He asked: "Why is it so clean?"

"It cleans itself. That is the nature of the crystal. It even repels dust."

"And how can it be used to control the weather?"

The old man said: "That is difficult to explain, but easy to show you. Come."

He stood up and went through the doorway. His son and grandson followed him. The captain hesitated, wondering if he was invited, but the troll child smiled and beckoned him. Only the trollwife remained behind, placing the child on a mattress in a basket, and began clearing the table.

Niall had to lower himself to the floor by grasping the edge of the table, and hurried after them. The crystal globe, as if responding to his excitement, sent tiny electric impulses through his hand. With their longer strides, the others were already halfway up the stairs. Scrambling up these waist-high steps, Niall experienced a sudden memory of childhood, when he was dwarfed by furniture that towered above him, and grown-ups who looked like giants.

As he reentered it, the crystal cave produced on him an even stronger impact of power and beauty. His contact with the trolls obviously had attuned him to its vibrations. It was as if he was surrounded by a sound like a rushing wind blowing through a forest. He glanced up toward the ceiling, almost expecting to see trees bending in the wind.

The others were at the rear of the cave, where the icy translucence of the crystals gave way to upright columns that looked like green glass trees with long spearlike leaves. Facing these was an object like a throne or an armchair carved from ice. In front of this was a green column, about a foot taller than Niall, that terminated in a cuplike hollow. Inside this cup something shone and glowed like a living light. It reminded Niall of the recently repaired lighthouse that stood at the end of one of the harbor arms to guide incoming ships at night.

The troll child was sitting on the chair, staring at the light as if hypnotized. As Niall approached, he noticed something strange about the globe in his hand; it was throbbing as if in sympathy with the light, and tugging at his hand as if trying to escape like a balloon. Instinctively he held it tightly against him.

At that moment, a crash like thunder startled him so much that he almost dropped the globe. The air was filled with a sharp electrical smell.

The young troll laughed and clapped his hands, and Niall realized that he was somehow responsible for the thunder.

The grandfather lifted the child from the chair, and gestured for Niall to take his place, helping him by lifting him under the arms. To Niall, the chair seemed gigantic; its armrests were as high as his head. The globe in his hands was now tugging so hard that he had to hold it with both hands. The tingling sensation was uncomfortably strong, like trying to hold something that was too hot.

The grandfather reached inside the hollow, and took out another globe about the same size as the one Niall was holding so tightly. He placed this carefully on the floor, where its light slowly died away. Then he took the globe from Niall's hand, and placed it in the hollow at the top of the column. Instantly, it began to shine with a light that was far more powerful than the one it had replaced—so strong that Niall had to shield his eyes, and the captain took a step backward. Then Niall experienced a compulsion to remove his hands and look directly at the light. As he did so, he felt its power flowing through him, as if he had also been transformed into a globe of light.

It was a strange sensation, at once frightening and exhilarating. He felt like a thirsty man drinking from a cup, afraid that someone would snatch it away. The light renewed a sense of inner strength that he had once experienced in the white tower.

The old man indicated the green column.

"This is the pallen, and it connects the globe to its environment."

Niall could sense that some form of energy was rising up the pallen, and causing the globe to glow like a lightbulb.

The effect on Niall resembled in some ways what happened when he used the thought mirror. But the thought mirror only seemed to strengthen his will. This magic globe also seemed to deepen his feelings and to increase his knowledge and insight. The thought mirror strengthened his mind; this force also extended it, so that he could feel the presence of the mountains, and of the Valley of the Dead.

As the powers of the crystal drew him into its world, he also began to understand its purpose and its history. The man who had carved it was a priest, and it had taken him a year to select a block of quartz that weighed more than fifty pounds, and to free from its crystal prison this globe that weighed less than a pound, and whose energies had formed over more than a million years.

It was no wonder the Magician wanted it so badly. With the crystal globe in his possession, his powers would be awesome, and the energy at his disposal almost infinite. For this crystal extended its filaments all over the Earth, like a spider's web, and the energy that was now causing the globe to send out pulses of light was the energy of the Earth itself, the same explosive force that was discharged in thunder and lightning. It was stored, as if in a battery, in the blocks of crystal that now surrounded him. And when he entered the world of the crystal globe, the force became available to his own mind. Without stirring from his seat—which provided a ready-made connection between his mind and the globe—he could have caused the Valley of the Dead to shake with thunderstorms, and made its lake overflow into a destructive torrent.

These insights raised an obvious question. He withdrew his mind from the globe, causing its light to grow dimmer, and asked the troll: "Does the karvasid possess a globe like this?"

"Yes, but it is far less powerful."

"Where did it come from?"

"He made it himself, with the aid of a boca he had enslaved." The troll anticipated Niall's next question. "A boca is a nature spirit who lives in silver and copper mines, and who can take human form. They are the great craftsmen of the deva world."

The picture the old man transmitted was unappealing. The boca looked like a man whose skin has been flayed off, showing the muscles. It was very tall, and had a thin, cadaverous face and red-rimmed hollow eyes that looked menacing. To Niall's unspoken thought, the troll replied: "Yes, they can be very dangerous. But the karvasid enjoys showing his power."

"Where does your own globe come from?"

"My great-grandfather made it. It is not as powerful as yours because its crystal is less delicate." The mental image seemed to suggest that the crystal lattice was like fine lacework.

"May I try it?"

"Certainly." The old man removed Niall's globe and replaced the other. As the energy of the crystal chair saved Niall the trouble of establishing a connection, he saw instantly what the old man meant. This globe was not capable of concentrating the same quantity of Earth-force; its spider web was smaller.

Another question occurred to Niall.

"If the cave dwellers were carried into captivity, why did they not tell the karvasid where the globe was hidden?"

"No one knew but the priest, and he was killed."

Niall asked: "And did you never think of looking for it?"

The troll shook his head.

"I knew that if the karvasid could not find it, it must be very well hidden. Besides, if I had found it, I would have become the target of his greed."

"Just one more question: can you show us the best route to Shadowland?"

The troll said: "That will be unnecessary. You can learn all you want to from that." He pointed at the crystal globe. "So now I suggest we leave you alone, to learn how to use it."

He removed his globe from the top of the pallen, and replaced it with Niall's own. The light immediately became brighter, and Niall experienced a sense of inner contraction that was like the effect of the thought mirror.

A few moments later he had been left alone in the cave. He had a sense that the captain was glad to withdraw: its energies still made him uncomfortable.

Although Niall had been glad to be left to himself, he now found himself feeling oddly at a loose end, unsure of what to do next.

His first thought was to reestablish contact with his mother, to learn the latest news about Veig. He relaxed until he became aware of the threads of awareness that stretched around him, then repeated the mental trick he had learned in the tower of Sephardus, causing something to click in his brain, and envisaging his mother's room.

It worked so quickly that he was taken unaware. Suddenly, he was standing in his mother's room in the other wing of the palace. He was standing with his back to the door, and she was sitting in her chair, darning a child's garment.

Sensing his presence, she looked up, and he saw that she was about to scream in alarm. He quickly shook his head and raised his finger to his lips.

She started to say: "What are you doing here . . ." then the question trailed off, and Niall realized she was trembling, and her sewing had fallen on the floor. Because he was transparent, and she could see through his body, she thought he was a ghost.

He said quickly: "Don't worry, I'm all right."

She looked out of the window, where the night sky was full of stars. "It's the wrong time . . ."

"I have another way of coming to you. How is Veig?"

"He is the same—still very weak. But where are you now?"

Niall had a sudden desire to laugh. It seemed absurd to be in the same room with her, and for her to be asking where he was.

"In a cave in the Gray Mountains. But don't worry. I'll come again tomorrow."

Then Niall found the scene fading; a moment later he was back in the cave. What had happened, he realized, was that he was not putting enough concentration into the mental act, but was relying too much on the power of the globe. It taught him an interesting lesson: that without the mental effort, the powers of the globe were greatly reduced.

N iall had no idea of how to even begin learning about Shadowland. But as soon as he entered the world of the crystal, he was aware that he was at the center of a web, and that, like a spider, he had to learn to read its vibrations. Not far from this center, where he was now sitting, there was the outside world, and the rock-strewn valley from which he had entered the underground world of the trolls. This valley was in darkness; but after a few moments, it lifted like a fog, and he could see the landscape as clearly as if in daylight.

This was not quite the daylight of normal perception. There was a strange quality about it that made things seem gray and unreal. In fact, he had noted something of the sort when he had been speaking to his mother, but had attributed it to the poor lighting in the room. Now he saw that it had to do with the energies of the crystal, which could penetrate solid matter, so that dense objects became almost transparent. It was not unlike the "double vision" he had experienced after speaking with the goddess of the Delta.

Like a spider, his mind used the energy threads as it climbed upward. Soon he was above the valley, following its course northward. It was, as he had feared, virtually impassable. To walk seven leagues— twenty-one miles—over such difficult terrain would take two hard days.

As he gazed down on the valley that stretched north, he experienced a strong suspicion that these broken and piled rocks were not entirely the work of nature. True, they obviously had been swept down by a tremendous flood. In this case, why was there not even a stream in the valley? Moreover, there were many places where the cliffs had collapsed into the valley. What could have caused such landslides, when the cliffs were made of forms of granite?

The answer, he suspected, was that this road north was the main approach to Shadowland. Since it would be the obvious route for an army marching north, to make it impassable would be to block the main access to the Magician's underground kingdom.

What, then, were the alternative routes? With a mental effort, Niall projected himself still farther above the landscape.

He was familiar with its outline, since he had seen it so clearly through Asmak's imagination. Far ahead, where the mountains looked as if they had been carved into needles by wind and sleet, he recognized the plateau between two peaks where Skorbo had crashed. One of these peaks—probably the higher one on the right—was Skollen.

A river descended from the center of this plateau and ran south through a green valley, then flowed southwest to plunge in a spectacular waterfall over the cliffs of the Valley of the Dead and run westward to the sea. Obviously, then, the best approach to Skollen lay along the river valley. And this could be reached by returning the way they had come, then turning north somewhere above the cliff dwellings.

By this less direct route, the journey to Skollen was at least thirty miles—a long day's march. So far on this journey he had covered only half that distance in a single day. His thoughts turned to the possibility of less arduous ways of travel—the oolus birds, or even summoning a spider balloon—only to reject both. Either would be too obvious and risky; any watchman on the top of Skollen would be aware of their approach from far off.

But were there sentinels? He projected himself across the intervening landscape until he could see that what looked like a river running from the plateau was actually a ribbonlike waterfall. Then he was looking down on the bleak, inhospitable plateau, and on the razorlike rocks where, according to Asmak, Skorbo's balloon had come to grief. And again he found himself speculating how Skorbo had found himself so far north of the Great Wall. Even with gale-force winds, he should have been capable of flying in a slow arc that would have taken him south again—Niall himself had done something of the sort on his way back from the Delta, and so knew it could be done.

Hovering above the rocky summit of the eastern mountain, he could see that it was the crater of a dead volcano, with a lake a few hundred yards wide in its center. The mountain was far higher than it looked from afar. But as far as he could see, there was no sign of a lookout. He then projected himself a thousand feet above the summit, from which he could survey its steep, bramble-covered slopes, hoping to discover the cave where, according to the troll, Sathanas and his followers had taken shelter. From the east, it was possible to see why it was called "Skollen," for hollows in the rocks near its summit gave it the appearance of a skull.

But these hollows were not caves. He examined all the faces of the mountain without success, then went lower and looked more closely. Finally, he saw what looked like a cave, half-hidden by bushes, and by a broken thorn tree that leaned across it. Directly above it, extending all the way to the summit, was an unscalable mass of gray rock. The cave faced northeast, so would have been useless as a lookout for the southern approach.

He tried looking inside it, but could see nothing but a mass of dark shadows. He surveyed it for a long time, but saw no sign of movement.

Finally, he yawned, realizing that these mental efforts were more tiring than they seemed. It was probably close to midnight, and he wanted to leave early. So he pushed himself off the crystal seat, jumping the eighteen inches to the ground, and made his way back down the stairs.

The room in which he had eaten was in silence and in semidarkness; only the trollwife sat close to the light, and sewed some child's garment—Niall smiled at the thought that all mothers seemed to perform the same tasks.

She asked: "Are you ready to sleep?"

He said gratefully: "Yes, I am."

Carrying the light, she led him through the arch that led to the kitchen, and down a corridor with uneven granite walls. She paused to show him a toilet behind a door of coarse planks, then led him into his bedroom next door. This was basically a small cave that had been hacked out of the rock; only the floor was relatively smooth, the walls and ceiling showing the marks of tools. Carved wooden toys in a basket revealed that this was a child's bedroom; its only furniture was a wooden bed, and a chair whose seat was four feet off the ground. His own backpack lay on the chair. In one corner of the room, on a flat circular cushion, the captain was already asleep, his legs bunched underneath him.

The trollwife gave her cheerful, gap-toothed smile, and withdrew softly, leaving him in darkness. Niall guessed she was glad to get to bed. He was also relieved to clamber into the great wooden box of a child's bed, which was large enough for three persons of his size, and to make himself comfortable on a mattress that seemed to be full of dried beans or peas.

Before pulling the coarse blanket over him, he groped in the dark and removed his watch from the pack; the phosphorescent dial showed that it was a quarter past midnight. He wound it under his blanket, so as not to wake the captain, then placed it on the chair, where its loud tick was oddly comforting. A faint breeze on his cheek made him aware that, far from being airless, the room had some kind of ventilation, which he guessed to be associated with the distant thunder of water from below. He tried to work out what day it must be, but fell asleep before his mind could come to grips with the problem.

He was awakened by the noise of the children, and by thumps that suggested they were having a pillow fight. He looked at his watch and saw that it was half past six. He felt fresh and well rested, which he attributed to the energy of the crystals. The captain was also stirring, and Niall could tell, without having to ask him, that he was also feeling rested and refreshed.

Half an hour later he was seated at the table, eating a section of a massive hot sausage that steamed in a pewter dish; it contained grains of sweet corn and cereal as well as sausage meat that tasted like venison. They drank a creamy warm milk poured from a wooden jug, and Niall guessed that the animal that provided it had been milked within the last half hour. When the trollwife offered him more sausage, Niall had to shake his head and pat his stomach.

The captain ate in the kitchen; he had been given an uncooked sausage and a saucerlike plate of the milk.

The two male trolls applied themselves to their breakfast with serious determination of purpose, consuming most of the remainder of the sausage. The strange beast on the floor lay watching the children, who occasionally threw it tidbits.

Breakfast finally over, the grandfather turned to Niall: "Have you decided on your route?"

"I think so. The river valley seems the best approach." He tried to convey a mental picture of the valley.

"No. You could be seen for miles. But if you follow this road for half a league, you will find a steep path up to the cliff top. It has been made by cattle. Follow this trail to the top, and you will find a gully that has been made by water. At the end of the summer it will still be dry. If you follow this, you will be able to approach Skollen with less chance of being seen."

Niall asked: "Are there lookouts on Skollen?"

The old man and his son considered this. The younger man replied: "I do not know. It is many years since I visited Skollen."

"And even more since I was there," said the old man.

The trollwife suggested: "Why not send the children to guide them to the cattle trail?"

Her husband shook his head.

"No. The karvasid is vindictive. He cannot do us much harm, but it is well not to risk drawing his attention."

It made Niall suddenly aware of something that had not struck him before: that in giving him shelter like this, the trolls were exposing themselves to the vengefulness of the Magician.

Another question troubled him, and he addressed it to all three of them: "Do you think I should take the crystal globe with me?"

All shook their heads simultaneously, and the old man said: "If it fell into his hands it would make him invincible. That is why he spent so much effort trying to find it. If he knew you possessed it, he would not rest until he had taken it from you. That is why it would be best to leave it here."

Niall inclined his head. "If you think so." But the thought of losing this marvelous tool he had so recently acquired caused a pang of regret.

The trolls sensed this, and the husband remarked: "You are not leaving it behind. It belongs to you, and has now adjusted itself to your vibration."

The old man added: "Before you leave, I will show you how to maintain contact with it."

Niall said: "I am afraid I must go soon. We have a long journey ahead, and for the short legs of a human being it is even longer."

For some reason they found this funny, and all the trolls—including the children—laughed uproariously.

Niall said: "There is another question that I have been thinking about. You say that the karvasid hates spiders. Would the captain be risking his life in coming with me?"

The spider said immediately: "That is my choice. I shall go wherever you go."

The old man turned to the captain: "He is right. The karvasid is a madman. You are welcome to remain here with us."

The spider said: "I go with him. If I lose my life, I have lost it in the service of the goddess."

Niall made a movement that the spider would recognize as a formal act of thanks. "Then I shall be glad of your companionship." He turned to his hostess. "I thank you for your hospitality," then to his host: "And you for rescuing us from certain starvation." The troll smiled his good-natured smile, and shrugged.

"With the help of the goddess, you would have found some way of escape." His tone made it clear that he meant it.

The grandfather stood up. "First let me show you how to establish contact at a distance. It is very simple."

Moving with the slowness of a giant statue, he led the way upstairs. This time Niall had plenty of time to scramble up each step.

In the hall of crystal Niall was again lifted into the thronelike chair. He fixed his eyes on the globe, and felt its instant response. It was like switching on a light. Once again the pleasant trickle of vitality flowed through him, filling him with delight.

The older troll nodded approvingly. "You have learned to enter sympathetically into its vibration."

In fact, Niall found that it came so easily and naturally that it was like recognizing someone you had known for years. It was strange how a piece of inanimate crystal could be so oddly like a person.

The elder troll no longer bothered to transmit thoughts; it was as if his mind had gently taken control of Niall's will, and was guiding it. First, he urged Niall to enter the world of the globe. But at that point he instructed Niall to withdraw part of his mind, so that he was no longer wholly absorbed in the power of the crystal.

While remaining in semicontact with the globe, Niall was directed to establish contact with the mind of the younger of the troll children. This was easy, since Niall found the child sympathetic and likable.

The next stage was to unite the two contacts—with the child and the crystal globe. They immediately fused together, providing a third point of reference. Since it was easier to establish telepathic contact with a child than with the globe, Niall realized that he now had a simple way of tuning in to the wavelength of the crystal. Moreover, since the wavelength was the same for the whole family, Niall now had five potential ways of tuning in to the globe.

To demonstrate the method again, the troll now led Niall to repeat the performance, this time using the mind of the captain as his point of entry.

Niall was then sent downstairs into the room where the trollwife was removing the breakfast dishes. From there, he established contact with the mind of the child, then with the globe.

This exercise made him aware of something else. Lying in bed that morning, he had been thinking that life for the troll children must be very boring, restricted most of the time to an underground cave. Now he realized why this was untrue. The trolls were part of a network of communication with their own kind. In effect, the trollwife could pay a mental visit to the wife of the troll of the sacred mountain, just as two wives on the city of the beetles could call on one another for a midmorning gossip.

Moreover, the trolls had, just as casually, included the captain in this network of contact. For them, contact was natural, and the loneliness and exclusivity that humans accept as part of their condition was a kind of ignorance.

And now he understood why the trolls disliked and distrusted the Magician. He had carried being alone to the point of mania; with his hatred and paranoia, he represented a danger and source of disruption—not just for the trolls' world, but for the whole world of nature of which the trolls and the chameleon men were a part.

This, Niall now guessed, was why the trolls made no attempt to dissuade him from exposing himself to this danger. They hoped that his intervention might be the beginning of the downfall of the Magician.

Half an hour later, they were ready to leave. Niall had refilled his water bottle with sparkling water from the crystal cave, and the trollwife had presented him with a parcel of food wrapped in a cloth.

Her husband asked: "Do you have a rope?"

Niall shook his head. "Do we need one?"

"It is always best to be prepared." He turned and disappeared down the stairs.

Meanwhile, the old man explained what to do if they were again attacked by the combative sheep—that these animals had learned that their best chance of survival was to attack, reprogramming their natural impulse to flee. But if their aggressor failed to retreat, primeval instinct would reassert itself, and they would lose their nerve. Recalling his and the captain's ignominious flight of two days ago, Niall was grateful for this advice.

The troll returned with a bag made of sackcloth.

"Take this, and do not be afraid to entrust your weight to it."

Niall opened the top of bag and saw why the troll had felt the need to reassure him. The coiled rope was silky to the touch, and very thin—the whole package hardly weighed a pound.

Reading Niall's thoughts, the troll said: "It is made of the web of the hairy tree spider. Nothing can damage it except fire."

As a final gift, the old man presented Niall with a walking stick.

"This will shorten your journey." He twisted the top where it was encircled by a metal band, and the stick came apart. He shook it, and a fragment of rose-colored crystal fell into the palm of his hand. "This is mimas crystal, which is attuned to your nervous system. It works best with an empty stomach. So when you feel hungry, do not eat, but take a few drops of this zacynthus essence in a cup of water." He handed Niall a metal flask in a net of woven string; it was small enough to fit comfortably into the pocket of his tunic with hardly a bulge. "Then you will feel its virtue. But do not take it on a full stomach—it will make you sick."

Niall thanked him, and examined the stick and the flask. The stick had been made so skillfully that no line was visible where the top and bottom joined. As to the flask, it seemed far too delicate to have been manufactured by the huge hands of a troll.

Niall swung his haversack onto his back, and again thanked his hostess. In the few hours he had known her, he had come to regard her with lively admiration; she possessed a warmth and vitality that reminded him of Merlew, but without Merlew's irritating egoism; he reflected that if he could find such a woman built on a human scale, his objection to matrimony would vanish. He was delighted when, as he held out his hand to her—well above his head—she picked him up like a child and kissed his face, pressing him against her full breasts.

She and the children stood in the doorway of the cave, waving good-bye, while the grandfather accompanied them as far as the flight of steps out of the other side, raising his hand in a gesture Niall had come to recognize as a troll blessing, after which their host led them through the tunnels to the open air. Niall was pleased to see that this time the captain passed through the quartz barrier without the slightest hesitation.

Outside it was a disagreeable day. The north wind was chilly, and was blowing before it clouds of mist and a fine drizzle. Niall turned to wave good-bye to the troll, and thought for a moment that he had already gone back inside. Then a shimmering of the rocks told him that he had made himself transparent, and on this dull, rainy morning was virtually invisible.

Niall wrapped his cloak around him, pulling up the hood, glad that it was waterproof; he reflected that the spider, with his armor plating, was rather better protected than he was.

The road up the valley was just as rough as he had expected, with small, irregular rocks that twisted under his foot, and boulders that had to be skirted or clambered over. Within half a mile, both his knees were bleeding, and the palm of his hand had been scraped when he tripped and fell headlong. Even the spider, with his longer stride, found the going difficult.

The morning was silent, except for the distant bleating of sheep; the misty drizzle seemed to muffle all sounds. Ahead, the mountains were invisible through the gray swirling vapor. If, as Niall suspected, the Magician was using birds as spies, their approach should be unobserved.

At least the stick prevented Niall from tripping as often as he might have done.

The point where they left this exhausting road was about two miles from their starting point, and it took them more than an hour to reach it. The track that ran obliquely up the high bank was muddy and slippery, and covered in hoof marks; Niall had to walk bent almost double to prevent himself from slipping backwards. But finally, after a quarter of a mile, he was able to straighten up on level ground and draw a deep breath. For a moment, the mists parted enough to catch a glimpse of Skollen, which towered up like a fortress. Niall would have been glad to sit down and rest his aching legs, but there was nothing to sit on but the wet, windswept grass, so he plodded on.

By now he was tempted to push back the hood to lower his temperature, or even to open the front of the cloak; but he knew that if he did this, he would be soaked within minutes. He envied the spider, whose short hairs were so covered in water droplets that he was a silvery color.

But when Niall's mind reverted to where he had been on the previous day, and he recollected that if it had not been for the chance discovery of the crystal globe, he and the captain would still be trapped in the cave, his tiredness vanished, and he trudged forward with a new will, noting once more how the idea of misfortune could serve as a stimulant.

An hour later, the rain stopped, and the sun began to break through the mist. Water had run down Niall's neck and soaked the front of his tunic, and he was glad to open the cloak and give himself an opportunity to dry out, although the wind was cold through his wet garment. The route they had been following ran parallel to the rock-strewn valley; they were on a cattle track that led toward the eastern flank of Skollen. They could now see that the troll had advised them well, for the track dipped up and down, often shielded by bushes, and they were far less exposed than if they had followed Niall's chosen route along the river in the center of the plain.

As the Sun became warmer, he sat on a low bank and folded the cloak, stowing it in his backpack. A drink of the sparkling water produced a shock of pleasure that made him realize how far the wind and rain had depressed his energies.

The captain, relaxing in the sunshine, said: "Here is your friend." A bird flew low overhead and landed a dozen yards away. The captain was right; it was the raven. Niall was glad to see it; by now, he thought of it as an old friend, and was afraid he had seen the last of it. He took a biscuit from his pack, and tossed half of it to the bird. He was hungry, but decided to follow the troll's advice, and to take a few drops of the zacynthus essence when his stomach was empty; nevertheless, out of curiosity, he looked inside the cloth-wrapped parcel that the trollwife had given him. It proved to contain slices of bread, a segment from a globular red cheese, some huge radishes, and the end of a joint of uncooked beef, obviously intended for the captain. The spider held this by the end of the bone and ate it standing by the side of the path; the fact that he did so in Niall's company indicated how far he had come to accept the presence of a human being.

A quarter of an hour later, now feeling less tired, Niall transferred himself into the mind of the bird, and directed it to fly up into the air. Delighted to be sharing Niall's consciousness, it soared up for a quarter of a mile, so he could see the central plain to their left, with its swift-flowing river, and the strange, twisted mountains that lay ahead, their peaks covered in snow. The wind up here was icy cold. Skollen was one of the less impressive of the peaks, being about a thousand feet high, with a shape like an eroded volcano.

While the bird was still aloft, Niall took the opportunity to find out whether there was some place near Skollen where they might camp for the night. But the terrain was uninviting, empty, and featureless; a mile or so ahead, it rose toward the mountains. It looked as if they had no alternative than to press on to Skollen, now probably about twenty miles—or four hours' brisk walking—distant. Since it was still at least two hours to midday, they would probably be at the foot of Skollen by midafternoon.

Half an hour later, he was less sure. The land was rising steeply, and the grass had given way to bare rock that was twisted, and hard on the feet; Niall guessed it to be weather-eroded lava—even the sure-footed captain stumbled more than once. There was also a faint smell in the air that he did not recognize, but which reminded him of the burning coke the night watchmen used in the brazier that warmed their hut on the harbor.

When his foot went into a crack and he left his sandal behind, he sat down to pull it loose. The projection of rock he was sitting on had a sharp edge, cutting into his buttocks, and he shifted his weight to make it less uncomfortable, at the same time staring down into a pool of rain that had formed in the crevice. Oddly enough, bubbles of gas were rising through the water, with a sulfurous smell. At that moment, his mind vaulted into the past, and he was suddenly remembering the dream he had experienced in the cave of the chameleon men. He was peering down into a crack in the ground—very much like this one—and feeling the same discomfort from the sharp edge of rock he was sitting on, and a sweet smell, like burnt caramel, was issuing from the crevice.

It lasted only a moment, but caused a curious flash of happiness.

He was now hungry; and since his stomach felt empty, he decided it was time to try the liquid the troll had given him. Unscrewing the cap, which was the size of a small cup, he poured into it a few drops of the zacynthus essence, which smelled oddly medicated, then filled it up with water. The flavor was surprisingly bitter, but he grimaced and swallowed it down. His stomach lurched and convulsed, and for a moment he wondered if he was going to be sick. Then the nausea passed, and was succeeded by a sense of relief.

A moment later, as he stood up, he was surprised to find that his fatigue had vanished completely. He bent to pick up the stick, and was even more surprised when, as he touched it, a tingling surge of energy passed through him. This energy was not flowing from the stick, but seemed to come from the ground itself; the stick seemed to act as a contact. He had experienced the same flow of force in the crystal cave, but this was far stronger. It reminded him of an electrical device that was popular among the children of the beetle city, which consisted of two metal cylinders attached to a hand-cranked generator. When the handle was turned, anyone who held the cylinders received a mild electric shock that was like a buzzing vibration in the hands. This Earth-force that now flowed through him, although clearly of a different nature, produced a similar sensation.

He was suddenly filled with an extraordinary zest. Five minutes before, his view of this plane of twisted rock had been jaundiced; now it struck him as extraordinarily interesting—like this whole strange and eventful journey. The cold wind that blew from the mountains, far from seeming disagreeable, now felt as pleasant as a spring breeze.

The captain, sensing this change of mood, looked at him with curiosity. Niall said: "I don't understand why, but this stick fills me with energy. Try it."

The spider took it in its claw, and promptly dropped it. "I find it unpleasant."

Niall realized that the crystal inside the stick was attuned to his own human vibration, and that he might feel just as uncomfortable if he had suddenly found himself turning into a spider.

As they continued on their way, the feeling of being able to draw upon enormous energies filled him with exhilaration. But what struck him most clearly was that this energy was all around him, like the air he breathed; he was absorbing it just as he was breathing the air.

The odd thing was that his hunger had vanished; this energy seemed to be serving as a kind of food.

He felt as fresh as if he were just setting out in the morning, and walked with such a long stride that it became unnecessary for the captain to slow his pace. A sense of rising energy made him feel that he could easily have broken into a jog.

The energy also caused his brain to seethe with ideas. Now that Skollen was visibly closer, he found himself speculating on why the Magician was so consumed with hatred. Of course, a man whose family had been killed by the spiders could be forgiven for hating them. But that was a long time ago, and he had achieved a satisfying revenge in causing the disaster of the Valley of the Dead. Why was the hatred unappeased? What was his purpose? If Niall could understand his aim and his motivations, then he could also understand his weaknesses.

One thing puzzled him deeply. How could the Magician maintain such hatred? Niall recognized instinctively that it was a poison that was as bad for the hater as for the hated. So how had he managed to escape its consequences?

Again, Niall had always pictured the Magician as a man who stood alone, an absolute ruler, with no friends or intimates. But no living creature is designed to stand totally alone. Niall had once believed that the Spider Lord was such a being, until he discovered that all spiders are a part of a communal web, and that even great rulers like Cheb are never truly alone. So how could the Magician endure the loneliness that is the destiny of tyrants?

But what if Niall was as mistaken about the Magician as he had been mistaken about the Spider Lord? In that case, why should there not be peace between the spiders and the inhabitants of Shadowland?

As if to terminate these speculations, a deafening clap of thunder was followed by an instant downpour of freezing rain. For a few minutes it fell so heavily that it was impossible to walk on. Niall crouched down on the ground, but before he could unfold his cloak, he was soaked to the skin. There was no shelter, not even a rock to break the wind.

The captain contracted himself into a ball with his legs bunched underneath him. Niall sat on his backpack to avoid the sharp rocks, and placed his cloak over his head like a tent. And although it was water-proof, the rain, which blew against him with a sound like hail, had soon penetrated it. Within minutes he found that he was crouching in a stream of water that ran down the rocks like a small river. Niall found himself entertaining the notion that the Magician was opposing their attempts to reach his kingdom.

The rain finally stopped, but the wind continued to blow. And since there was no point in staying there, they continued to walk on, up a thirty-degree slope that had turned into a series of parallel streams that seemed determined to wash them downhill.

Half an hour later they reached the top of the escarpment, and the sun came out. The wind was still as cold, so that Niall felt numb from his head down to his feet. But at least they could now see where they were and where they were going. To the west, perhaps five or six miles away, they could see the point where the river plunged down from the plateau, creating a kind of broken waterfall. It was probably as well that the troll had advised them to take the easterly route, for there was no obvious path up the slope. This way, at least, they only had to contend with a steady uphill slope toward Skollen, and with a wind that seemed determined to prevent them from moving forward.

On either side of the river hundreds of sheep were grazing. If these were as aggressive as the ones they had already encountered, Niall was glad they had avoided them.

A few hundred yards to the east, on top of the ridge, there was a rocky outcrop that had been carved to a point by the weather. They hurried toward it, and huddled under its shelter. Being out of the wind actually made them feel warm. Niall sat with his back against the stone, and in spite of his wet clothes, almost fell asleep. That, he knew, would be disastrous—he would wake up too numb to move.

The relative comfort also made him aware that he was hungry, but he had no intention of eating. Instead, he unscrewed the top of the zacynthis flask, poured a few drops into it, then filled it up with water and drank it down. This time the feeling of nausea was less severe—he suspected that his empty stomach was glad of any kind of nourishment—and a few moments later he felt a return of the tingling energy. As circulation was restored, and his cold flesh began to warm up, the sensation was almost painful.

Niall could sense that the captain, in spite of the legendary endurance of spiders, was also beginning to feel depleted. He refused Niall's offer to taste the zacynthus essence, but accepted some of the goat cheese and buttered bread, and devoured them hungrily—the first time Niall had ever seen a spider eat anything but meat.

A glance at his watch showed Niall that it was half past one—about five hours to dusk. Reluctantly, they moved on, first of all along the edge, to a point where it was easier to descend into a shallow valley, then back onto the slowly rising escarpment. Full of energy once more, Niall strode into the wind, determined to reach Skollen before nightfall.

An hour later, the wind had dropped, and his clothes were dry. The summit of Skollen loomed directly above them. But Niall was aware that the cave they were seeking was on the northeastern face, and therefore stayed on the lower slopes. Fortunately, these slopes were in places almost flat, resembling the brim of a hat, and by the time the sun was within half an hour of vanishing behind the mountain, they were at the foot of the northeastern face.

Here, below a dense thicket of brambles, they paused to regain their breath. The past few hours had been the most strenuous Niall had ever experienced in his life, and he was aware that he would not have reached Skollen without the troll's stick and flask of zacynthus essence. Even the captain was visibly tired.

They had been there only a few moments when they were rejoined by the raven. Niall had not seen it since the onset of the storm, and had assumed that it had either been battered to the ground or forced to take shelter, but from its liveliness as it pecked at bread crumbs, it obviously had found some other way of surviving the wind and rain. Niall transferred his consciousness behind its eyes, and induced it to fly upward. A mile up the slope, Niall saw the cave, and the brambles that made it virtually unapproachable from below; he also saw how these could be bypassed by taking a diagonal path up the mountain, then scrambling up a rocky slope where brambles had not succeeded in gaining a foothold.

Since the light was already turning gray, they set out immediately. Without previous reconnaissance it would have been impossible to find their way—and as it was, there were several points at which they became lost and had to retrace their steps. As they struggled slowly upward during the next two hours, Niall's leg muscles burned as if they were on fire, and he felt that he never wanted to see another mountain for the rest of his life.

Dusk was falling as they reached the level at which the spiky bushes had been unable to advance any farther up the slope. From there they followed the line of bushes to the left until Niall saw the broken thorn tree that half covered the entrance to the cave.

If there were guards in the cave, they certainly would have been warned of Niall's approach by the sound of rocks dislodged by his feet— one enormous boulder had crashed all the way down the mountain. But some instinct told Niall they were not being observed. When they finally halted a few feet below the cave entrance, Niall took the flashlight from his pack, turned its beam up to maximum, and shone it through the narrow entrance. There was a wild flutter of wings, and a flock of cave pigeons rushed out past them, startling them both.

The light beam revealed walls that were ribbed with ledges containing nests, and a floor that was white with bird droppings. Niall turned the thought mirror on his chest, to be prepared for any sudden attack, then clambered over the tree trunk, the captain close behind him.

At first glance, the cave seemed to be about thirty feet deep, the roof sloping down at the back to join the floor. The place was obviously empty. Niall suppressed his disappointment. If this was not the entrance to Shadowland, then they would have to conduct another search in the morning. At least they had found a shelter for the night. But as he made his way farther, another bird flapped past him, and he realized that what looked like the end of the cave was actually a left turn that plunged downwards. Behind him, he heard a squawk from the bird as the captain pinned it down with his will. A faint snapping sound indicated that the spider had secured his supper.

Niall shone his flashlight down the tunnel. It was low—not more than five feet high—and descended at an angle of about forty-five degrees. Niall guessed it to be an outlet from the volcano, whose crater must be a quarter of a mile above them. It looked dangerously steep, so he turned and went back into the cave, where the captain was engaged in removing the feathers from a fat pigeon.

It was clear to Niall that this cave had never been used as a human habitation. If it had, there would be signs of a fire, and smoke on the walls.

Outside, the sky was dark, and the first stars were appearing. The pigeons began returning one by one. It was colder here; Niall could smell winter in the air.

He was so tired that he could have fallen asleep on the bare floor. But he decided to follow the captain's example, and eat before he slept. He unfolded the sleeping bag and laid it out on the floor as a tablecloth, then opened the parcel of food that the trollwife had given him.

The bread was still fresh, and the butter was creamier than that of the spider city. The portion of red cheese made a pleasant change from the goat cheese he had eaten so far, and the huge radishes were crunchy and slightly peppery. He washed all this down with a mouthful of mead, which made his stomach glow. Then, soothed by the sounds of pigeons, he crawled into the sleeping bag, and slipped into the deep sleep of exhaustion.

PART TWO

He woke up in the night, and lay there in the pitch blackness, which was so silent that he could even hear the captain's breathing. No stars were visible through the cave entrance; evidently the clouds had returned. The pigeons were sleeping silently, unaware that a few yards away slept a predator who would probably eat one of them for breakfast.

The floor was uncomfortable—Niall had not bothered to inflate the sleeping bag—and as he turned over onto his other side, he began to think of the problems that faced them on the morrow. The first was the sloping tunnel. Among the variety of information implanted by the sleep-learning machine was a diagram of a volcano, showing vents branching out of the central shaft; forty-five degrees seemed to be the typical angle at which they joined the pipe. If this one became any steeper, he would certainly find it impossible to keep his footing, and would arrive in Shadowland like a bomb.

His thoughts reverted to the Magician. Was he really an adept of the magical arts? According to the Steegmaster, magic was a superstition of the unsophisticated. But then Torwald Steeg certainly would have regarded elementals and trolls as superstitions, and the magical control of the weather as an outrageous absurdity. On the whole it might be best to keep an open mind.

But what of Qisib's statement that when the Magician spoke to Madig, no breath issued from his mouth? Surely that was an impossibility? How could a man utter words without breath? Niall began to experience a sense of being lost in a sea of frightening improbabilities.

Eventually, tiredness overcame him, and he fell asleep again.

He was awakened by the sound of the pigeons, and saw that the sky outside was gray. Soon after that the birds took flight, except for one who remained on the ledge, obviously unable to move under the captain's gaze. To avoid having to watch it being devoured like a large fly, Niall crawled out of the cave and into the cold, clean wind that blew from the north.

The night before, he had noticed a pool of water in a depression on the rock ledge. This was now covered with a thin film of ice. He drank some of it, crunching the ice, then washed his hands and face in the freezing liquid. After he had dried them on his tunic, he sat on the ledge and watched the sun rise, gilding the face of Skollen until it ceased to look bare and bleak, and became beautiful. Then the light touched the slopes of the northern mountains, and turned their twisted spires into a fairy-tale landscape. Suddenly Niall understood why they were called the Gray Mountains; even in the morning sunlight, they were a misty gray that verged on blue.

When the captain—now looking replete—emerged to enjoy the sunlight, Niall decided to escape the wind, which was raising goose pimples on his arms, and went back inside. There he ate some bread and cheese, wrapped the rest of the food securely in its cloth, and tied the mouth of the haversack, having first taken out the flashlight and secured it to his wrist. Even though he now knew how to share the captain's ability to see in the dark, he might still need a brighter light.

A few minutes later they set out. The captain went first, his climbing skills making him the obvious leader. Twenty yards into the tunnel, the wisdom of this arrangement became clear when Niall, in spite of using the stick, lost his footing on a smooth patch and slid for a dozen feet before the captain, perceiving the problem with his rearward eyes, halted the movement with his hind legs.

Fortunately, the lava under their feet was full of cracks that had formed as it cooled, and once Niall decided that it would be safer to remove his sandals and progress backwards on all fours, he felt more secure. The stick he fixed across the top of the pack by using the ends of the drawstring.

He was prepared to crawl for a long time, although it was painful to his knees. So it was a pleasant relief when, after less than half an hour, the captain halted and said: "Now we have to go down." They had arrived at the main chimney in the heart of the mountain.

It was an awesome sight, being about a hundred yards wide. But the flashlight beam showed that its sides were even rougher and more covered in projections than the vent they had just descended. Although Nial disliked heights, he could see at once that any good climber could have made his way down it without a rope.

One thing puzzled him. Was it conceivable that the fugitives from the spider city had come this way? If so, did they know what they were seeking? For surely no one in his right mind would descend a volcano chimney merely to see what was at the bottom.

He was peering into the chimney as he lay on his stomach, holding on to an extrusion like a dog's ear on the edge of the drop. Now he sat up, reversed his position so his feet were braced against it, and took the rope out of his pack. Not anticipating that he would need it, he had not even bothered to remove it from its container of sacking. Now he untied the rope that held it in a loop, and began to measure its length by paying it out, using the length of his arm as a measure. It took him a quarter of an hour, and he was amazed to learn that he had more than four hundred yards of the light, soft rope.

The problem, he could see, would be how to recover the rope once he had tied it round a projection. But when he explained this to the captain—in the form of an image—the spider instantly saw the answer: to loop the rope around the dog's ear and then use it doubled. This, of course, would halve its length, but since there were so many projections, this hardly seemed to matter.

Niall expected the captain to lower himself by extruding web from his spinneret—a process Niall had witnessed many times in the spider city. But the captain preferred to crawl over the edge and then move down headfirst, walking as comfortably as on a horizontal surface. The answer, Niall realized, was that the captain was concerned in case he did not have enough silk to reach the bottom.

Niall, after stowing the flashlight in the long pocket of his tunic and heaving at the dog's ear to make sure it was solid, lowered himself over the edge. He refused to let himself think of what was below, and took care not to let his eyes stray downward, as he moved down hand over hand, gripping the two strands of rope between the sole of one foot and the instep of the other. The spider silk stretched under his weight, but showed no sign of snapping. Since it retained a vestige of stickiness, the two strands stuck together, relieving Niall of his anxiety about what would happen if, in an absentminded fit, he released one of them.

Niall's main problem was the roughness of the chimney. Projections and excrescences forced him to push away from the surface again and again. And within fifty feet he found his descent blocked by a jutting lump of lava so large that he had to swing himself sideways to get off it. Only then did he see a sharp edge, over which the rope was now stretched, and try to climb back. But the struggle made him so breathless that he decided to risk it, hoping that the captain would save him if the rope was severed.

With twenty feet of rope still left, he found another large projection, shaped like a wart, and was able to sit comfortably, his legs on either side of it, while he tugged at one side of the rope to free it. The stickiness was less of a problem than he expected, and it fell down and on past him, so he had to heave it back up again. Then he once more looped it over the wart, stood up, pressing the two sides together, then lowered himself carefully over the edge.

During the next two hours he repeated this procedure seven times, calculating that he must have descended about a quarter of a mile. But he was becoming increasingly tired, and once even found himself yawning. However, when he was halfway through the seventh lap, and was just beginning to wonder what would happen to his endurance if the chimney was another half-mile long, a telepathic message from the spider announcing that he had reached the bottom renewed Niall's concentration. And when he was paying out the rope for the ninth time, the spider told him he was close to the bottom, and Niall felt immense relief.

In the last few yards of the descent he suddenly found his feet swinging inward, without a wall to stabilize them, and realized that he must be lowering himself past some kind of cave or tunnel. And since he was now so close to the bottom, he decided to risk clinging with one hand while he groped in his pocket for the flashlight. Making sure it was looped around his wrist, he shone it into the hollow. As he suspected, he was looking into another volcanic vent, which rose at a steep angle. It looked as if their descent down the chimney had been unnecessary— there was probably another entrance lower down. Niall realized that he should have asked the trolls for more precise directions.

Five feet farther down, his feet touched solid ground. He had been promising himself that when he finally arrived at the bottom he would fling himself down and rest until his limbs had ceased to ache. But this was impossible since the bottom of the pipe was blocked by an immense plug of lava with an irregular concave surface, and he was, in effect, standing on top of a hill that was fifty feet high and whose sides, beyond the first ten feet, were almost vertical. There was a gap of a few feet between three sides of the plug and the wall of the chimney.

Since there was no sign of the spider to advise him which side to descend, Niall sent out a telepathic signal that was the equivalent of a shout. This brought the captain catapulting out of a tunnel. It apparently had not struck him that Niall might have any difficulty climbing the last fifty feet.

By this time, Niall had examined the surface of the plug for any projection round which he could loop the rope, but had found none. The only solid-looking projection was thirty feet above him, on the wall of the chimney.

The captain solved the problem by climbing the side of the plug with absurd ease, taking the rope in his pedipalp, and climbing the wall to the projection. Niall was then able to lower himself the final distance to the ground. When he was down safely, the spider unlooped the rope and walked down the wall as easily as a fly.

Niall asked: "Where now?"

The captain led the way into a low tunnel, and Niall's fatigue disappeared when he saw crude steps carved in its surface, the first sign they had seen so far that other men had preceded them.

Twenty feet farther on there was something that excited him even more. Where the tunnel turned a corner, he could see light reflected off the rock. Moments later they were standing at the top of a long slope, in a pale light that tinged everything blue. Niall was startled by a flash like lightning, accompanied by a crackling sound; for a second, everything became brighter. He was puzzled when the lightning flash was not followed by the usual burst of thunder.

The sky was full of a blue-green vapor that rolled and billowed like mist, and which made visibility poor—it was like standing on a hillside covered in fog. Above the tunnel from which they had emerged, the slope continued upward until it was lost in mist. Niall noticed that the rocks higher up the slope, where it vanished into the cloud, were covered in blue moss.

The temperature was warm, the equivalent of a spring day. There was a strange, sharp smell in the air, which reminded Niall both of the smell of the sea and of burning sulfur. When, a moment later, another flash occurred, the smell increased, and he realized it had something to do with these electrical discharges.

He sat down on the ground, his back against a moss-covered rock, and allowed himself to relax for a few minutes, until his legs ceased to ache. The moss was thick and spongy, and when Niall tore off a handful, he was able to squeeze a cloudy liquid out of it.

He replaced the flashlight in his backpack, drank a mouthful of water, and followed the captain down the rocky slope. Visibility was about the equivalent of a bright moonlit night on Earth. The steady blue-green light cast no shadows, and Niall found himself wondering why this place had become known as Shadowland.

Ten minutes later they were below the ceiling of cloud, and he caught his first clear glimpse of the landscape. Half a mile below him there was a bleak plain that stretched into the distance, and that looked like the kind of rocky terrain that extended for miles around Skollen. Somewhere in the middle distance there was a flat expanse of blackness that might have been a lake, although in this light it was hard to tell.

Visibility here was roughly equivalent to a rainy day on Earth, although the cloudy sky was blue rather than gray. It was strangely even, like some artificial light, and the only sounds were the periodic crackling of the lightning and distant cries that sounded like birds. But if birds could live in this bare landscape, what did they eat?

Niall found that it was necessary to walk carefully to avoid twisting his ankle on the uneven surface. He tried to imagine how all this must have seemed to Sathanas and his companions when they first came here, looking for some place of refuge from the spiders. Basically, Shadowland seemed to be a giant chamber or cave, like the land below the sacred mountain, formed by volcanic activity. It should have been as black as night, but some unknown electrical activity kept the air glowing like an aurora.

Curious to know whether this was some form of magnetism, Niall sat down on a rock and removed the expanding metal rod from his haversack. He had been intending to use it as a dowsing rod, but now observed that it was tingling as if with a mild electric current. He pressed the button to open it, and instantly regretted it as there was a blue flash that gave him a powerful shock and made him drop the rod with a clatter. He hastily pressed the button to make it retract. In its expanded state, it obviously acted as an aerial to the electric force.

Instead, he looked at his watch, then at the compass. The watch showed that it was half past eleven in the morning. The compass needle swung around wildly and refused to settle.

And what, he wondered, would the Magician and his companions have done when they found themselves in this place of unvarying blue light? They must have decided to go on, hoping that this bleak land could afford them some kind of refuge, and presumably some form of nourishment. And since they had settled here, they must have found both. This meant that not all Shadowland was as a bare and inhospitable as the landscape he could see.

The thought spurred his curiosity, and he marched on downward, reaching the foot of the slope half an hour later.

There, for the first time, he observed a vapor rising out of a crack in the ground; he placed his hand in it, and it felt warm and steamy. A quarter of a mile further on, he saw a pool that bubbled, with steam rising from its surface. He dipped his hand in it and found that it was warm. And since his feet were aching, and both were sore from the chafing of the rope as he climbed down, he asked the captain to wait while he sat down and dipped his feet into it. It made him sigh with pleasure, then yawn. If there had been something to lean on, he would have fallen asleep. He was tempted to remove his tunic and take a bath—the captain, as usual, was waiting with apparently inexhaustible patience—but he decided that it would be more sensible to move on.

As he swung the pack onto his back, the stick came loose and clattered on the ground. He picked it up by the metal band, and he felt a tingle that reminded him it had been many hours since breakfast and that his stomach was rumbling with hunger. He unscrewed the cup and half filled it with water, added a few drops of the zacynthus essence, and gulped it down.

The nausea was so powerful that it caused his sight to blur. This lasted about half a minute, causing him to concentrate on not being sick. But when the nausea subsided, he realized immediately that the effect of the zacynthus was far stronger then on the previous day. It filled him with such zest and vitality that he felt like turning somersaults. And when he shook the crystal out of the stick and held it in the palm of his hand, it flickered as if it contained a blue fire.

There was a sizzling hiss that made him jump, and lightning struck the ground a dozen feet away, leaving a strong smell of ozone. Suddenly he became aware of a blue, shining ball about a foot in diameter, bouncing toward him. He shrank away, and it rolled past with the light motion of a bubble and burst soundlessly. As it did so he felt a faint electric shock, and the blue crystal in his hand glowed like a spark. Niall had never seen, or even heard of, ball lightning, but he knew instinctively that it could be dangerous.

He replaced the crystal inside the stick and screwed on the head. But as they walked on, the energy began to make him feel uncomfortable. It was too strong, and began to give him a headache. As soon as he tied the stick across the top of his pack, this disappeared.

Looking at the lightning that illuminated the blue clouds, he began to formulate a theory to explain the phenomenon. Was it possible that

Shadowland, this gigantic cave beneath the Gray Mountains, was an amplifier of the Earth-force—not the vital force that filled the Great Delta, but some magnetic energy that sprang from the rocks? In that respect it would be like the crystal cave of the trolls, but far more powerful. He knew that in some sense he could not even begin to understand, the Earth was a vast dynamo whose current was spread unevenly. Perhaps in this enormous bubble called Shadowland, some freak of geology had created a concentrated vortex of force that discharged spontaneously in flashes of blue lightning and caused a permanent thunderstorm.

The ground underfoot was now smooth and hard; in places it reflected the blue light, and looked like some kind of dull metal. But half an hour later, this suddenly changed. The ground became softer, and when he stooped down to tie the leather thong of his sandal, he realized that he was walking on black earth. This puzzled him: what was earth doing in a giant cave formed of molten lava? Half a mile farther on, he saw the answer when a lightning flash was reflected off a sheet of water: rivers from above would bring down soil.

The water was the lake that Niall had seen from the hilltop, and it looked immense—perhaps ten miles across. They found themselves walking parallel to a river that flowed away from the lake, which Niall suspected of being the underground river below the cave of the trolls.

Soon they reached the point where the river flowed from the lake, and discovered that the water there was shallow. Since Niall was thirsty, he dropped onto his knees and tasted it. The water had a mineral flavor that was not unpleasant, and a rusty taste that indicated iron.

The spider waded on into the still water, and his peculiar air of concentration told Niall he was looking for food. Forty yards farther out, with the water now reaching his belly, he stood still. Niall watched with curiosity, aware that he was sending out some kind of signal.

The minutes passed. There was no sound except that of running water, and even that was almost inaudible. Then the spider's claw darted into the water, and came out with something that wriggled. A moment later it was in the captain's mouth. He evidently found it tasty, for a moment later his claw darted out again, and came out holding another wriggling fish. This was bigger, about six inches across, and from a distance seemed to be shaped like a ball. Again it was eaten in a few bites.

In ten minutes the captain had eaten a dozen of the creatures. Finally, he came toward Niall, holding something that squirmed, which he held out in his claw. Niall was surprised, for it was like no fish he had ever seen. It looked as if someone had taken it by the head and tail and squashed it like a concertina, so it was as high as it was long. The face seemed to be all mouth and eyes, the eyes being enormous ovals, and the mouth, which continued to open and close, bore an odd resemblance to the mouth of a pretty girl. The body was short and fat, and terminated in a tail that was several inches high and only about an inch long. The whole face was fringed with a kind of orange weed, and the huge eyes made it look as if it was startled.

The captain said: "Try it. It tastes good."

Niall shook his head. "No, thank you. I would have to cook it."

Without hesitation, the spider ate it whole. His jaw chewed with a sideways motion.

Niall waded out another ten yards, and felt a movement in the dark mud under his foot. He pressed down hard to prevent it from escaping, then bent down and plunged his hand into the mud. The fish wriggled, but less vigorously than Niall expected. He found himself holding a small version of the other fish, about three inches across. Its mouth opened and closed repeatedly, and the huge eyes stared at Niall as if begging him to put it back. Its body felt plump and fleshy, and Niall could understand why the captain had eaten so many.

Its enormous eyes obviously had been designed to see in the dark water, with hardly a glimmer of light. And when Niall let it go, expecting it to swim out of range, its short, fat body buried itself at his feet within seconds. These strange creatures obviously had evolved in this vast underground lake over hundreds of thousands of years. The feebleness of its struggles convinced Niall that it had few predators, and had never had to develop the speed of fish on Earth. In this strange, windless environment, lit by a dim blue glow not much stronger than moonlight, it lived an eventless life, opening and closing its mouth to take in fragments of weed.

Niall could understand its lack of sense of urgency. Except for the lightning, nothing ever happened in this quiet world. The lake was fed by a river that provided food, and there seemed to be no competition—unless, of course, the lake had more menacing inhabitants.

But Niall, at least, was aware of the passing of time. Somewhere ahead lay the city of the Magician, and he had to find it if his brother's life was to be saved. So he waded back to shore, tied on his sandals, and walked along the lake shore toward its far end.

Half an hour later, he saw something that caught his attention: a great mass of brown weed, in broad strips, floating near the surface. He waded out and picked up one of the pieces. It was very slippery, almost slimy, and had the same iodine smell he had observed in the weed in the house where Skorbo's assassins had lived. One side was smooth like wet leather, the other covered in sucker-shaped buds. So the weed in which Skorbo's killers wrapped their household gods had come from this lake. Its smell reminded him of the girl Charis, and he felt a twinge of sadness.

As he waded ashore, still in a state of relaxed sensitivity, he saw a shadowy shape from the corner of his eye; when he tried to focus on it directly, it had gone. Niall concluded that he had glimpsed an elemental, or some other semisupernatural being that regarded this place as its home. It had seemed to be a black shape, about the size of a child.

Knowing that it was pointless to try to see an elemental unless the elemental allowed itself to seen, Niall made no further effort. A few minutes later, when another shape flickered on the edge of his vision, he ignored it. The shape continued to play hide-and-seek, momentarily becoming more visible. Niall continued to ignore it. Finally, as if intrigued by his indifference, it ventured farther, and Niall was able to gain a clear impression of a black creature about the size of a monkey. The way that it was able to adjust its visibility convinced Niall that this was not a nature spirit, but something more intelligent—like the long-dead king he had glimpsed in the stone circle.

The captain had been waiting on the shore; if he was curious about what Niall was doing, his respect for the chosen of the goddess prevented him from asking. He evidently had caught no glimpse of the black creatures.

Niall tried to recall what the troll had told him about former inhabitants of Shadowland. He had said they looked like black apes, and that they were killed by poisonous fumes when the volcano erupted; ever since then, he said, the land had been haunted by their ghosts. So these black shapes must be . . . what had the troll called them? Then it came back: "troglas."

As if the word were a magic spell, one of them suddenly appeared on the edge of his vision, and remained there as he "looked sideways" at it. It was, indeed, one of the strangest-looking creatures he had ever seen. To describe it as a kind of black ape was, in a sense, quite inaccurate. Apes have receding chins and flat nostrils. This creature had a definite chin, and prominent—and broad—nostrils. It crouched, so it looked almost humpbacked, and had bent legs. Its dark eyes were undoubtedly intelligent. Niall would have remained unaware of it if he had not sensitized himself to the life-field of the fish.

As if it pleased them that this stranger understood the nature of spirits, more of them appeared, some only semitransparent, as if they could not make up their minds to become more visible. Suddenly Niall understood why this place was known as Shadowland—because it was inhabited by shadows.

He tried addressing the trogla who had first appeared.

"Can you speak to me?"

He was not using the telepathic language of the spiders, but the direct-meaning language of the chameleon men. But this was evidently not the language of the troglas, for what sounded in his mind was only a kind of echo, like someone speaking at a great distance. Niall tried hard to tune his mind to this communication, and asked again: "Can you speak to me?"

This time the answer was clearer, but equally baffling. It seemed to be: "Only in dreams."

Dreams? Niall was still trying to understand this when his attention was called to the present as the captain suddenly halted, staring into the distance. His senses were keener than Niall's, and he had detected something approaching. Niall understood this much through his telepathic empathy with the captain. But it was another ten minutes before he could see figures in the distance.

His first impression was that there were half a dozen horsemen coming toward them along the lake shore. He deliberately repressed the tension that made his heart beat faster at the thought of finally meeting representatives of the Magician. But while still a quarter of a mile away, the horsemen stopped. It was surely impossible that they had not seen Niall and the captain. Perhaps, for some unknown reason, the horsemen preferred to wait for them.

Five minutes later Niall and the captain were close enough to see that the horsemen seemed unaware of their presence. They were removing something from the backs of their animals, and Niall soon saw that it was a large net. They were stretching this out along the shore.

As Niall came closer, he became aware that these were not normal human beings. They seemed very short and powerful and, as far as Niall could see, were not wearing clothes. At any moment, Niall expected them to break off what they were doing to stare at the strangers. In fact, they continued working at laying out the net as if they were deaf and blind.

Niall remembered the living-dead man who had thrown himself into the river in the spider city, and was struck by a suspicion. And when finally he stood only a few feet away from the toiling men, it became a virtual certainty. These creatures were not alive.

In appearance they were almost identical to one another; they might have been cloned from the same embryo. All were baldheaded, and their powerful bodies were physically perfect, with thick, muscular arms and legs. The faces had character, with strong jaws, broad but well-shaped noses, and lips that would have been sensual if they had not been set in such a straight line. A regiment of them would have struck fear into the enemy. Yet the eyes had no expression. Except for the fact that they were obviously breathing, they might have been zombies or robots.

There was something else that confirmed that they were nonhuman: the area where males have sexual organs was as smooth and bare as a doll's.

As Niall and the captain watched, these creatures waded into the lake, dragging the net behind them. It was about forty feet long, and must have weighed at least a ton, yet they pulled it as if it were a piece of muslin.

A dozen yards from shore, they were up to their chins in the still water. But they went on until their heads vanished below the surface. Since he had observed the rise and fall of their chests, Niall assumed that they would reappear fairly quickly. But as the minutes went by, he realized he was wrong.

His attention now turned to their steeds, each of which had two large panniers slung across its back. It was immediately obvious that, in spite of bridles, they were not horses. Their heads were more like those of bulls, with short faces, but the large, bulging eyes added a touch of the frog. Their legs were short and obviously very strong, their backs broad and flat. It was apparent that they were bred for strength. Unlike their riders, they were clearly alive, and regarded the captain with suspicion. He, for his part, was not at ease with them—possibly remembering his encounter with the aggressive sheep.

Half an hour went past while Niall and the captain stared out over the smooth water, waiting for the heads to break the surface. In this world in which time seemed suspended, there seemed to be no good reason to move on. Finally, a ripple appeared, followed by the tops of bald heads. But their emergence was slow. The reason became clear as the rest of them became visible, dragging something behind them. The net was bulging with their catch. The creatures inside it were struggling feebly, yet without any real conviction; like the fish Niall had caught in the mud, they seemed almost indifferent to what happened to them.

Niall was astonished to see that the manlike creatures were breathing, and that water was gushing out of their mouths and noses. It seemed likely that when they submerged, they simply went on breathing water instead of air. By the time they reached the shore, the water had ceased, and they were breathing normally.

The net was dragged onto the hard-packed sand, and the apelike beings—Niall was already thinking of them as ape men—opened it. There was a violent movement, and a snakelike creature reared up from underneath the feebly struggling fish, and sank its teeth into the arm of one of the fishermen, then lashed around until it had torn out a chunk of flesh. Niall had seen one in the harbor, and recognized it as a moray eel. For a moment it looked as if the man was not going to react; then he grabbed the eel and squeezed. It divided into two halves as if made of soft putty, both halves falling at the man's feet. A little pale pink fluid was running down his arm.

The steeds were led forward, and the men began putting their catch into the panniers. Most of them were like the fish Niall had already seen, with plump bodies and huge goggle eyes. Some had the disklike shape of jellyfish, but were white in color, with thin tentacles that stirred protestingly when they were turned upside down. There were also small squids, like those in the sea at home, and black, shiny, sluglike creatures about a foot long, one of which clamped onto a man's thigh and was promptly peeled off and dropped into a pannier. When each pannier was full, it was covered over with a thick layer of the brown weed. Finally, the net itself was rolled into a long bundle, after which the men lifted it and tied it across the backs of all six animals, whose powerful legs sagged under the weight. Then they were led away by their bridles.

The captain paused long enough to pick up half of the moray eel, which was six inches thick, and tore chunks from it as he walked behind the slow-moving animals.

An hour later, as they left the lake behind, the ground once more became hard and gray, like the lava field they had crossed on their way to Skollen. The pace was necessarily slow, and Niall found himself yawning. It was like walking through a long, gray afternoon. But a few miles beyond the lake, the flashes of lightning became more frequent, and Niall was surprised when he felt drops of water on his face. He looked up at the sky. There was no sign of the rain clouds he would have expected on Earth; instead, the sky above was swirling, as if stirred by a breeze, and the blue electricity was crackling in it.

Niall expected a cloudburst, but all that fell was a light rain. It made his hair and his tunic damp, but was not heavy enough to soak him. Several bolts of lightning hit the ground within a few hundred yards, leaving behind an ozone smell.

This mild storm also had the effect of increasing the light, as if day was about to dawn. The result was that Niall could now see the first sign of a city on the horizon. It was difficult to estimate its distance in the strange twilight, but Niall guessed about two miles. For a moment he was tempted to walk ahead of the slow-moving animals, then decided against it. They obviously knew the best way into the city.

At one point the ground became rougher where the lava had formed runnels. The outermost animal stumbled, and a mass of weed fell off the pannier. The animals immediately came to a halt, and the man leading the nearest came back and replaced the weed on top of the load. Niall had been walking only a few feet behind, and the man's arm brushed him as he lifted the weed. As Niall had expected, his flesh was cold.

Half an hour later, Niall was able to see the city more clearly, and his heart began to beat faster. The captain, who could sense Niall's emotions, looked at him curiously, wondering what was exciting him. The answer was that what Niall could see ahead were pointed conical buildings that stretched up into the sky like tall, narrow pyramids. They resembled the buildings he had seen in his dream in the cave of the chameleon men.

As they approached closer, Niall was able to see that the city was sur-rounded by a dark-colored wall. This was about the same height as the old city wall that divided the spider city. At intervals of a few hundred yards, there were hexagonal towers with tall rectangular windows. It struck Niall as odd to have a wall around a city in this empty land. Who was it sup-posed to keep out? What it seemed to suggest was that whoever built it was paranoid about the fear of attack. Slowly, Niall became aware that the wall they were approaching was not built of stone. This wall had lines that ran parallel to the ground, and were about six inches apart.

There was a door whose top was pointed like a Gothic arch, and as they approached, a man came out. Niall recognized instantly that he belonged to the same race as Skorbo's assassins: he had a thin, very pale face, large dark eyes, big ears, a shaven head, and a receding chin. The nose was as beaky as a hatchet. This was a descendant of the original cliff dwellers.

The man glanced at the captain without surprise, as if he was used to seeing giant spiders every day. This made Niall wonder if they were expected, and it gave him an odd feeling of disquiet.

At close quarters Niall could see that the wall was made of metal—presumably iron—and that the parallel lines were joints where it had been welded. There was something rough and crude about the workmanship, which lent it an appearance of menace. In its way, it was as impressive as the Great Wall in the Valley of the Dead. Stretching for about a mile in either direction. it must have involved tremendous labor.

The guard pushed a heavy wooden gate wide open to admit the men with their animals. But it would have been impossible for six of them to enter abreast; the gateway was wide enough only for two. The men unloaded the rolled net, and two of them dragged it through the archway. The beasts were obviously relieved to have their burden lightened, and walked forward eagerly in single file. This was evidently something they did regularly.

When the animals and men had passed through the gateway, the guard glanced impassively at Niall and the captain. His voice sounded inside Niall's chest.

"What do you want?"

It was harsh and oddly toneless.

Niall replied: "To see the master of this city."

The guard stared at him woodenly, then turned and went back through the gate. A moment later, it closed. Niall and the captain looked at one another, wondering whether this was meant to be a refusal. It would be absurd to have traveled all this way to be denied entry.

Five minutes went by, ten minutes, a quarter of an hour. Everything was strangely silent except for the occasional crackle of lightning as it struck the wall. Then a door beside the gate opened. The guard was staring at them with a face whose blankness somehow conveyed hostility. Again his voice sounded harshly in Niall's chest.

"Are you sure you want to come in?"

It was asked as if it were a statement.

Niall said: "Of course." The question surprised him, until he reflected that it was probably some formal watchword intended for strangers.

The guard stood to one side to admit them. As they passed through the door, Niall thought he observed the flicker of a smile on his face.

On the far side of the archway there was a further door, which was closed. Niall and the captain found themselves standing in a narrow space. To one side of this there was a room, separated from them by a wooden counter that was highly polished. Behind this stood a man with the receding chin of the cliff dweller, but with a fatter face. He was obviously the superior officer of the guard, who now joined him by raising the flap of the counter.

The room was lit by a light on the ceiling, a glass cylinder containing a glowing wire. The men of Shadowland evidently had mastered electricity.

The officer's voice sounded inside Niall's chest. "What do you want?" It had a curious quality, as if echoing in an empty room.

Niall repeated: "To see the master of this city."

"Impossible. The karvasid sees no one." He looked outraged.

"Then is there someone else I can see?"

The man stared at him, as if about to refuse. Then he said: "Very well. Come with me."

He raised the counter and emerged. Niall could now see that he was distinctly better fed than the guard who stood behind him.

He opened the inner door, and Niall caught his first glimpse of the city of the Magician. It was disappointing. There was a great empty space—not a square, because it stretched away like a road. A few hundred yards away there was one of the conical buildings like that of his dream. The difference was that this was gray, like the flat plane. There were other conical towers, some tall, some short, some oddly lopsided. The plane between them might have been regarded as a central avenue, except that no buildings defined its sides. There were occasional benches, which looked as if they were made of a dark marble, but they seemed to be set at random among the buildings. In places, steam rose from cracks in the ground.

Lightning struck the nearest conical building, hitting a lightning rod that rose out of its apex. Steam suddenly hissed out of vents close to the top, looking like smoke. For a moment Niall thought it had caught fire, but after a moment, the steam ceased.

Their guide strode on silently, offering no explanation of where they were going. Niall glanced at him; his face seemed impassive. Was it possible, Niall wondered, that in spite of appearances, he was also some kind of robot? Gently, afraid of provoking an angry reaction, Niall tried probing his mind, looking at him as he did so, so that if the man noticed, it might appear accidental, as if he had casually brushed against him. But there was no reaction.

It was strange: although the man seemed unaware of what Niall was doing, his mind was virtually a blank. A normal human mind would have contained a continual flow of feelings and impressions and thoughts; this man's mind was little more than a reflection of his surroundings. It was almost as blank as some of the minds of the female guards in the spider city. Was this because, like these women, it had been violated so often that he no longer noticed it?

Then Niall observed a reaction of annoyance, and, thinking he had been caught out, quickly withdrew his probe. But when he looked ahead up the avenue, he saw that he was not its cause. Some kind of vehicle, drawn by two of the horselike animals, was crossing the avenue at a great speed, and vanished behind one of the conical buildings. It was the clatter of its iron-shod wheels that had annoyed the officer.

Niall said: "Where are we going?"

He sensed the man's irritation at being questioned, and for a moment thought he did not intend to reply.

Then the guard said: "To see the prefect." His voice was flat, almost metallic, in Niall's chest.

It struck Niall that the man had some of the characteristics of the officers in the Spider Lord's entourage; he had been trained to behave and think mechanically. So there was a sense in which the regime of the Magician resembled that of the Spider Lord. Usually, when one intelligent creature spoke to another by means of telepathy, the words carried a background of meaning, of feeling. Niall had now come to know the captain so well that his voice in Niall's head had an individual tone. But this officer's voice might have been reproduced by some mechanical device.

They had been walking a quarter of an hour, and had seen no one. Then Niall observed two more of the horse-drawn vehicles in the distance. They were proceeding more slowly, and did not provoke their guide's displeasure. It was hard to see who was in them, but whoever it was seemed to be wearing gray garments.

Partly out of curiosity and partly out of boredom, Niall began probing the mind of their guide again. It seemed incredible that he was unaware of it, for if it had been a normal human being, Niall's mental probe would have been as intrusive as someone leaning on his shoulder. But there was still that puzzling blankness. In fact, it was worse than blankness. Seen through the eyes of their guide, the street was as gray and featureless as a snowy landscape at dusk. Even the outlines of the conical towers seemed blurred.

Now intrigued, Niall tried increasing his concentration. The effect was immediate: the outline of the cones became clearer and sharper.

The problem, then, was that their guide's senses were dull and mechanical; he was suffering from a kind of permanent boredom. Niall and the captain looked more distinct; but that, Niall realized, was because they were novelties in a world of perpetual sameness.

Now fascinated by this experiment, Niall made an intense effort of concentration, trying to force their guide's senses to perceive everything more sharply and clearly. The result startled him. The buildings not only became more sharply defined, but became colored with bright stripes. The same thing happened to the road.

There was a hiss that made him jump, and a cloud of steam issued from a crack in the ground. But now, the warm steamy smell, which had reminded Niall of a laundry, had become sweet and pleasant, like children's candy.

At that moment, their guide responded with a feeling of pleasure, and his face broke into a smile.

Niall was baffled by this phenomenon. Was the road really gray or really colored? Did the air smell like cotton candy, or like steam from a laundry?

Niall was struck by another thought. The raven had enjoyed having Niall behind its eyes because it made it feel more alive. And this, presumably, was why their guide was now smiling. But this flicker of insight still left Niall as unenlightened as ever.

Back again behind his own eyes, Niall continued to experiment. The road and buildings were once again gray, and the air smelled of steam. But when he stared at the cones and concentrated hard, their outlines instantly became sharper and somehow more real. Then, remembering how he had perceived them a moment earlier, he tried to restore them to color by wrinkling his face and concentrating hard The grayness faded, and for a moment the buildings took on faint red, blue, and yellow stripes, which vanished almost immediately. The road, however, remained gray. He tried again, making a more sustained effort. This time, nothing happened. Somehow he realized, it was not a question of willed effort, but of some odd mental trick.

He imagined again being behind the eyes of their guide, and instantly saw what he was doing wrong. He was failing to make the *assumption* that the buildings were actually colored.

He tried again. It was as if he had pressed a control switch; everything instantly became colored, and the air was full of the sweet smell. The scene was now virtually identical with Niall's dream in the cave of the chameleon men.

The road and the buildings had ceased to look dull and dreary, but seemed to glow with a friendly warmth. And as a cart passed by a hundred yards ahead, he could see that the two people in it were clad in striped, colored garments. The beast that pulled it was also wearing some kind of colored decoration, as if part of a carnival.

Niall could now see that the cart contained a man and woman, and that the woman was holding the reins. He could even see her face. Although it was not pretty, being rather too thin, he found something oddly attractive about it.

He also noted that, if he concentrated hard, the colors deepened. He tried this, screwing up his eyes and wrinkling his forehead. It had the effect he recalled in the dream: the colors deepened and became more attractive, intensifying the feeling of gaiety. The light also became stronger. The effect was rather like sucking a piece of honeycomb, or some tasty and slightly acidic fruit, in that it induced a shiver of pleasure. But when he concentrated harder still, it had the disconcerting effect of making everything become gray, while the sweet smell disappeared and was replaced by the laundry smell. Since he greatly preferred the colored effect, Niall concentrated less hard, and again found himself surrounded by rich colors and pleasant smells. Some of them, like the cooking smell that issued from the palace kitchen at home, reminded him that he was hungry.

He noticed that their guide's smile had faded; he tried looking at the world through his eyes again, and discovered that everything had become gray and dull, which induced a sense of repetitiveness and boredom.

Now he was certain of at least one thing: the Magician dealt in illusions.

They had been walking for at least two miles through the empty streets, with no sound but the occasional crackle of lightning or hiss of steam. At last, there was a change in their surroundings. They could see, beyond the tower they were approaching, a long, rose-colored building with pointed towers about three times the height of the building. At least a mile beyond this, they could see people moving around.

Ten minutes later they stopped in front of the rose-colored building, which might have been a palace. It looked reassuringly like the larger buildings in the spider city—in fact, oddly like a house that had been a hostel for women—who, until Niall became ruler, had been kept segregated from males. They approached a wide but low flight of steps, at the top of which a guard stood in front of a wrought iron gate of elaborate design. He looked typical of the cliff dwellers, with a wide, sensuous mouth and a chin dark with a two-day growth of beard. His face seemed oddly familiar; then Niall remembered why. He looked like one of the assassins who had come to the spider city to kill Skorbo—and who had committed suicide rather than be taken alive. Niall could still remember the nausea he had experienced after being struck to the ground by the killer's will-force.

Their guide addressed the man telepathically—Niall was unable to hear what was being said. But the guard stood aside and pushed open the gates, which were well oiled and silent. There was a wide courtyard with a fountain in the middle, which sprayed colored water; Niall was puzzled to see that the color of the water changed from moment to moment through red, blue, green, yellow, and violet, yet in the bowl of the fountain, it looked light green. This, presumably, was another of the Magician's illusions.

Behind the fountain was a glass-paneled door. As they approached, this swung open, and a man came out. He was tall and thin, but the face was quite unlike those of the cliff dwellers, being distinctly handsome, with ascetic features and thin gray hair over a domelike forehead. He looked displeased to see strangers, and stared incredulously at the spider. Then, to Niall's surprise, he spoke aloud in human language.

"What is this?" The voice was sharp and authoritative.

Their guide said something telepathically; again, Niall was unable to tune in to it.

The thin man's face suddenly lost its stern expression, and became almost friendly. He looked at Niall and the captain with steely blue eyes.

"I am Typhon. What is your name?"

"I am Niall, the ruler of the spider city. This is my bodyguard, the captain."

The man turned to their guide. "You may go." Then he held out his hand to Niall, and they exchanged a handshake that involved pressing forearms together and grasping the upper arm. Niall observed that Typhon was wearing a gold band around his wrist, and that on this there was a small clock.

Typhon said: "It is a long time since we have received visitors." His voice was clear and well modulated, the voice of an educated man. "So I am unprepared. But please come in."

The room they entered might have been one in the palace of the late King Kazak, except that it contained items of furniture that had not been used in the spider city for many centuries: armchairs. Niall was also intrigued to see a clock on the wall, pointing to a quarter to eight. The Shadowlanders obviously had a preoccupation with time.

"Won't you sit down?" He turned to the captain. "Please do whatever you prefer." He spoke telepathically as well as aloud. The spider's response was to make the typical gesture of thanks, and remain standing.

Niall took a chair, whose cushions yielded pleasantly. It was a relief to sit down. He could hardly believe that he was in the city of the Magician, and was speaking to a human being who seemed as civilized and cultured as Simeon.

"Are you hungry?"

Embarrassed, Niall shook his head.

"When did you last eat?"

"This morning."

"Then you must be hungry." He sent out a powerful telepathic signal. A moment later, a servant girl entered the room. She was wearing a plain blue dress like a smock. Although obviously descended from the cliff dwellers, she was almost pretty, with long, dark hair and dark eyes, and tiny protruding front teeth like a rabbit's; only the weakness of her chin spoiled the effect. She stared at Niall and the captain with astonishment. Typhon said: "Bring food, Katia."

"Yes, lord." She replied telepathically. Niall was impressed; in the spider city, no servants could send telepathic signals.

"Wine?" Typhon lifted a carafe of ruby liquid from the sideboard.

"Thank you. Only a little." He was afraid that, in his present state of fatigue, he would become drunk.

Typhon poured wine into two long-stemmed glasses, and placed one on the table in front of Niall. He sat down opposite.

"And what brings you to our city?"

Niall took a sip of the wine; it was dry, and was as good as any he had tasted in his palace.

"I came to ask help for my brother. He cut himself on an axe that came from your city, and now has a fever."

Typhon looked concerned. "I am sorry to hear it. I am sure the karvasid will be able to help."

Niall experienced a surge of delighted relief. He could hardly believe that he had solved the problem that had worried him most.

"Thank you. I would be deeply grateful." It was a phrase he had learned from Simeon, but he meant it.

The girl came back carrying a tray, which she placed on the table. It contained an oval plate full of tiny fishes, and a dish with slices of a yellow fruit that Niall did not recognize.

Typhon asked the captain: "Can we offer you food?" Niall was impressed that he spoke with the same courtesy as if addressing a human being.

The captain said: "Thank you. I am not hungry." After seeing him gorge himself on lake fish, Niall could believe it.

As the girl was bending over the table, the wooden serving fork fell on the floor, and her mouth fell open with dismay. Niall was shocked to see that she had no tongue. She glanced nervously at Typhon, but he only smiled at her.

Typhon said: "Please eat." He took a plate and helped himself to some of the fishes, then to the yellow fruit. Niall did the same. The fishes were warm, and had a flavor that was slightly oily and salty; the fruit had an acid taste that complemented it. Niall ate hungrily, washing down the fish with wine.

Typhon said: "Forgive me saying so, but you seem very young to be the ruler of a great city. Do you mind telling me how old you are?"

"I am not certain. About eighteen."

"Ah, just a third of my age. I envy you. And how did it come about?"

Niall realized he was being invited to tell the story of his life, but he felt no inclination to do so. He was tired, and it would take too long. Besides, he was the ruler of a city, and Typhon—as far as he could make out—was merely the second in command of the Magician. So he confined himself to saying: "I was appointed by the goddess."

If Typhon was disappointed by this strange reply, he did not show it; he was clearly intelligent enough to see that Niall did not wish to be patronized. He said: "Then you must be a remarkable young man. As to me, I was appointed prefect because my father and grandfather held that office before me." He refilled their glasses, saying: "Then let us drink to a closer friendship between our cities."

Niall had not drunk a toast since he was in Kazak's underground city by the salt lake. He raised his glass and drank. The wine was causing a pleasant glow in his stomach, and the knowledge that he had saved his brother's life made him feel almost lightheaded. He asked: "Would the karvasid wish to make peace with the spiders?"

"Why not?"

"I was told that he hated them."

"By whom?"

Niall smiled faintly. "Cheb the Mighty."

"Why do you smile?"

"Because you must think I am insane."

Typhon shook his head. "On the contrary, it is obvious that you are telling the truth."

Niall acknowledged the compliment with a smile. He was beginning to like Typhon. There was something about him that reminded Niall of Simeon. He said: "But after all, the spiders drove the karvasid from his home."

Typhon shrugged. "That was a long time ago. Hostilities cannot go on forever, and neither would we wish them to. Our citizens would be glad to travel freely."

"Can they not do so now?"

"Of course. There is nothing to stop them. But most of them are afraid." Niall raised his eyebrows. "Of being killed by spiders."

Niall knew what he meant. A hungry spider would eat first and ask questions later. But he only said: "If we had a peace treaty, that could never happen."

Typhon smiled. "Good. That is what I was hoping you would say."

Niall asked: "When could I meet the karvasid?"

Typhon looked embarrassed and cleared his throat. "That is difficult. . . ." He hesitated, obviously looking for the right way of putting it. "He is old, and rather set in his ways. He dislikes meeting people. So I run this city for him, while he remains absorbed in his work." He sensed the question in Niall's mind. "He is a philosopher and a scientist. You have seen the animals who draw our carriages?"

221

"Yes."

"He made them." He laid special emphasis on the word "made." "They are precisely adapted to the conditions in Shadowland. Once we had horses, but they were afraid of the lightning. So the karvasid created the gelb. He is a very great scientist." His tone carried sincerity and conviction.

Niall said: "And those strange men who can breathe underwater?"

"The yobis? They are not men. They are machines—machines made of flesh." He sent out a signal, and the girl came in. "Send the moog in."

A moment later, the door opened, and a huge creature came in. Like the fishermen Niall had seen by the lake, he was naked and baldheaded. But his muscles were immense, and his shoulders looked as if they could have supported the weight of a horse. His hands must have been a foot wide.

Typhon addressed him telepathically: "Show them."

The monster went to the door that led outside, and grasped the doorknob with a finger and thumb, opening it with a gentleness that was almost feminine. He vanished outside. Moments later, he returned, carrying a balk of timber six feet long and six inches thick; it must have weighed a hundred pounds. He advanced to the center of the room, and grasped the timber in the center with his huge right hand, then squeezed. His fingers sank into the wood as if it was made of sponge. Then, having created a groove, he grasped the timber with his hands apart, and snapped it in half like a dry stick. After that he stood like a great statue, awaiting his next order.

Typhon said: "Show him," indicating Niall.

The giant held out half the broken beam, and Niall reached out and touched it. It was undoubtedly solid wood.

Niall said: "But surely his flesh must be softer then the wood?"

Typhon smiled. "Show him." The moog held out his hand, palm upward, and Niall touched it. It was as unyielding as hard leather. After that the giant held out his hand to the captain, who touched it gingerly with his tarsal claw.

Typhon said: "The karvasid is a scientific genius. He is one of the greatest inventors the world has ever known."

Nial stared up at the moog's powerful face; the hard blue eyes were obviously able to see, yet stared ahead as if made of glass.

Typhon nodded to him, and the moog went out.

Niall came to the subject that was at the forefront of his mind.

"When can I find out about my brother?"

"I shall speak to the karvasid tomorrow."

"Thank you."

"When did this accident happen?"

"Just over a week ago."

"Then there is more than enough time to spare. The poison of the trekuta tree takes twenty-eight days to do its work."

"Is there an antidote?" Niall was thinking how long it would take him to return home to administer it.

Typhon shook his head. "It is unnecessary. The karvasid can cure your brother from a distance."

"By magic?"

"No. By a science based on thought vibrations." He took another of the fishes. "Perhaps you might be able to meet the karvasid tomorrow. In the evening we have an assembly for members of the council, and the karvasid will be present. I shall ask him if you can attend."

"Thank you." But as he spoke, Niall felt misgivings. He remembered his last meeting with the Magician, when he had experienced the sensation of a crablike creature clinging to his chest and making him gasp with pain.

The door opened, and a young man came in. Niall was instantly struck by his resemblance to Veig—the same beard and dark curly hair, the same round, cheerful face. He looked startled to see the captain.

"Ah, Gerek." To Niall he said: "This is my assistant, Gerek. Gerek, this is Niall, who is the lord of the spider city. And this"—he indicated the captain—"is his escort and guard, the captain."

Niall stood up, and he and the newcomer clasped arms. Niall noted that, like Typhon, Gerek was wearing a gold armband with a clock on it. Gerek had a cheerful grin, and smelled of machine oil; he also had a black smear on his nose. After clasping Niall's arm, he turned and inclined his head toward the captain. Again, Niall was struck by this courtesy.

Typhon said: "Wine?"

Gerek said with feeling: "Please." He accepted the full glass and half emptied it, then smiled cheerfully at Niall. "Oof, I needed that."

He flung himself into a chair and helped himself to a handful of the small fishes.

Typhon asked him, with affectionate solicitude: "Hungry?"

"Ravenous."

"Then we may as well eat." He sent out a signal, and the girl came in. "Bring in the dinner, Katia."

Niall thought they had already eaten, and was glad to hear that the fish had been merely hors d'oeuvres.

Gerek asked Niall: "How did you get here?"

"On foot."

"How long did it take?"

Niall did a quick calculation. "Seven days."

"You did well. But why didn't you use one of those balloons?"

Niall said: "I was afraid I might crash, like Skorbo." He wanted to see how they reacted to Skorbo's name.

But Gerek took it quite casually. As he helped himself to more wine, he said: "He didn't crash."

"No?"

"No, we brought him down. At least, the karvasid did. He won't allow anyone to fly over us."

Niall got the feeling that Typhon was not entirely happy with this conversation. But before he could ask further questions, Katia came in, pushing a trolley with wheels—Niall had seen only one before, in Doggins' home. She began laying dishes on the table, much of the food being the same as the food Niall would have expected in his own palace: dishes of nuts, meat, fruit, stuffed small birds, and fishes cooked in a crisp batter. There were also some of the plump fishes with large eyes, such as he had seen in the lake, and little squidlike creatures no longer than a finger, also cooked in the batter. The drink was a flask of golden mead. Watching Gerek eying all this with undisguised greed, Niall was reminded again of his brother. The resemblance became even stronger when, as Katia withdrew, Gerek's eyes followed her with a predatory gleam.

Niall took a plate and helped himself. As before, they ate with their fingers.

In this relaxed atmosphere he felt he could ask a question that had been troubling him.

"Why does Katia have no tongue?"

It was Typhon who replied.

"Here most women have it removed in childhood. The karvasid wanted to force them to learn to speak with their minds."

Niall said: "But doesn't it hurt to cut out the tongue?"

"No. They are in a drugged sleep when they have the operation."

Gerek said: "I still think it's cruel."

Niall was relieved to hear him say this; the thought of women having their tongues removed outraged him.

Typhon said to Niall, in a tone of apology: "You see, the karvasid is oversensitive to noise."

Gerek shook his head. "But why not make a law that forbids women to make a noise around the palace? It would be just as effective."

Typhon nodded. "I agree. But you know the karvasid. He likes to do things his own way." He addressed himself to Niall. "When he was building this city, the karvasid was convinced that our land would be invaded by spiders, and this made his temper explosive. No one should condemn him who does not know how it felt to have his city invaded and many of its people killed and eaten." He turned to the captain. "I hope you will forgive me for speaking frankly."

The captain replied: "I understand."

Typhon turned to Gerek.

"But now there will be a peace treaty between our cities, and the days of mistrust will be over."

"Wonderful!" Gerek smiled at Niall. "But are you certain the spiders will agree?"

It was the captain who interrupted. "He is the master of our city."

Typhon added: "He was appointed by the goddess."

Gerek looked astonished; he stared at Niall, but said nothing, evidently tongue-tied.

Niall felt the need to add some comment. "It is a long story, and I will tell it to you some other time."

Typhon smiled at Gerek. "So now let our guest eat and drink. Perhaps you could take charge of him tomorrow, and show him the three levels? I have to spend the day with the karvasid."

Niall said quickly: "And you will ask him about my brother?"

"I promise." He signaled to Katia: "Bring us more wine—this time something less sweet."

As they ate, Typhon told them the story of the discovery of Shadowland. This was obviously to relieve Niall from the necessity of talking; in fact, he was so fascinated that he almost forgot to eat. So was the captain, who had by now learned enough of the human communication wavelength to follow the story, and who listened with close attention. Even Gerek, who must have been familiar with it, listened closely—although it soon became obvious that the food and drink were making him drowsy.

Typhon described how Captain Sathanas, commander of the guard, had escaped with twelve companions from the downfall of the city of Korsh. They had tried to take with them the ruler of the city, Vaken the Fair, but he had been among the first to die when the spiders swarmed over the walls. The Faithful Band, as Sathanas and his companions called themselves, escaped through underground tunnels below the city, and sailed down a river that came out to the east. One of the band was drowned in the torrent—their first loss. (Niall found it all too easy to imagine how this happened, and shuddered.)

Through harsh winter weather they made their way north to the Gray Mountains. Two more of their number died in a landslide, and another was swept to his death over the great waterfall when he was trying to catch fish in the river. And finally, a snowstorm drove them to take shelter in a cave on the Mountain of the Skull. They remained there for two days without food, knowing that if they ventured out, they would freeze to death.

Noticing that some birds flew out of the depths of the cave, they went to investigate, and found a chimney that descended into the heart of the mountain. But they had no means of climbing down, and—of course—no wish to, since they had no idea what lay at the bottom.

Finally, when the storm abated, one of their number, a soldier called Vosyl, went out hunting, hoping to catch a snow-hare. He followed tracks into a thicket at the bottom of the mountain, and there found a cave, where he killed the hare. The sound of the gunshot startled the birds, and some of them flew inward, deeper into the cave. When Vosyl returned with the hare, he described what he had seen. The next day, they all went into the cave with torches and, more than a mile down a steep tunnel, discovered the lower entrance to Shadowland. And ever since that time men have used the phrase, "as lucky as Vosyl."

Later that same day, the Faithful Band found their way into Shadowland. Some of them were afraid to go on, because they saw the ghosts, but Sathanas told them that if they went back, they would face certain death. And Shadowland was warmer than the world outside. So they went on, and when they found the great lake, they knew they were saved. That night they dined on fish until they could eat no more, and then slept the sleep of the weary.

The Faithful Band made their first permanent encampment by the side of the lake, and for six months they lived on nothing but fish and blue moss. They discovered that the moss on the higher slopes could be eaten, and that when dried out, it could be ground into a kind of gray flour from which they could make batter.

Niall recalled the spongy blue moss; it had not occurred to him that it might be edible. He also realized that the crisp batter he was now eating must be made from its flour.

Each day, Typhon continued, they explored Shadowland. They discovered the western cliff, where the birds nested, and the small northern lake, with its edible weed. And one day, they traced the river to its source, and discovered the northern entrance to Shadowland in the Black Gorge—a route that became impassable when the river was in flood in midwinter. They called the valley beyond it the Vale of Thanksgiving, because it was there that they first saw the sun after more than six months.

The Faithful had now been reduced to seven, since one of them had been struck by lightning. Five of the remainder wanted to move out into the sunlight again. But Sathanas advised against it. He knew that if the spiders learned of their existence, they would not rest until they had killed them all, or taken them back into captivity.

The captain interrupted to ask: "But why? You were no danger to them."

Typhon nodded. "That is true. But the karvasid was sure they regarded us as a threat."

Niall could understand the captain's question. With a newly conquered city to organize, Cheb would have had better things to do than search for a few men who had escaped. Besides, spiders, being lazy, are naturally peaceable.

Then it struck Niall that the troll had given him the most important clue when he said that Sathanas seemed possessed by a consuming hatred. Such a man could never believe that he was safe from the spiders.

Although Gerek was now dozing, Niall was impatient to hear more of the story.

"And did they spend the second winter by the lake?"

"Yes. But they were no longer alone. By that time they had brought women to Shadowland. The karvasid sent a raiding party to the city of Cibilla, and they saw women working in the fields. They kidnapped four of them and brought them back to Shadowland. And the following year, the first babies were born here."

Niall asked: "And when did they raid the cliff dwellings?"

"Oh, that was a long time later—more than a century."

"But if you already had women, why did you need more?"

"It was not women we needed, but men. By that time we were building this city, and needed workmen. The karvasid also felt that our population was not increasing fast enough—we needed settlers to farm the land below the Vale of Thanksgiving."

"Was the karvasid no longer afraid of being discovered by the spiders?"

Typhon shook his head. "Not after he learned to control the weather. Many spider balloons were wrecked over the Gray Mountains, until they stopped coming. But of course, the karvasid's greatest triumph was to make the spiders decide to build the Great Wall. They thought they were doing it for their own defense." He chuckled. "They did not realize they were doing it for ours."

At this point they were both startled by a loud snort from Gerek, who awakened with a sudden start. He rubbed his eyes.

"Sorry—I've had a long and hard day."

"Then you should go to bed." Typhon turned to Niall and the captain. "Would you like Katia to show you to your rooms?"

"Thank you." The idea of sleep was certainly marvelously alluring; this had been perhaps the most eventful day of his life.

Gerek said: "Let me show them."

Typhon said good night, and Gerek led the way from the room.

Although less spacious than Niall's palace, having only two stories, Typhon's villa was beautifully designed, with wide corridors lit by electric light; the stairway had a balustrade of fine wrought ironwork. There were also, Niall observed, many wall clocks.

Niall's bedroom overlooked a garden at the rear of the house, in which there were small trees with a purple fruit that looked like eggplant.

Gerek showed Niall how to close the blind, pulling a lever that caused its slats to close and cut off the perpetual blue daylight, and how to turn off the electric light.

The captain was waiting in the doorway. Gerek said: "Your room is next door."

The captain looked round Niall's spacious room. "I would prefer to sleep here."

"Of course." Gerek seemed unsurprised. "If you're sure you'll be comfortable. I am two doors away, in case you need me." He indicated the clock on the wall, which glowed with some form of internal light, and now showed half past ten. "I will wake you at half past seven—we have a long day tomorrow. And we have to be at the palace of the karvasid at seven in the evening."

When Gerek had said good night, Niall went into the bathroom. It was as well appointed as anything in his own palace. He was tempted to take a bath, but suspected he would fall asleep in it, so contented himself with sponging himself in warm water.

The captain had moved a thick rug to a corner of the room, and was standing by it—Niall suspected he felt it would be impolite to retire first. Niall climbed into bed, and regretted for a moment that he was not alone, so he could close his eyes immediately. He forced himself to ask politely: "What do you think of Shadowland?"

The captain hesitated. "I have not yet made up my mind."

Something in his tone—telepathic communication carried far more overtones than ordinary speech—made Niall suddenly alert.

"Why?"

"We arrived unannounced, yet I had the feeling that we were expected."

Now Niall understood why the captain had preferred this room: he wanted a chance to talk to Niall. He said: "That is possible. It often occurred to me on our way here that we might be expected."

The captain, who had continued standing, said: "But why?"

The telepathic comment, which would have been ambiguous if spoken aloud, implied many questions: why should the Magician want to lure Niall to Shadowland, how had he done it, and what was his ultimate intention?

Niall answered the last of these.

"Perhaps, as Typhon said, because it would suit him to make peace with us."

"Then why did he not send ambassadors? Why, instead, did he send assassins to kill Skorbo?"

Niall had to agree that the captain had a point. He still had no idea why Skorbo had been killed. He said: "Perhaps he felt Skorbo had betrayed them in some way." His inability to answer the question emphasized the lure of the soft pillow.

The captain sensed his tiredness. "I am sorry—you want to sleep."

He obviously found these human beings peculiar, with their need to switch off consciousness like a light every sixteen hours or so. Spiders could remain in a state of semisleep for days or even weeks.

Niall smiled. "I promise I will think about what you say."

The captain lowered himself onto the rug, and bunched his legs underneath him.

"Perhaps I am mistaken. Perhaps they really want peace."

Niall turned off the light. Lying in the darkness, he reflected that it surely made no difference whether they were expected or not. All that mattered was that the Magician wanted a peace treaty, and would cure Veig.

The thought made him glow with happiness, and the happiness carried him into sleep.

N iall woke from a deep sleep soon after six o'clock; in the spider city it would have been half an hour before dawn. The room was silent except for a faint humming made by the clock, and the sound of the captain's breathing. Underneath the bottom of the blind, Niall could see the unchanging blue daylight of Shadowland.

As he lay there, he reflected on what the captain had said before they went to sleep. It was, of course, quite possible that their arrival had been expected. The Magician probably had spies in the spider city—that was why Niall had left by the underground route. But once he was out in the open, nothing could shelter him from prying eyes.

But could the captain be correct in suggesting that Niall had been deliberately lured to Shadowland?

He recreated in memory the scene in which Veig had cut the ball of his thumb with the ax. The overseer Dion had brought it to the palace, wrapped in sacking, from the garden where Skorbo had been struck down.

Of course, whoever left the ax behind in the garden would expect it to be taken to Niall. And if Veig had not been present, Niall himself would have unwrapped it. And, seeing its razor-sharp edge, would almost certainly have tested it, just as Veig did, with his thumb.

And so it would have been Niall himself who was stricken with the poison. And he certainly would have been in no position to make the journey to Shadowland.

So the captain must be wrong. There was no obvious way in which Niall could have been deliberately lured to Shadowland.

The wall clock was showing half past six. Niall decided to try to contact his mother. He sat up in bed, propped a pillow behind his back, and stilled his mind.

Nothing happened for several minutes, while he remained passive, as if listening. Then he became aware of his mother's presence, as she would be aware of his.

She asked him: "Where are you?"

"In Shadowland, in its capital city."

Her voice was as clear as if she was in the room.

"Are you safe?"

"Yes. I am a guest of the Magician."

"What kind of a man is he?"

"I have not yet met him. I shall be introduced to him this evening."

"When will you return?"

"Soon, I hope. How is Veig?"

"The same as before. He sleeps a lot."

"Tell him I hope we can cure him soon."

The closeness of the contact diminished; it required total freshness of mind to stay in touch. He only had time to say, "I will speak to you soon" when the connection was broken.

The captain was still sleeping. Niall tiptoed to the bathroom and ran himself a bath. It seemed strange that it should be so like a bathroom in the spider city, until he recalled that the Magician had come from the spider city, and that this place had been built in its image.

When Niall returned the captain was awake. Niall asked: "Are you hungry?" and the answer came back in the form of a feeling rather than words; it conveyed: "Yes, very."

Niall opened the blinds, and looked out at the soft blue daylight. Now he could understand why there were so many clocks in Shadowland. In the world above, life was governed by the seasons, by night and day. Here it would be all too easy to lose count of time, and drift into a kind of perpetual present.

As he stood there, a woman came into the garden with a basket under her arm, and began picking some of the eggplantlike fruit. She had her back to Niall, and her movements were so graceful as she bent to put the fruit in the basket that Niall watched them with pleasure. As she turned sideways, he saw that she had a pretty figure and well-shaped breasts. Her hair was fashioned into a bun on the back of her head. Then she turned toward him, and her face became fully visible. Niall saw, to his surprise, that it was the face of an old woman, with wrinkled cheeks. At that moment she became aware of Niall's gaze, and smiled up at him. Her mouth had only three teeth. The odd thing was that her smile was still charming; moreover, despite the wrinkled cheeks, Niall still found her oddly attractive.

A few minutes later, her basket half full of fruit, she went back indoors, having first made a little curtsy to Niall.

He was intrigued. Ever since arriving in the spider city a year ago, he had become accustomed to pretty girls and attractive women. When he lived in the desert, Niall would have found it impossible to believe that he would have failed to respond to most of them. Yet because his telepathic abilities meant that he was aware of their minds as well as their bodies, he found most of them uninteresting. They had been bred for physical attractiveness, not for intelligence or vitality. He enjoyed being pampered by Nephtys and Jarita, having them wash him when he took a bath, then dry him and rub his body with oil. Sometimes Jarita looked up into his face and he knew she wanted to be kissed; but he felt that this was a borderline that he was unwilling to cross, for it would have soon reached the ears of the other maidservants—Jarita would have made sure of that—and created discord. So unlike Veig, for whom every woman was a mystery that filled him with longing, Niall preferred to preserve a delicate balance, and to absorb from the women a subtle essence, like the scent of a flower.

So it was strange that, in this city of the Magician, his response to women was becoming more like Veig's. Was it simply that he was missing the daily contact with the girls of his entourage? Or was it, like the mystery of the colors and scents, another sign of the Magician's power to create illusions?

There was a knock on the door. Gerek called: "Ready?"

The breakfast had already been set out on the table, and there was a jug of some steaming liquid. At the side of Niall's plate was a golden armband containing a clock.

Gerek said: "Typhon wishes you to accept this gift."

This was the thought that had flashed into Niall's mind as he saw the armband, and he was delighted that he was correct.

"Wonderful! A clock to wear on my wrist!"

"They are called watches."

He clasped it on his forearm, noting that the time was a quarter to eight. He had been in Typhon's house precisely twelve hours.

In the corner of the room, on another table, there was a plate full of slices of red meat, which Niall guessed was intended for the captain's breakfast.

Gerek said: "Typhon has already gone out. We shall see him later. Please help yourselves to breakfast."

Niall experienced a tingle of excitement at the thought that, even now, Typhon might be speaking to the Magician about Veig.

Katia poured liquid from the jug into glasses; it was red, and smelled of raspberries. Niall had a strong intuitive sense that she found him attractive; she often smiled at him, and as she leaned over him to pour, her breast brushed his temple, and Niall experienced a sudden glow of sensuous warmth. But at close quarters he observed something that struck him as odd; the bare skin of her arm was not smooth, like that of Nephtys or Jarita, but covered in fine wrinkles. He found himself wondering if this was due to lack of sunlight.

The food was simple: fruit, fish, sliced meat, and a dark brown bread in which Niall detected the now familiar taste of the flour made from fungus. There was even a kind of yellow jam made from the acidic fruit Niall had tasted.

Standing in front of his own table in the corner, the captain was eating with the total absorption that spiders always displayed at meals. But he was picking up the meat with his tarsal claw rather than setting the plate down on the floor in the manner Niall knew he would have preferred. He drank by lifting an earthenware vessel of water in both claws.

Niall asked: "What are your plans for today?"

"To show you our city. And then, if you don't mind a long walk, to see the Vale of Thanksgiving."

"I would like to." Niall sensed that this had a special meaning for the inhabitants of Shadowland.

Niall ate a good breakfast, and washed it down with the warm raspberry drink, which was unsweetened; his week of travel had given him a powerful appetite.

As they left the room, Gerek said: "Katia suggests that you leave your tunic behind and let her wash it for you. You can borrow one of mine."

Niall accepted the offer gratefully; his own tunic had become grubby and wrinkled.

When they emerged from Typhon's villa, a cart drawn by two gelbs was standing at the bottom of the steps. The animals stood silent and unmoving. Gerek turned to the captain.

"There is room if you would like to ride."

The spider said drily: "I would look ridiculous." This was the first time Niall had seen him display a sense of humor.

Gerek took the reins, and Niall sat in a well-padded seat beside him. As the cart drove off down the multicolored avenue, he experienced the satisfaction of a child on holiday. The gelbs trotted at about twice a man's walking pace, so the spider had no difficulty in keeping up with them.

Periodically, jets of the sweet-smelling steam blasted out of the ground, but the animals did not flinch. They remained indifferent even when lightning struck a conical tower as they passed it, and they were showered with fragments of colored stone. Niall tasted one of these; it was sweet, and had a peppermint flavor. But it did not dissolve in his mouth, and he finally spat it out. The taste, it seemed, was another of the Magician's illusions.

He asked Gerek: "What is the purpose of these towers?"

"The karvasid built them as lightning conductors. They also collect electricity."

This struck Niall as a novel idea. He had never thought of electricity being collected like rainwater.

He also noted that Gerek had said he "built them," as if the Magician had constructed them personally.

"But why do they have colored stripes?"

Gerek smiled. "To lift the spirits of our citizens."

As they trotted silently along the avenue—the hooves of gelbs made almost no sound—they saw a few more carts drawn by gelbs and, farther along, a strange device that Niall had never encountered before: a single large wheel with someone balancing astride it and riding it along the flat surface. Niall had never even encountered a cycle, much less a bicycle with only one wheel.

Clearly, the citizens needed some form of transport to cover these enormous distances. Niall asked: "Why is there so much space in your city?"

"The karvasid feels that it looks more attractive. But we have not yet reached the living quarters."

Ten minutes later, the scenery began to change. The conical towers came to an end, and there were rows of wooden houses, with alleyways in between them. These alleyways were at right angles to the road, and were bounded on either side by a kind of wooden wall, behind which were brown two-story houses with flat roofs.

They began to encounter more of the one-wheel cycles, and carts drawn by gelbs—usually one to a cart. There were also men and women who looked at first glance very like the people who could be seen around the spider city, except for their bright-colored garments. They evidently found Niall and the captain objects of curiosity, and stared at them intently.

Niall was surprised when they came to the end of the street with wooden houses, and found themselves approaching a bridge across a river. On its parapet there were lighted lamps on columns. Niall, who knew about the cost of municipal lighting, asked: "Do you keep them lit all the time?"

Gerek gestured at the sky. "We have plenty of electricity."

Niall was fascinated by the river. It was a light turquoise blue, and was flowing swiftly. With sunlight reflected from its surface, it would have been beautiful. But even in this pale blue light, its flowing wavelets, with their loud rippling sound, were almost hypnotically attractive.

On the other side of the bridge, on top of a hill, there was an impressive building of dark green stone, with rounded towers and buttresses. Niall guessed what it was even before Gerek pointed and said: "The palace of the karvasid."

Having noted that the rest of the city was completely flat, Niall asked: "Is that a natural hill?"

"No. It took a thousand workmen twenty years to construct it."

"A thousand men?" Niall was startled. His main impression so far was of a city with a small population.

Gerek understood what he meant. "There were more people at that time."

Niall was about to ask what had happened to them when the cart halted at the edge of a large open space with a market. Strings of colored lights gave it an atmosphere of festivity, while the stalls were covered in glittering silver cloths that reflected the light. On the far side of the square there was a curious structure that he instantly recognized as the "circus tent" of his dream, with its clumsy multistory shape. It made him wonder for a moment whether he was at present asleep or awake.

Gerek halted the cart on the edge of the square, and they climbed out, leaving their vehicle at the end of a row of stationary carts with gelbs in harness. All these animals stood unmoving; they might have been mistaken for statues made of wood.

There were more people in the market than he had seen so far; even so, it was not as crowded as the market in the spider city. For the most part the men and women seemed oddly pale, like Skorbo's assassins; sometimes their complexions were a light shade of yellow. And when Niall came close, he noticed that the skin was covered in fine lines, like Katia's arm.

By far the strangest thing about this scene was that it was so silent. This, of course, was because the people were addressing one another telepathically. But even their feet were almost soundless; the most popular form of footwear seemed to be a shoe made of soft white leather, of the kind that many children wore in the city of the bombardier beetles. The total effect was bizarre: a bustling market with hardly a sound.

All around the edge of the square were striped booths that served food and drink, and the air was full of pleasant cooking smells. The market stalls themselves contained a remarkable variety of goods: clothes, shoes, household articles like wooden buckets, clothes pegs, and stepladders, as well as food such as cheese and butter, apples, pears, plums, and the eggplantlike fruit Niall had seen in Typhon's garden. There were even one-wheeled cycles for sale.

Niall was suddenly struck by an interesting realization: he had not so far seen a single child. Neither were there animals like dogs or cats. Yet some of the meat on sale looked like large rats.

Niall pointed to the "circus tent."

"What is that?"

"It contains amusements. Would you like to see inside?"

With a disquieting sense of déjà vu, Niall advanced toward the entrance that looked as if it had been created by cleaving the canvas with a knife. Directly beyond this flap there was a gray space that was even more like Niall's dream. But when another flap was pushed aside, the similarity vanished. The inside of the enormous tent was lit by electric lights that were brighter than the daylight outside. And the people inside were speaking in normal voices, chattering and laughing. There was also soft and pleasant music, played on some kind of stringed instrument. Around the walls there were booths separated by thin walls made of woven strips of wood, and machines with flashing lights.

The bright lights also showed clearly that most of the people had fine wrinkles—so fine that they would scarcely be visible in daylight—while the predominantly dark hair of the men and women was frequently powdered with gray. What was so odd was that their bodies showed no sign of aging; the majority of the women had good figures and firm breasts, while the men looked strong and athletic. No one he had seen so far looked overweight. Niall thought of the woman he had watched from his bedroom window, with her wrinkled face and youthful figure, and was baffled.

Niall's appearance, followed by the captain, caused a stir; but the tent was so big that the chattering continued unabated. And those who gazed with astonishment at the spider quickly lost interest when they saw Gerek and recognized that he was in charge of the two guests; within a few minutes, no one was paying them any more attention.

Niall asked Gerek: "What is this place?"

"It is the Hall of Entertainment."

Niall looked around him with interest. His committee had discussed providing something of the sort for the inhabitants of the spider city, and he was on the lookout for ideas.

"What are these machines?" Each booth contained an upright metal box in which there was a circular opening about a foot in diameter, and each one had a comfortable seat of metal tubing attached to its front.

"We call these reality machines. Come and see."

He led Niall into one of the booths, and said: "Excuse me." An attractive young woman looked round at them with wide eyes. For a moment, Niall thought she was startled by the sight of the captain, then realized that her eyes were actually circular. Again, Niall experienced a disturbing sense of déjà vu, then remembered where he had seen such round eyes: in the white ghostlike creatures of his dream.

The girl smiled charmingly at them, looking at Niall with particular interest, and Niall experienced again the glow of attraction that he had felt when Katia had pressed against him. The women of this place seemed to radiate a kind of erotic energy.

A label on the side of the booth said: "Scene by Moonlight." Gerek gestured at the circular opening, and Niall sat down and placed his face against it. He found himself looking at a picture of a cobbled road that ran beside a river or canal, with trees on either side, and neat-looking houses. A crescent moon hung in the sky, and was reflected on the water of the canal. A girl in a low-cut dress was walking along the road. A well-built young man who looked like a laborer was walking toward her.

It was a delightful picture, and Niall looked at it with appreciation. Then, as he stared, it became three-dimensional; he was looking at a real road, and the trees were stirring in a cool night breeze. A moment later, he found himself standing on the road and feeling the breeze against his cheeks and looking at clouds drifting past the moon. Everything was real: the rippling water of the canal, which reflected the moon, and a leaf that drifted down from a tree. A cat emerged from a garden gate. The man passed the young girl without even glancing at her.

What was so odd about this was that Niall was conscious of himself in two places at once: standing in front of the machine, and being on the moonlit road. This produced a curious surge of pleasure, a sense of control.

Gerek said: "If you want to restart it, push the orange button."

Niall did as he suggested. Instantly, the picture reset itself. The man and the girl were again twenty feet apart, the trees stirred in the breeze, the cat slipped out of the gate. Niall wondered why Gerek had suggested restarting it. He looked at the girl's attractive features, and the bosoms that almost emerged from the neckline of the dress, and it passed idly through his mind that it was a pity that the young man did not ask her for a kiss.

A moment later, as they passed one another, the man turned, slipped his arm round her, and gave her a kiss. The girl seemed to enjoy it.

Niall found it hard to believe that his own spontaneous thought had caused the change. He again pressed the reset button, and watched the two approaching one another. But this time, he changed the scenario in his imagination. And a moment later, as the two drew closer, it was the girl who stepped in front of the man and placed her arms round his neck. The two stood pressed tightly together in the moonlight. Niall felt like a voyeur as he watched them.

Niall said: "That's amazing!" Gerek smiled, obviously pleased. "But how can my thoughts change what is happening?"

"I don't know. It's one of the karvasid's early inventions. I don't understand the principle behind it."

Niall stood aside and invited the captain to look. After a moment's hesitation, the spider peered through the round hole. His body suddenly became rigid, and Niall knew that he had found himself standing on the moonlit road.

A few seconds later, the captain also reset the machine. This time, the eyes around the back of his head closed, obviously to enable him to concentrate better. Niall was curious about what had interested him. Then it came to him: the cat. The captain was looking at it as a potential meal. The thought made him smile.

Niall asked Gerek: "Could I make it do anything I wanted? Make the moon fall out of the sky or the trees walk along the road?"

"Certainly. It responds to your imagination."

Something in the way Gerek said this made Niall realize that he found it all rather boring. He probably had looked into all these "reality machines" dozens of times.

When he looked into the machine in the next booth, Niall understood why, after their initial surprise, no one paid much attention to the spider. The label on the booth said "Korsh," and inside the machine was an exact representation of the main avenue of the spider city—the one that ran south out of the square—with spider webs stretched overhead, and slaves and female overseers on the crowded pavements. Niall found himself standing on the curb, and had to admit that it all looked totally real. As he stood there, a spider dropped out of its web, seized a slave, and carried him aloft.

Niall said to Gerek: "This is out of date. Spiders are no longer allowed to eat human beings."

Gerek looked surprised, but said nothing.

Entering again this panoramic scene, with the river in the background, Niall was struck by another inaccuracy. The female overseers had been coarsened and robbed of some of their femininity. These women were beautiful, but also looked ill-natured and stupid. They strutted around looking as if they might beat and trample on a slave out of sheer spite.

Niall thought he began to understand. The inhabitants of Shadowland were allowed to familiarize themselves with the spider city, but it was represented in such a way that they felt no envy for its inhabitants. It looked overcrowded and dangerous.

They strolled between rows of booths, and Niall paused frequently to read the labels. Warfare seemed very popular, and at least two dozen machines were dedicated to great battles of history including Salamis, Actium, Agincourt, Lepanto, Austerlitz, Waterloo, and many Niall had never heard of. As he passed these machines, Niall could hear the thunder of cannon, the shouts of charging armies, and rousing military music. The men who peered into them were obviously soldiers, and some wore blue and red military uniforms. It was apparent from their total stillness that each was physically present on the battlefield.

Many of the machines were twice as wide as the others and had two seats attached. These were clearly designed for couples, and without exception they were occupied. Gerek explained that they enabled couples to share adventures, and that many of the men and women who gazed into them were strangers to one another.

The sheer number and variety of the dream machines was overwhelming—it would have been possible to spend weeks in this vast hall. It also became clear that the machines presented the citizens of Shadowland with an outlet for every kind of impulse and daydream. By merely look-ing through a circular aperture, they could experience virtually anything: forests, rivers, mountains, strange cities, bizarre landscapes, mythical creatures, amazing love affairs, heroic battles, even voyages around the solar system.

Other machines were devoted to extraordinary surrealistic fantasies. Niall was particularly amused by a giant naked woman who seemed to be built of bricks, and who ate houses as if they were cream cakes. And the captain was obviously fascinated by a swamplike dreamscape with indeterminate creatures who changed continually from plants to reptiles to birds, animals, insects, and crustaceans, while never being wholly one or the other. Niall found its landscapes oddly repellent and oppressive, but the captain stood in front of it for a quarter of an hour without stir-ring. It made Niall realize how little he understood the spider mentality.

They had been inside the Hall of Entertainment for more than an hour, and Niall's appetite for its amazing variety was beginning to flag out of mere fatigue. So when Gerek asked if he was ready to leave, he nodded.

Next to the exit there was a bright, silver-colored machine that was slightly larger than the others. As they approached, the man who was peering into it turned around, and Niall saw that this face was glisten-ing with sweat. Niall asked Gerek: "What's that?"

"That is a new exhibit. It is for testing the power of the will."

"How does it do that?"

"Why not try it?"

Hesitantly, Niall peered into the machine, then sat down. He imme-diately felt himself drawn into its powerful ambience, as if by a kind of suction. This suction did not operate on his body, but somehow on his perceptions.

He found himself looking at two glittering railway tracks that extended about fifty feet toward a square red building, into which they disappeared.

The illusion took about a minute to build up, like a picture that was completed piece by piece. Niall then realized that he was standing on a platform, beside a red trolley whose metal wheels rested on the tracks. A small door stood open. After a moment of hesitation, Niall obeyed his impulse to climb in and sit down on a wooden seat. As soon as he pulled the door closed behind him, the trolley began to move toward the red building. Two doors swung inward to admit it, and he found himself inside a kind of hut whose brightly colored walls were covered in pictures of the planets. A soft and soothing music was playing out of small holes in the walls.

The wagon stopped, and a metal band passed around Niall's waist, confining him to the seat. Then the trolley moved smoothly toward a blank red wall. But just before it was about to strike it, two more doors slid open, and Niall found himself perched on top of a slope that plunged downward toward a small blue lake that covered the tracks, and then steeply upward again, and around a curve. A moment later, the trolley was moving down the tracks at an increasing speed toward the water. Niall felt a surge of alarm, even though he knew this was an illusion, and that he was actually standing in front of a machine.

He closed his eyes as the trolley, now traveling faster than he had ever traveled in his life, swooped into the water. The was a tremendous splash, and a wall of water surged into the air; he could feel drops of icy-cold water on his face. When he opened his eyes, the trolley was hurtling up the slope, slowly losing speed. It swept round a curve, pulling him sideways in his seat and pressing him tight against the metal band. When he opened his eyes again, the trolley was at the top of another slope, at the bottom of which a cavern straddled the line. Again, they plunged down, and he ducked his head to avoid the low entrance. Then he was in a roaring darkness, deafened by the clamor of the iron wheels.

He was surrounded by a purple glow, and saw ahead of him a white giant wielding a scythe. He ducked frantically, and the scythe passed over his head, brushing his hair and causing bits of hair to fall down his cheeks. Then they were traveling along a curving track that followed a hilltop, in a tumultuous wind. Dim lights enabled him to see the steep sides of a slope that plunged down to the sea. Huge breakers were rolling in, surging up the slope, and turning into spray only a few feet below where Niall was sitting, so he could feel the spume. Again, he had to soothe his rising panic by telling himself that all this was an illusion. Yet when he tried to become conscious of his body standing in front of the dream machine, he failed. He was only aware of himself sitting in the trolley, held tightly in his seat by a metal band. It was like being trapped in a nightmare.

They were roaring around another bend and down a slope. A great breaker swept in, struck the slope, and surged up toward him. Cold water dashed against him, soaking his clothes and taking his breath away. Then they were plunging down again, this time toward a forest, in which two giants were swinging hatchets at a tree. The tree fell, and Niall closed his eyes in horror as it landed across the track. But long branches prevented it from touching the ground, and the trolley hurtled out of the other side of the branches.

Wondering how much more of this his nerves could take, he closed his eyes and felt the air rushing past him, his body hurled upward at one moment as they swept downhill, then squashed down in the trolley seat as it surged up again. More spray dashed into his face and he tasted salt. He was aware that at this speed, he could be knocked unconscious if some projection struck his head.

To his immense relief, the trolley began to slow down. Ahead of him he saw the red building in which he had started this journey. Then the car halted, the band withdrew from around his body, and the door opened. Feeling stiff and badly shaken, Niall staggered out onto the platform. As soon as he did this, he became aware of his body standing in front of the machine. He raised his hand to his tunic, convinced that it would be drenched in seawater. But it was perfectly dry. Only his face and hair were wet, and as he touched it with his fingers, then tasted it, he realized that the salt was perspiration.

He turned to Gerek. "That's terrifying. But why do you say this tests the power of the will?"

"Because you can resist the illusion if you want to."

The captain was now standing in front of the machine, peering into the circular hole. His body became perfectly still, and it was obvious that he had been dragged into the scene against his will. Watching him, Niall recalled that feeling of total absorption, like being sucked into a vortex. It seemed to be some form of hypnosis, with something in common with a spider's ability to induce paralysis. In that case, the trick of resisting it surely must depend on maintaining awareness of his body standing in front of the machine?

After less than a minute, the captain turned away. In answer to Niall's question, his mind conveyed a clear picture of the impossibility of squeezing his long legs into the trolley.

Intent on testing his theory, Niall immediately sat down again in front of the circular opening. But this time he concentrated hard, resisting the sense of being sucked into a vortex. It was as if he had interfered with some mechanism. The scene with the trolley and railway lines remained somehow unreal and static. Niall had to decrease his resistance before he experienced the sense of being pulled into it.

As the scene built up around him, like a jigsaw puzzle coming into existence piece by piece, Niall maintained the sense of contact with his body. It was as he was opening the door and climbing into the trolley that he felt his mind become blank for a split second, and realized that this was the moment when he had lost awareness of his body and become part of the illusion. He made a mental effort, as though shaking his head, and immediately became conscious of his body again.

As the trolley moved forward, he made another effort of will, and at once interfered with the mechanism; the trolley stopped and the whole scene became static. The illusion, he realized, depended on his becoming hypnotized by the motion of the trolley. When he resisted, it was as if someone had snapped his fingers in front of his face, breaking the spell.

He ceased resisting, and the red doors slid open, admitting him to the small building. This, he realized, was the crucial moment; he was about to be hurled into motion. He shook his head and clenched his teeth, restoring the sense of his body standing in front of the machine. The next set of doors opened, but the trolley remained motionless at the top of the steep slope, and remained motionless until he relaxed his will, and allowed it to rush forward.

Swooping down toward the water, he found it more difficult to maintain control. He kept his teeth clenched, and as he hit the water, forced himself not to blink. As a result, he saw that what actually happened was a flash of blue light, accompanied by strong puffs of cold wind on his cheeks.

As they approached the cave entrance, he held his neck rigid, refusing to give way to the impulse to duck. The result was a momentary darkness as his head passed through the stone, again accompanied by a violent puff of air that made him wince.

Ahead of him was the white giant swinging the scythe; it cost an effort not to duck, but all that happened was a flash of light and puffs of wind on his cheek, simulating hair that had been sliced off.

As the car clattered around the curve of the hilltop, he looked down on the roaring sea, aware that this was an illusion of light and sound, a kind of cinema projection. He was almost taken in as they were struck by the wave, but realized that this was merely a blast of freezing air. And when the two giants made the tree fall across the track, he simply braced himself as the trolley passed through the gap in the branches.

Now he kept his eyes open, ignoring the rocks and trees that rushed past him. And as the change in the rhythm of the wheels told him that he was close to the end of the journey, he once again concentrated until he became aware of his body. There was a flickering confusion, and the trolley jerked and then stopped. The metal band withdrew from around his body, but he made no attempt to stand. Instead, he concentrated on his body. There was a flash, followed by darkness, and he was suddenly sitting in front of the machine. The light inside it had gone out.

In that moment, Niall experienced a sudden insight, whose precise nature eluded him but which left behind a glow of exhilaration.

Gerek said: "You seem to have blown the fuse."

This had happened, Niall realized, because he had aborted the last part of the operation, and so confused the preset pattern that governed it.

Gerek was bending over a tube of flickering green light, in which a black line wavered up and down. He said: "That was impressive." But Niall thought he detected a note of anxiety in his voice. When the light inside the machine came on again, he looked relieved.

For a moment, Nial experienced a painful twinge of headache. The events of the last few minutes had left him tired, and colors were dancing in front of his eyes. He looked around for somewhere to sit down again.

Gerek, reading his mind, said: "Let's go and have a cup of coffee."

He led the way out of the exit. Next door there was an open area with tables and chairs, and a counter.

"Sit down and I'll get you something to drink."

The table tops were circular and in bright primary colors, each supported by a single metal leg with seats attached to it. Niall sat down with a sigh of relief, and gradually began to feel better. The captain, as usual, stood there motionless.

The cafe was about half full. Many of the women, he noticed, had the same round eyes as the girl he had seen in the booth. As they were still waiting for Gerek's return, a man and woman, dressed in the usual brightly colored clothes, came in through the street entrance. They walked past them with only a perfunctory glance at the spider. It was only after they had passed that it struck Niall as odd that two strangers should walk into the Hall of Entertainment, find an eight-foot spider standing at a table, and pass by with hardly a glance. Could the inhabitants of Shadowland be all that familiar with real spiders?

Gerek returned, carrying a tray.

"Sorry I've been so long. They had to slice more meat."

He had brought a plate of underdone beef for the captain, and coffee and biscuits for himself and Niall. Since Niall had never tasted coffee, he had no way of knowing that the hot liquid he was now sipping was a substitute made of chestnuts.

He asked Gerek: "Why do some women have round eyes?"

"They are an experiment of the karvasid. Since the light here is less bright than on the surface, he thought that round eyes would help them to see better."

"But why only women?"

Gerek smiled, and lowered his voice. "He thought round eyes made men looked silly, whereas it made women prettier."

Glancing at a blue-eyed girl at the next table, Niall had to agree that her round eyes made her attractive; the effect of astonishment made her seem vulnerable and innocent. On the other hand the men, many in military uniform, and mostly of the cliff-dweller type with pale faces and stubbly blue chins, would have looked absurd with round eyes.

Niall finished the last biscuit and drained his coffee. He asked: "Where are we going now?"

"I thought you might like to see a little more of Shadowland."

As they emerged into the blue daylight—which seemed oddly depressing after the bright lights of the Hall of Entertainment—Niall was fascinated to see that the road was cobbled. But there was otherwise no resemblance to the scene of his dream. These houses were strikingly quaint, with steep, red-tiled roofs, and upper stories that projected above the lower; their windows were made of small leaded panes. And the people here bore no resemblance to the white-haired, ghostlike creatures of his dream.

He asked Gerek: "Have you ever seen creatures like this?" And he projected a telepathic image of the white ghosts.

Gerek nodded. "They are called graddiks."

"And where do they come from?"

"Come from?" Gerek looked at him in astonishment. "They don't come from anywhere. They don't exist. They are purely mythical."

"And what about troglas?"

"Oh, they existed once. They were the original inhabitants of Shadowland, but they were all killed in a volcanic eruption long before men came here."

"And is it true that their ghosts still haunt Shadowland?"

Gerek shrugged impatiently. "Of course not. Ghosts don't exist."

Niall could see that Gerek was of the same mind as Torwald Steeg.

Looking around the corner of another cobbled street with quaint houses, Niall asked: "What kind of people live here?"

"This is a district called Freydig, which is for our better-off citizens. It is based on a city called Krakow in medieval Poland. That's the Town Hall." He pointed to a building that might have been a ducal castle. "It also has the best restaurant in the city."

The people of this quarter certainly looked plumper and better dressed than those in the wooden houses on the far side of the bridge, and one tall, beautiful woman was wearing a cloak of white fur. Niall was curious.

"Why are they better-off?"

Gerek laughed. "A good question. In fact, the karvasid thought that it would be better if our city had different classes, the rich and the poor. A city where everybody was alike would be less interesting than a city with class differences. As it is, the poor dream of moving to this side of the river, near the palace."

"And what do the rich dream of?"

"To be allowed to travel to the surface. That is why the karvasid wants to make a peace treaty with the spiders."

Niall said: "You astonish me."

"Why?"

"Surely real travel would be boring in comparison to the Hall of Entertainment."

"Ah no. You see, dream machines fail to satisfy the sense of reality."

They now had walked around the enormous circus tent, and were back in the market square. It was even more crowded than before, and again Niall was struck by the silence.

Their gelbs, which were waiting in the row of stationary carts, looked as if they had not stirred an inch in the past two hours. Niall and Gerek climbed in, Gerek took the reins and turned the cart, and they drove off smartly, turning left along the road that followed the river. Glancing back over his shoulder, Nial saw that many people were staring after them. It seemed they were not as indifferent as they appeared to be.

The captain, with his eight-foot stride, had no difficulty keeping abreast; in fact, they were traveling at about the speed that spiders preferred. Niall therefore settled back in his seat and allowed himself to relax and enjoy the scenery.

Not far beyond the marketplace they passed another enormous square, in which a squad of soldiers was engaged in rifle drill. This was the first time Niall had ever seen soldiers on parade, and he was fascinated by the machinelike precision of their movements as they snapped to attention or presented arms; all of this—since he could not hear the telepathic commands—seemed spontaneous and full of astonishing vigor.

He asked Gerek: "Why do you need soldiers when you have no enemies?"

"The karvasid believes in being prepared for attack. Besides, the training is good for our menfolk."

This city was larger than the city of the spiders, yet obviously had a far smaller population. This was apparent from the small number of people they saw. Yet its buildings were as impressive as those of spider city, and far more varied in style. One great square building looked like an old-fashioned office block with outside columns that seemed purely for the purpose of decoration, and a flat roof with a parapet. Yet through its large windows Niall could see only one solitary woman sitting at a desk. Another building along the riverfront had a series of arcades, and in a kind of interior courtyard he could see trees—rather squat trees whose vegetation was the dark color of seaweed.

On the far side of the river there were rows of terraced houses looking like those on the outskirts of the spider city. Niall saw a man emerging from one of these, and blinked with astonishment, suspecting that his eyes were deceiving him. The man seemed to have a square head. Niall pointed to him.

"Is there something wrong with him?"

"No. That is one of the karvasid's experiments. He thought that a man with a different-shaped head could be made more intelligent, but he proved to be wrong. They are very stupid."

Niall noticed something else—open spaces with great piles of square stone blocks in the center. These piles looked as if they had been tumbled haphazardly from the back of some huge cart. He pointed: "And what are they for?"

Gerek said briefly: "Building blocks."

"But you seem to have more buildings than you need."

"That is why they were not used."

They were crossing another bridge built of stone, with lighted lamps along the parapet. Beyond this, Niall could see the city wall, with its strange hexagonal towers and tall windows, and another city gate—obviously not the one he had entered by, for there were no conical towers in sight.

Niall said: "I don't understand. Was the population once far greater than it is today?"

He thought Gerek seemed troubled by the question, but in fact, he answered casually: "Oh, yes. Even a century ago there were four times as many people."

"What happened to them?"

Gerek hesitated before replying: "I was not born then, but I suspect that the karvasid made one of his rare mistakes. He was afraid that the population would outgrow the food supply, and ordered many woman to be sterilized. So the birth rate fell steeply. But then the sterility seemed to spread. Now no baby has been born for twenty years. I was one of the last."

Gerek seemed disturbed, and Niall felt sorry to have asked an embarrassing question.

A few minutes later they arrived at the gate. The guard who opened it for them stood to attention and saluted Gerek. Niall observed that he watched the spider curiously out of the corner of his eye. Then they were out in the featureless landscape of Shadowland, with its flat, hard surface. Yet the only visible difference from Niall's approach of the day before was that a smooth gray road stretched ahead of them. In the black earth on either side of the road, Niall observed occasional cracks, from which steam was issuing.

Gerek said: "You promised to tell me how you became the ruler of the spiders."

And since the road ahead vanished into the unchanging distance, and they were obviously going to be on it for a long time, Niall took a deep breath and began.

"I was born in the desert on the other side of the great sea. . . ."

If he had tried to tell of his journey to Kazak's underground city, and how he had killed a spider with the expanding metal rod, it would have taken all day. So instead he compressed it, describing simply how he had returned from a hunting trip to find his father dead, and his family taken captive by the spiders. Gerek listened with total absorption, and so, oddly enough, did the captain, who was becoming increasingly skilled at following human mental imagery.

Niall spoke of his rescue of the spider that fell overboard during the crossing from North Khaybad, and how in consequence he was well treated on arriving in the spider city. To describe the white tower and all he had learned there would again have made the tale overlong, so he spoke only of his journey to the city of the bombardier beetles. He condensed the account of how Doggins had lost his complete supply of explosives on Boomday, and only described how he and a group of young men had set out to find the hidden arsenal in the Fortress. Gerek was clearly fascinated by Niall's account of the Reapers.

"We have some of these in the castle armory. I understood they were invented by the karvasid."

"No, they date back to olden times, before the spiders came."

After talking for an hour, Niall became tired of the sound of his own voice, and so abridged the account of his trip to the Delta. But when he spoke of the empress plant, Gerek interrupted with amazement: "And you actually spoke to the goddess?" Niall nodded. "What was she like?"

Niall said, enjoying the sense of anticlimax: "A giant vegetable sticking out of a hilltop."

But when it came to speaking of his conversation with the goddess, Niall experienced an odd reluctance to go into detail. An instinct checked him, and since he always obeyed such instincts, he confined himself to explaining that the empress plant had been brought to Earth by a comet from another galaxy; after that, he went on to describe his return to the city of the beetles.

By now, they were traveling by the side of a lake whose surface was almost entirely covered by a bright yellow weed, while on its far side was a vertical cliff, perhaps a thousand feet high. At the top of this was a blue-covered slope that stretched into the vapors of the sky. The ledges on the cliff face were full of birds.

Now extremely hungry, Niall abbreviated the next part of his tale even more. He said nothing of the fact that the Spider Lord proved to be a female, for he felt this should not be spoken about in front of the captain. Neither did he speak of the direct intervention of the goddess. Instead, he explained that he had told the spider council about his encounter with the goddess, and that this was why he had been elevated to the position of ruler of the spider city.

Gerek asked incredulously: "And they believed you?"

"Of course. They could read my mind."

Gerek was silent. Niall obviously had given him much food for thought.

A few minutes later he brought the gelbs to a halt. "Do you feel hungry yet?"

"Very!"

The borders of the lake were covered with thick blue moss, which cushioned their feet. Gerek released the gelbs from the shafts, and they immediately began to eat this. More surprisingly, they also waded into the lake, and began to take mouthfuls of the yellow weed, which hung down from their faces like beards.

Gerek said: "This is called grilweed, and is regarded as a great delicacy. Try it."

He kicked off his shoes, waded into the water, and took a handful of the weed, some of which was a quarter of an inch thick. Niall accepted it dubiously, but was agreeably surprised. Grilweed was crunchy and had a delicious flavor, like a slightly peppery form of sweet corn.

Gerek said: "The flavor disappears when it is transported to the city. It seems to be due to some peculiar electrical property of the cliff."

It was true that the weed produced a light electrical sensation on the tongue.

Niall removed his sandals and walked into the water. He was immediately aware of a much stronger electrical current, and when he immersed his hands it became stronger than ever.

The captain tasted a fragment of the grilweed, but obviously did not find it to his taste.

Gerek said: "The lake is also well stocked with fish."

The captain immediately showed more interest, and waded out into the water. But his legs soon became entangled in the grilweed, which formed a thick mat on the surface. Gerek went to the cart and opened a compartment under the seat; from this he took a blue device that seemed to consist mainly of a flat piece of metal about a foot square. It had a handle, not unlike that of a saw. Niall and the captain watched curiously as Gerek waded cautiously into the water, where the gelbs had cleared a space in the grilweed, and plunged the metal sheet down to arm's length. He pressed a switch, and there was a humming sound.

"What does that do?"

"Attracts the fish."

After about a minute, Gerek reached into the water with his other hand, and it came out with a plump fish, which he handed to the captain. It was a foot long and, like the fishes in the other lake, made only feeble attempts to escape. The captain waded ashore, turned his back for the sake of politeness, and ate hungrily.

Gerek meanwhile caught two more fishes, which he left to wriggle on the moss. He returned to the cart and took from the compartment a blue device that might have been a short rapier with a handguard dividing the handle from the blade. He pushed the blade down the throat of one of the fishes and pressed a button on the handle. There was a humming sound, and within a minute, the air was full of the appetizing smell of freshly cooked fish. From the cart Gerek took two plates and cutlery, then switched off the rapier, and slid the fish onto a plate. He handed this to Niall.

"Try it with the grilweed—they go well together."

He was right. The perfectly cooked fish was juicy, but needed something to give it flavor; the crunchy, peppery grilweed complemented it perfectly.

They ate their meal in a leisurely manner, stretched out on the thick moss. Niall twisted off a handful of this and tasted it; the consistency was like raw cauliflower. He washed it down with lake water, which was clear and sweet, and prickly on the tongue. After eating two large fishes, the captain fell asleep. Niall himself placed his head on a mossy stone and closed his eyes. The silence was broken only by the crackling of lightning, which frequently struck the cliff. The gelbs, having eaten their fill of the weed, stood there without stirring. Gerek also lay down with his head on a clump of moss.

Niall asked: "How old is the karvasid?"

Gerek yawned. "No one is quite sure. He came here about four hundred years ago."

"How has he been able to live so long?"

"He says that anyone can live to any age they like. He told Typhon that prolonging old age is just like staying awake when you feel sleepy. You have to make sure that you stay interested in something. And then you get a kind of second wind."

All this struck Niall as perfectly plausible. He asked: "Do the people of Shadowland believe in the goddess?"

"Oh no. At least, not in the superstitious sense."

"What is the superstitious sense?"

"Well, believing that she's a supernatural being." He closed his eyes, then opened them suddenly. "Incidentally, the karvasid will be very interested to hear that the goddess is simply an intelligent vegetable from another planet."

Niall had a feeling that Gerek had missed his point, but felt too pleasantly drowsy to bother to correct him. He asked: "What did the karvasid think she was?"

"Oh, just a silly superstition of the spiders." He glanced across at the captain, but he was obviously sound asleep after his long morning's walk.

The karvasid, Niall reflected, was obviously another total skeptic.

He closed his eyes and allowed himself to fall asleep; when he opened them again, Gerek was harnessing the gelbs.

The captain was taking advantage of the delay to eat another fish. But he was obviously not really hungry, and left it half finished.

As Niall took his seat, Gerek said: "We have only about a mile to drive, then we have to get out and walk."

Beyond the point where the river flowed into the lake, the drive was uphill. Like the slope above the lake, the hillside was covered with a thick and particularly bright layer of the blue moss, obviously a major source of the city's food supply. The gelbs plodded up the steep slope with no sign of strain—it was obvious they were built for strength and placidity rather than speed.

The river that ran alongside the track had become a cataract. Finally they reached a point where the cart obviously could go no farther. Here a level space had been cut into the hillside, only a few feet from the water that thundered past, filling the air with drops of spray. Horses would have been nervous, but the gelbs stood there as if they were deaf.

From the box under the seat, Gerek now produced two tubular objects, each six inches long, which Niall recognized as electric flashlights. He handed one to Niall and dropped the other into his own pocket.

Ahead of them lay a narrow and twisting path that became increasingly steep and slippery with spray from the stream that roared deafeningly past a few feet away. Birds were flying in and out of the spray, enjoying the shower bath. After climbing for half an hour, the sight of the drop below made the skin contract on Niall's scalp.

By now, they were all soaked from head to foot. Then, to Niall's relief, the path and the stream diverged. Looking up, he could see the point, fifty feet above them, where the water issued from the cliff. But their own path was becoming harder—so steep that steps had been cut into the rock face. Finally, to Niall's relief, they encountered a metal rail that had been set into the cliff, and Niall clung to it until his knuckles became white.

The most frightening moment occurred when lightning struck the cliff face twenty feet above them, and started a miniature avalanche. As stones bounced past him and alarmed birds flew up from below, Niall clung to the rail with both hands. He was relieved that the lightning had not struck the rail.

Steps finally led them into a cave entrance on a level with the emerging stream. Again, alarmed birds flew out past them. Tool marks on the walls and ceiling of the cave showed that it was not natural, but had been cut out of the rock. Niall scrambled ten feet into the darkness, then sat down on the floor, his back against the wall, relieved to be able to rest. He was breathless, and his knees ached. Gerek sank down beside him. Even the spider, whose head and back were scraping the ceiling, was breathing heavily.

The captain suddenly reacted with a hiss, staring into the depths of the cave. This was dark, since the pale blue daylight failed to reach more than a few feet beyond the entrance. As Niall gaped with horror, a huge figure loomed out of the darkness.

Gerek said: "Don't worry—it's only the guard."

But what astonished Niall was that the naked moog, looking like some great marble statue, had no head. He found himself laughing simply to release nervous tension.

"He seems to have lost his head."

Gerek shone his light on the moog, and Niall saw that the creature had one eye, in the center of its chest. This was staring at them unblinkingly.

Gerek said: "That is to make him more frightening to intruders."

Niall asked with astonishment: "Do you have intruders?"

Gerek grunted. "Sometimes people try to escape to the upper world."

The words startled Niall. He had taken it for granted that the moog was there to guard the northern entrance of Shadowland from possible invaders. The notion that it was also there to prevent Shadowlanders from escaping came as a surprise. "Escape" seemed to imply a prison.

But he only had to look at Gerek's cheerful, open face to feel reassured. Such a person could never be involved in cruelty or oppression.

With Gerek leading, they squeezed past the moog, whose vast bulk occupied most of the narrow cave. Then the tunnel made a left-hand turn, and the roaring of the water became deafening. A dozen feet farther, and they found themselves on a kind of bridge that had been carved out of the rock; the stream rushed below them, creating a continuous flow of wind. Always fascinated by rushing water, Niall halted to gaze down, and was interested to see that the stream divided into two. Half of it flowed under the bridge, toward the point where it emerged from the cliff, while the other half plunged down into a kind of sinkhole.

"Where does it go?"

"To the lower levels."

Across the bridge, the path turned uphill, and they were soon walking with the stream on their right. There was a drop of ten feet to the surface of the water. This cave, whose ceiling was only a few feet above their heads, obviously had been carved out of the rock by the water, which had gradually widened and deepened it.

In effect, they were walking on a riverbank that ascended toward the surface. The water had worn it smooth underfoot, but rock projections above meant that continued vigilance had to be observed if they wanted to avoid striking their heads. But finally a point came where the walls of the tunnel stretched above them, and they could walk comfortably upright. It was no longer a tunnel but a kind of underground canyon, where the river had to make its way around giant rocks that had collapsed from the ceiling. No longer reflected off the walls, the roar of the water became less deafening.

At one point the river plunged over a waterfall fifty feet high; but a tunnel with steps had been carved into the rock, and they climbed up as if inside a tower, and came out where the water flowed over the fall. Niall preferred not to look down; this ascent was beginning to make him breathless.

The spider, with his ability to see in the dark, had been walking ahead, probably impatient of the slow progress of the short-legged humans. A few hundred yards beyond the waterfall, Niall sensed the captain's excitement, and caught his first glimpse of daylight far above them. At the same time, he sensed the spider's flash of alarm, and shone his flashlight into the darkness. The massive form of another headless moog, even bigger than the first, was standing guard by the side of the path. The solitary eye in its chest followed them as they went past.

A quarter of an hour later, daylight was streaming down into the canyon, whose precipitous dark sides showed why it had been called the Black Gorge. There Niall caught his first glimpse of the sun in two days. It was early afternoon in the world above, and the sunlight was reflected on the river, which was now flowing peacefully into the gorge. Niall had never thought that he would feel so glad to see the sun again, and to feel its warmth on top of his head. Suddenly he understood why this valley to the north of Shadowland had been called the Vale of Thanksgiving.

Half a mile farther, and they had emerged from the canyon into a broad meadow that was, in effect, a saddleback between two peaks. The grass was damp—evidently it had recently been raining—and sent up a light mist. The air was fragrant and remarkably warm for October, and full of the sound of birds. Niall found himself laughing spontaneously out of sheer exhilaration. He could imagine how Sathanas and his companions had felt when, after their first winter underground, they emerged into the spring sunshine.

The warmth and sunlight had already caused his tiredness to dissolve away, and he walked with long strides as he followed Gerek through the soft grass toward the lower of the two peaks, which faced north. This was not more than five hundred feet high, and when they stood on top of it, he was able to look down onto a steep slope that plunged down to a valley a mile below. The wind from the snow-covered peaks to the north was chilly, and made Niall shiver—he was covered in perspiration—yet this green valley between the two peaks trapped the sun, so that its temperature was that of a summer afternoon.

The captain had taken the opportunity to fold his legs underneath him and drowse in the sunlight. When they descended again, Niall and Gerek did the same, flinging themselves down on the damp grass; Niall lay with half-closed eyes, soothed by the sound of birds.

A few yards away, two sparrows were quarreling over a worm, stretching it out like a piece of elastic, when a larger bird swooped between them and stole it. The glossy black feathers and yellow beak seemed familiar, and when it settled on a bush a few yards away to eat its prize, Niall probed its mind; it was, as he thought, the raven. But it obviously felt some doubt about approaching him with another human being lying within a few feet. And when Gerek suddenly yawned and stretched, it flew away.

Gerek sat up, and pointed at the other peak.

"Are you ready for another climb?"

Niall would happily have stayed where he was, but heaved himself to his feet and followed Gerek.

This ascent took longer; but when they reached the top, Niall understood why Gerek had taken them there. Down below to the south lay fertile slopes with orchards, vineyards with trellises, and patches of brown that were obviously cultivated fields.

Gerek said with pride: "This is the larder of Shadowland." He pointed to a wooded hillside across the valley. "And that is our wood supply."

"Do you burn it?"

"Oh no!" Gerek looked almost shocked. "That would be a waste. Besides, we have plenty of coal and electricity."

A river glittered far below, and Niall could hear the distant lowing of cows. The opposite mountainside was covered with sheep. Between here and the next peak, there must have been thousands of acres of rich farmland.

Gerek said: "Now you can understand why people sometimes try to escape." The breeze blew his hair across his eyes. "You can also see why the karvasid wants to make a truce with the spiders."

Gazing across the valley, Niall could not even glimpse the southern part of the gray mountains; Skollen was a hundred miles away, and too many tall peaks stood between them. This secret place, with its meadows and orchards, and with mountains to the east and west, was a perfect refuge. No wonder the Magician had been so delighted when the spiders built the Great Wall and guaranteed that his haven should remain undiscovered.

Niall said: "We shall be glad to make a truce. Then your people and ours can get to know one another."

Yet even as he heard himself saying these words, a sudden doubt crossed his mind like a shadow. Would the Magician really want the people of Shadowland to mix freely with other human beings?

Half an hour later, they were again entering the cool shadows of the Black Gorge and starting the descent to Shadowland. The captain led the way, and this time Niall decided to establish contact with his mind so that he could also see in the dark. The increased visibility, and the fact that they were now traveling downhill, made the return journey pass quickly, and in what seemed an amazingly short time, they had emerged on the steep slope above the lake where, only three hours earlier, they had stopped to eat. Soon they could see the gelbs a quarter of a mile below them, as motionless as if carved out of wood.

It was soon after three o'clock when they climbed back into the cart. Niall asked: "Where now?"

Gerek pointed to the southeast. "Can you see that smoke?"

"I think so." He could see something that looked like mist or fog.

"That is the entrance to the lower levels."

"And what are the lower levels?"

"I suppose you could say they're the industrial heart of Shadowland."

Since the spider city had no industry, the phrase meant nothing to Niall.

When they were once more on the flat plain, Gerek urged the gelbs to a fast trot.

"We don't want to be late. The karvasid is an obsessive about punctuality."

It amused Niall to hear him talking in this vaguely disrespectful way about the Magician, indicating that he regarded him as fallible.

Half a mile beyond the lake, they turned left onto a road that was less well marked; the hard surface looked as if it had been worn by the wheels of carts. Now the smoke that Gerek had pointed out was clearly visible, although it looked less like smoke than a broken and irregular column of semitransparent cloud, stretching upward like the outline of a ruined tower.

A mile or so farther on, Gerek pointed upward, and Niall was surprised to see an immense hole in the smoky blue sky, stretching upward like a giant chimney.

Niall leaned back and peered up. "What is it?"

"The pipe of a volcano we call Holkerri. It means the cloud-scraper."

The column of broken cloud stirred something in Niall's memory; then he remembered: it was the cloud he had seen in his dream, stretching upward like a shimmering curtain of beads.

This broken mist was rising out of a crater at least five miles across. Niall felt a twinge of alarm as they passed over its rim, for although the slope beyond was not steep, there was a wide hole at its center, from which the steamlike smoke was issuing as if from a volcano. But the gelbs trotted on as briskly as if they did this journey every day.

A moment later, Gerek confirmed Niall's suspicion when he said: "This is where I come to work."

As they drew closer to the hole, Niall was relieved to see a wooden building balanced on its edge. From the depth below came a roaring sound, like an underground river. The smoke, which was slightly but not unpleasantly sulfurous, hung around them like a fog.

The door of the hut was opened by a moog, whose marble face was expressionless. The gelbs trotted inside, and the moog closed the door behind them. Gerek dismounted from the cart, but as Niall started to do the same, said: "You may as well stay where you are." He led the gelbs to the far side of the hut, beckoning the captain to follow.

Suddenly the walls of the hut began to rise into the air, and it took several seconds for Niall to realize that the floor was descending. They passed a giant pulley wheel set in the side of the gulf, and continued down slowly to the bottom of the shaft, a distance Niall judged to be about a quarter of a mile. As they descended, the roaring noise became louder, and when the lift stopped, it was deafening. They drew level with another giant pulley wheel, whose surface was covered with thick black grease, and Niall stared at it with awe. He had never before seen a mechanism on this scale.

As the wooden floor jarred to a halt, Niall was able to see that the roaring noise came from a tall metal structure at the bottom of the shaft. The steam-colored smoke was pouring out of a chimney in its roof; the roaring noise was evidently an immense fan.

Niall was glad to see that this lower level of Shadowland was lit by the same blue glow, although it was appreciably weaker than up above. Gerek climbed back into his seat and shook the reins, and the gelbs trotted forward.

The air down here was full of a smoke that stung his eyes and made him cough. It was billowing into a semicircular tunnel, whose roof was twenty feet above their heads, and whose walls were covered in soot. The wind that blew in their faces carried fragments of grit like sand, and Niall had to remove a cinder from his eye. A quarter of a mile farther on, the tunnel came to an end and so did the wind, which obviously was being sucked in by the fan at the bottom of the shaft.

The road they were now following was a few yards from a railway line, on the far side of which there were sidings with dozens of V-shaped metal trucks. On the other side of the road there was a deep quarry, twice as big as the one near the city of the bombardier beetles, with more railway lines across its floor; these vanished into a tunnel in its far wall.

His ears still ringing from the roar of the fan, Niall pointed at it and asked: "What's that?"

"The entrance to the third level. That is where we mine coal and iron. If we have time I'll show you."

Niall received this promise without enthusiasm; he was already finding the second level cold and depressing. The air made his eyes sting and constricted his lungs.

He asked Gerek: "Where do you work?"

"Everywhere." Gerek gestured all around. "I supervise the machinery in the factories."

For a moment Niall failed to understand what he was talking about. Then a fragment of knowledge implanted by the learning machine came to the surface, and he remembered that a factory was a building where goods were manufactured.

The factories Gerek was pointing at were long, low buildings with chimneys from which smoke issued.

He asked Niall: "Would you like to see inside one?" Without waiting for a reply, he turned the gelbs into a factory yard, and climbed down. Niall did the same; the ground underfoot was made of hard-packed cinders that crunched as they walked. On the far side of the yard were huge metal sections that Niall recognized immediately as part of the iron wall that surrounded the city above. Dozens of them were stacked together against the factory.

Niall and the captain followed Gerek across the yard. The building was constructed of square gray blocks with a rough surface. Gerek grasped a handle and pulled with both hands; a door slid open, and they were surrounded by the noise of machinery and the smell of grease. The workshop beyond was brightly lit by tubes attached to the ceiling, and men and women in gray clothes stood in front of machines of many kinds: tall, upright machines, low, flat machines, machines with metal domes and flashing lights. Niall was interested to observe that some of the men had square heads, like the man he had glimpsed that morning, and that most of the women had circular eyes.

The woman who stood at the nearest machine glanced around as she felt the draft from the door, and her mouth fell open in shock as she saw the captain. Gerek smiled at her reassuringly, and she turned back to her machine, which was grinding out iron rivets. Niall pretended not to have noticed her reaction, simulating interest in the lights on the ceiling. But her shocked face made him aware that she had never before seen a giant spider. Comparing this with his observation in the Hall of Entertainment, when the couple had entered from the street and had not even given the spider a second glance, he drew an inescapable conclusion: that they had been prepared, and the woman in the factory had not.

Niall was not surprised when, a moment later, Gerek beckoned them out into the yard and slid the door behind them.

They drove further along the road, past the squat gray shapes of more factories. One building on the corner was quite different; it was smaller, and painted in bright colors, which were now fading under the grime that had settled on it.

"What is that?"

"It used to be the nursery school."

The thought of a nursery in this gloomy place was somehow unsettling.

The cart turned a corner, and Niall found himself looking at the most impressive building he had seen so far. It was many hundreds of yards square, and at first glance seemed to be a palace. It was three stories high, but in each corner there was a square tower that was twice as high. The whole building blazed with lighted windows, while a long walkway with colonnades and lighted lamps ran along its frontage.

Gerek explained: "This is the living quarters of the workers."

There was a note of pride in his voice, and Niall could not help feeling impressed. No workers in the spider city had living quarters as magnificent as this.

"But why is it so huge?"

"It was built in the days when we had more labor."

Gerek led the way up the steps and through a double door in the center of the front. What lay beyond was a hall-like space with comfortable chairs, and a floor covered with a thick gray carpet. Niall was reminded of a similar building in the spider city; it had once been a hotel, but was now deserted, and full of remnants of past splendor, such as chandeliers and tall mirrors.

Gerek led them across the floor and out of a door on the far side; they found themselves in a wide, carpeted corridor. An attractive girl came out of a door carrying a handbrush and shovel, and went off in the opposite direction. She was wearing a gray skirt and blouse, and Gerek looked appreciatively at her shapely legs.

He then led them to the far end of the corridor and pushed open a door. A pleasant smell of cooking wafted out.

"The kitchen." It looked rather like the kitchen in Niall's palace, but bigger, and with more cooks bustling about. These were all dressed in white smocks and tall white hats.

There was a sudden loud, continuous hooting sound that made Niall jump. "What on earth's that?"

The noise stopped.

"The signal that the day's work is finished."

Niall looked at his watch; it was five o'clock. In the spider city the working day did not finish until six.

Gerek opened another door. "And that is the main dining room." It was enormous, with long wooden tables and wooden chairs. "And here," he opened another door, "is the gymnasium and swimming pool."

Rather overwhelmed, but feeling that some response was required, Niall said: "You treat your workers very well."

Gerek said with a smile: "I don't think they have anything to complain about."

Suddenly the corridor was filled with men and women, who streamed through the door from the lobby. Many of the men had the square heads that Niall had already noted, while the majority of the women had round eyes. All had the relaxed and cheerful air of workers who have finished a long day. What struck Niall was that they were speaking aloud, and not communicating telepathically. Yet there was none of the clamor that filled the slave quarter in the spider city when the day's work was finished; these workers spoke in quiet, controlled voices, like people coming out of a lecture in the city of the beetles. All went up a flight of stairs at the end of the corridor. Niall was curious to note that none of them paid the least attention to the captain.

Niall said to Gerek: "They speak aloud here?"

"Ah, yes. That is permitted on the second level. Not, of course, if they come to our city. There they have to follow our rules."

Soon the corridor was empty and silent again. Niall had observed that the men had turned to the left at the top of the stairs, and the women to the right. A speculation occurred to him.

"Where are they all going now?"

"To their rooms to change out of their working clothes. Dinner is at six."

"And why do the women all go one way, and the men the other?"

"Because the women's quarters are to the left and the men's to the right."

"They live separately?"

"Oh yes."

So Niall's guess had been correct; men and women were kept apart here, as in the spider city before Niall became ruler.

"Why is that?"

Gerek shrugged. He seemed surprised that Niall had bothered to ask. "It has always been like that. I think perhaps it dates to the early days of Shadowland, when there were far more men than women. It would have been unfair to allow one man to have a woman all to himself, so the women were shared."

"But . . . don't some men and woman live together as husbands and wives?"

"No, that is not allowed."

A second wave of workers poured down the corridor and, like the previous ones, separated at the top of the stairs. Niall persisted: "Don't couples ever prefer to live together?"

"For what purpose? They are fed here, and there is nothing to stop them from spending the night in one another's rooms. So why should they want to move in with one another permanently? It would only be an inconvenience to both."

"But don't they ever fall in love?"

Gerek looked amused.

"The karvasid regards that as a form of illusion. Surely no man wants to spend his whole life with the same woman? It takes away his freedom."

Niall reflected on his own preference for remaining unmarried, and had to agree that there was something to be said for Gerek's view.

"But what about in the days when couples had children?"

"The children were taken away from them and brought up by specially trained carers."

Niall was disturbed. So far, he had been impressed by what he had seen of Shadowland, but Gerek's words aroused unpleasant memories of the spider city in the days when men and women were kept apart.

Gerek seemed to read Niall's thoughts. He gestured at a new wave of workers flooding through the doors.

"Do they look unhappy?"

Niall had to admit that they didn't.

"You see? The karvasid regards family life as unnatural. Every man wants more than one woman."

"What about the women?"

"They prefer more than one man."

Niall was thoughtful as Gerek showed them over the second floor—recreation rooms, living quarters, even a reading room, although there were very few books, and what there was looked very old. By now, most of the people they saw had changed out of their working uniforms and into their leisure clothes, which were dark blue.

Finally, Gerek looked at his watch.

"It's time we returned to the first level, or we shall be late."

As they were leaving the building, they encountered another crowd of workers. Since it was now half past five, these evidently worked to a different schedule. They also looked quite different from any Shadowlanders Niall had seen so far, having longer necks and elongated heads that reminded him of lightbulbs.

Gerek explained: "They are another of the karvasid's experiments. After the failure of the square heads, he decided that people with long necks are more intelligent than those with short necks. He proved to be right. They are particularly good at calculating, so they are used as office workers."

As they were about to climb into the cart, a pretty, pale-haired girl of the long-neck type approached them. Her circular eyes were blue. Gerek glanced at her nervously.

"Not now, Dimpney. I have to go."

But the girl was not to be put off. She placed her hand on his arm with a pleading gesture, and after a muttered "Excuse me," Gerek withdrew out of earshot, and listened as she talked earnestly. Finally, he spoke quietly but intensely for a few moments, then shook his head and turned away from her. The girl hesitated, and walked away. Gerek climbed into the cart, and sighed.

"There is an example of why men and women do not live together in Shadowland. She is my secretary, but she is becoming possessive."

"You regard that as bad?"

"In Shadowland it is regarded as a serious fault."

He shook the reins impatiently and the gelbs trotted forward.

Niall was amused. He had often seen Veig in similar situations. With a touch of good-humored malice, he said: "What do you intend to do about her?"

Gerek snorted. "Get myself another secretary."

The gelbs obviously knew where to go; they turned back the way they had come. Gerek occasionally shook the reins to make them go faster, looking at his watch.

The road back past the factories was now deserted, although they occasionally passed a solitary pedestrian, still wearing the gray work uniform. Niall pointed at one of these, a thin, baldheaded man with a gray mustache.

"Where do you suppose he's going?"

"I don't know. Some people like to walk around when they've finished work. I once asked one of them where she was going, and she said she didn't like being among a crowd all day." He shook his head in bewilderment.

"Isn't that natural?"

Gerek looked surprised. "I don't think so. The karvasid goes to a great deal of trouble to make sure the workers are comfortable and well fed. Why should they want to be alone?"

They were passing the quarry with the entrance to the third level, and Gerek interrupted himself to say: "I'm afraid we shan't have time to go down there after all. But I don't think you would have enjoyed it anyway."

"Why not?"

"It contains nothing but mines. Even I try to avoid it as much as I can."

Soon they entered the wide tunnel, with its throat-catching smell of soot and coal smoke. A few minutes later, the gelbs halted at the bottom of the shaft, with its giant fan that still belched clouds of white smoke. The lift was where they had left it. Gerek drove the cart onto the platform and pressed the button. As they began slowly to ascend, he suddenly looked more cheerful.

"Ah, this is the part I always enjoy." He turned to the captain and spoke telepathically. "I hope you have enjoyed your tour of Shadowland?"

The captain replied with formal courtesy: "Thank you. I found it very instructive."

Niall suspected that he meant more than the words conveyed.

I t had been a long day, and as the cart rattled across the flat landscape toward the city, Niall reflected that it seemed strange to be
surrounded by the same even blue daylight when his body clock
told him it should be approaching dusk. In fact, the light here was so
much brighter than on the second level that it created an illusory sense
of dawn.

His mind reverted to a question that had occurred to him in the factory hostel.

"Don't the workers object to wearing the same dull clothes all the
time?"

"Why should they?"

"Well, women, for example, prefer pretty clothes, like those worn
by the women in your city."

Gerek smiled.

"Ah, but they are not real colors. They are created by the illusion
machines." When Niall looked blank he said: "You asked me this morning about the conical towers and I explained they store electricity. But
they affect your sense of sight, so you see colored stripes. They also
affect your sense of smell, so you think you are breathing pleasant
scents. What scent do you smell when you are near the towers?"

"A sweet smell, like cotton candy."

Gerek turned to the captain. "And you?"

"The smell of flies that have been trapped in a web for a week."

Gerek smiled at Niall. "You see?"

Niall asked Gerek: "And what do you smell?"

"A scent like roses, my favorite flower."

Niall asked: "Why does the karvasid not build illusion machines on
the second level?"

"It would be too costly. Besides, the workers have been taught to
enjoy the smell of smoke."

"Taught? How?"

Gerek chuckled.

"That is one of his secrets. Ask Typhon—he understands it."

They had passed over the rim of the crater, and since, on this flat terrain, there was no reason to stick to the northern track, Gerek was driving the cart directly toward the city, which Niall guessed to be about ten miles away.

What Gerek had said interested him deeply. Now that he understood about the illusion machines, Niall found himself thinking about the old woman he had seen from his bedroom window that morning, who in spite of her wrinkled face had struck him as oddly attractive. Then there was the woman he had seen driving in a cart the day before, and toward whom he had again experienced that same instant feeling of attraction. Was this the effect of the illusion machines?

If so, what about his brother Veig, who fell in love at least once a week, always with the same kind of pretty face? The girls who attracted Veig might have been created by the same doll maker. Clearly, he was hopelessly susceptible to illusions.

At this point, his complacency was disturbed by the thought that his own response to Princess Merlew was equally automatic. He knew she was spoiled and self-centered, yet he experienced the same powerful attraction every time he looked at her. Surely her attractiveness was real—some magnetism that had been bestowed on her by nature, not by his own mind?

Or was nature itself a trickster? That thought disturbed him deeply, unsettling the foundations of things he took for granted.

Then he had a thought that restored his cheerfulness: that when the guard was leading him to Typhon's house, he had been able to control the intensity of the illusions. If he concentrated hard, the colors became richer and deeper. So he was not simply being sucked into a web of deception: his own mind played an active part. And in the same way, Veig was not simply being taken in by pretty faces; he wanted to be taken in. With that insight, his momentary pessimism evaporated.

Half an hour later, the pointed shapes of the conical towers appeared on the horizon. At this distance they were gray. He watched them closely as they approached, waiting for the first sign of color. When they were a few hundred yards from the gate—the same gate by which Niall had entered before—faint red, blue, and yellow stripes appeared. This faintness was not the effect of distance, for a moment later they deepened into full color.

The guard opened the gate and saluted. This was not the same man as yesterday, and as they went past him, Niall tried probing his mind. The result was disappointing. The guard obviously was unaware of what Niall was doing; but his mind was a blank, conscious only of the present moment, and of vague anticipations of his next meal.

As soon as they entered the avenue of the conical towers, Niall observed a change in the atmosphere. Most of the towers had steam issuing from vents close to the top, and the colors were undoubtedly brighter, giving them a festive air. Since Niall now knew that they were "illusion machines," he recognized that the towers themselves must be responsible for this effect. Even the sky above them looked different; it seemed to shimmer with a brighter blue.

People were sitting on the benches; one-wheeled bicycles lay on the ground, and many carts with gelbs were standing nearby. These citizens had clearly made special trips to be close to the towers at this evening time of day. As their cart passed one of the towers, Niall experienced a warm glow, a sudden feeling of lightheartedness, which became fainter when it was behind them, but increased again as they approached the next tower.

Meanwhile, the atmosphere was heavy with steam that was hissing from the cracks in the ground, so that a thin layer of moisture condensed on Niall's face. The steam had the typical sweet cotton candy smell, but there was more than that. As he breathed in deeply, Niall seemed to be able to detect other scents: for example, the rose petals Gerek had mentioned, and many more. This, surely, was the Magician's way of compensating his subjects for living in this rather dreary land? The total effect was intoxicating.

It was also fascinating and mysterious. Niall had experienced illusions before—auditory as well as visual—when he was in the Delta; but those were some kind of hypnotic force exuded by the plants. The illusions of Shadowland were an effect devised by the Magician. Could it be due to some chemical substance in the steam? Or to some subtle vibration that affected the brain?

The gelbs halted in front of Typhon's mansion, and the guard threw open the gate. As they entered the courtyard, the fountain leapt higher, as if greeting them with a glittering array of color, and once again Niall responded with a sense of delight.

Katia came toward them with a tray with glasses of a sparkling orange-red drink. She was obviously delighted to see them again—perhaps bored with being alone—and her smile made her tiny protruding front teeth seem charming. Only this morning Niall had thought she was pleasantly attractive but certainly not pretty; now she seemed delightful, and the weak chin no longer seemed to matter.

Gerek took her earlobe between his finger and thumb and said: "You're looking lovely this evening."

She laughed with pleasure and replied telepathically: "That's not me. That's just the karvasid's machines."

Her reply surprised Niall. So the illusion machines were common knowledge?

But as he drained the glass—the atmosphere of the second level had made his throat dry—he reflected that it was better to see a girl as pretty rather than only minimally attractive. After all, falling in love had the same power.

In his room he found his own tunic on the bed; it had been washed and ironed. Although it was of coarser material than the one he was wearing, he decided to change into it. It reminded him somehow of his purpose in being in Shadowland. As, half an hour later, they prepared to leave for the palace, Niall asked: "Will Typhon be returning here?"

"No. He will be at the palace until dawn."

The captain asked: "Would it not be better if I remained here?" Niall sensed that he felt uncomfortable at the thought of mixing with a crowd of humans.

"Oh no. The karvasid would wonder where you were."

As they left, Katia stood at the door; she looked at Niall with a sad expression.

"You're lucky to be invited to the palace. I've never been there."

As they were climbing into the cart, Niall asked Gerek: "Couldn't you arrange an invitation?"

Gerek seemed slightly shocked.

"Oh no. Servants are not allowed."

When they reached the bridge across the river, Niall was surprised by the number of carts drawn by gelbs, and by the crowds of pedestrians on the sidewalks. Even the blue-green waves of the river seemed to share in the holiday atmosphere. The only thing that seemed strange was that it was all so silent. This, he knew, was an illusion, since all these people were engaged in telepathic communication.

Niall asked Gerek: "Who are the people who have been invited?"

"Some are privileged citizens—those who have contributed to the welfare of the city. Then there are many guests from the two levels— overseers, managers, supervisors."

"Any workers?"

"Yes, one from each factory. They are the ones who have achieved the highest production."

"And what is this reception for?"

"Twice a year all the managers and overseers present their reports in a general meeting. This should be ending about now."

"Does the karvasid preside over the meeting?"

"No. He dislikes dealing with people. Typhon acts as his intermediary. The karvasid will make an appearance later."

They took the road that led directly to the palace, whose green front was illuminated by floodlights. With its Roman arches and strong, thick columns, it looked like something built in antiquity. The road itself was made of a sandy-colored stone speckled with white and black, and since the surface was smooth and unbroken, Niall assumed it was some form of cement. Five hundred yards along, the road was divided by a roundabout, in the center of which stood an enormous dark tree, whose trunk must have been five feet in diameter. Its seaweed-colored leaves gleamed in the light of the circle of lamps that surrounded it. Its huge branches seemed carved out of stone.

Niall asked: "What kind of a tree is that?"

Gerek said: "It is not a 'kind' of tree. It is *the* kalinda tree, which was planted by the karvasid before the city was founded." He smiled, as if he wanted Niall to know he did not blame him for his ignorance.

"Where did it come from?"

"The Vale of Thanksgiving."

A moment later, as they passed the roundabout, Niall experienced an unmistakable sense of power that emanated from the tree, so strong that it made his nerves tingle. He asked: "What are those women doing?"

Several woman, scarcely visible in the darkness under the branches, were facing the trunk, and apparently embracing it.

"Hoping to conceive. They think it has magical properties."

The road that led from the kalinda tree to the palace was impressive, for it was the only road in this city that ran uphill. At least a hundred carts with gelbs were waiting in line along the road, but Gerek drove straight past them all, over a drawbridge across a moat, then through two farther gateways to ten-foot-high bronze doors that stood wide open. The Magician, Niall reflected, liked to impress his subjects.

Close to these gates, the carts had formed something of a traffic jam; this was due to the fact that two of them had locked their wheels. As Niall watched, two very tall men emerged from the gates and strode over to the obstruction. Niall guessed their height to be seven feet. Both had gaunt, angular faces and big ears; their hair was bright red. The purposeful way they strode suggested that the drivers of the carts were in trouble.

What happened then was that each of the men grasped a cart on the outside and gave a violent heave. The interlocked wheels both came off and rolled down the slope, while the unbalanced carts tilted over, spilling out the couples who had been in them. The two guards pointed back down the hill, and their meaning was unmistakable. Even from twenty yards away, Niall could see that both couples looked shattered, and that the women—who were wearing bright party dresses—were close to tears.

Niall asked Gerek: "Can't we do anything for them?"

Gerek shook his head. "Unfortunately, no."

"But don't you have the authority?"

"Not here. That's the man in charge." He pointed to a big man with a black mustache and jutting chin, who waved at Gerek. "Jelko's the commander of the Palace Guard. But even he wouldn't dare to show partiality. You see, everybody must obey the law. When you've been here a few days you'll begin to understand."

The two couples were walking back down the hill looking listless and miserable. Niall was saddened—so much so that he felt he had lost all appetite for the party.

The two seven-foot giants were directing the carts to a large courtyard to the left; their manner struck Niall as rude and peremptory. They saluted Gerek and allowed him to drive into an empty courtyard to the right, although one of them looked as if he intended to question the captain's right of entry. But since even this giant stood six inches shorter than the spider, he seemed to change his mind.

Niall was not mollified by their special treatment; he was still thinking of the disappointment of the two couples who had been turned away. He asked Gerek: "Why are they so rude and irritable?"

Gerek said evenly: "That is their job. They are here to keep order."

At close quarters, Niall could see that the stone of which the palace was built was not natural. Like the material of the approach road, it was flecked with black and white fragments, and consisted of blocks three feet long and eighteen inches tall. Niall nevertheless had to acknowledge that it was more impressive than the black marble of the Spider Lord's palace.

They dismounted and went through the nearest door. The room was evidently an office, with a desk and file cases. Since the walls were made of undecorated green stone, this looked incongruous.

Gerek said: "This is Typhon's office." He motioned Niall to take the comfortable chair behind the desk, and opened a cupboard, from which he removed a carafe of golden wine and some tumblers.

"We don't want to go in yet. We'll only have to make conversation." He looked at his watch. "The committee meeting should be over by now." There was a sound of footsteps in the corridor. "Ah, this should be Typhon."

Typhon seemed surprised to find them there. Niall thought he looked tired and preoccupied. Nevertheless he smiled at Niall and the captain, and Niall was again struck by his good manners.

Gerek poured wine into a tumbler and held it out to him. Typhon shook his head. "No, I won't drink."

Gerek looked surprised. "Why not?"

"It wasn't a good meeting. Nearly everyone had failed to meet the new production targets."

Gerek groaned. "Oh no! What went wrong?"

"I don't know. But the karvasid is going to be displeased."

Gerek was looking concerned.

Niall asked: "What are the new production targets?"

"There are still five miles of the city wall to be built. It was supposed to be finished by January. Now that's impossible."

Niall was puzzled. "I don't understand. Surely a wall is to keep out enemies? And if the treaty is signed, it won't be necessary."

For a moment, Typhon and Gerek looked blank, as if Niall had said something incomprehensible. Then Typhon smiled.

"Yes, you have a point." He turned to Gerek. "I'll have that drink after all." He accepted a tumbler from Gerek and raised it. "To the peace treaty."

Niall raised his glass and drank. But he still had a feeling that there was something that had not been said.

After what he considered a polite interval, he asked the question that had never been far from his thoughts: "Did you speak to the karvasid about my brother Veig?"

"Indeed I did. He says he will speak to you about it later. But when I told him that it happened a week ago, he seemed to feel there was no urgency."

"And did you speak to him about the peace treaty?"

"Of course. And like me, he was baffled by how a boy like you became ruler of the spider city."

Gerek said: "I can explain that. Niall told me the story as we were driving out to the northern lake."

"I shall be fascinated to hear it." He turned to Niall. "But now, I wonder if you would excuse us while we go into the next room to discuss some business?"

"Of course."

When they were alone, the captain said: "You realize that something strange is going on?"

"Strange?" Niall's thoughts had been preoccupied with Veig, and with his meeting with the Magician. "In what way?"

He was speaking aloud, and the captain said: "It might be best to speak with our minds."

"Very well. But what makes you suspicious?"

"To begin with, I am sure we were expected."

"I think it possible. But why are you so sure?"

The captain hesitated. He did not find it easy to express his thoughts on the human wavelength; it was obviously like speaking a foreign language.

"In this city, no one has seen a spider before. To them, we are legendary monsters who might eat them alive. Yet no one has shown any surprise at seeing me—except one woman in the factory."

"Yes, I noticed that. But there may be some other explanation. Perhaps she was simply startled to look round and find us there."

The captain projected a sense of polite skepticism.

"And does it not strike you as strange that, when you have come so far to see the Magician, he keeps you waiting a whole day? If an ambassador arrived in the spider city, he would be received immediately. The Magician could have cured your brother today if he had wanted to—Typhon said he could do it from a distance. So why is he keeping you waiting? What does he hope to gain?" He broke off. "They are coming back."

The spider must have been able to pick up their physical vibrations from some distance, for it was at least half a minute before Typhon and Gerek returned. By that time, Niall had poured himself another tumbler of wine, and had dismissed from his mind the mood of doubt, which would otherwise have lingered like an unpleasant smell. But he was aware, from the lingering traces of their own mood, that Typhon and Gerek had been discussing something that had disturbed them.

Typhon said: "Would you like to look over the palace?"

"Very much." Niall had been hoping for this invitation. Aware that his own palace was basically a commercial building, he was curious to know what a real palace was like.

He found it deeply impressive. The floors were tiled with wooden bricks, and the corridors were covered with carved panels of fine workmanship. Having supervised some repairs in his own palace, Niall was aware that this one had been created by skilled craftsmen who must have devoted years to the task.

One thing aroused Niall's curiosity. On either side of the corridor, at regular intervals, beads of green glass were set into the paneling, and as they walked past, these glowed like the eyes of a cat.

"What are these for?"

"They are mechanical eyes. Through them, the karvasid can see whoever is in the palace."

As they walked through a labyrinth of corridors, Niall was struck by the variety of the styles. Some rooms and passageways were decorated in nature motifs, others in an abstract style full of curves, others with patterned tiles whose style he recognized as Moorish. It was as if the karvasid had changed his mind periodically and ordered a different mode of decoration. Many of the rooms had walls of the original green stone—or artificial stone—and dark, heavy furniture; Niall found them impressive but slightly gloomy. In other parts of the palace, the green stone was invisible under paneling.

Niall remarked on this variety of style; Typhon's reply was: "It would be pointless to build a palace without variety." Niall was not convinced. His own palace was simply a comfortable place to live in, like a home. This was more like a museum.

The next room, in fact, was a museum, with glass cases. Niall was struck by a case that contained a lay figure wearing a suit of fine chain mail over a black leather jerkin; the trousers were also made of a kind of wrinkled leather.

Typhon said: "This is the armor worn by the karvasid when he was Captain Sathanas. And these are the leggings he wore during the winter journey to Shadowland."

Niall stared with deep interest at the face, but it might have been a tailor's dummy. It had a forked black beard.

The next case immediately drew Niall's attention. It contained another figure in chain mail and black leather jerkin, taller and more heavily built than Sathanas. The face looked oddly lifelike, although the skin might have been polished wood; the brown eyes were obviously made of glass.

"This is the karvasid's comrade in arms, Vosyl, who discovered the entrance to Shadowland."

"A statue?"

"No. The body is mummified."

Niall stared at it with morbid fascination.

"Are his other comrades here?"

"Not of the original Faithful Band. But that is Darvid Grubin, the grandson of Vosyl, who was commander of the strike force at the time we expected Cheb to invade. He is known as the Hero of Cibilla." Niall gazed at a massive figure that looked as if it was about to stride out of its glass case. "And those are his favorite weapons."

Niall stopped to point. "Isn't that a Reaper?"

The atomic blaster looked oddly out of place among broadswords, battle axes, and other items of medieval weaponry.

"Why, yes." Typhon seemed surprised. "You know about Reapers?"

But before Niall could reply, Gerek had interrupted: "I told him they were invented by the karvasid."

Niall decided that it might be tactful not to pursue the subject, and so simply did his best to look impressed.

The figure in the next case was quite clearly a mummified human being, but was shockingly grotesque. The head was wider at the bottom than at the top, with a huge, flat nose spread out across it as if it had been hit by some heavy object. The thick lips looked as if they were made of rubber, while the tiny eyes, with large bags under them, had difficulty peering out of layers of obesity. The fat body sagged, like a balloon full of water, and the bow legs filled the black leather trousers so tightly that a seam had split apart. It was probably the ugliest human being Niall had ever seen.

Typhon said: "Yes, that is the karvasid's chief steward, Zamco. He served him for thirty years—the best steward he ever had."

Gerek chuckled. "And he couldn't keep his hands off the maids. He got every single one of them pregnant."

"But what was wrong with him?" Niall assumed he was suffering from some disfiguring ailment.

"Oh, nothing. He was one of the karvasid's most successful experiments."

"Experiments?"

"It was once called genetic engineering. But the karvasid made a great discovery—that the genes can be influenced by the unconscious mind, and that the unconscious mind can be accessed by means of vibrations. Have you ever heard of sleep-learning?" Niall nodded. "This is a similar principle."

"But why did he make him so ugly?"

"Because he was testing a theory that ugly people may become the most intelligent. Vosyl was the ugliest member of the Faithful Band, yet the most intelligent and hardworking. He felt he had to compensate for his ugliness by developing other qualities."

Niall looked with distaste at the mummified Zamco.

"I think this was going too far."

Gerek, staring at the mummy, said: "I'm inclined to agree."

"Ah, but it worked. Zamco was the best of servants."

Niall began to wander along the exhibits, but felt no inclination to pause for more than a moment before any one of this gallery of freaks, some fat, some thin, but all deformed or misshapen. He asked: "Why are they all so ugly?"

"Because at that stage the karvasid was working on simple genetic variations, and individual variations tend to be unattractive." He gestured at an exhibit with a nose like a giant strawberry. "Beauty is harmony of many different parts. Introduce one misshapen nose and it turns to ugliness."

"But did he ever create *anything* that wasn't ugly?"

"Oh, many things. In fact, at the risk of sounding immodest, he was responsible for me and Gerek. Both our mothers went through the process of unconscious conditioning."

Gerek smiled. "But Typhon's mother wasn't as suggestible as mine."

Typhon pretended to hit him in the stomach.

As they passed a case containing an object like a short, flesh-colored snake with a half-developed human face, Niall averted his eyes; he preferred not to ask about it.

Only one of the remaining exhibits aroused his interest, a large brain in a container of transparent fluid. Typhon spoke with real enthusiasm:

"This is one of his most remarkable achievements. This brain was grown outside a body. The karvasid believed that it should be possible to provide all the stimuli through currents of energy. The person to whom this brain belonged—a paralyzed child called Rufio—never realized that he did not possess a body. By stimulating the neural circuits, the karvasid was able to make him believe that he did all the things that a normal child does— eat, drink, go for walks, mix with other people, even learn to swim."

Gerek interrupted: "Even fall in love."

This caught Niall's interest. "Fall in love?"

"Indeed. When Rufio reached puberty, the usual sexual hormones were administered, then the image of a pretty girl was fed into his circuits. He not only fell in love, but the brain began to grow at an amazing rate. In a year it had almost doubled its size. You see the implication? Unrestricted by a human skull, it simply went on growing! The karvasid had created a superbrain which lived entirely on illusions!"

Niall was impressed. "What happened to him in the end?"

"Oh, he went insane."

Niall asked: "Boredom?"

"Oh, no. Boredom depends on the physical body. It is an appetite for stimulation. But Rufus got all the stimulation he needed."

Gerek said: "Except sex."

"Oh, he had that too, in the form of electrical stimuli."

Gerek said: "It can't have been as much fun as a real girl."

"How can we tell? It may have been more." But Gerek's interruption obviously had broken his train of thought; he looked at his watch. "It's time we joined the others."

Niall asked: "Will the karvasid be waiting?"

"No. He will be in his own apartments. At this age, he finds people very tiring."

Niall could understand. He remembered how his own grandfather, Jomar, had lost all interest in life a few months before he died. And the karvasid was many times his age.

As they approached the reception room, Niall was surprised to hear the sound of music. It was not until they were about to pass through the wide-open doors that he realized that the music was not physically audible, but was sounding inside his head. It was marvelously infectious, creating a bubbling sense of gaiety.

The room was crowded; Niall estimated there must be three hundred guests. On a platform in the center of the ballroom, an orchestra was playing—a dozen men dressed in silver and blue uniforms. But the platform was covered with a transparent dome, on top of which there was a device consisting of circular metal plates connected in parallel; this was obviously transforming the music into a telepathic wavelength that was audible to everyone in the room. And since everyone was engaged in telepathic conversations on the same wavelength, the effect was exactly like a normal party with chattering guests.

When Niall made a mental effort to block out this sound, he was astonished to realize that the room was silent except for the shuffling feet of the dancing couples and the distant lilt of a waltz through the dome. The sense of gaiety also vanished—only to return as soon as Niall tuned in to the music. It was an odd sensation—like stepping out of brilliant sunshine into a rainstorm, then back into sunlight again.

Typhon placed his mouth close to Niall's ear. "If you don't mind, I'll introduce you as Colonel Niall. Most of the men here have a military rank."

"Of course. Whatever you think best."

"And I'll describe you simply as an envoy from the spider city. Telling them the truth would make everyone ask you how it came about. Or would you prefer that?"

"Of course not." Niall was only too glad to avoid attention.

Typhon asked the captain: "Do you have a name we could use?"

"Among my own people I was known as Makanda."

"Then let it be Captain Makanda."

As they entered the ballroom, Niall paid special attention to see whether the spider's presence would arouse interest; if not, it would support the captain's suspicion that they were expected. But what happened was much like their earlier experience in the Hall of Entertainment. Eyes turned on them as they entered, and people stared with open curiosity; but it lasted only a few moments, and normal conversation resumed. Once more, Niall's impression was that Shadowlanders were too polite to stare.

Typhon said: "Let me introduce you to our mayor, Major Baltiger."

The mayor was a tall, thin man with a snub nose and a white scar on his cheek; he beamed at Niall and said cordially: "My dear sir!" Instead of clasping forearms, he shook hands in an odd, jerky manner. "We don't see many outlanders here." Niall guessed that outlanders meant strangers.

Typhon said: "Colonel Niall is an envoy from the spider city."

The mayor said heartily: "Wonderful!" He obviously was sincere, but Niall suspected that his cordiality was connected to the huge glass of wine he was holding.

Looking around the room at the dancing couples, Niall was struck by the high level of beauty in the women, and masculinity in the men. There was not a corpulent figure among them. It seemed that the guests at the karvasid's reception were chosen for a certain distinction.

A moment later, Typhon introduced Niall to a tall, pretty woman whose fine blond hair stood out from her head like a ball of cotton wool. Her circular blue eyes reminded Niall of pools of water. At a distance she looked as if she was in her late twenties, but at close quarters, the fine lines on her skin made it clear that she must be twice that age. Nevertheless, Niall noted that she was radiating the same curious sexual attraction as the old woman he had seen in Typhon's garden. Her pretty, bow-shaped mouth seemed to be inviting a kiss.

When she told him she was the mayoress, Niall said that he had just met her husband. A look of alarm crossed her face.

"Major Baltiger is not my husband. In this city . . ." She blushed as if unable to continue.

Niall, feeling he had embarrassed her, hastened to interpose: "Of course, I forgot."

She said nervously, her face still pink: "He has been my lover many times, but we are *not* married." Her huge blue eyes looked as if they were about to overflow with tears. Niall observed that at close quarters, circular eyes looked as if they were bulging.

The odd thing, Niall noticed as she turned to be introduced to the captain, was that she had the figure of a young girl. So did many women in the room. He made a mental note to ask Typhon how the women of Shadowland kept their bodies so shapely and athletic.

He watched her talking to the captain with fascination. Most women who were talking to a giant spider for the first time in their lives would look nervous, or at least self-conscious. Yet she was talking to the captain as if he was simply another male, and continued to exude the same slightly helpless sexual attraction.

Of course, they were speaking telepathically, and therefore she was more aware of the captain's mind than of his appearance. Yet as Niall observed her attitude, her unconscious movements, he could see that she was responding to the captain simply as a female responds to a desirable male. The captain was aware of this, and Niall could see he enjoyed it.

Typhon was already introducing Niall to another woman he called Herlint. She was plump, had brown eyes of the normal shape, and was probably in her twenties. But for the sallow complexion, she might have been considered pretty.

She asked Niall: "Are you staying here long?"

"Only a day or two. Then I have to return."

"You're so lucky!" She glanced round to make sure Typhon was not listening, then said in the telepathic equivalent of a low whisper: "I'd love to come with you." As she said it, she suddenly exuded the same sexual attraction as the mayoress. It was as if she had turned it on by pushing a button.

Niall felt flattered. "You'd like to travel?"

"Of course! Everyone would like to travel." Her face became sad. "But I don't suppose I shall ever get the chance."

Out of a desire to give pleasure, Niall said: "You may."

She gazed into his eyes with an intensity that embarrassed him.

"Why do you say that?"

"Because I'm here to discuss a peace treaty."

Her eyes widened. "With the spiders?" He nodded. "Oh, that would be wonderful! Wonderful!" He realized that if they had been alone, she would have flung her arms round him.

Now worried in case he had been indiscreet, he said quickly: "It's still supposed to be a secret, so please don't tell anyone."

She gazed at him reproachfully. "I wouldn't dream of it!"

At that moment, to Niall's relief, Typhon interrupted them. He wanted to introduce Niall to a big man wearing a red uniform with gold brushes on the shoulders. He was introduced as Lieutenant Vasco, head of the fire-fighting service. Vasco had a magnificent blond mustache, a deep scar across his forehead, and when he smiled, he showed excellent white teeth.

For a few minutes their talk progressed along predictable lines—how long Niall had taken to reach Shadowland, how long he intended to stay, how he liked their city. Niall tried to change the direction of the conversation by inquiring about his scar. Vasco's smile clouded over, and for a moment, Niall was concerned in case his curiosity might seem discourteous. Vasco smiled with his magnificent teeth and said casually: "Dueling with our best swordsman." The offhand tone concealed a certain pride.

Niall asked whether the city had many fires. Vasco looked somber. "Too many."

"Due to lightning?"

Vasco shook his head.

"Too many for that."

Niall was surprised. "But why?"

The fire chief made an expressive gesture that meant: "Your guess is as good as mine."

Gerek interrupted by offering Niall a plate with a meat sandwich, and a glass of wine balanced on it. Lieutenant Vasco bowed slightly and took his departure, and for a few minutes, Niall was left to eat and drink undisturbed. He was, in fact, very hungry, and his fellow guests, although obviously anxious to engage him in conversation—several women smiled at him with wide, inviting eyes—obviously felt he should be given time to eat.

As he ate, he watched the fire chief, who was gazing into a woman's wide violet eyes, and wondered what he meant about too many fires. Was he hinting that they were started deliberately? And if so, why, and by whom?

Looking at the mayoress, he also found himself wondering about her embarrassment when he had assumed her to be married to the mayor. She had seemed genuinely upset. Yet she admitted without shame that they had been lovers. Was it possible that she had been somehow conditioned to regard marriage as shameful, or at least, rather discreditable?

In that case, why?

The shadow of an explanation crossed his mind. The impulse to marry is based on the biological instinct to have children. In a land where women had become sterile, such an impulse could only lead to deep frustration.

Conditioning people to regard marriage as shameful would certainly be an effective way of defusing it. . . .

But how could it be done? Of course, the spiders had conditioned human beings to regard themselves as slaves. But that took generations of selective breeding.

As Niall looked around at this scene of almost feverish gaiety, he began to formulate some disturbing insights. It was obvious that Shadowland was full of a seething and undirected energy. Men were subjected to endless military discipline, and fought duels and carried themselves with an air of masculinity. And women exuded an intense femininity—presumably to keep the men preoccupied.

All this seemed to suggest that one of the major problems of Shadowland was a rising tide of boredom.

Is that why the Magician wanted a peace treaty with the spider city—to stave off the collapse of his own empire?

At this point Niall experienced a vague intuition, a feeling that someone was staring at the back of his head. He turned round to find Typhon standing there holding a bottle.

"More wine?"

"Not now, thanks. I still have plenty."

Typhon smiled and moved on, pausing to offer Gerek a drink. A moment later, Gerek came over to Niall.

"Enjoying it?"

"Yes, thanks."

"In a few minutes it's the big moment."

Niall felt oddly apprehensive. "Big moment?"

"The karvasid will present the awards."

Niall realized why he was feeling apprehensive. He was recalling what Typhon had said about failing to meet production targets.

Gerek leaned forward and said quietly: "By the way, please don't mention the peace treaty to anyone."

Niall felt a twinge of guilt.

"Is it supposed to be a secret?"

"Oh, no. But Typhon intends to announce it at the end of the evening. We don't want to spoil the surprise."

On the far side of the room, Herlint was talking animatedly to the mayoress and another woman, and all three were looking toward him. He had a feeling that he had already spoiled Typhon's surprise.

At that moment, the music stopped. The sound of conversation died away, and the room fell silent. The band played a solemn chord, and everyone turned to face the far end of the hall. The whole wall began to slide across like some huge door, until it had vanished into the wall. Behind it, in the center of a raised platform, was a throne of green stone, on either side of which were two half-naked moogs. Around the back of the stage was a row of the Magician's guards, all standing rigidly to attention; the sallow faces and blue chins indicated that they were descendants of cliff dwellers.

Niall's heart began to pound as he recognized the figure on the throne; his cheeks were burning, and he experienced a buzzing noise in his ears. He felt as if he was about to suffocate.

The Magician looked exactly as Niall had seen him in his vision in the white tower, dressed in a long black garment like a monk's robe. But he was smaller than Niall expected. Since the light came from above, his face was only a dim blur inside the cowl, but Niall felt that the eyes were fixed on him.

He was startled when the pounding of his heart subsided and was replaced by a glow of happiness and warmth. It took a moment or so before he understood: he had become caught up in the enthusiasm that surrounded him. The whole audience regarded the Magician with something like adulation. This feeling was such a relief after the acute feeling of apprehension that he allowed himself to relax into it.

Instantly, it became far stronger, and he found himself gazing at the figure in the black robe with a curious sense of awe and sympathy. Surely a man who loved his people, and was in turn loved by them, could not be such a monster?

On either side of the stage, two large gray screens emerged from the floor; each was about six feet high. Then, to Niall's surprise, the audience began to clap and applaud—Niall was aware how much the Magician hated noise—and this rose to a deafening clamor as the Magician reached up with long white hands and pushed back the hood, revealing his face, which was skull-like. He had a small forked beard, but no mustache. His ears were covered with black muffs, obviously noise-excluders, held in place by a metal band that passed over the massive dome of his head, and because Niall was in deep sympathy with the audience, he knew instantly that these were intended to cut out all sound. But as the Magician raised his hands to his ears, the applause died, and by the time he had removed the bands, the room was completely silent. At that same moment, the face of the Magician appeared on the screens, filling them both.

It was, Niall felt, the most impressive face he had ever seen. Its most striking feature was the pair of black and penetrating eyes, which stared from either side of a thin, curved nose. The high forehead reminded him of the chameleon men, except that it was smooth, marked with only a few faint parallel lines. The head was completely bald.

The black eyes seemed to be gazing straight into his own—in fact, into his soul. But Niall was aware that everyone in the room felt the same.

A moment later, the Magician began to speak telepathically, and Niall understood the reason for the screens. Because the lips were not moving, the eyes had to do the work of communication. Without the magnification, this would not have been possible.

"My people." The tone was very clear and sharp; this was in no sense an old man's voice. "I welcome you to this two hundred and twelfth celebration of productivity."

This, Niall realized, meant that these gatherings had been going on for a hundred and six years. The thought that the Magician himself was several centuries old was awe-inspiring. He was aware that this feeling was shared by everyone in the audience as they gazed at that remarkable face with its hypnotic eyes.

"We also have present tonight two envoys from the city of Korsh, where I was born, and from the spiders who now rule that city." Everyone looked at Niall and the captain. But Niall was puzzled by the last phrase. Surely the Magician must be aware that he was not a mere envoy, but the ruler of the spider city?

"You all know that it is four hundred and thirty-two years since I led my followers into Shadowland, and set up our first camp by the lake." Niall felt the audience relax, like children listening to a story; this must be a familiar part of the Magician's speech. "At this time the land was occupied only by ghosts and troglas, who hated our intrusion." Niall felt the shiver that went through the audience at the thought of this sinister menace, for the Magician's words were accompanied by the projection of visual images.

From this point on, the karvasid began to use images as much as words—Niall now thought of him as the karvasid, since "Magician" seemed somehow disrespectful, suggesting a trickster. His words evoked a bleak and unwelcoming land, whose skies seemed much darker than today's. Even the surface of the lake seemed menacing.

He went on to describe how four of their group had been killed, and the hardships of their first winter, when they had survived on fish and sphagnum moss. Niall had heard all this from Typhon, but the karvasid's account was infinitely more real. His power to convey images made them relive the whole adventure.

Niall's latent hostility to the Magician, dating back to his vision in the white tower, soon gave way to sympathy. This man with his hatchet-like face and precise, businesslike manner was obviously a hero, a being who deserved to be regarded as a model of strength and determination. His face showed marks of suffering in the sunken cheeks, the hollows under the eyes, the lines at the corner of the mouth.

If this great ruler was willing to cure Veig, then Niall felt prepared to offer him his complete loyalty. He was obviously by far the greatest man Niall had ever known, and it seemed almost too much to hope that he might become Niall's friend and mentor.

It was a long speech—at least half an hour—yet although the audience was standing, no one stirred a muscle. Even the captain, who was directly in front of Niall, was obviously totally absorbed.

When the karvasid concluded by stating that he intended to exchange ambassadors with the spider city, the surge of enthusiasm from the audience made Niall feel as if he was to be swept off his feet. For a moment he expected them to burst into cheers, then remembered that the karvasid hated noise. He noted, though, that most people were staring at the captain rather than at himself.

When he had finished speaking, the karvasid again placed the noise excluders over his ears, and the room exploded into frenzied cheers. Men and women waved their arms; some embraced and kissed, with tears running down their cheeks. Niall had not seen such enthusiasm since the people of his own city became free. This, he realized, was due to the announcement of the exchange of ambassadors, and he felt a rush of pride to be the bearer of such good news.

Since everyone was smiling at him, he expected to be summoned onto the stage; the thought of having to stand before the karvasid filled him with a curious anguish. A moment later he exhaled with relief when the karvasid raised his hands for silence, and Typhon strode onto the stage and announced that he would now present the productivity awards. People began to move across the room and form a line in front of the stairs that led to the stage. The mayor and mayoress were the first of these, followed by the fire chief.

In any normal gathering, this relaxation of the tension would have been the opportunity for excited whispers. Here everyone was too aware of the importance of the occasion for idle chatter. There was not even telepathic communication. But the air was electric with a feeling of excitement and happiness.

While the line formed, Niall permitted himself a sense of self-congratulation. His journey to Shadowland was responsible for this happiness. For the first time, many Shadowlanders would feel the sun on their faces and the wind in their hair. The cheeks of these pale-skinned men and women would lose their pallor and begin to glow. And when that happened, perhaps the curse of sterility would disappear.

The presentation ceremony began. Two moogs had carried onto the stage a polished wooden box with legs, which seemed to be full of rolls of paper tied with ribbon. This was placed beside the karvasid's throne. Gerek climbed up on stage and stood behind the box. Typhon took a scroll from his pocket and read from it in his reverberant actor's voice: "The first prize goes to Major Baltiger, our esteemed and resourceful mayor!"

The mayor obviously was popular, for there was loud clapping. On one of the two screens, the major's face appeared, smiling happily but nervously. Gerek took a scroll from the box and handed it to him. The major fell on his knees in front of the throne and pressed his lips fervently to the karvasid's hand. On one screen, the karvasid smiled graciously, while on the other, the back of the major's head could be seen as he kissed the long-fingered hand. The mayor levered himself clumsily to his feet, and walked off stage on the other side.

"Lieutenant Vasco, whose brave firefighters have saved twenty-three houses in the past six months!"

Again, there was hearty applause.

Vasco dropped athletically to his knees, pressed his lips against the karvasid's hand, then sprang up with exactly the right mixture of reverence and panache, and strode off stage holding his scroll aloft.

"Madame Selena Hespeth!" This was the mayoress, with her strange fluffy hairstyle, who was being honored for her services to the women of the city. She blushed attractively, and on the screen her face looked radiant. As she fell to her knees and kissed the karvasid's hand, her whole posture somehow exuded adoration; she looked as if she would like to die kneeling in front of him.

Niall's nervousness had begun to subside, but the thought that he would sooner or later have to stand in front of the karvasid revived it. This sinking feeling in his stomach seemed absurd; he had never suffered from stage fright in his life, and his position as the ruler of the spider city had given him a self-confidence that made it seem unlikely he ever would. Yet his cheeks were now burning, and he again felt as if the room was too hot. The mere sight of the karvasid's calm face on the screen made his heart pound so he felt sick.

It was, he realized, an effect of this atmosphere of worship and reverence. He concentrated his will and tried to struggle free of it, but it was impossible. Now he wished that he had slipped the thought mirror into his pocket before he left the house.

Every time the audience applauded, his misery increased. His throat felt dry and painful and he longed for a glass of cold water. But the only thing he could see was his wineglass, standing on a small table. As he reached out and picked it up, he was ashamed to observe that his hand was shaking. He raised the glass to his dry lips, at the same time glancing around him in the hope that no one had noticed his shaking hand. Dividing his attention was a mistake; the wine went down the wrong way, and he began to cough.

He did his best to smother it with a handkerchief, but it was no good. Red wine had spilled down the front of the white tunic. As people around glanced at him sympathetically, he hastily put down the glass in case his coughing made him spill more. The convulsion blocked his aural passages, and the room suddenly became soundless.

The result surprised him. It was as if he was swimming under water. The applause continued, but sounded oddly distant. Then his ears cleared, and the room became normal again. But in those few seconds of deafness, his attack of nerves had vanished.

He knew immediately what had happened. He had been cut off from telepathic contact with the people around him, just as, when he first came into the ballroom, he had detached himself from the music that sounded in his head. This was the same effect: he had ceased to be a part of the audience and its enthusiasm.

But now, as he felt himself being drawn again into the communal emotion, he experienced a sudden feeling of resistance. It was as if his critical faculties had awakened from sleep, and he was viewing the enthusiasm around him with a kind of irritable disdain.

He glanced up at the captain, and realized that the spider had sensed his change of mood, and was regarding him with the tiny bead-like eyes in the back of his head. As his own eyes met them, he realized that he had mistaken the captain's stillness for fascination when, in fact, the captain felt exactly as he did. He was also looking at this scene of emotional fervor with ironic detachment and amusement.

When Niall looked up at the face of the Magician on the screen, his whole view had changed completely. A few minutes earlier it had seemed noble and distinguished; now it seemed merely complacent and self-absorbed. The lines that Niall had taken for marks of suffering looked more like irritability and cruelty.

What exactly had happened? What strange sorcery had made him see the Magician—it now seemed ridiculous to think of him as the "kar-vasid"—as a kind of god? Was it the same kind of magic that made him see every woman in the room as attractive?

He decided to try an experiment. He relaxed, opened his mind, and deliberately allowed himself to be drawn into the telepathic wavelength of those around him. There was a momentary revulsion, which soon passed, and then once again his viewpoint changed. He was glad to be among these warm, friendly people, and to be present at this assembly at which the great master of Shadowland condescended to show himself to his people. Now it was self-evident that the karvasid was a great and benevolent being who loved his subjects and was loved by them. Niall's intellectual recognition that a moment earlier he had seen him as a char-latan now seemed absurd.

It was amazing. He quickly realized that, now that he had discov-ered the trick, he could change his point of view at will, seeing the Magician either as a cold-hearted manipulator or as the compassionate father of his people. Niall had never before recognized so clearly that our perceptions are governed by our assumptions.

His view of the people around him changed too. In his receptive state, he saw the women as deliciously attractive and the men as brave and honest. When he changed his viewpoint, the women became silly and vain, and the men posturing idiots.

He quickly realized that he preferred his detached viewpoint; it seemed pleasanter and healthier, like a vigorous breeze on his cheeks. That warm, intimate glow of feeling that came when he switched viewpoints began to seem increasingly counterfeit, spurious, and somehow sugary.

At that point he was struck by a disquieting thought. Sooner or later he was going to have to talk to the Magician, and had no doubt that he had remarkable telepathic abilities; he would be able to read Niall's feelings at a glance. When he first came to the spider city, Niall had quickly learned to hide his thoughts from the spiders—but that was different. The spiders were accustomed to human beings with blank minds, and made no attempt to probe what lay behind the facade. The Magician would not be so easily deceived. It therefore would be more sensible of Niall to share the enthusiasm of the others.

Accordingly he attuned himself to the telepathic current around him, and plunged into a sea of comradely unity that was like jumping into a heated swimming pool.

There was plenty of time to reflect on these strange insights. As the ceremony proceeded, the well-dressed upper classes of Shadowland were succeeded by factory overseers who had achieved new levels of productivity. Several workers who had produced more than their quota received promotion, and one who had actually doubled it was even allocated a house on the first level. His delight was so immense that the whole audience felt warmed by it and burst into cheers, while even the Magician smiled benevolently. A few minutes later, a female worker who had served as the manager of a women's shoe factory for twenty years was also promoted to the first level. It evidently came as a surprise, and the screen showed her radiant smile. All this, Niall could see, was designed to make the workers feel that in this benevolent, democratic society, any of them could move into the upper ranks of society.

After the workers came the miners from the third level. Their ill-fitting clothes reminded Niall of slaves in the spider city. They looked undernourished, and most of their faces were as pale as corpses. Some of them were so overawed to be in the presence of the Magician that they trembled as they knelt to kiss his hand, and one of them tripped, and had to be helped to his feet by a moog. This man was so upset that tears ran down his cheeks, and he could hardly walk as he hurried off the stage. The whole audience vibrated with sympathy, for it was obvious that the man's only fault was to regard the Magician with the awe he deserved.

As he watched all this, Niall found himself reverting to his critical frame of mind, and wondering why the Magician allowed himself to be treated with this absurd reverence. Niall himself had experienced it when he first became master of the spider city, and had found it an embarrassing nuisance. Now most of his subjects recognized that he genuinely disliked public displays of devotion, and some had even learned to pass him without signs of recognition. Niall looked forward to the day when everyone did the same.

But then again, perhaps the Magician was not really egocentric. Perhaps all this was necessary to prevent the inhabitants of Shadowland from becoming discontented with their boring lot, confined perpetually underground. This was obviously the reason for the militarism: it encouraged discipline. Even King Kazak had encountered this problem of boredom in Dira, in spite of the constant threat of being overrun by the spiders.

At last the awards were over, and Niall could see that the audience was beginning to lose concentration. Yet he could also sense that something further was expected; even though it was two in the morning, the night was not yet over.

All heads turned as another group of people came out of the other room and formed a line. They looked nervous and worried, and Niall guessed that they were due to receive some kind of reprimand. This seemed odd at the end of the award ceremony, but on second thought, Niall could see that it was logical. The virtuous had been praised and received their rewards; now it was the turn of the sinners.

These miscreants, nine in all, were not divided into social groups, like their predecessors in the award ceremony. This, Niall guessed, was part of their punishment: to be herded together like prisoners who had no status.

Everyone stared at them with morbid curiosity. The first of these was a worker in gray cheap clothes like those of the slaves. Niall recognized him; the tall man with the gray mustache he had seen walking alone as he left the second level. Behind him was a gray-haired woman, also of the worker class. But the man and the woman behind them were obviously upper class, since the man had a military bearing, while the woman had a large and shapely bosom and striking blond hair tied with a black ribbon. At the back of the line, behind half a dozen factory workers and miners, was an overweight, big-chinned man in a worker's uniform.

The tall worker was the first, and the screen showed that he was perspiring with fear. Typhon read out the charge in a flat, level voice: that this man, called Pobrek, constantly absented himself from his hostel, and preferred to avoid communal activities like games. This nonparticipation gave his fellow workers the impression that he disdained their activities.

Pobrek fell on his knees and begged forgiveness, explaining that he had recently been ill and depressed, and could find no woman who was willing to offer him companionship. He ended by bursting into tears and prostrating himself at the feet of the Magician, who had removed his sound-excluders and was listening with his eyes hooded.

Typhon looked at his master to see if he had any comment to make, and when the Magician gave no sign, turned to the accused and explained gravely that in a happy community like theirs, nonparticipation was perceived as a criticism, which introduced a note of discord. Since this was a first offense, Pobrek would be fined three months' wages, but if the offense was repeated, he would go to prison.

The prisoner, who had been dragged upright by two moogs, immediately prostrated himself again at the Magician's feet and kissed them, then crawled offstage on all fours. And the audience, who had been following this drama with breathless attention, looked as relieved as if they had also escaped punishment.

Next came the blond woman and the man with the military bearing, who had the physique of a wrestler. Their offense had been to spend twenty-six nights together, in contravention of the regulation against cohabitation, and to devise a plan to take a three-day holiday together in a remote part of the Yevakian Plain. (Niall had no idea where this was.) Had they any defense to offer? Both shook their heads silently.

After glancing at the Magician, and again receiving no signal, Typhon went on to say that he had no alternative than to order the statutory punishment: six months in the mines.

The woman gave a cry of despair, while the man looked crushed. He knelt at the feet of the Magician, kissed his foot, and begged for leniency. This time the Magician's face was seen to nod slightly. The woman burst into tears of relief. Typhon stated that the couple had chosen corporal punishment, and this would be duly carried out: three strokes for the man, two for the woman.

Once more the man turned his face to the Magician, and in the total silence that followed, asked in a husky voice whether he could not be allowed to take the punishment for both of them.

Once more Typhon looked at the Magician, whose face had become stern. In the silence, he spoke in his thin, clear voice: "In that case, the woman would escape punishment. But I will make one concession. You will both receive three lashes each. Silence!" This last was an admonition as a sigh went up from the audience.

Both prisoners looked shocked; the man went so pale that he seemed on the point of collapse.

A moog came forward and lowered himself onto his knees, with his back toward the man, then raised his arms level with his shoulders. Niall was puzzled; since he was still in his detached state, he had no idea of what was coming. But the man himself obviously knew, and stretched out both arms under those of the moog. The moog then lowered his arms, trapping the man's arms on either side of his barrel-like chest. The man gasped with agony, and seemed to faint. The moog then stood up, raising the man's body off the ground, so he hung down the heavily muscled back, his feet dangling like those of a rag doll.

The other moog stepped forward, raised a cat-o'-nine-tails, and brought it down so hard that the thud made everybody wince. A red wheal appeared across his back, which immediately began to bleed. The man hung there motionless, obviously feeling nothing. Two more blows followed, each leaving a red mark, from which tiny rivulets of blood ran like tributaries. After that, the moog raised his arms, and the man dropped onto the floor.

The woman moaned and tried to fling herself on her lover. Something held her back, like a wall of glass, and Niall knew that the Magician had interposed his will. Now the moog with the whip reached out and grabbed the back of the woman's white dress. A single tug ripped it down to the waist, where it was held in place by a belt. The upper half of her body was naked.

Curious to know whether the audience found this as distasteful as he did, Niall relaxed his mind and allowed himself to share their feelings. A moment was enough; he was shocked to be engulfed by a mixture of fear and erotic pleasure, with the pleasure predominating. A woman who stood close to him was staring with open mouth, her breast rising and falling like an exhausted runner's.

The moog knelt and again raised his arms, and the woman allowed her own arms to be trapped. A moment later, the moog stood up, and she was dangling from his back. It was obvious that she was still conscious as the first blow fell, for she gave a short, choked scream. Her skin must have been more delicate than the man's, for there was far more blood, which stained the lower part of her back. She writhed as the second blow struck but made no sound. When the third blow fell, she was silent, obviously unconscious.

The moog allowed her body to fall onto the man's. The two moogs from the other side of the throne came forward and dragged both bodies off the stage by the arms.

After them it was the turn of the gray-haired woman, a catering manager who was accused of wasting tons of meat by failing to keep it refrigerated. Her reply to the charge was inaudible, but no one cared; her face was thin and unattractive, as was her scrawny body, and seeing her flogged would give no one satisfaction. Niall knew in advance that she would be given a warning, and he proved to be correct.

The next three cases were also dealt with quickly. Two miners accused of chronic laziness and underperformance were able to produce doctor's certificates stating that they were suffering from weak lungs, and they were ordered to report to the city hospital for medical tests. And a machinist from the second level was accused of persistent insubordination, and defended himself by arguing passionately that the foreman picked him out for undeserved harsh treatment. Typhon answered that, whether or not the foreman was at fault, the stability of their society depended on obedience to authority, and he therefore sentenced him to six months in the mines. The Magician nodded briefly to confirm this sentence.

The last man in the line was the big-chinned worker, whose rounded stomach suggested that he belonged to the privileged group who could eat as much as they liked. He was identified as Drusco, the overseer in charge of wall construction. The charge against him was that his team had fallen behind in their work, so that the city wall would not be completed by the New Year. This in turn meant that a regiment of soldiers had to remain on duty to guard the gap in the wall.

Asked what he had to say for himself, Drusco had to clear his throat several times before he could speak, and even then, his voice was hoarse. He said that it was not his fault, but was that of the overseer in charge of production on level two, who was failing to deliver the segments of the wall on schedule. Typhon asked if he had asked the overseer the reason for this delay. Drusco said he had, and that the overseer blamed the workers in the copper mines. Typhon asked whether he had addressed an inquiry to the overseer of the copper mines, and Drusco admitted that he had not done so. Why not? asked Typhon, and Drusco replied that he thought this was the responsibility of the factory overseer.

During this exchange the Magician's face had darkened, and it was obvious that he was having difficulty keeping his temper.

Typhon intervened quickly to avert an explosion: "No, it is your responsibility, since you are in charge of building the wall."

Drusco nodded dumbly; on the screen, his thick lips twisted as if he was about to burst into tears.

Typhon looked at the Magician. "Six months in the mines?"

The Magician shook his head angrily. "No, no. Too lenient. Six strokes of the whip and six months in the mines."

Drusco went pale and looked on the point of collapse, and everyone sensed that he intended to throw himself at the feet of the Magician and beg for mercy. Typhon forestalled this by nodding at the moog, who knelt down with his back toward Drusco. The audience watched intently; Drusco evidently was known to all of them. Finally, with a gesture of despair, Drusco reached out his arms. But he failed to reach out far enough, so that when the moog stood up, Drusco slipped down his back and onto the floor.

The Magician snapped: "Seven strokes," and the sheer menace in his voice made Drusco recognize that his life hung by a thread. The next time the moog knelt down, he reached out until his chest was pressing the moog's broad back.

Niall averted his eyes; he preferred not to see what happened next. But it was impossible not to hear the thud of the cat-o'-nine-tails, and Drusco's scream of pain. After the third stroke, he stopped screaming, and Niall guessed that he had lost consciousness. But the blows continued, and seemed to become softer. When Niall looked up, he saw why. Drusco's back was such a mass of bleeding and torn flesh that the sound was muffled.

By the time this was over, Niall knew there was no point in trying to control his feeling of disgust—if he tried, he felt it would choke him. The flogging of Drusco had been stupid and sadistic—and moreover, pointless, since the peace treaty would make the wall unnecessary. He now regretted that he had agreed to make peace with such a monster, since, as a fellow sovereign, he would be obliged to assume a mask of courtesy.

Drusco's unconscious body had been carried offstage by a moog, and now Typhon was speaking again.

"Before we conclude, I have an announcement to make. The karvasid has already told you that we have with us two envoys from the city of Korsh.

He has also authorized me to tell you that we shall soon have a peace treaty, which will permit travel and commerce between our two nations."

The audience burst into enthusiastic applause, and a path opened up to allow Niall and the captain to approach the stage. The applause continued until Typhon had to raise his hand for silence. He said: "Please welcome Captain Makanda and Colonel Niall!"

As, surrounded by beaming faces, Niall followed the captain toward the stage, he felt his irritation dissolve; so much warmth was irresistible. The moment this happened, he ceased to feel hostile toward the Magician, and saw him once again as the benevolent ruler of a friendly people. This came as a relief; about to confront the ruler of Shadowland, he preferred to feel friendly.

Faced with the steps that led up to the stage, the spider hesitated. His eight widely spaced legs were not intended for climbing stairs. He obviously would have preferred to climb straight onto the stage but felt that this would be failing to show respect. Confining his feet to the narrow stairway, he mounted to the stage. Niall followed, and stood awkwardly beside him, facing the Magician, who remained seated. At close quarters, Niall could see that his skin was gray and unhealthy, and covered with a fine network of lines that made it look like some kind of expensive leather.

The Magician smiled at them, then extended his hand to the captain. This was clearly intended as an invitation to kneel and kiss it.

The spider hesitated. Niall could see that this was not because he objected to making the gesture, but simply because he was unsure about the mechanics. The spider stood at least two feet above the Magician, looking down on him. Bending his front legs would involve tilting forward at an impossible angle, while bending all his legs would cause his body to vanish in the middle of them. The spider solved the problem by bunching all his legs underneath him, as if about to fall asleep. His mouth finally performed an approximation to a kiss. The audience was silent, obviously overwhelmed by the extraordinary sight of this dangerous monster paying homage to their ruler.

The Magician held out his hand to Niall, still smiling. Suddenly, Niall's sense of involvement with the audience disappeared, and gave way to anger and disgust. He was, after all, the ruler of his own city, and to treat him merely as an envoy seemed a calculated insult. Niall turned to look at Typhon, about to say: "Does the karvasid not understand that I am the ruler of the spider city?"

Typhon looked helpless and apologetic, but this eyes said quite clearly: "Go on, for heaven's sake, do it."

Niall knew what he must do. He looked into the Magician's eyes, shook his head firmly, and said: "No."

What happened next was so fast that he had no time to anticipate it. The Magician's smile changed to an expression of dangerous fury, and a tremendous blow struck Niall on the side of the head, making him see stars. He felt his other cheek strike against the floor, and for a moment he lost consciousness.

When his vision cleared, the captain was struggling against two moogs, who were obviously immune to his will-force and poisonous sting. One of the spider's claws gripped a moog by the elbow, and the forearm fell onto the floor; no blood ran from the stump, and the moog went on fighting as if nothing had happened. The two other moogs joined in, and within moments, the spider had been smashed to the ground by a tremendous blow on the head.

Niall tried to raise himself on all fours, but had no strength. The Magician's face was demoniacal with rage and hatred, and for a moment Niall thought he was about to die. Instead another blow drove the breath out of his body and filled him with nausea. For a bewildered moment he was in the air about ten feet above his body, then swooped down into it and spun into blackness.

W hen he woke up, he was a mass of pain: his body, his head, his face, his cheeks. His lower lip seemed as large as a balloon, and he felt as if he had no skin on the left side of his face. His stomach hurt as if someone had kicked him in it, and all his ribs felt bruised. It was so agonizing when he tried to move that he lay still again. He could hear a loud wheezing noise, then realized it was his own breath.

He was also cold. When he opened his eyes—although only the right would open fully—he realized why. He was lying on a stone floor in a prison cell. A dim yellow light shone through a barred hole in the door. Light also leaked through a grating behind him, and a draft indicated that there must be a window there. Below this there was a wooden bed suspended from the wall by two chains.

He forced himself to his hands and knees and pulled himself up by the bed. His hands encountered something soft—a blanket. When he climbed onto the bed, he found a wooden block intended as a pillow. He covered himself with the blanket, lay down facing the door, and fell into an uneasy sleep.

When he opened his eyes again, the light outside his cell door had been turned off. By the gray daylight from behind him, he could see that the wall was made of green stone blocks, which told him that he was probably still in the palace. He knelt on the bed and peered upward through the grating. On its far side, there was a sloping ramp of stone, at the top of which was a barred window. He tucked the blanket more closely around him, in an attempt to conserve his body heat, and lay there passively, feeling the throbbing of the bruises on his left side, and a larger bruise on the right side of his head where he had been struck.

Suddenly he felt the presence of his mother; she was repeating his name. In his completely quiescent state, he could hear her as clearly as if she was in the room.

"Are you all right?"

He knew she would not be deceived if he said yes. Since she was inside his head, she could feel his discomfort as if it was her own. He said: "No. I'm in prison."

"But why?"

"I offended the Magician by refusing to kiss his hand."

He could sense that she wanted to ask him more questions about this, and so was glad when she asked instead: "Are you hurt?"

"Bruised. And very cold."

There was a silence. Then she said: "Yes, I can feel it. Shall we send spider balloons to try and rescue you?"

Niall knew the answer to that. If the spiders threatened to invade Shadowland, the Magician would respond by killing him.

"No. I don't think I'm in any immediate danger, so don't worry."

"But what does he want?"

Niall said with feeling: "If I knew that I'd feel better!"

"Is there anything I can do?"

A thought occurred to Niall.

"Do you have a fire in your room?"

He knew that his mother lived on the windiest corner of the palace, and that her maid Deberis liked to start the day by lighting a large fire.

"Not here, but in the next room."

"Please stand by it and get as warm as you can. Then try to transfer some of it to me."

Niall had no idea if this was possible, but a minute later he could actually experience the glow of the fire on her legs and body.

"Can you feel that?"

"Yes."

"Wait a minute and I'll put my heavy robe on."

Within a few moments, he was as warm as if he was also standing in front of the fire. He knew that his mother must be uncomfortably hot, but was too grateful for the warmth to worry about that. At last he was beginning to feel human again. Then the glow began to fade, and he realized that she was becoming tired.

She asked: "Can this Magician read thoughts?"

"Yes."

"Then you must be very careful." Her voice was becoming faint, and her next words were almost inaudible. "I will try and communicate this evening."

Then her presence faded completely.

Now feeling more cheerful, Niall swung his feet off the bed and sat up—and gave a gasp of pain as his bruises were reactivated. The discomfort was as intense as trying to lower himself into a bath that was too hot, and made him grit his teeth and curse under his breath. He pulled the blanket round him like a cloak, and moved to the foot of the bed, where the draft was less strong.

But at least the pain had made him concentrate, and reminded him of the ability he had discovered through the thought mirror. He closed his eyes, concentrating hard, screwing up his face, and immediately felt relief. Moreover, the concentration revived the warmth his mother had communicated. This made the bruises and scratches throb more than ever, but the warmth made up for it.

A slight sound from behind him made him turn and peer upward through the grating; a bird had hopped through the bars of the outer window. Instantly, he knew it was the raven, and chuckled with delight, then glanced over his shoulder at the cell door to make sure he had not been heard.

The bird now fluttered across to the grating, on which it perched looking down at him. Niall's telepathic contact with it told him that it recognized he was in trouble.

He lost no time transferring his consciousness to its brain. It cost him more effort than usual, no doubt because he was tired; but as soon as he found himself behind the raven's eyes, he felt much better. Looking down at his own face, he became aware of the bruise that was turning purple and the skin missing from his left cheek. Then he urged the bird to return to the window, and to fly upward.

They were in a circular inner courtyard, with barred windows all around it. The raven flapped upward until it was hovering above the palace, and Niall could see that it extended over a wider area than he had realized. It was built in the form of a medieval castle, with three parallel circular walls. He directed the bird to perch on the topmost turret, then looked around to take his bearings.

The courtyard with the dungeons was in the center of the palace, and it was obvious that even if a prisoner could escape through his cell window, he would still be trapped. The only door out of the courtyard led to a narrow passage between two buildings, at the end of which there was another wall with a door.

The bird was perched on the guttering of the turret. A number of other birds were also perched on the roof and in cornices; this was understandable, since the palace towered above the city; by normal day-light, it would have afforded a view to the northern cliffs, but even in the dull light of Shadowland, the view was spectacular. Birds, Niall real-ized, enjoy looking down from a height. Niall himself disliked heights, but looking through the bird's eyes, felt the same pleasure as the raven.

Was this central tower, he wondered, the Magician's quarters? The window immediately below him was covered with a cage of black metal, and he directed the raven down to perch on one of its crossbars, taking the precaution of making it choose the end rather than the middle, to make itself less conspicuous. A few feet away from him, their backs to a doorway, two armed guards stood rigidly at attention in a dimly lit cor-ridor. They were so still that Niall found himself wondering if they were dummies. Then he saw, on the wall facing them, two green lights glow-ing like the eyes of a cat—the mechanical eyes that Niall had noted in the corridors of the palace. Their purpose clearly was to make everyone feel under constant observation.

Niall directed the bird to fly onto the next window, and again to perch at the end of the crossbar. This room was well lighted and, as he had expected, it was the Magician's chamber. The walls were covered with glass cupboards containing scientific apparatus, but the room's most striking feature was a column of light that stretched from floor to ceiling, shining with a soft, blue glow that seemed almost alive. It reminded Niall of a similar column in the center of the white tower, although this was less wide. Clouds of darkness, like rising bubbles, drifted toward the ceiling as if through a liquid.

At a bench near the far wall, the Magician was standing, his back to the window, holding a test tube close to his eyes and gently shaking its contents.

Overcome by an illogical intuition of danger, Niall made the bird leave its perch and fly down to the top of a crenellated wall above the courtyard. There he watched an officer addressing a squad of men, all typical cliff dwellers, who were standing at ease. Niall observed immedi-ately that they had Reapers rather than rifles propped against their sides.

The officer, whom Niall recognized as Jelko, the commander of the Palace Guard, was talking to them with a fierce earnestness that was reflected in their attentive faces. Unfortunately, the raven's brain was poorly adapted for telepathic reception, and Niall was unable to catch more than the occasional word. He would have given a great deal to know why they were all looking so serious.

A soldier in the front row asked a question, and this time Niall could hear the reply quite clearly: "Shoot back, but be careful. These things are deadly."

At that moment, a large magpie tried to settle beside the raven, which squawked angrily at this invasion of its space. Jelko glanced up at the birds, and suddenly gazed intently. To Niall's horror, the raven became paralyzed, held in a concentrated beam of will-force. Its legs buckled; but since it was standing in the crenelation, it was prevented from falling. The magpie toppled and dropped to the ground. Niall instantly exerted his own will-force and broke the spell; the officer gazed with astonishment as the raven flew away.

Niall had learned an important lesson: that in the Magician's palace, not even a bird was safe.

For the next quarter of an hour, he directed the raven to fly all around the rooftops of the palace. He was curious to know why it was so big. The reason, he soon discovered, was that it was virtually a town in itself. The courtyards were thronged with women, as well as men, all obviously cliff dwellers. Again, everything was unnaturally silent. But it was clear that the men and women were allowed to live together, for several large buildings were obviously married quarters, with washing lines strung across the courtyards.

Beyond the back of the palace, on the far side of its outermost wall, there was a gray, utilitarian building that looked oddly out of place; built of square concrete blocks, it might have been a factory or warehouse on the second level. From inside came the hum of machinery and the clink of bottles. Niall directed the raven to perch on the windowsill.

Beyond the grimy glass, half a dozen women were working on either side of a moving belt that carried bottles; these were being filled with a white liquid that flowed from a pipe above the belt. Niall, totally unfamiliar with factories and conveyor belts, had no idea what he was looking at.

At this point he was abruptly drawn back to his body and its bruises. Someone was trying to probe his mind. His first thought was that it was his mother, attempting to restore contact, and he opened his mind to become receptive—a state similar to listening intently for some faint sound. But after half a minute, the sensation went away. Then the light outside his cell door was turned on, and there was a sound of a bolt being withdrawn.

The man who came in was a hunchback, and even in this poor light it was obvious that he was one of the Magician's "experiments." One eye was normal; one was so large that it stuck out of his face like a tennis ball. His nose was also grotesquely large, and twisted to one side. He was carrying a tray, which he placed on the bed. This contained a small piece of bread and a cup of water.

Niall realized suddenly that his watch was missing. He asked: "What time is it?"

He spoke telepathically, but the jailer replied in normal speech: "I can't tell you that."

Niall asked: "Why? Don't you know?"

The man said stolidly: "I can't tell you that."

He had some speech impediment, as if his tongue was too big for his mouth. Without a further word, he turned and left the cell. The light outside went out.

Niall was hungry. In spite of the swollen lip, he ate the bread quickly and drank the water. This had an unpleasant taste, like oil. A few minutes after drinking it, he began to feel sick, and had no doubt that it had contained an emetic.

In the corner of the cell there was a bucket covered with a wooden lid. Niall fell on his knees in front of it and vomited. It must have been a strong emetic, for the convulsions continued long after his stomach was empty. After this he sat down with his back against the wall, shivering and exhausted.

He staggered across the cell, stretched out on the bed, and covered himself with the blanket. He was still feeling weak, and drifted into a semisleep.

While he was lying there, feeling completely exhausted and vulnerable, he experienced a sudden vivid memory of Veig. It was so clear that it was as if Veig's face was looking at him from the semidarkness. Niall started; in the events of the past few hours, he had forgotten all about his brother. Now he experienced a despairing sense that he had betrayed Veig and condemned him to death.

This brought back the memory of Typhon asking him how many days it was since Veig had been poisoned, and when Niall told him, replying: "There's still plenty of time." Did Typhon know what was going to happen? Was he involved in this plot to throw him into prison? And if so, how about Gerek? Niall could have sworn that both were honest, but as he lay there thinking, he began to experience doubts. The result was a sinking feeling that drained him of energy.

And why *was* he in prison? Because his pride had revolted at the idea of being treated as one of the Magician's subjects. But he was not one of his subjects. He and the Magician were fellow sovereigns; he had every right to be treated with respect.

And then, of course, there was the odd fact that the Magician wanted his people to think that Niall and the spider were merely envoys. What was his motive?

With his head buzzing with fatigue and his stomach still churning with nausea, Niall found it hard to think clearly, or to make the logical connections that might show him the solution to these problems.

To distract his mind, he tried working out how long it had been since Veig had cut himself on the ax. It had happened on a Friday, and early on Sunday morning he had left for Shadowland. . . . By recalling the events of each day, he was able calculate that this must be Monday, and that his brother had only eighteen days left.

At this thought, his cheeks began to burn, and his heart pounded until he was afraid it would burst. For the next ten minutes, he felt more depressed and helpless than he had ever felt in his life. It began to look as if the Magician had won, and Niall would be forced to do whatever he wanted.

His problem, he could now see very clearly, was that he was too young and immature to possess the mental toughness that would enable him to withstand the pressure of a man whose greatest obsession was forcing others to do his will. To develop this inner strength required long self-discipline, of the kind possessed by the monk Sephardus.

The thought of Sephardus had the effect of focusing Niall's attention and halting the slide into discouragement. After all, Sephardus had spent years alone in his cell, learning to control the powers of his mind. And one thing about the Magician was certain: he had never learned the discipline of self-control. The murderous rage on his face when Niall had defied him proved it. In that respect, he was vulnerable.

Niall remembered the crystal sphere that was at present in the cave of the trolls. The elder troll had taught him how to reestablish contact. This involved creating a connection with one of the troll family, dividing his attention, and then allowing his mind to blend with the crystal. In order to reverse the process, he had to achieve contact with one of the trolls.

Niall envisaged the female troll and imagined that she was there in the room. But there was no feeling of contact. It struck him then that it was, after all, somewhere in the middle of the day, and that probably she was busy cooking or doing housework. It would have been pointless trying to contact his own mother at that time of day.

Next he tried envisaging the grandfather, but again the effort was unsuccessful. It was like knocking on a door when no one was at home.

Finally, for the sake of making one more effort, he tried envisaging the younger child, for whom he had felt a natural sympathy based on his feeling for his own sisters. This time it worked, and he was suddenly able to see the child as clearly as if he was in the room. Moreover, he knew the boy was aware of his presence. He seemed to be playing some kind of game involving wooden blocks, so his mind was passive and receptive.

Before the child's attention could wander, Niall did what the grand-father had taught him—detached a part of his mind and directed it toward the crystal. At once, he experienced the electrical, tingling sensation. A moment later, his energies had blended with those of the crystal, and he felt as if he was at the center of a web, which transmitted waves of power.

Unfortunately, this influx of energy also brought agonizing pain. He had adjusted to his cuts and bruises, but this electrical force was like pouring salt into his wounds. He whistled, and groaned aloud. As this happened, he once again felt that his mind was being probed. That meant someone was listening outside his cell.

A moment later, the door opened, and the hunchback came in. He said: "What's going on?" Niall made no reply. The hunchback came over to the bed and peered down into Niall's face, then grunted and went out.

It was clear to Niall that his attempts to establish contact with the crystal must be left until he had recovered some of his strength.

But the knowledge that he could call upon the energies of the crystal restored his optimism. Feeling much better, he closed his eyes and relaxed, then drifted into sleep.

He was awakened as the door opened again. This time it was not the jailer, but a brown-haired girl, dressed in the plain blue dress of a servant, who was carrying a tray. As she came into the cell, Niall saw that, although obviously a descendant of the cliff dwellers, with the typical receding chin, she had circular eyes, which, as usual, gave her a look of startled innocence. As with Katia, the overall effect was one of flawed prettiness.

She smiled shyly at Niall, and asked telepathically: "Are you hungry?" The voice that sounded in Niall's chest was clear and gentle.

Niall sat up and swung his feet onto the floor, leaving room to set the tray on the bed. He looked suspiciously at the food—a slice of dry bread, a small piece of cheese, half an apple, and a cup of water. But he was very thirsty. He raised the water to his nose and sniffed it.

The girl asked: "What is it?"

Niall grimaced. "The last lot made me sick."

Her reply was to take the glass from him and sip it herself, then hand it back. Niall tasted it, and was glad to find that it had none of the oily flavor.

He asked the girl: "What is your name?"

"Umaya. And you?"

"Niall."

She was looking intently at the abrasions on the left side of his head. She asked: "Who did that?"

"I don't know. Somebody knocked me down."

She reached out and touched a scratch with her fingertip; Niall winced.

Then, to Niall's disappointment, she turned and left; the bolt slid back into place behind her. Yet Niall had a sense she would be back. He sipped more of the water, resisting the temptation to empty the cup, then ate the dry bread with the apple and cheese. It left his hunger unappeased, but he felt better.

Umaya came back, this time carrying a white box, which she placed on the tray. It contained bandages, jars of ointment, and a white tube about six inches long with a brush at its tip. She was also carrying a damp, warm cloth, with which she delicately cleaned the abrasion on his left cheek. Her fingertips were cool, and as she leaned close to him, the blue smock smelled as if it had just been washed and ironed. Her hands, he noticed, were pretty and shapely.

When she had dabbed the abrasion dry with a handkerchief, she picked up the white tube and pushed a slide on its side; it made a faint humming sound. She placed the tip against Niall's face, and he winced as he received the buzz of a mild electric shock. She smiled and shook her head, and as he looked up at her open mouth, he saw, as he expected, that she had no tongue.

She reached around his head, and gently pulled it against her smock, then again applied the brush. After the initial sting, it tickled rather than shocked. Feeling the warmth of her bare arm against his temple, he relaxed, exactly as he did with his own female body servants, and enjoyed the contact. As she changed the position of his head against her, he could feel that the breast under the blue smock was bare.

He asked: "What is it for?"

"To heal you, and liquify the blood."

This last statement left him puzzled, but he was too relaxed to ask what she meant.

A few minutes later, she went around to his other side, and this time applied the brush to the bruise from the blow that had knocked him down. At first, the vibrations made it hurt, but gradually, this gave way to a soothing sensation. He seemed to see tall trees swaying in the wind, and was reminded of something that eluded him. After five minutes, he could no longer feel the bruise. Finally, she pushed his head away from her, smiled at him, and then pressed the bruised spot with her fingertip. To Niall's surprise, there was not even a twinge of discomfort.

He pointed to the tube.

"What is this force?"

"It is vrees." She seemed to expect him to know the word.

"What is vrees?"

She seemed surprised. "You do not know? It is a force that comes from the Earth."

Now he knew what it reminded him of: the force of the crystal that the troll had enclosed in the walking stick. It seemed the Magician had found some way of capturing and storing Earth-force, as a battery stores electricity. It was hard not to admit that he was a remarkable inventor.

Umaya then applied a green ointment to the other abrasions on his face, which took away their sting and throbbing heat.

She replaced the ointments in the box and closed the lid, then asked: "Why are you in prison?"

He was surprised. "Don't you know?"

"No. My father is only the jailer. They tell him nothing."

He said: "I am in here because I refused to obey the karvasid."

She looked horrified. "Refused to obey! But why?"

"Because he was ordering me to do something I did not want to do."

He could tell that she was so shocked that she preferred not to pursue the matter. She picked up the tray and hurried to the door. But as she pushed it open, she turned back toward him, and asked in a tone of formal inquiry: "Is there anything you want?"

"Yes. Can you tell me what happened to my companion, the spider?"

She hesitated, and he could see that, like her father, she had been ordered not to answer questions. But she allowed good manners to override her doubts.

"He is well."

"Uninjured?"

"Yes."

Standing there, with the tray held in front of her, she reminded him irresistibly of Jarita and Nephtys, and he found himself thinking that he would enjoy taking a bath with her, and feeling her delicate hands soaping his body. As this thought crossed his mind, she blushed a deep red, and he realized that she had read his thoughts. A moment later she hurried from the room, and he heard her setting the tray down and bolting the door. Her feet ran up a flight of stairs as if anxious to escape.

He was puzzled. She had read his mind, apparently without effort. Yet the image of being bathed by Jarita and Nephtys had merely flashed through his brain as an idle reflection. It astonished him that she had picked it up.

Twice that day, Niall had felt someone trying to probe his mind. He had assumed it was the hunchbacked jailer. But could it have been Umaya?

He dismissed the idea immediately. Even the slightest contact with her made it clear that she was as sincere and guileless as Veig. So whoever was trying to read his thoughts, it was not Umaya.

All the same, it was strange that she had read his mind so easily.

After the food and drink, he was already feeling sufficiently recovered to try again contacting the crystal. This time it was easier. He envisaged the younger of the two children, conjuring up the red hair and red cheeks and the gap between his teeth, and immediately became aware of him; the child was sitting in front of the fire, playing with a dragon carved out of wood.

Niall then divided his awareness, established contact with the crystal, and immediately found himself standing beside it in the cave. The grandfather troll was only a few yards away, towering four feet above Niall. He was polishing a rose-colored crystal with a cloth, and was clearly unaware of Niall's presence.

The odd thing was that the troll and the cave seemed transparent, as if made of a watery fluid. Looking down, Niall seemed to himself perfectly normal and solid. He reached out and touched the troll; his hand went through his hip. Niall reached up and waved his hand in front of his eyes; the old man did not even blink.

The troll stopped polishing, and placed the crystal in the hollow at the top of the pallen, where it instantly began to glow with a rosy light. Niall was surprised that he could not only feel its warmth, but could experience a rippling sense of vitality emanating from it. This felt so pleasant that he moved closer to absorb a little of the energy.

At that moment he noticed that his own crystal globe was lying on the floor, swathed in a black velvet cloth. Even through the cloth he could sense its energy. As soon as he bent over it, he automatically tuned in to this energy, and felt it responding.

The old man sensed that something was happening, and looked over his shoulder. His eyes widened as he saw the globe disentangling itself from its cloth and then rising into the air. He reached out to the chair to steady himself, then sat down with a bump.

Niall, totally focused on the crystal, was not even aware of the shock he had produced. What delighted him was that the crystal was responding to him exactly as if he was present in his physical body.

At that moment, the grandfather said something in the guttural troll language, and Niall looked at him, and suddenly grasped the effect of what he had done. At the same time, the old man understood what had happened. Speaking telepathically, he asked: "Where are you?"

"Here." Niall found it hard to believe that the old man was unable to see him, since his body seemed quite solid.

The troll reached out and removed the rose-colored crystal from the pallen, and its light went out like a snuffed candle. Niall reached up and replaced it with the crystal globe, whose dazzling white light instantly filled the cave with its blinding glare, causing the troll to shield his eyes. As this happened, Niall's surroundings lost their transparent appearance and became visibly more solid, although still several degrees less so than Niall himself. At the same moment, Niall realized he had become visible to the old man.

The troll peered down at him, scratching his nose.

"Where are you now?"

"In prison in Shadowland."

The old man muttered: "I thought that might happen. What excuse did he use?"

"I refused to kiss his hand."

"Good." He smiled grimly. "But you'd better return to your prison. You are in great danger here."

Niall asked in astonishment: "Why?" Nothing seemed further from the truth.

"Because if he knows you have the crystal, he will stop at nothing until he has it. He'll torture you until you tell him where it is."

This was an unnerving thought. For, as Niall instantly realized, if the Magician knew where it was, the trolls would also be in danger.

The troll seemed to understand that the warning had produced a greater effect than he intended, for he added: "But don't be afraid. That is the worst thing you can do. So long as you hold on to your courage, he can't harm you. Now listen. For the next week I will leave your globe on the pallen, in case you need to use it."

"Thank you."

"Now you'd better be gone."

Niall transferred his attention from the light and back to his body, and immediately found himself in his own cell, lying on his back and again aware of his throbbing bruises. It seemed a poor exchange for the crystal cave.

The troll was right, of course. If someone now probed his mind, his increased vitality would immediately give him away. The thought of the Magician's learning about the crystal globe made his stomach turn a somersault and his cheeks flush. Then the reflection that his journey to Shadowland had been a failure, and that he had condemned his brother to death, made it worse, causing an abrupt plunge into gloom. He sat down on the bed, and felt his energies leaking away, bringing a sense of total vulnerability. In his sudden despair, he even found himself wishing that he had kissed the Magician's hand. What difference would it have made? Instead, absurd pride had led him into this dangerous and hopeless situation. . . .

Was it, he wondered, too late to send the Magician an apology? But the very thought revolted him. The Magician was like an evil child, totally spoiled by power. The thought of kneeling in front of him made Niall feel physically sick.

For the next half hour, he felt as if he was trying to extricate himself from a swamp of black mud, and as if every attempt only caused him to plunge in deeper. He sat with his head in his hands, trying hard to find something to feel optimistic about, and failing.

When he felt it would be difficult to sink any further, he heard a faint movement outside the door. His stomach lurched; he suspected that someone was spying on him. Anticipating an attempt to probe his mind, he ordered himself to become passive and empty. He lay down, closing his eyes as if trying to relax into sleep, and pulled the blanket over him. During the next few minutes, he heard further sounds, including the clink of a bucket handle. Then the bolt was drawn back, and footsteps entered the cell. He kept his eyes closed until the sound of his waste bucket handle told him that whoever it was had his back toward him. He opened his eyes and saw a short, sandy-haired man, who gave a grunt of disgust as he raised the lid that covered the bucket.

Now certain this was only a servant, Niall tried probing his mind, ready to withdraw instantly if he reacted. But the man's mind was a blank, merely conscious of its surroundings. The handle clinked again as he went outside with the bucket, poured it into another bucket, then came back and replaced it on the floor.

Lying on his back, appearing to be asleep, Niall could tell that the man was looking across at him. Then the door was opened, and the footsteps went out again. But as the door closed, Niall was able to catch the thought that crossed the man's mind, and was amazed that one of its components was a sense of grievance against the Magician.

As the steps receded up the stairs, Niall reflected on this, and the more he thought, the more incredible it seemed. This man, apparently a menial whose task was to empty buckets of human waste product, was actually feeling irritable and disgusted toward the master of Shadowland.

Why? Niall tried to recall his impression of a moment ago. The man had looked across at Niall on the bed, and then . . . experienced a spontaneous surge of irritation toward the Magician.

There could surely be only one explanation. He knew that Niall was one of the envoys who had come to propose a peace treaty with the spiders. And everyone in Shadowland was longing for such a treaty. It would mean the end of isolation, of the boredom of living in a permanent blue twilight, of eating a monotonous diet of fish and blue moss. And the Magician had thrown all this away in one of his childish fits of rage.

No wonder this emptier of buckets was disgusted. It meant the end of his hopes of a less dreary form of existence.

Suddenly Niall was unable to lie still. He sat up on the bed and threw off the blanket, his energies renewed by a sense of hope. This lasted only a few moments, until he reflected that the Magician was the despot of this land, and that there was no one who would dare to challenge his authority; nevertheless, it was a welcome change from the despair of half an hour before.

His stomach was again growling with hunger. He had become accustomed to hunger when he lived with his family in the desert, but his body was now used to regular meals. To take his mind off it, he closed his eyes, and thought about their home in North Khaybad, under the branches of the euphorbia cactus. With no great effort he could conjure up the sound of the wind blowing through them. Little by little, he relaxed, and ceased to care about the protesting noises from his stomach. Then he set out to recall the country of the ants, and how, for the first time in his life, he had sat up to his neck in running water and listened to its rippling sound. Soon his nose itched, and he scratched it—a sure sign he was drifting toward sleep—and a few moments later was dozing.

The doze became a kind of dream in which he was aware he was asleep. Someone was lying beside him, and it seemed that it was Umaya. In his half dream state, he could actually feel her body pressed against his and her arms around him. For some reason, it seemed important not to let her know he was awake, so he lay there breathing quietly. She was massaging him, just as Jarita did after a bath, and her hands ran from his shoulders down to his knees. He also knew that she wanted to kiss him, and since she thought he was asleep, there seemed to be no harm in this. Her lips brushed his own, after which she kissed him more firmly and lingeringly.

Her hands were very cool, and there was a soothing quality about their touch. He began to experience a sensation of lightness and acquiescence, a desire to let her do whatever she liked. And what she wanted to do, he realized, was to drink his energy as dry earth drinks water. The sensation of his energies flowing into her was one of the sweetest he had ever experienced.

He was shocked out of this by a sudden shout. He knew who it was: the woman with the long brown hair, whose face lacked eyes and a nose. In the same moment, he knew that he was not lying in bed beside Umaya, but beside one of the vampire-like creatures with pointed teeth.

As he woke up, he felt for a moment totally confused, as if he no longer knew who he was. Then he found himself lying alone on the bed, with his cheek bleeding where he had scratched it on the hard pillow. But there was none of the usual pleasure of waking from a nightmare; on the contrary, he felt that the nightmare was continuing, even though he was now awake. It was as if he was still entangled with some entity that was draining his energy, and that was determined not to let go.

For a moment he experienced panic, then realized that was a mistake. It only increased the sense of vulnerability. During the past year, he had acquired a certain degree of self-discipline, and now he called upon it and concentrated his mind. There was a moment of struggle; then he experienced relief.

His face was hot, and his heart beat painfully. It seemed absurd to feel so hot when the cell was cold. He turned his attention inward and tried to analyze what was happening. The energy leak was still there, but less obvious than before—now it was little more than a kind of drip. Yet although imperceptible, it could still drain him until he was exhausted.

He tried closing the leak by concentrating hard; it only increased the hot flush, and made his heart beat faster. What he needed, he realized, was the kind of soothing coolness he had experienced when Umaya had dressed his bruises. But if Umaya was so telepathic, he ought to be able to call her. Using the technique he employed when trying to contact his mother, he envisaged her clearly, then tried to send a signal.

For the next five minutes he tried to slow the beating of his heart. Every time he began to succeed, he experienced a spurt of anxiety, and his pulse rate increased. It began to seem that the more effort he made, the more energy he would waste.

A sound in the corridor caused a flash of hope; when it was followed by sound of the bolt being drawn, he knew that it was Umaya.

She crossed the floor to the bed.

"You were calling me?"

He nodded without opening his eyes; he was already beginning to feel better. She reached out and touched his moist forehead.

"You have a fever."

"Something is stealing my energy."

She placed her hand at the junction of his throat and chest; her palm immediately became cooler.

"It is a graddik."

He felt too tired to ask how she knew.

She said, with a touch of reproof: "But you must have invited it inside you."

This time he knew exactly what she meant. He nodded.

"I was dreaming. I thought it was you."

She said: "That is dangerous. When you have invited a graddik inside you, it is hard to get rid of."

"Can you get rid of it?"

"I don't know. Perhaps."

She left the room, drawing the bolt behind her.

Five minutes passed while he lay passively, listening to his heartbeat and feeling his energy draining away like a dripping tap.

When she returned, she was carrying an oblong box, which she placed on the floor at the foot of the bed. A moment later, the cell was full of an odor he recognized: the iodine smell of the lake weed.

She pulled back the blanket, then began to unbutton his tunic. He knew exactly what she intended do, and the thought made him breathe slowly and deeply with relief. He sat up to allow her to draw the tunic down over his feet.

When he was naked, she took the mat of weed from the box, and placed it over his body as if spreading an eiderdown on the bed. It was cool, and made him shiver. But the sense of losing energy stopped at once, as if someone had turned off the tap.

He heard the rustle as she removed her dress, then felt her weight press down on him. She adjusted herself, with both arms bent on either side of his chest, and lowered her right cheek against his face; her brown hair fell into his mouth. It took a few minutes for the mat to become warm. As soon as this happened, the flow of energy began, as quietly and as naturally as a blood transfusion. He breathed in slowly as his energies began to revive.

He had been afraid that the graddik would steal the energy as fast as it flowed into him; but during the energy transfer, he could see that this was impossible—as difficult as to steal the water someone was drinking.

As with Charis, this energy exchange made his nerves tingle with pleasure, so that he felt himself being sucked down into a vortex. They had ceased to be two separate beings, and had blended together, so that both became part-woman and part-man. They no longer had individual histories; her past and his had blended together, as intimately as if they had spent days describing their lives to one another. Yet in another sense they remained apart, for she was not giving herself, but doing this as a nurse, to restore him to health.

After a quarter of an hour, he felt as refreshed as if he had just awakened from a long night's sleep; he would have been perfectly happy to shoulder his knapsack and begin the journey back home. Umaya pushed herself away from him, swung her legs onto the floor, and picked up her dress. He could sense that his maleness had refreshed her exactly as her female energies had revitalized him. As she slipped on her dress, which she had unbuttoned down the front, he found himself admiring her shapely breasts and buttocks without a trace of erotic attraction. She was like a nurse who had just changed his bandages.

He was struck by a sudden thought.

"Does your father know you are doing this?"

"Of course." She smiled at him as if she found the question naive. Her nonverbal thoughts, which he could now read, went on to indicate that this was simply a part of her job.

"And do you have to do it very often?" The question was accompanied by a twinge of jealousy.

"Not often, but sometimes." She must have noted the jealousy, for she added: "I had to do it last night, or the man would have died."

Niall did not have to ask the identity of the man; he could read in her mind that it was Drusco, the overseer who had been flogged for failing to meet his production target.

She smiled at him and went out; the bolt slid into place.

Niall felt curiously disturbed, half-troubled by some thought that refused to emerge into the light of full consciousness.

Now that he was feeling better, the cell seemed intolerable—cold, damp, and drafty. Was this why the Magician had allowed Umaya to restore his energies—to make the place twice as unbearable? But at least his mind was now feeling alert again, and could return to the question of how he could escape.

The first possibility was Umaya. Yet although their close physical contact had made him aware that she found him attractive, she was undoubtedly too afraid of the Magician to help him.

It was as he was thinking about her that he realized that their minds were still in contact. He was aware that she had now climbed two flights of stairs and was about to enter the guardroom, behind which lay the two small rooms that she shared with her father. With a little effort, Niall was able to watch her close the door behind her, then place the box with the lake weed in a drawer and lock it, hanging the key on a board next to the door. He was also able to see the clock on the guardroom wall, which showed half past five.

This reminded him that it would be dusk in the spider city, and that his mother would now be thinking about contacting him. He therefore turned on his back, closed his eyes, and immediately became aware of her presence. He was not surprised by the coincidence, having become accustomed to such things when his mind was alert.

Because she was inside his mind, she could sense his condition.

"Good. You feel better."

"Yes, the jailer's daughter gave me energy."

"I can feel her presence." Her voice suddenly became urgent. "Please be very careful."

"Careful?" But as he spoke, she disappeared.

He was completely bewildered. This had never happened before. Sometimes his mother had lost contact because the energy of communication faded. But that could not have happened, for her voice had been strong and clear.

His first impulse was to try to reestablish contact. But some instinct told him not to do this.

What had she meant by: "Be very careful"? Did she mean Umaya? Why should he be careful of Umaya?

The more he thought of it, the more certain he became that his mother had broken off the communication. But why should she?

He reconstructed what had happened in his mind. He had told her that Umaya had given him energy, and she had replied that she could feel her presence. She had warned him to be careful and broken off communication.

Suddenly he understood.

If she could sense Umaya's presence inside him, then she must have realized that Umaya could read his thoughts.

And if Umaya could read his thoughts, then so could the Magician. For, like the Spider Lord, he could read the minds of any of his subjects.

This, he now realized, was why the Magician allowed her to give energy transfusions to prisoners like Niall and Drusco. It meant he had access to what they were thinking.

Completely unaware that she was doing so, Umaya was serving as a telepathic link with everyone in the prison.

Niall felt stunned at his own stupidity, and at the same time, relieved that the consequences had not been more serious. If his mother had not grasped the danger, the Magician would have learned about the crystal globe. For only moments before he had spoken to her, Niall had been about to turn his thoughts to the problem of escape. And the trolls and the crystal globe would inevitably have played a major part in those reflections.

And that would have been a disaster. When Niall had asked the trolls whether he should take the crystal globe to Shadowland, the grandfather had replied: "No, for that would make him invincible."

Nevertheless, there was still one possibility that troubled him. It was now obvious why his mother had broken off communication—because she was afraid that the Magician might have direct access to Niall's mind. In which case he might, at that very moment, be listening to their conversation. She was afraid what Niall might reveal.

Fortunately, Niall knew her fear was unfounded. The Magician had no direct access to Niall's thoughts. After six months among spiders, Niall became instantly aware if someone tried to probe his mind.

But was it possible that the Magician had already learned about the existence of the crystal globe through Umaya? That thought turned his heart to lead. For as they had been engaged in a mutual exchange of energies, their minds had been completely open to one another, as if they had exchanged identities.

But a moment's thought reassured him. Niall knew enough about telepathy to be aware of its limitations. Unless a thought was very close to the surface of the mind, like a fish swimming on the surface of the sea, then it was unlikely to be noticed. After all, the depths of the sea contained millions of fishes. While they had been exchanging energy, Niall had been given full access to Umaya's past life. He understood a great deal about her history, and what kind of a person she was. Yet he did not even know the answer to such obvious questions as whether she had ever been in love, or whether her mother was alive. And his own thoughts had been far from the trolls and the crystal globe. It had been wholly focused on the relief of absorbing energy. So it was virtually impossible that she knew anything about the globe.

Even so, the realization of how close he had come to betraying his secret made Niall shudder. It was obviously pure luck that had saved him.

This thought engendered a strange glow of optimism, accompanied by a flash of insight. The optimism sprang from the sudden realization that he had always been lucky. Even as a child he had never been afraid of the dangers that surrounded their desert habitat—giant scorpions and tiger beetles and saga insects—because he had an odd sense of invulnerability. He had, it is true, experienced despair when his father had been killed and his family abducted by spiders, yet when he found himself treated as a privileged hostage in the palace of King Kazak, and held Merlew in his arms, he realized that his luck had never deserted him.

And now he knew how close he had been to betraying the trolls and the whereabouts of the crystal globe, he once again had the feeling that some providence was looking after him.

The conclusion was equally clear. All Niall had learned about human history in the white tower had convinced him that the Magician could not win. Such people always brought about their own downfall.

The question that now interested him was how that that downfall would come about, and whether he was destined to play any part in it.

N iall was dozing when Umaya brought his supper. This consisted of a cup of water and a slice of bread—although he was pleased to see that the bread was buttered. As she turned to leave, she reached into the pocket of her smock and placed something wrapped in cloth on his plate. It proved to be a small but plump fish, still slightly warm. It was oily and salty, like the fish at Typhon's house, but Niall was so hungry that it tasted better than any fish he had ever eaten.

He had deliberately not spoken to Umaya; he was afraid that she might divine that he was shielding his thoughts from her. It was unlikely, but since he now felt so close to her, it was a risk he dared not take.

After eating, he lay down, still hungry, and set out to induce a state of calm. What he wanted to achieve was the point of deep relaxation that he had experienced in the cave of the chameleon men. He began by conjuring up the taste of the earthy water and the sense of peace that followed, then emptied his mind, and focused on achieving a deeper and deeper state of tranquillity. After a few minutes, all tensions dissolved away, and he entered the timeless state of total relaxation. His mind was now attuned to the processes of nature: to the slow drift of clouds, to rain falling on leaves, to roots that absorbed the energies of the Earth. His heart was beating so quietly that it seemed to have stopped, and he had a strange sense that his body did not belong to him.

It was at this point that he realized that his cell was full of presences. They seemed oddly familiar, and at first he thought they were nature spirits. Then he remembered where he had encountered them: by the side of the lake, on the first day he came to Shadowland. These were the wraiths and ghosts that gave Shadowland its name.

Because he had passed the point of deep relaxation, he was able to look at them directly. Most of them were little more than shadows, and Niall could sense that they were living in a state that was akin to a dream, in which reality dissolved and fluctuated. They were here, in the dungeons of the Magician's palace, because they wanted to cling to something that was solid and familiar. He observed a woman dressed in a ball gown, as if on her way to one of the Magician's receptions, and a tall man in military uniform. Both were so transparent that he had to blur his focus to see them.

Then he noticed the black figure standing near the door, almost invisible against the dark background, and recognized one of the troglas.

Remembering the difficulty of communicating, he addressed it in the direct-meaning language of the chameleon men: "Can you speak to me?"

As before, the answer was like the echo of a distant voice.

Niall said: "I cannot understand you."

The trogla took a step toward him. If he had not been certain that it meant no harm, it would have made his heart beat faster. It walked in a crouching position on legs that seemed too short for its body. The nostrils were wide and slightly flattened, and in its black face the teeth, which were pointed, looked unnaturally white. But the eyes, which were yellow and very large, were obviously intelligent.

When it spoke, its voice still sounded blurry and out of focus, but the meaning was clear. It was saying that its kind had lived here for centuries before the coming of human beings.

Niall asked: "How did you die?"

The reply surprised him: "We were killed by your people."

Niall was puzzled. The troll had told him that the troglas had died from poison gas in a volcanic eruption.

"But why?"

"For meat. They made clothes of our skins."

Niall recalled the black leather garments that he had seen in the karvasid's museum. In a less relaxed state he would have felt nauseated.

"When did this happen?"

The reply was like a shrug, which he interpreted to mean: "The dead have no sense of time."

"But before this city was built?"

There was a long pause, and Niall wondered if the trogla had understood him. When it finally came, the answer puzzled him more than ever.

"In the time of the karvasid Sathanas."

Niall was beginning to tire, and was losing the ability to maintain the state of deep relaxation. The other ghosts had already become invisible, and seconds later, the trogla also vanished.

He lay down on the bed and closed his eyes. One thing seemed obvious: he needed sleep. Without sleep he remained vulnerable. Even as this thought came into his head, he yawned until his jaw cracked.

He pulled the blanket over his shoulders, and as he did so, the slightly musty smell reminded him of the earthy taste of the water in the cave of the chameleon men. This in turn reminded him of the words spoken by their leader just before their parting: "If you wish to return to us, remember this taste." His tiredness vanished immediately. He imagined himself staring into the water, with its tiny fragments of moss, and conjured up its smell and taste. Instantly, without transition, he found himself back in the cave, sitting where he had sat before, and with a vessel of the earthy-tasting water beside him. The others were also around him, exactly as before.

Was he dreaming? It hardly seemed to matter. What was important was that he felt he was surrounded by friends, and that they were obviously conscious of his presence.

As before, his sleepiness had vanished completely. This was because his mind was in contact with their minds, and they were wide awake. And, as before, their minds communicated with him as if they were one person.

They repeated what they had said before: "Show us how you fall asleep."

So Niall closed his eyes, imagined that he was switching off the light, and allowed himself to float into quiescence. But this time he was aware that he was no longer drifting into sleep; there was a strong sense of being deliberately and carefully guided. Moreover, it was clear that the state he was being guided toward was only one of dozens of possible states.

Within moments, he was descending into confusion, in which voices, images, and thoughts floated around as if they were fish swimming in a pond—fish that existed quite independently of his mind. Then he became aware that he was asleep and dreaming. Yet his surroundings looked oddly real. He was standing in the street, outside Typhon's house, and the guard who looked like one of Skorbo's assassins was standing at the top of the steps in front of the gate. He was staring woodenly ahead, although at one point he wrinkled his nose and expelled his breath, obviously suffering from boredom.

Niall was not afraid of being noticed, for he was invisible even to himself. He could feel his own body, and even the material of his tunic against his skin, but when he looked down there was nothing there.

He tried clearing his throat, to see if he could be heard, but the guard continued to stare into space with the same dull expression.

Suddenly possessed of an absurd suspicion, Niall mounted the steps and reached out to touch him. His fingers went straight through the man's arm.

Niall touched a metal bar of the gate. Although his fingers were invisible, he could feel them passing through it, as if the gate was made of gossamerlike threads. Now convinced that his body was on a different wavelength from his surroundings, Niall walked through the closed gate.

As he passed the fountain, the spray fell on his cheek, but he felt nothing whatsoever.

The front door was closed. He stopped automatically to knock, and again had the gossamer feeling as his knuckles failed to connect. He took a step forward and walked through the door.

There seemed to be no one at home. He crossed the dining room and turned left toward the kitchen. The moog was standing outside the kitchen door, his arms by his side. Unlike the guard, he did not look bored, but his eyes simply stared at the opposite wall. His chest was not even rising and falling.

To see whether it could be done, Niall walked through the wall instead of the door, and found himself in a large, well-appointed kitchen with cupboards of shiny, dark wood, and a marble floor. The clock on the wall showed half past eight. Katia was sitting at the table, drinking coffee, while the older woman with the body of a twenty-year-old stood at the sink washing clothes by hand. They were speaking telepathically, and Niall observed that, in this dream-body state, he was almost painfully sensitive to thought waves; it was rather like being naked in the rain.

As Niall entered, Katia was saying: ". . . find themselves in trouble."

The woman at the sink replied: "I'm not saying I agree with them. But I can understand why they think there are too many rules and regulations."

Unlike Katia, whose voice was that of a working girl, the woman's voice was unexpectedly cultured.

Katia said: "What do they expect? They're soldiers."

The woman replied: "Yes, but we're not."

"What's that supposed to mean?"

"Why doesn't he allow marriage? You're all right. You've got two lovers. I haven't even got one. Men and women *need* someone to share their bed. I want a husband!"

Katia looked around nervously and said "Sshh!"

The woman said: "Why? There's nobody here."

There was the sound of a door closing with a crash. Katia said: "That must be him. And he's in a bad mood. He always slams the door when he's in a bad mood."

The older woman turned back to the sink and began diligently wringing out clothes.

Katia went to the door, walking straight through Niall. As this happened, he noticed that he experienced a momentary feeling of pleasure. This intrigued him. It showed that, although bodiless and apparently insubstantial, he could still experience the human life-field.

He followed Katia into the dining room. She had been right. Typhon looked irritable and disgruntled. He threw his cloak onto a chair, then flung himself down in the other. Without asking him, Katia sat down at his feet and began unlacing his boots. When she had pulled them off, and began massaging his feet, he said: "Never mind that. Get me a drink." He spoke in verbal language.

She went back to the kitchen. Niall followed her as she went to a cupboard and removed a wide-necked carafe of golden wine, which she placed on a tray with two glasses. As she stood at the table, Niall stepped up behind her, then took an additional step so he blended with her body.

It was a curious sensation. For a moment, he felt like a drop of rain that has fallen on a dry sheet on a washing line and remains on the surface for a moment before being absorbed. As soon as this happened, there was a feeling of warmth, and a pleasantly erotic sensation, and then Niall actually became Katia, her sensations and feelings replacing his own.

As she picked up the tray and went out of the kitchen, Niall followed her and watched her place it on the table in front of Typhon, who poured himself a full glass of wine, then drank most of it in a deep draft. Again, Niall was able to sense his feelings: tiredness, impatience, anger. Katia stood silently, waiting for further orders. Niall was tempted to step inside her again, but resisted the urge; if he could feel her presence, she might be able to feel his.

She asked: "Would you like something to eat?"

Typhon said irritably: "No. I'll wait for Gerek."

She went out, and Niall followed her back to the kitchen. He had decided to wait for Gerek, hoping to learn why Typhon was in a bad mood.

The older woman was still standing at the sink, although she was now gutting fish on the draining board, while Katia was preparing food at the table. Niall stood behind the woman at the sink, then stepped forward into her body.

He immediately experienced the same pleasantly sensuous warmth as with Katia, but far stronger. Suddenly he understood why she had said she needed a husband: her body was tingling with erotic energy. Moreover, she instantly became aware of Niall—not, like the moog, as an alien presence, but as a male energy that she absorbed eagerly.

Mildly stimulated, and feeling a little guilty at this intrusion into her body, he hastily withdrew. Yet in that brief contact, he had caught a glimpse of something that intrigued him: a feeling of intense hostility toward the Magician. He therefore overruled his feeling of guilt, and stepped once more inside her.

He experienced at once the same sense of complete identification that he had experienced earlier in the day with Umaya, giving him total access to her memory. But in the case of Umaya, he had been aware that she had the same access to his own thoughts and feelings, whereas this woman did not.

Her name was Quinella, and she was fifty-four years old. Like all the other women in this city, she took daily doses of a medicine that delayed the onset of age. But the medicine only affected the body; the head, and to a lesser extent, the neck, aged normally.

One side effect of this medicine was that it stimulated physical desire, so that Quinella was as sensually alive as an adolescent. And since, like many women of her age, she had no lover, the frustration often became intolerable. When this happened, on average once a week, she went to the kalinda tree and embraced it, allowing it to drain away her erotic energies.

Now, suddenly, Niall understood why a group of women had been embracing the tree when they had passed it in Gerek's carriage. But why had Gerek told him the women were hoping to conceive, as if implying that it was just a superstition?

Niall also understood why Quinella was angry with the Magician. When she had heard about the plan to make peace with the spider—news that had spread almost instantaneously, since everyone was telepathic—she had been stunned with incredulity and delight; like every other inhabitant of the city, she had felt that it signaled a new era. So the news that Niall and the captain had been imprisoned aroused furious resentment, and the end of her hopes of finding a husband.

The sound of voices from the other room indicated that Gerek had come home. Katia placed the food on the tray with another carafe of wine, and went out.

Gerek was sitting opposite Typhon, and was already draining a glass of wine. Niall could sense that, like Typhon, he was weary and impatient. When Katia tried to kneel to unlace his boots, he waved her away.

As the door closed behind her, Typhon said bitterly: "He says it's all my fault, of course." The strength of his feeling was so great that it made Niall wince.

"But why you?"

"Because he says I announced the peace treaty without consulting him." Typhon drained his glass and stared morosely at the floor.

Gerek said: "But you *always* make public announcements."

"That's what I told him. He claims it was a calculated piece of treachery."

But Niall suddenly knew the Magician had been correct. Typhon had made the announcement with the aim of forcing his hand.

Gerek said: "That's absurd."

"Of course it's absurd. And now he's just making the situation worse. He doesn't know how to cope with disagreement. He's too pig-headed."

Gerek looked around nervously, then went to the front door and peered out. As he came back to his chair he said: "I wouldn't like to see you land in one of his dungeons." He sat down again. "Tell me what's happened."

Typhon made an obvious effort to calm himself.

"After you left this morning, Baltiger and Vasco came to see me. They wanted me to talk to the karvasid. I told them there'd be no point— once he's decided on something, he never changes his mind. So then they asked me if they could go and see him—the whole Citizens' Committee."

Gerek sat up. "My God!"

"Yes, quite. How can I explain that he won't see anybody because he hates people? They think he's wise and kind, and that's because I've told them so until I'm blue in the face. So how can I suddenly tell them the truth?"

Gerek said: "But after last night they must realize that he's got a short fuse."

"Yes, yes, they realize that all right. But Baltiger's the mayor, Vasco's the chairman of the Citizens' Committee. They think they've got the right to express their opinions."

Gerek clutched his forehead in a parody of despair. "So what did you tell them?"

"I said I'd pass on their views to the karvasid. So they finally rode with me as far as the kalinda tree, then went to a meeting at the Town Hall. I promised I'd go there later and tell them his decision."

"And what were you supposed to tell our master?"

"Oh, what you'd expect. That everybody in Shadowland wants a peace treaty, and perhaps it's not too late."

"And what did *he* say?"

Typhon smiled grimly. "He almost foamed at the mouth. Sent for Jelko and ordered him to arm the guards with Reapers."

"What!" Gerek was horrified.

"Oh, they're not the real thing. They fire a kind of laser beam. They could give you a bad burn, but that's about all."

"Thank God for that!"

Typhon shrugged. "If we had the real thing, he would have invaded Korsh a long time ago."

Talking to Gerek obviously had made Typhon feel more relaxed, and he began helping himself to food.

Gerek asked: "And what did you tell Baltiger and whatshisname when you went to the Town Hall?"

"I haven't been yet."

"You haven't?"

"What's the point? I'd only have to tell more lies—tell them the peace treaty will be signed next week or next month. Let him tell his own lies. He's better at it than I am."

Niall was not deceived by this tone of injured innocence. Typhon was saying that he was sick of the Magician. Like Quinella and the guard who emptied the slop bucket, he felt that it was time the despot was relieved of his power. Merely expressing his irritation aloud to Gerek increased its force.

This, Niall realized, was the problem with a city in which everyone was telepathic—public opinion could change in a moment.

As Katia pushed in the trolley, Niall decided he had heard enough. It was time to find out what was happening at the Town Hall.

He walked through the door and down the steps, into the street. The city center was half a mile away, and he had no desire to walk—to begin with, walking without a body was an oddly unsatisfactory experience—since he was weightless, it made him feel like a ghost.

He decided to try raising his arms to see if he could fly. At first nothing seemed to happen; then, quite abruptly, he found himself in the market square.

Suddenly, Niall understood the meaning of the phrase "as quick as thought."

The market was crowded, as he had expected; yet there was none of the gaiety and bustle he had noticed on his previous visit. Now there was a feeling of tension; it was as if everyone was waiting for something to happen.

Walking through the market gave him one of the strangest sensations Niall had ever experienced. It was unnecessary to push his way through the crowd, since he was able to walk straight through people. But as he stepped in and out of someone's body, he felt a slight frisson, a tingle like an almost imperceptible electric current.

He was interested to note that there was a quite clear and distinct difference between men and women. Female energy created a sense of warmth and attraction—sometimes so strong that he occasionally turned to look at the woman he had just walked through. He absorbed this energy like food, and observed that it produced an effect akin to sweetness. Male energy, on the other hand, seemed somehow "dry" and nonabsorbent, sometimes even with a touch of bitterness, like the smell of wood smoke.

He also observed that every individual had a different "flavor," which was the essence of each personality. This difference would have been impossible to put into words, but was like a series of differing tastes or smells, each one defying description. Niall realized suddenly how much we miss when we know people only from the outside.

Sometimes the contact was minimal, as when his shoulder passed through someone else's. But if his body corresponded for a moment with another body, he received the full "flavor" of the personality. And if he spent more than a few seconds in someone's body—which happened if they were walking in the same direction—he became aware of what they were thinking and feeling, and something of their history.

Without exception, everyone was thinking the same treasonable thoughts about the karvasid.

Under different circumstances he would have enjoyed spending hours wandering in and out of so many individuals—particularly since this involved a continual shock of surprise to realize that other people were as real as he was. But for the moment, he shared their feverish curiosity to know what was happening in the Town Hall, and what conclusions the Citizens' Committee had reached.

He recognized the man standing at the top of the Town Hall steps as Vasco. He was staring anxiously into the distance and tugging his mustache. The mayoress was standing beside him, her round blue eyes making her look permanently astonished. She was saying: "Shall we send a messenger to his house?"

"I've already done it. The doorkeeper says he's not home yet."

"I wonder what can be keeping him?"

Niall guessed they were speaking about Typhon, but to confirm it, he walked behind her and stepped into her body. The sensation was pleasantly erotic, both for her and for him. She had been suffering from a headache, but his masculine energy immediately caused it to disappear.

He also knew that her name was Selena, that she was thirty-nine years old, and that she and Vasco were lovers. This, of course, was perfectly normal in Shadowland society. What was not permissible was that they spent far more time together than the law allowed; both would be sentenced to the mines or flogging if they were found out. This, Niall realized, was why they were so anxious for a peace treaty with the spiders; they intended to seize the first opportunity to leave Shadowland and marry.

Niall's access to her memory also gave him instant knowledge of the history, geography, and social organization of Shadowland. There was far too much to absorb at once—he would have had to spend a morning inside her to grasp it. At least he now understood the many dissatisfactions that seethed beneath the surface of this isolated society.

Even so, her memory provided no answer to the question that puzzled him most: why the Magician refused to permit marriage.

Since he knew that they were wasting their time waiting for Typhon, Niall placed into her head the thought that they should go inside. Unaware that it was not her own idea, she touched Vasco's arm and said: "Let's go inside. He's sure to come soon." They climbed a marble staircase to the council chamber used by the Citizens' Committee.

The place was crowded, and dozens of heads turned as they opened the door; Niall could sense their disappointment that Typhon was not with them. Selena and Vasco took their places on the platform, where Baltiger and a dozen other men and women were seated around a table covered with a green baize cloth. Selena sat down beside the mayor and whispered in his ear. He nodded, then stood up, clearing his throat.

"A messenger has been sent to the prefect's house, but he is not at home."

He sat down, and the members of the Committee began talking to one another in low voices. There was a general air of uncertainty and indecision. Without Typhon's advice, no one knew what to do next. Yet all had a feeling that some change was at hand.

Vasco coughed and stood up.

"I have a proposal to make. I suggest that I and a few more senior members of the Committee should go to Typhon's house and wait until he returns." He looked around hesitantly. "Perhaps it would be better if everyone else went home. Will anyone second that?"

There was a silence. Everyone knew that if they all went home, the moment of rebellion would be over, and tomorrow would once again be like yesterday and the day before.

Niall realized it was time for him to act.

As Selena said hesitantly: "I wonder . . ." everyone looked at her. She was not a self-assertive person, and the thoughts that now came into her head frightened her. But since she was accustomed to speaking in public, Niall's suggestion that she should stand up made her rise automatically to her feet. And suddenly, to her own surprise, she knew precisely what she wanted to say.

"Is there really anyone in this room who wants to go home?" She looked around at their faces, and the answer was obvious. "I certainly don't." There was a murmur of approval. Encouraged by their support, her voice grew stronger. "There are certain matters that this Committee would like to put to the prefect, and that we would like the prefect to put to the karvasid on our behalf. To begin with, we would like to tell him that every citizen of Shadowland wishes to offer full support for the idea of a peace treaty with Korsh. Is there anyone here who disagrees?" There was silence. "In that case, and since the prefect is not here to take our message, I suggest that we take it ourselves. Are you willing to follow me?"

From any other audience there would have been a roar of approval, but Shadowlanders had been disciplined to observe restraint. Nevertheless, the spontaneity with which the audience rose to its feet made their answer clear.

Vasco had caught Selena's eye. He looked stunned. He had never seen her like this. In effect, he was asking her: Do you know what you're doing? And in effect, she was replying: It makes no difference—it's too late to change our minds.

Niall also knew what Vasco was thinking: that to march on the palace was futile because it could achieve no result. The Magician held all the cards and they held none.

Yet like Selena, Niall knew that it had to be done; it was time to show the Magician that all his subjects disagreed with him. After all, he could not have them all flogged or sent to the mines. This rebellion was not a rational conviction, merely an instinct.

As she descended from the platform, the audience opened up a passage to allow Selena and the Committee access to the door. Then everyone followed her down the stairs and out into the street.

Niall was fascinated by what now happened. Unlike the spiders, Shadowlanders had no collective awareness; their telepathic abilities were restricted to individual communication. Yet as the audience from the Town Hall overflowed into the marketplace, every one of the waiting crowd already knew what had happened, and was ready to accept Selena and the unwilling Vasco as their leaders. Niall estimated the total number at five hundred, of which half were women. Many men were dressed in their military uniforms, although none were carrying weapons.

As they reached the end of the bridge, it became clear that the road to the palace was blocked by soldiers carrying Reapers. Behind them, up the hill that led up to the kalinda tree, were perhaps a hundred more, spaced at regular intervals.

Without hesitation, Selena led the way across the bridge. The soldiers, Niall observed, were looking nervous as the crowd drew closer.

As they reached the center of the bridge, Niall noticed the kalinda tree. The air around it was illuminated by a shimmering light that flowed in waves, and reminded him of the sun trying to break through on a misty morning. Its branches looked as if it was illuminated by pale blue flames. For reasons he could not understand, the sight filled Niall with a strange sense of vitality and happiness.

In front of the soldiers, Jelko, the guard commander, was staring impassively at the advancing crowd, his Reaper pointing at the ground. On either side of him stood the two seven-foot giants who had directed traffic at the Magician's reception. Jelko was a big man with square shoulders and a commanding presence. Since his face conveyed no hint of what he was thinking, Niall chose the simplest way to find out. He stood behind Jelko, then took a step forward into his body.

The "flavor" of masculine energy was overwhelming, and this, he recognized, was because Jelko was so concentrated on the crisis at hand. The crowd, although peaceable, stretched beyond the other end of the bridge, and although they were unarmed, they had an air of quiet determination that was as intimidating as open rebellion. Although Niall's knowledge of the spiders should have prepared him for it, he was once again astonished at the extent to which a crowd could behave like a single individual.

It came as a pleasant surprise to discover that Jelko felt no hostility toward these marchers, and that this was due to the fact that he and

Selena were lovers. Now, as she strode toward him, the captain of the Guard was feeling she was looking particularly attractive. Niall had to agree that, with her bow-shaped mouth and bright eyes and halo of blond hair, the mayoress looked like a romantic heroine.

She halted ten feet in front of Jelko, and the crowd behind her came to a halt as if someone had shouted an order.

Jelko asked stiffly: "What is happening?"

Selena said: "The Citizens' Committee would like to see the karvasid."

"Have you spoken to the prefect about it?"

"No. We think he is in the palace."

Jelko shook his head. "He left hours ago."

She looked him in the eyes.

"In that case, perhaps you could take the message?"

"What is it?"

"That the Citizens' Committee, with the full support of our fellow citizens, wishes to recommend that the idea of a peace treaty should be actively explored."

The mayor added: "And that an ambassador should be sent to Korsh as soon as possible."

Although his face showed no sign of it, Jelko was uncertain how to proceed. His inclination was to order the crowd to disperse, but since it was led by the mayor and mayoress, he wondered whether it was within his authority. Niall did his best to reinforce his doubts by suggesting that Jelko should simply obey orders. But it was Selena who added the final touch of persuasion by saying: "The Citizen's Committee will take full responsibility."

Jelko said: "Very well, I will take the message." He turned to one of the red-haired giants. "Captain Zadin, I'm leaving you in charge. If anyone tries to advance beyond this point, order the guards to fire." And having once more asserted his authority, he turned and strode up the hill.

Niall, still seeing the world through Jelko's eyes, found his reactions surprising. Jelko was aware that what he was doing amounted to an act of insubordination that might cost him a flogging and demotion. He knew that he should have ordered the crowd to disperse, and advised the Citizens' Committee to go and find Typhon.

Why had he not done so? Because, Niall realized, like everyone else in Shadowland, Jelko was hoping to see the downfall of the karvasid, or at least some erosion of his authority. This act of defiance was his own attempt to bring it closer.

Yet twenty-four hours earlier, such an idea could not even have entered his head.

It was, Niall realized, he himself who was responsible for all this. His act of saying no to the Magician had made the citizens of Shadowland realize something they had so far not even dared to think: that life would be easier without this tyrant they had always regarded as their benefactor. What they really wanted was change.

Niall could see that, in a sense, this was unfair. In his own irritable and self-centered way, the Magician *did* have the interests of his subjects at heart. He spent a great deal of his time thinking of ways of keeping them occupied and amused. Compared to the slaves in the spider city, his subjects were very well treated. He was not wantonly cruel and sadistic—merely an obsessive egotist who lacked self-control. Power had turned him into a monster. Niall was not sure whether, under similar circumstances, he would not be the same.

Jelko was approaching the kalinda tree. From behind his eyes it looked normal. But as soon as Niall stepped out of Jelko's body, it turned into the surging mass of pale blue flame he had seen from the bridge. Once again, he was filled with happiness and vitality.

This lasted for only as long as it took him to realize that some invisible force was pulling him toward the tree. He grabbed at a bush at the edge of the path, but his hand went through it. In that moment he felt as helpless as when he was being swept along the underground river. As he found himself rushing toward the tree, he flung both hands in front of his face to protect it.

There was no impact, and what happened next was too fast to understand. He seemed to be sucked into the tree, as if into the center of a whirlwind, and hurled upward like a leaf. After that he was catapulted out of the top of the tree in a shower of energy like sparkling beads of light, and swept toward the palace. The pale brown road flashed underneath him, and he glimpsed Jelko walking uphill. After that he was flying toward the top of the central tower, in a roaring vortex of energy that made his head spin.

Suddenly the energy turned blue, and he was looking out through a wall of glass, and staring into a face that filled him with dread.

H e was standing inside the glass cylinder that stretched from floor to ceiling, and waves of darkness rose around him like bubbles in a liquid. The glass, about an inch thick, was as clear as water.

The face that stared into his own was not, as he had feared in his first wave of panic, the Magician, but an enormous crouching creature with yellow eyes and blue-black lips, which were drawn back in a snarl. That it could see him was apparent, for it was obviously as startled as he was. It had no nose—only two holes—and the jaw was flat and shallow like a beast's. The yellow canine teeth looked like curved needles.

Then he knew he had seen it before—not in actuality, but in the mental picture conveyed to him by the troll. This, he realized, was the boca, the demonic entity enslaved by the will of the Magician. And this room he recognized as the Magician's laboratory, which he had glimpsed through the eyes of the raven. To his relief, there was no sign of the Magician.

The face of the boca resembled a skull covered in a thin layer of dark flesh; its scrawny body must have been eight feet tall, so that even in its crouching position it looked down on Niall. The huge hands had black, swollen knuckles and claws instead of nails. Over the hips and belly the taut skin was almost concave. As it stared at him, the yellow eyes, with their black pupils, were intelligent, but their expression made Niall feel glad there was a sheet of glass between them. He felt like a mouse being watched by a hungry cat.

He pressed his hands against the glass, to reassure himself it was solid; it felt quite firm and unyielding. In his state of invisibility, this seemed odd, since in the past hour it had begun to seem natural to be able to walk through obstacles. Then the answer came to him. This tube had been built to contain living energy, vibrations that had passed straight through the walls of this room. It therefore had to be of some special substance that was impermeable to living energy.

Next he tried the method that had worked for him so far—envisaging himself elsewhere. Closing his eyes, he imagined himself back in Typhon's house. But when he opened them again, he was still inside the tube. He tried envisaging himself back in his cell. That also failed to work. With rising apprehension, he tried conjuring up the smell of the earthy water and imagining himself in the cave of the chameleon men. But even as he did it, he was aware that his inner tension made it impossible to achieve the necessary state of relaxation. There was a distinct feeling of resistance.

Further experiments were cut short as the door opened and the Magician came in. Niall braced himself, expecting to be discovered immediately, but as the Magician glanced at the boca, then around the room, he evidently noticed nothing unusual. He turned to the bench, where there was a polished wooden box, and opened the lid. He took something from it, then sat down at the bench and became absorbed in an object that was concealed by his body.

The boca, meanwhile, had withdrawn to the farthest corner of the room, where it sat crouched beside a black wooden armchair; with its hands between its raised knees, it looked like some giant stick insect. Since the Magician had come in, its air of menace had disappeared, although it continued to eye Niall warily. Niall, who had been terrified that its fixed gaze would warn the Magician of his presence, permitted himself to relax. Even so, he continued to feel an irrational fear that the loud beating of his heart would give him away.

At any minute, he calculated, the commander of the guard should be arriving. The half-mile walk uphill should take about ten minutes. After five of these had passed, he began to look around the room, looking for ways of escape in the event of getting out of the tube. Meanwhile, in total silence, the blue energy bubbled and surged like boiling water, making his skin tingle and producing a burning sensation. Its smell reminded Niall of sea air on a stormy day. He had no doubt of its nature, for he had detected its presence in Quinella, Selena, and every other woman with whom he had recently been in contact. It was pure erotic energy, and in this undiluted form it produced in him a feeling of elation mixed with mild nausea.

This explained why women pressed themselves against the kalinda tree; it alleviated the discomfort. And that, he suddenly realized, must be the reason the Magician refused to allow marriage among his subjects. Frustration increased the feverish sexual energy that pervaded the air of the city like a fine moisture. In effect, the kalinda tree acted as a demoisturizer that absorbed it and transferred it to the laboratory.

Niall was startled by a tap on the door. The Magician grunted with irritation and went to answer it. As he did so, Niall's attention was caught by something on the bench that reflected the light. It was a crystal sphere, about the same size as the one he had found in the cave of the cliff dwellers. This was the object that had absorbed the Magician's attention.

Niall heard the guard at the doorway say: "Commander Jelko to see you, sir. He says it's urgent."

The Magician snapped: "What do you want?"

Jelko, his voice trembling with nervousness, said: "Excellency, the Citizens' Committee is asking to see you."

"What!" The voice was a shriek of incredulity. "How dare they? Tell them I don't see *anyone!*"

"There's a great crowd behind them, sir. They're blocking the whole bridge."

With two strides the Magician crossed to the window. When he spoke again his voice was ominous. "What do they want?"

"To see you. . . ."

"I know that, idiot. What about?"

"I think it's the peace treaty, sir. . . ."

There was a silence, then the reply came in a cold, hard voice. "Tell your men to open fire on them."

"Kill them all?" Jelko sounded stunned. He was so shocked that he forget to say "sir."

"I don't care how many you kill. The fools have got to be taught a lesson."

Niall was still sufficiently in tune with Jelko to know what he was thinking: that Selena would be the first to die. He also knew exactly how Jelko would react: in his present state of mind, he would prefer to kill the karvasid.

Jelko's voice sounded oddly calm as he said: "Wouldn't it be better if I ordered them to disperse?"

It was then that Niall knew that Jelko was preparing to fire. This questioning of his master's orders was calculated to draw an angry refusal.

But the Magician must have sensed this too. He turned to the boca and said something in a language Niall did not understand. With a speed that made Niall wince, it sprang across the room like some monstrous grasshopper and gripped Jelko's throat. There was a snapping noise as it broke his spine. Finally, it twisted Jelko's head around so it faced the other way. Then it dropped the body on the floor and turned toward its master.

The room exploded with a radiance that made Niall shut his eyes. When he opened them again, the Magician was holding out the globe, and the boca was backing away, its huge hands over its eyes; it returned to crouch in the corner, looking oddly like a beaten dog.

Niall had no time to wonder what had happened, for the Magician was staring at him, and he was suddenly aware that the blinding glare had made him visible. His body was shining as if it had become luminous.

The Magician came slowly across the room, holding out the radiant globe. Niall tried to move, but found he was paralyzed.

"You again." He nodded his head slowly. "I might have known you'd be behind this."

Niall felt like a fly trapped in a bottle, and braced himself for whatever might happen next.

What happened was that the Magician held out the globe, whose glare was painful to the eyes. Since Niall was paralyzed, he could not close his eyelids. The globe seemed to be changing, as if it had turned into a spinning planet. Then it seemed to be turning itself inside out at a bewildering speed. Finally, it expanded until it filled the room.

At that point it ceased to be a globe, and became the face of the Magician, which also seemed to fill the room. It was immense, like the face of some giant statue, and the huge eyes were staring into Niall's, so that tiny red veins were clearly visible.

Niall realized he was inside the globe, looking out at the Magician, who was holding it between the palms of his hands. The gigantic face was smiling at him.

"It was kind of you to come to see me. It saved me the trouble of coming to see you."

He placed the globe on the bench, then bent over it, so his face once again filled the room.

"Don't look so anxious. We are going to be friends and allies. Aren't we?"

Niall nodded. It happened without his volition. And he knew suddenly that he was trapped: not merely his body, but his brain and his whole being.

Oddly enough, he no longer felt afraid of the Magician. The giant face seemed to exude trustworthiness and kindness. A small part of Niall's brain was astonished at this transformation. But the rest of him—including his consciousness—felt fixed and rigid, as if transformed into stone. This part of him had become the Magician's puppet, with no willpower of its own. To be so completely controlled would have been a terrifying sensation, if there had been enough of him left to feel terror.

The Magician said: "Who taught you to make the spirit walk?"

"Simeon."

"Who is Simeon?"

"A doctor from the city of the bombardier beetles."

The Magician was now probing his mind.

"Who taught you how to find your way to Shadowland?"

"The trolls."

For a moment, the tiny free portion of Niall's consciousness was afraid he was going to be forced to betray the trolls. But since he was so rigidly confined in the grip of the Magician's will, he was unable to feel the fear that might have betrayed him.

While their minds were in contact, Niall was also conscious of the Magician's thoughts and feelings, the most dominant of them being satisfaction: a sense of good fortune that Niall had fallen into his hands so easily, and that his mind was so pliable. Like the easygoing Typhon, Niall would make a good servant.

Niall himself felt no alarm at the prospect. He felt he was completely under the domination of a being whose intentions toward him were benevolent, and who would probably become a friend. Resistance would have seemed folly.

The Magician said: "Another question. Are you really the chosen of the goddess?"

"Yes." The word was unnecessary, since the purpose of the question was to get Niall to bring the answer to consciousness, where the Magician could inspect it. He nodded slowly.

"Amazing!"

What he saw clearly interested him deeply, and he would have liked to pursue it further. But at the moment he had other things to attend to. The chief of these was the revolt of his subjects. And since he was now in a good humor, he would deal with it strictly but justly. He was, after all, the benevolent father of his people. Nevertheless, they had no right to question his judgment, and must be made to understand that.

He said to Niall, almost affectionately: "You will have to remain here while I attend to the matter."

He raised the globe, and it once more filled the room with light. Then Niall found himself back inside the glass tube. The Magician slipped the globe into his pocket, and left the room.

A rivulet of blood was running across the floor from Jelko's neck. Moments later, the two guards came in, and looked down at Jelko's body with undisguised revulsion. The guards, obviously fighting the urge to vomit, grabbed the corpse by the ankles and wrists and dragged it outside. Since they had paid no attention to the boca, Niall deduced that they could not see it.

Alone again, Niall felt curiously placid and contented. All desire to escape had vanished. He and the Magician were reconciled, and there was nothing more to worry about. Veig would be cured, the peace treaty would be signed, and he would return to govern the spider city with the help and advice of his friend the Magician. It had all turned out well after all.

Five minutes went past. The clock on the wall showed twenty minutes past nine. It was a pity he was confined in the glass cylinder—he would have liked to look out of the window and see what was happening.

The boca, still crouched in its corner, was gazing at him intently. Why was it watching him so carefully when he had no intention of trying to escape? Niall stared into the yellow eyes, and was again struck by their intelligence.

Without any conscious decision, Niall tried probing its mind, and was surprised to realize that it was feeling pity for him. That seemed absurd. What was there about his situation to arouse pity?

Then, as if suddenly remembering something he had forgotten, he understood. The Magician had allayed all his fears and anxieties and made him feel free.

Why, in that case, was he still a prisoner?

It was then that Niall realized he had been in a state akin to hypnosis, and had wasted seven minutes, during which he ought to have been thinking about how to escape.

There was still one method that he had not tried.

He closed his eyes, and envisaged the younger of the troll children. There was still a slight feeling of resistance, but it vanished when he increased his attention. Then there was the unmistakable sense of contact with a living person, and he became aware that the child was asleep in his cot.

The fact that he was asleep made no difference to his effectiveness as a psychic link, for the boy was merely a steppingstone. Using him as his focus, Niall divided his attention, and reached out to the globe. Then he was in the troll cave looking at the crystal sphere on top of the pallen.

As if it sensed his presence, the green spark glowed in its center, then the globe began to radiate light. The troll, who was standing at the back of the cave, turned his head in surprise.

Contact with the crystal was instantaneous; it was like meeting someone he knew intimately. The globe responded to his mental vibration, and his mind flowed into the spider web of awareness as if causing its strands to light up. The sense of relief was enormous: not only of escaping from his glass prison, but of escaping from his everyday consciousness and entering the world of objective reality.

The troll, communicating in direct-meaning language, said: "Back again? What is happening now?"

"The Magician is about to order his soldiers to fire on the crowd."

The troll said dryly: "That sounds in character."

"What can I do about it?"

"Does he have his crystal with him?"

"Yes."

"Then use your own to neutralize it. That should distract him."

"How?"

"Ask it."

Niall reached up and took the crystal from the pallen; it produced a mild shock as its energies mingled with his own. He sat on the edge of the step below the chair, and allowed his mind to blend with the globe. This, as usual, produced such a deep sense of relaxation and absorption that he had to warn himself to remain alert. As soon as he focused on the question of neutralizing one globe with another, the answer became self-evident; it was merely a matter of bringing the two within one another's vibrational radius, and allowing energy to flow from the stronger to the weaker.

He asked: "Are you sure the karvasid's globe is less powerful than mine?"

"Quite sure."

"But how can I bring them close together?"

The troll pointed to Niall's crystal. "Take it with you." Seeing Niall's expression of puzzlement, he said: "Look."

He reached up and placed his own globe in the top of the pallen, where it immediately began to emit a rosy light. He said: "Watch."

He placed both his hands on either side of the pallen, about two feet below the globe, then slowly moved them upward. As his hands covered the globe, the rosy light seemed to spill over them as if it were some kind of liquid. The troll moved his hands farther apart, then slowly raised them. The light stayed inside his hands, while the globe itself became dull, like a gaslight that has been extinguished. The troll held out his hands to Niall. Between them, glowing like a red planet, the sphere of crimson light was suspended.

"Crystal has an energy body, just as you have. Now do what I have just done." He carefully held his hands above the pallen, then lowered them on either side of the globe. When he removed them, it was glowing once more.

The troll removed the globe and placed it in its black cloth on the floor. Niall took his own globe and placed it on the pallen, where it continued to glow. He tried to imitate the troll's movements precisely, placing both hands on the pallen and cautiously sliding them up. When they reached either side of the globe, he could feel the glow against his skin, as if he were touching a living thing. His palms were at least two inches from the surface. When he raised his hands further—as far above his head as he could reach—the light continued to glow between them, while the globe itself ceased to shine. Niall chuckled aloud at the sensation, which was rather like holding some soft, furry animal. It made his arms glow all the way to the shoulders.

As he closed his eyes, the troll said: "Good luck."

When he opened them again, he was a hundred yards below the kalinda tree, and saw that he was just in time. The Magician was already past it, striding toward the bridge. Niall found it easy to read his thoughts, for they were dominated by pleasurable anticipation at the punishment he intended to inflict on these stupid children who had dared to question his authority.

For a moment Niall's heart sank when he found there was no sign of the energy globe, although his palms still tingled from the contact. But as soon as he focused on the space between his hands, it glowed and re-formed. Intuitively, he knew that this was some kind of projection of the globe in the troll's cave, although in another sense it would have been equally true to say that the globe existed everywhere that its web extended.

Niall concentrated on it, and drew some of its energy into himself. Then he closed his eyes, envisaged being on the bridge, and instantly found himself there.

The mayor and mayoress were standing where he had left them more than half an hour earlier, when Jelko had set out to walk to the palace.

The crowd was totally silent as they watched the Magician walking toward them. All recognized the underlying air of menace, and wished they were elsewhere.

He halted, and stared at them, then asked, with dangerous civility: "Who wanted to see me?"

There was no sound, and everyone avoided his eyes. Although the Magician looked calm, everyone felt they would be inviting instant violence by answering.

The Magician looked at Selena. "You?"

She was obviously too frightened to speak. Niall felt instinctively that the Magician would select her as the first victim, and that he had to do something before that happened. He touched the globe with his hand, absorbed some of its power, then directed it against the Magician like throwing a stone. It was intended to shock and cause a diversion.

What happened was instantaneous. The Magician turned, and lashed out with the rage of an angry snake. Niall's physical body would have been carbonized by the bolt of energy, but his dream body only experienced a numbing shock before the force was absorbed by the crystal. Even this deflected blow was enough to stun him so that his senses seemed to fly apart.

When his vision cleared, he saw that the Magician was lying on the ground, and that the two red-haired guards were bending over him. What looked like the top of the Magician's head had fallen off and was lying nearby; for a moment Niall assumed he was dead, and was puzzled at the lack of blood. But when he took a step forward, walking straight through the nearest guard, he saw that the Magician's eyes were open, although the face was as pallid as a corpse. What lay on the ground a few feet away was not the top of his head, but a kind of hat shaped like a human cranium. The Magician's skull was, in fact, of normal size and shape, and covered with stubbly gray hair; what had fallen on the ground was a domelike false cranium.

The spectators were looking bewildered. They had seen the Magician twist around, then collapse as if shot. Niall could sense that, like him, they hoped he was dead. He also knew that when they realized he was still alive, they would almost certainly panic, knowing from experience that he would blame them. With five hundred people packed shoulder to shoulder, anything might happen.

Niall acted swiftly. Striding across to the mayoress, he entered her brain and suggested that she should take charge. Selena brushed past the

Reapers of the guards, and said in a clear voice: "The karvasid is ill. Carry him to the palace."

The two giants who had been bending ineffectually over the fallen man now raised him between them by placing their arms under his. He hung loose for a moment, his feet off the ground like a rag doll's, until two more guards took his feet and two more raised the middle of his body. The six men began carrying him, headfirst, up the hill. Niall walked beside them for a moment, long enough to ascertain that the Magician was still alive, although obviously dazed and stunned.

Major Baltiger had now taken the initiative, telling the crowd telepathically: "Please disperse to your homes." Niall felt relieved when they began to drift away—he was still afraid the Magician would recover enough to order the soldiers to open fire.

The blow and the shock had left him feeling oddly disconnected, but since he was weightless, he could stand without dizziness. He still had no idea what had happened and why the Magician had collapsed.

He removed the globe from the pocket of his tunic, noting that his fingertips felt tender, as if burned. Until his hand touched it, it felt as insubstantial as a ball of cotton wool, but as soon as he held it between his palms, it became solid and pleasantly cool, soothing the burned fingers. As soon as he focused on it, the disorientation vanished, to be succeeded by a glow of energy. The pain in his fingertips immediately disappeared.

As he entered the world of the crystal, he became aware of the damage. The lattice had been ripped apart by a force too powerful for its strands to absorb. It reminded Niall of the web of a domestic spider through which some child has thrown a stone.

And now suddenly he understood exactly what had happened to the Magician. Like Niall, he knew how to draw energy from the crystal, and to launch this energy like a thunderbolt. Niall shuddered as he thought of what would have happened if he had not been carrying the crystal globe; the force would have destroyed him like a dry leaf in a bonfire.

But since his hand was resting on his own crystal, the force had been instantly absorbed, as if by a lightning conductor. It had then gone on to drain the energy from the Magician's globe. As the conduit through which this tremendous force had passed, the Magician had also been drained of energy and knocked unconscious.

As always, Niall felt soothed and refreshed by his contact with the crystal. When his mind came back to the present, he was alone, and the bridge was empty. The Magician and the soldiers who were carrying him had disappeared uphill; only two soldiers had been left on guard at the bridge.

Niall started to walk toward the palace. But as he approached the kalinda tree, and began to feel its force sucking him toward it, the absurdity of again being trapped in the glass cylinder made him smile. He closed his eyes and imagined the inner courtyard of the palace. When he opened them, he was there.

It was strangely empty and silent. The great brass-studded door that led into the Magician's tower stood open, and for a moment, Niall wondered if he had already been carried inside. Then, through the arched tunnel that led to the outer courts and the drawbridge, he saw the Magician approaching. He was walking slowly, but was unsupported by the two red-haired guards on either side. His hood was turned back, and he was again wearing the false cranium, which transformed his head into a gigantic dome.

His face looked older than when Niall had last seen it, and the skin had taken on a yellow tinge. His slow steps made it clear that he was weak and tired. Then, just as Niall was beginning to feel sorry for him, he stumbled on a projecting paving stone and turned furiously on the guards. "Get that repaired immediately." Clearly, his temper was as short as ever.

The guards were ordered to wait outside, and Niall followed the Magician as he mounted the stairs alone. The progression up five flights of spiral staircase was slow, and Niall kept his distance. The last thing he wanted was to have his presence detected; he reasoned that the boca would only attack him on the Magician's orders, and therefore that while the Magician did not know he was there, he was safe.

Surprisingly, the Magician seemed to gain strength as he climbed, and by the time they reached the fifth floor, was walking almost normally. His personal guards were still in the corridor, and one of them hastened to open the door. The Magician hurried past him, limping with exhaustion, and slumped into the armchair. For a moment the skin of his jaw became slack, and he looked like a man close to death. Then, as the guard was about to shut the door, he said brusquely: "Wait. Go down and send Captain Zadin to me."

A few minutes later, the red-haired giant was stooping to enter the door, obviously wondering whether he had caused offense. The Magician asked: "Do you know the names of those people who were at the front of the mob?"

Standing rigidly to attention, the captain said: "They were members of the Citizens' Committee, sir."

"I want you to arrest them. Bring them all back here and take them to the cells."

With a sinking feeling, Niall realized that his hopes of peace and reconciliation had been unrealistic. The Magician was as full of malice as ever.

As soon as the guard had gone, the Magician closed his eyes and leaned his head against the backrest; the sallow skin was wrinkled and flabby, and the eyelids looked as if they were made of decaying rubber. For a long time, as the silence lengthened, he stared into space.

Niall now noticed for the first time two nearly transparent troglas who were hovering in the vicinity of the black cabinet. Their motion seemed oddly purposeless, like the fluttering of moths round a candle flame. The boca, which was still crouched by the armchair in the window corner, was watching them intently. It was obvious that the Magician was unable to see them.

After perhaps a quarter of an hour, he opened his eyes, forced himself painfully to his feet with his hands on the chair arms, and hobbled to the black cabinet. He opened a bench drawer, took out a key, and unlocked the door. Its inside seemed to be covered in hoarfrost. The two troglas fluttered closer, as if trying to force their way inside.

From the top shelf, the Magician removed a flask half-full of some blue liquid, and unclipped a metal catch that held its lid in place. A blue vapor rose from it, and the troglas pressed closer. As they did so, they became more visible, and their hands and feet could be seen. The ozone smell of the liquid filled the room: the smell of the life-fluid.

The Magician poured a few drops into a beaker, raised it to his lips, and took a sip. The effect was startling. Within seconds, his cheeks had lost their yellowish tinge and the wrinkles vanished as the skin of his face seemed to tighten on the bones. Moments later, spots of color appeared on his cheeks and his eyes became almost feverishly bright. Suddenly he was twenty years younger.

He drained the beaker, and returned the flask to the cabinet with the firmness of a vigorous and healthy man.

In a sudden insight, Niall understood the purpose of this laboratory and of the glass cylinder. The Magician's driving purpose was to learn the secret sought by philosophers since Cornelius Agrippa: the elixir of life. Even the troglas looked more alive after inhaling its vapors.

After locking the cabinet, the Magician, his movements now firm and decisive, took from his pocket the crystal globe and raised it within a few inches of his eyes. As he held it by the fingertips of his left hand, it began to glow, but no longer with the same fierce light as before. Although it illuminated the room, it was no longer with the blinding radiance that had driven the boca to retreat.

Niall looked nervously down at this own body. To his relief it remained invisible. The globe obviously had lost most of its strength.

The Magician crossed to the glass cylinder and held the globe close to it. His expression made it plain that he was baffled by Niall's disappearance, and again his thoughts were as clear as if spoken aloud. He asked the boca: "Is there someone else in this room?"

Niall's heart seemed to stop. Without raising its eyes, the boca said: "Yes."

"Who?"

The boca said: "The dead." Its voice had an unreal, rustling quality, as if made by dry leaves rather than vocal cords.

"Where?"

The boca pointed at the troglas, which were still hovering around the cabinet.

The Magician held out the globe and made an obvious effort of will that caused it to shine with something like its former brightness, but the light seemed to drive the troglas before it like a strong breeze, so they ceased to be in the place where he was looking. Almost immediately, the globe became dull again.

The Magician held it between his palms, a few inches from his face, and his expression showed he had grasped the extent of the disaster. Suddenly looking tired, he went went back to the chair. He said to the boca: "You must make me another."

The boca made no reply, and its face remained expressionless.

The Magician said: "Do you hear me?"

"Yes." It spoke with its eyes on the ground, but from where he was standing, Niall could see they were full of hatred.

The Magician's eyes came to rest on a dark patch on the floor: the place where Jelko's blood had spilled. He sent out a powerful telepathic signal that was the equivalent of an angry shout, and a guard immediately appeared in the doorway. The Magician pointed to the ground.

"Clean this up before it stains."

The man saluted, and appeared moments later with the mop and bucket. Niall watched with a touch of amusement as he scrubbed frantically at the brown patch which, under a film of water, became darker than ever. Finally, he went out and returned with a scrubbing brush, which also made no difference.

The Magician said wearily: "Go away, you fool. Didn't you know blood has to be washed away while it is wet?"

Hardly able to believe his good fortune, the guard picked up the mop and bucket.

The Magician said: "When the prisoners arrive, I want the mayor and mayoress brought here."

The man saluted and hurried out.

As the Magician sat in his chair, his mind was again easy to read, and Niall could see that he was again brooding on the problem of Niall's disappearance. He blamed the protesting mob for interrupting at the crucial moment. Thoughts of revenge and cruelty seemed to fill the room with a sense of violence that was like the smell of a slaughterhouse.

This glimpse into sadism was a new experience for Niall. When he had first come to the spider city he had believed that the spiders took pleasure in cruelty; now he knew that it was only a form of the satisfaction predators take in disabling their prey. But in this Magician he could sense a murderous sickness that went beyond anything he had ever encountered. The Magician had fed on power until it had turned him into a monster.

This monomaniac had indulged his whims until he had come to believe that his will was a law of nature. To Niall's astonished perceptions, he seemed to have lost all contact with reality and gone insane.

Something caused the Magician to start and look toward the window. A moment later, Niall also heard the popping sounds that the Magician's acute hearing had detected first. Never having heard gunfire, Niall was at first baffled by the series of bangs that sounded like bursting balloons.

By the time he reached the window, the Magician was already there. From this point on the central tower, it was possible to look downhill to the bridge, which was partly obscured by the kalinda tree. From there, they could see the crowd that was pouring onto the bridge, and soldiers who were firing their rifles into the air.

The telepathic shout of rage was so loud that Niall winced. As both guards rushed into the room, the Magician pointed out of the window with a hand that shook.

"What's that?"

They clearly had no idea what he meant, and one of them hurried to the window. What he saw obviously bewildered him, and he shook his head dumbly. The other guard succeeded in looking past him by standing on tiptoe.

"Well?"

The guard stammered: "I don't know, sir."

Niall knew beyond all doubt that if the Magician's globe had been operating at full strength, both soldiers would have been struck dead.

His voice shook as he said: "Send for Captain Zadin."

When the men were gone, the Magician sat in his chair and gazed straight in front of him. His face left no doubt of what he was thinking: that his powers were fading and he was suddenly in actual physical danger. Niall was surprised that he was not feeling triumphant about his enemy's undoing. He even found room for regret that he had been its cause. Nevertheless, his chief emotion was intense curiosity. What did such a man do when he knew his power was gone, and that he might end in one of his own dungeons?

Niall was also interested to note that the troglas no longer seemed to be wandering aimlessly. They were watching the Magician, as if waiting for something to happen.

There were sounds in the corridor, and a knock on the door. The Magician shouted angrily: "Come in."

The red-haired captain was looking apologetic, yet there was something about his manner that Niall found hard to place.

"I'm sorry sir—I've only just come back."

The Magician snapped impatiently: "But what's happening?" He gestured at the window. "What's all this?"

Zadin said: "We tried to arrest them, sir, but they resisted. Then a soldier got shot. . . ."

"One of ours or theirs?"

"Theirs. Then it all flared up, and turned into a riot."

"How many men did you take?"

"Twenty, sir."

"And didn't they open fire?"

Zadin was looking strangely embarrassed, and avoided the Magician's eye.

"Well?"

Zadin said: "They joined them, sir."

Niall knew what was odd about the captain's manner. In spite of his deference and servility, he was enjoying being the bearer of bad news.

Niall expected the Magician to explode with his usual uncontrolled rage, and was surprised when he asked in a calm voice: "What do they want?"

Sensing danger, the captain redoubled his deference.

"To rescue the two envoys from Korsh."

The Magician went to the window. The sound of firing was closer. Niall was puzzled by his calm. "And how many do you think are loyal?"

"I don't know, sir."

The Magician said ironically, "So perhaps just you and me?"

Suspecting a trap Zadin said: "I don't know, sir."

"No? Then I'm going to give you a chance to prove your loyalty. That boy from Korsh. I want you to go down to the dungeons and kill him."

Niall knew this was intended to test Zadin's loyalty, and that he should have the sense to salute and withdraw.

But the captain failed to recognize his danger, and said with shocked sincerity: "Is that a good idea, sir? These people are coming to rescue him, and . . ."

"And when they arrive, they'll find him dead, won't they?"

Zadin said: "Yes, sir, if that's what you want."

The Magician shouted: "What I want is loyalty!"

Niall knew what was about to happen, and braced himself. The globe in the Magician's hand shone with a brilliant light. But the bolt of energy that struck the captain was not strong enough to destroy him outright. Instead, his mouth opened wide with pain, and his clothes burst into flame. His scream made the Magician wince and cover his ears.

In the same moment, Niall directed the energy of his own globe at the Magician's hand. The Magician's globe went out like a light that has been extinguished. He gaped in astonishment at the crystal in Niall's hand, which now filled the room with light, and looked with astonishment into Niall's eyes. Then there was a blur of movement, and the boca was holding the Magician by the throat. For a moment the creature looked like a giant grasshopper that has seized some smaller insect. Then Niall watched at close quarters what had happened to Jelko. The huge left hand gripped the throat, while the right covered the lower half of the face completely, and twisted the Magician's head around to face the other way. For a moment there was no sound; then the neck snapped. The boca's teeth were bared in a smile that made it look demonic.

Niall preferred not to stay and watch what was going to happen next. He stepped over the captain's body, with its smoldering clothes, and through the door, walking straight through both guards, who were listening with their ears pressed against it. Then he remembered that he could be wherever he liked by using the power of thought, and envisaged his cell.

When Umaya unlocked the door, Niall was sitting on the edge of the bed. He was shivering because, in his absence from his body, the blanket had slipped onto the floor. When he had heard the footsteps on the stairs, he had been trying to restore his temperature by concentration.

Selena and Vasco were the first to enter his cell, followed by Major Baltiger. Behind them the stairway was crowded with faces he now recognized as members of the Citizens' Committee.

Behind Umaya stood her father, wearing his customary sullen expression. His thoughts were so obvious that it was as if he was saying aloud: "When the karvasid finds out, you're all going to pay for this."

Niall was charmed as Selena threw her arms around him and kissed him with warm lips.

Vasco was wringing his hand over her shoulder, saying: "My God, you're frozen!"

Baltiger, shaking the other hand, asked: "Are you all right?"

"Yes, thank you. Just cold."

"There was a rumor you were dead."

Vasco said: "Come and get warm, and have something to eat."

Niall said: "First I must find my companion, the spider."

"Ah, yes, Captain Makanda." Vasco turned to Umaya. "Please take us to Captain Makanda."

She glanced nervously at her father, who looked as if he was about to have apoplexy. "Does the karvasid know?"

Niall said: "The karvasid is dead."

These words were heard by the people in the corridor, and repeated to those on the stairs. "The karvasid is dead!"

Then, to the jailer's obvious fury, the crowd was cheering.

Umaya asked her father: "*Is* the karvasid dead?"

He gazed into space for a moment, then his face drained of blood.

His daughter asked: "Is he?"

The jailer's shocked expression gave the answer.

Niall had been right. There had been a direct telepathic link between the Magician and his turnkey.

As Niall followed Umaya down the long corridor, Baltiger ordered the others not to follow; it was too low and narrow for a crowd. The captain's cell was at its farthest end, and as Umaya was unlocking it, it proved to be so small and dark that Niall could see nothing through the window in the door.

The captain was waiting for them, his back pressed tightly against the ceiling and his legs bent double so his belly touched the floor. He had already sensed the excitement that filled the air.

Niall experienced a rush of warmth as he saw his old traveling companion, and regretted that it was physically impossible to embrace a spider. But he knew the captain sensed what he felt, and that he was simultaneously pleased and embarrassed. Spiders were shocked by displays of affection.

As they emerged into the courtyard, a cheer went up from the waiting crowd—probably the loudest cheer that had ever been heard in Shadowland—and birds flew up in alarm from the rooftops. Niall looked up at the Magician's window, through which a light was shining, and was filled with pleasure at the thought that the citizens could now make as much noise as they liked.

With the captain and Niall on either side of them, the mayor and mayoress led the way down the hill and back across the bridge. Niall could see that the spider, obviously glad to be able to stretch his legs again, was bemused by the cheers that greeted him, feeling that he had done nothing to deserve them.

Niall asked Baltiger: "Has anyone seen Typhon?"

The mayor shook his head. "I imagine he might be afraid to show his face."

"But why? He hated the karvasid as much as anyone."

"Are you sure?" Baltiger obviously had assumed that the prefect would be shocked by the downfall of his master.

"Absolutely certain. He told me so himself."

"In that case, we must send someone to his house and invite him to the banquet." He turned to Selena and explained earnestly what Niall had just said, but the noise was so deafening that she obviously found it hard to understand.

As they approached the Town Hall, Niall was startled as colored rockets hissed into the air; he had not seen fireworks since the disaster over which Doggins had presided. These rockets did not explode with a bang—that would have been too much to expect in this city—but their reds, greens, blues, and yellows filled the sky, and seemed a visible expression of the joy felt by everyone in Shadowland.

As they were entering the banqueting hall, Niall was struck by a thought that turned his heart to lead: what would happen to his brother Veig now that the Magician was dead? Would Typhon know the secret that would reprieve Veig from his sentence of death? For the next five minutes Niall was preoccupied with trying to work out how many days ago Veig had cut himself on the sharp blade. But when he calculated that there were still eighteen days to run, he decided he could afford to relax and share the rejoicing.

The banqueting hall was, in fact, simply a large restaurant that would hold about a hundred people. Niall felt guilty about the crowds who cheered and waved outside the windows until Selena said: "They don't mind. They are all too happy to be free to care about not joining us." She raised her glass, full of a sparkling golden wine, and said: "Let us drink to our freedom."

Half an hour later, they had begun the first course when another burst of cheering broke out, and Typhon came in, followed by Gerek. Niall was surprised; he had expected Typhon to be received with a certain coolness. But it seemed that news of Niall's remarks had already spread throughout the crowd, and the prefect and his assistant were greeted as heroes.

Niall and the mayoress were requested to move apart, and two more chairs were placed between them.

Typhon, who was next to Niall, said: "Well, it seems that your coming started a revolution."

Niall shook his head. "Don't give me the credit. You started it by announcing the peace treaty."

Typhon said modestly: "I only did what I was told."

Niall smiled. "What you were *not* told."

Typhon only chuckled, and raised the glass that the waiter had just filled.

Gerek leaned forward and said to Niall: "By the way, you left this in your room."

It was the thought mirror, and Niall lost no time hanging it round his neck. Drinking wine on an empty stomach had already made him light-headed, and he was glad to have the means of controlling it.

It was Typhon who raised the question of Veig, by saying in Niall's ear: "By the way, you don't have to worry about your brother anymore. Now that the karvasid's dead, he'll begin to recover."

"Are sure of that?" This was all that Niall needed to share the euphoria of the guests around him.

"Quite sure. Your brother was being attacked by graddiks. Do you know what a graddik is?"

"Yes. I've been attacked by one too."

"Then you'll know they don't like being enslaved. At the first opportunity, they'll desert. By the time you return home, your brother will be quite well."

Niall laughed aloud in sheer relief; only the fact that their chairs were too close together prevented him from embracing Typhon. He raised his glass.

"I shall recommend that they appoint you ruler of Shadowland."

Typhon shook his head. "I suspect the Citizens' Committee has someone else in mind."

Niall was startled, almost dismayed, as he grasped Typhon's meaning.

"Not me. They can't choose me. That's absurd."

"Why? I think it's an admirable idea. You are already the most popular man in Shadowland, and you're the ruler of the spider city. You'd merely add Shadowland to your domains, and our people would automatically become citizens of your country. No need for ambassadors or a peace treaty or anything else. Doesn't that make sense?"

Niall said: "I'm not sure. Please let me think about it first." He was wondering how the spiders would feel about the influx of five thousand more human beings. "If you don't mind, please don't say anything about this for the moment."

Typhon said courteously: "Of course."

"Where did you hear this?"

"I've been talking it over with the messenger who brought me here. He tells me that everyone is saying the same thing. If you don't want it mentioned now, you'd better say so immediately. If I'm not mistaken, Baltiger's going to propose it before the evening's over."

Niall turned urgently toward his neighbor, but the mayor was already rising to his feet, and rapping the table for silence.

"Ladies, gentlemen, I wish to propose a toast to our honored guests, Colonel Niall and Captain Makanda. The captain is taking his meal in another room, but I am sure he is with us in spirit. So shall we all stand and drink to Colonel Niall?"

As the guests stood up and raised their glasses, Niall had a feeling he had been outmaneuvered.

Epilogue

In spite of a headache and lack of sleep, Niall was awake before dawn. He had stayed at Typhon's house, and the captain—as on the previous occasion—had slept on the rug in the same room.

Niall used the thought mirror to dispel the tiredness that was the result of only three hours of sleep. Then he sat up in bed, closed his eyes, and went into deep relaxation. He became immediately aware of his mother's presence, and realized that she must have been trying to establish contact at the very moment he had.

She asked: "Where are you?"

"I am back at Typhon's house."

"Ah, I knew you were free."

"How?"

"Your brother began to recover at ten o'clock last night, and insisted on sleeping in his own bed."

Niall was astonished. "As quickly as that? I calculate that the Magician died at about that time."

So Typhon was right: the graddiks had lost no time in deserting.

Niall made no attempt to describe what had happened in detail; it would have used up all his mental energy and tired his mother. But he told her that he had accepted the position of the master of Shadowland. He also asked her to contact Asmak, the director of the aerial survey, and arrange for three spider balloons to land at the top meadow of the Vale of Thanksgiving the following afternoon, to pick up Typhon, the captain, and himself. He felt that it was a matter of urgency, as well as courtesy, to introduce Typhon, now the deputy ruler of Shadowland, to the Spider Lord and his council.

The news that Veig was already on the road to recovery had filled Niall with joy and relief, and he was anxious to begin the new day, Shadowland's first day of freedom. But Typhon and Gerek were not at breakfast—they sent an apology with Katia and said they would appear later. Niall was sympathetic; without the aid of the thought mirror, he also would have preferred to spend the morning in bed.

Soon after half past nine, Niall and the captain set out for the palace, where Niall had arranged to meet the Citizens' Committee at midday. There were many things Niall wanted to find out before he met them, and he intended to address his questions to Kvaran, the brother of the red-haired Zadin, who was now in the hospital suffering from burns.

Kvaran, a lieutenant of the palace guard, was waiting for him at the drawbridge, and greeted Niall and the captain with a military salute. His cheeks were drawn, and in response to Niall's question he told him that his brother was now sleeping under sedation, after a healing ointment had been applied to his burns by the palace doctor. He would be permanently scarred, but was expected to make a full recovery. Niall was intrigued to learn that Zadin had been trying to crawl down the stairs when Kvaran had found him. The fact that he was still conscious revealed just how much the Magician's crystal globe had been depleted by his attempt to destroy Niall.

On Niall's orders, the central tower had been locked after the Magician's body had been removed. As Kvaran unlocked the heavy door, Niall observed that he looked nervous. Niall guessed the reason, but asked nevertheless: "Is something troubling you?"

"Yes, sir." Kvaran obviously was glad of the opportunity to voice his fears. "The guards saw the animal that killed the karvasid. It was so horrible that one of them has gone mad."

Niall was puzzled; it seemed unlikely that the guards had been able to see the boca.

"What did it look like?"

"A great crimson monster with no eyes."

Suddenly Niall understood. "Was the body badly torn?"

"As if by a wild beast."

The boca obviously had been covered in blood, but since it was invisible, had seemed to have no eyes.

Niall said: "If you would rather wait here, I will go up alone."

Kvaran looked relieved. "Thank you, sir. I'm not afraid of any human foe, but this thing sounds like a demon from the pit."

Kvaran's fears were groundless, as Niall had known they would be. There was no sign of the boca. Niall had no doubt that, after centuries of bondage to a master who was sick with the lust of power, it had lost no time in returning to its home in the silver mines of the north.

But the room was as horrible as Niall had expected, and made him feel sick. Although the body had been removed, dried blood covered the walls and ceiling, and the place smelled like a butcher's shop on a hot day.

Strangely, there was no blood on the glass cylinder, in which the blue gas still bubbled with black clouds. Like the crystal sphere, this glass, it seemed, could cleanse itself.

This was no longer true of the Magician's globe, which lay underneath the bench; it was brown with dried blood, and when Niall picked it up, the bottom was wet. Niall washed the blood off his hands under the laboratory tap, then cleaned the globe with a wet towel.

This is what Niall had meant to ask Kvaran about; he had awakened in the night and wondered if it would still be there. For although the globe felt dead to his touch and was probably drained beyond hope of recovery, Niall knew that the information it stored was almost certainly indestructible.

He left the laboratory, glad to escape its stench, and found the guardroom at the end of the corridor; this contained a table and two chairs, and a large sink. The room was too small for the spider to enter, and he stayed outside in the corridor.

Niall drew the curtain, sat at the table, and cupped the globe in his hands. Then he emptied his mind and tried to tune in to the crystal. The result was a stinging shock that made him drop the globe, so it rolled across the floor. Clearly, it had been booby-trapped in case some unauthorized person should attempt to use it. If its force had not been so weak, Niall probably would have been stunned or knocked unconscious.

He placed it on the table, stared into it, and tried to gauge its wavelength. Because he was now accustomed to his own globe, he knew how it should respond. And finally, by allowing himself to be guided by intuition, he began to feel his way into its world.

The first impression was unfavorable. His own globe was like a universe, with immense galleries that stretched in all directions, and it somehow conveyed an impression of light, as if it was housed under a giant glass dome. The Magician's globe was more like entering a dark building full of badly lit corridors and airless rooms. It was not only claustrophobic, but somehow frightening and stifling. The sphere was permeated by the personality of the Magician, and that personality was terrifying in its capacity for vindictiveness.

But all this was forgotten as Niall grasped the truth about the Magician and Shadowland. What he now learned left him feeling utterly bewildered. The man whose baleful presence filled the globe was not Sathanas, the soldier who had led his small band of warriors into Shadowland, but his lineal descendant, Sathanas the Fourteenth. The first Sathanas was the original builder of this palace, who had lived until his ninety-seventh year and fathered eleven sons and seven daughters.

This, Niall now realized, was why the interior of the palace was built in so many different styles. It also explained why the palace was so vast, a virtual citadel, with as many rooms belowground as above it. Here each later Magician lived his solitary existence, and guarded his closest secret: that he was not the Sathanas who had founded Shadowland, but one of his descendants.

But what was the purpose of this strange charade? It had started, Niall learned, by chance, and continued because it happened to suit the obsessive characters of each ruler of Shadowland.

When the first Sathanas died, his death was kept secret, because he had believed that the spiders would invade Shadowland if they knew he was dead. So his son, also called Sathanas, who was then aged forty, had taken his place. This second Magician had been a remarkable intellectual, undoubtedly a man of genius, who had devoted his life to the study of science and magic. It was he who had lured the warriors of Cheb the Mighty into the Valley of the Dead, and then drowned most of them in the Great Storm. It was this Sathanas who had created the globe that Niall was now holding, and enslaved the boca that had killed his thirteenth descendant.

His son, Sathanas the Third, had lacked his father's intellect, but had possessed a natural talent for agriculture. It was under him that the Vale of Thanksgiving became the center of rich farmlands that could support ten thousand people. From his father he learned the secret of controlling the weather, and the spider balloons that were occasionally blown over the Gray Mountains were invariably destroyed before they saw the fertile valleys with their orchards and wheat and vines.

Sathanas the Fourth was something of an adventurer, who had met the monk Sephardus, and was reputed to have visited the spider city in the guise of a slave. The globe revealed that he had speculated about the possibility of making peace with the spiders, but concluded that it would be too dangerous.

At this point, Niall's fatigue was beginning to undermine his concentration, and when he looked up at the wall clock, he realized that he was already late for his appointment with the Citizens' Committee, and hastened to wrap the globe in a soft leather duster, which he stowed in his pocket.

He need not have hurried. The Citizens' Committee had been comfortably installed in the Committee Room in the palace, where a large meal had been prepared on Typhon's instructions. Most of them were so tired after the revels of the previous night that some were dozing in armchairs when Niall arrived. But the presence of their new ruler revived them, and lunch was followed by a lively discussion that lasted until four in the afternoon.

There was an interesting diversion from their main business. The captain, as usual, had been placed in a separate room. Niall had just started to eat a mushroom tart when a maidservant whispered that the captain wanted to speak to him. Niall went next door and found a room with several large birdcages containing live birds, which had been provided for the spider's lunch. One contained a bustard, another several magpies, starlings, and other birds, and a third larks and sparrows. Niall felt sorry for the birds, but knew they would be paralyzed before the spider ate them.

When the spider indicated the second cage, Niall peered into it and recognized the raven, looking cowed and terrified, crouching on the floor. As soon as Niall opened the cage it recognized him, and perched on his outstretched fingers, the sharp claws causing him to wince. Niall raised his arm and let it walk onto his shoulder. There it remained throughout the meal, by which time it had gained the confidence to walk down onto the table, and it wandered around inspecting the plates of the guests and eating leftovers. Selena had no difficulty coaxing it onto her shoulder, where it gently took the lobe of her ear in its beak and tweaked it.

Everyone found the bird fascinating—Niall learned later that all pets were forbidden in Shadowland—and when it climbed back onto Niall's shoulder, it seemed perceptibly heavier.

After lunch, the discussion centered on the problem that most deeply preoccupied them: what freedom meant to them, and how it might best be used. It soon became clear that most of them would have liked to move to the spider city immediately. Niall did not confide to them his misgivings about how the spiders might react to the arrival of thousands or so human guests, but after granting general permission to travel to the surface, went on to suggest that they should wait at least until the spring.

Seeing their disappointment, he relented, and invited the Citizens' Committee to visit Korsh at some time during the next month. This was welcomed with delight, and Niall became clearly aware of something he had so far only half registered: that when a group of Shadowlanders came together, their telepathic abilities continually changed their mood. Although telepathic contact was person-to-person and not collective, as with the spiders, their feelings and emotions were transmitted by a process of induction; so when they became downcast—as when Niall told them they would have to wait till spring—the room was filled with dejection, whereas as soon as he suggested that the visit should take place next month, the atmosphere sparkled with elation.

This, Niall realized, presaged an evolutionary change. Within a few generations, everyone in Shadowland would experience collective consciousness.

Typhon arrived at four o'clock, and the whole assembly stood up to salute him. Niall was not sorry to leave, for the Citizens' Committee had plunged into an ideological argument about whether, now that the Magician was dead, all the old laws should be rescinded and citizens allowed to do as they liked, or whether the old laws should be left in force for the time being. Most of the women took the latter position, while Major Baltiger and most of the men were in favor of total freedom. As the head of his own Town Council in the spider city, Niall had heard it all before, and knew that if they decided to abolish all the laws, they would probably have to reinstate most of them in six months. But he knew it would be pointless to interfere; they had to learn for themselves.

In the courtyard, the raven flew off his shoulder and soared up to the roof. Niall could sense that it had had enough of behaving like a tame bird.

They now moved to Typhon's office, which was on the top story of the palace, and Niall was interested to see that there was an elevator—the only one he had ever been in, except for the one in the white tower. Why, he wondered, had the Magician never installed one in his own tower? Then he saw the answer. The Magician's laboratory had been built in the early years of Shadowland, long before Typhon's wing of the palace, and had remained unaltered.

The view from Typhon's office was even finer than from the laboratory, for it had two windows, one of which looked due north. This reminded Niall to tell Typhon that they would be departing from the Vale of Thanksgiving the following afternoon, and should therefore leave early.

The moment they left the council chamber, Niall had asked about the dynasty of karvasids. Typhon explained that his own family had been in their service since the first Sathanas. During his final years, that first karvasid had become increasingly paranoid, and refused direct contact with everyone except his prefect; Typhon's ancestor had even had to taste his master's food and drink. From that time on, the prefects were the only persons allowed direct contact with the karvasids. In effect, the karvasids became monks—at least, in all but one respect: they kept a harem of concubines in a closed wing of the palace.

The ninth karvasid, the one who had created the gallery of freaks and the superbrain called Rufio, had learned the techniques of mind-control through vibrations, and from then on, there had been no problem in convincing the inhabitants of Shadowland that their ruler was immortal and infallible.

Niall and Typhon had many things to discuss before they prepared to leave for Korsh. Everyone in Shadowland, from the mine workers to the aristocrats of Freydig, would be demanding change. For example, the workers on the second level were already suggesting that Drusco, the overseer who had been sentenced to flogging—and who had been released, together with all the other prisoners in the dungeons—should be appointed their leader and representative, and made a member of Niall's privy council; this, and dozens of other such matters would have to be handled by Gerek until Typhon's return.

So the day passed—not in celebration, as with most inhabitants of Shadowland, but in discussion about organizational details. This continued in the evening when Gerek returned from his day at the second level. He described how the workers had found it almost impossible to believe that the karvasid was dead, and were therefore more subdued in their response than the inhabitants of the city. But by the time Gerek had left at six o'clock, the news had sunk in, and the workers had been preparing for a long night of celebration.

During supper, Gerek raised an interesting question: the future agriculture of Shadowland. The agricultural workers had developed a remarkably efficient system for keeping their fellows supplied with vegetables and fruit. These workers were much envied by everyone in

Shadowland for their access to the open air, and there was much competition to join them.

The envy was based on a misconception, for the truth was that for eight months of every year they lived arduous and difficult lives in an enclave close to the northern exit from Shadowland, and had to walk to the surface every day and down again in the evening, carrying their produce on their backs in baskets. The remaining four months of the year they spent among the factory hands on the second level, working at menial jobs.

That afternoon, Gerek had been speaking to their representative, who wanted to transfer their underground enclave to the Vale of Thanksgiving, and suggested building a road that would run all the way from the Vale to the city. This could be done during the winter months, when there was no work aboveground. Gerek was acute enough to see that this would take far more than a single winter, and a greater force than two hundred laborers, and wanted to ask Niall about the possibility of transporting slaves from the spider city. Typhon agreed that this was one of the matters he would look into during his trip there.

This suggested to Niall an interesting possibility. The spider city would soon be needing more agricultural land—for Niall foresaw a steady increase in the human population now that the slaves had ceased to be the main staple of the spiders' diet. Shadowland had more agricultural land than it needed, excellent for cattle grazing as well as for crops. Here was a chance of an important trade link between the two cities.

All this was so absorbing that Niall forgot to contact his mother at dusk. He had been meaning to suggest delaying their departure by twenty-four hours, to give Typhon more time for final arrangements. But as he climbed into bed at one o'clock in the morning, it struck him that it would be better to leave things as they stood. At the end of twenty-four hours, there would certainly be more reasons for delaying until the following day, and then the day after that . . .

At dawn Niall spoke to his mother. Veig, apparently, was making remarkable progress, and it had taken Simeon's authority to persuade him not to go out for a walk. And the spider balloons would be leaving for the Gray Mountains soon after dawn. There was a northwest wind, but even with tacking, it should take them about five hours to reach the Vale of Thanksgiving. The homeward journey should take an hour less than that.

Two hours later, Niall and Typhon climbed into a cart pulled by two gelbs. As they were about to start, Niall was startled to see Umaya approaching. She had walked all the way from the palace to present Niall with a bag of cinnamon cakes she had baked for his journey. As Niall kissed her, he realized that she was probably closer to him than any woman except his mother. He felt sad as he looked back to see her waving from the street corner.

Typhon said: "Why don't you invite her to Korsh?"

"Yes, I think I will."

But as they drove toward the north gate, he thought about all the complications that would ensue with other women in his household, and decided to delay his decision until his next visit to Shadowland. It seemed ironic that the ruler of two great cities should be afraid of antagonizing his womenfolk.

The drive out of the city filled him with the excitement he always felt when starting out on a journey, and he could sense that Typhon felt the same, and that even the captain was looking forward to his return to the spider city. It must seem strange, Niall reflected, for a man of fifty to be leaving his native land for the first time in his life, aware that, now that his master was dead, life would never be the same.

Once the cart was out of the city, traveling through the featureless landscape of northern Shadowland, Niall asked Typhon the question that had been in his mind for two days.

"Did you hate the karvasid?"

Typhon considered this for some time.

"Not really. It would not have been sensible. I had to work for him and do his bidding, and knew I had to make the best of it. In fact, there were times when I was almost fond of him, particularly in the early days. I suppose I was what you might call his only friend. And everybody needs friends."

"Weren't you afraid of him?"

"No. When you've worked for somebody for thirty years, you get to know him pretty well. I often had to oppose things he wanted to do, and he accepted that. Besides, when he first became karvasid, he was a completely different person. You see, he worshipped his father, who was a man of iron self-control, and tried to be like him—Sathanas the Thirteenth lived like a monk and practiced asceticism, breath-control, and self-flagellation."

That brought back to Niall a question that had puzzled him.

"Breath-control? Is that why the karvasids didn't seem to be breathing?"

"All the karvasids had a natural gift for it. Sathanas the Thirteenth could hold his breath for a quarter of an hour. But my karvasid couldn't manage it for more than five minutes. I think he exhausted himself trying to live up to his father. And toward the end, he simply gave up, and his temper got worse and worse. There were times recently when he became insufferable."

Niall thought of the cool, murderous fury the Magician had displayed at the end of his reception, and was suddenly overwhelmed by the certainty that his death had been a necessity.

"How was it possible to like a man as cruel and selfish as that?"

Typhon said seriously: "You've got to understand the problems he faced. As you must have realized, people just don't like living underground. They build up a longing to escape, and they blame their ruler for stopping them. But it wasn't his fault. If it hadn't been for the spiders, he would have let them travel as much as they liked."

"But why didn't he think of approaching the spiders about a treaty?"

"He did. Our spies were always slipping into Korsh disguised as slaves. That's how he learned that you'd become the ruler. That made him very thoughtful, and I could see his mind brooding on what could be done. He brought down Skorbo's balloon so he could learn more about the spiders. He wanted to see if their minds could be altered by vibrations. And of course, he thought he'd succeeded. Then Skorbo began to change as the effects wore off, and the karvasid knew he'd have to die. That was when he decided to try to bring you here."

It came as no surprise, but Niall was interested to hear Typhon confirming it. "So he planned it?"

"Yes. He told the assassins to leave that ax in the garden. He knew somebody wouldn't be able to resist feeling the edge with his thumb."

"But what if it had been me instead of my brother?"

"In that case, your brother would have come to Shadowland to try and save you, and that would have been just as effective—perhaps more."

"So you knew I was coming all along?"

"He was tracking your progress with his crystal and with trained birds. Mind, there was one point where he thought he'd lost you—when you almost got swallowed by a metexia . . ."—Niall looked puzzled—

". . . a mass of slime. He told me you managed to escape on your own before he could make it dissolve. But he thought he was going to be too late."

This, Niall realized, was why he had occasionally had a sense of being watched, particularly on open moorland.

"So his main goal was to replace me as the ruler of the spider city?"

"That was his ultimate goal. Meantime, he thought he could control you until you became a kind of glove puppet."

Niall did not like to tell him how close the Magician had come to it.

Typhon said: "But there were other things he wanted. Since women stopped giving birth, there was a feeling of growing revolt, and he knew it could only get worse. He either had to find more women to bear children, or grant everyone more freedom. He knew that everyone needed new goals, new purposes, new distractions. At first he thought those fantasy machines were the answer. But they made things worse. They made people dream about distant places."

Thinking of his own travels, Niall said: "I think many of them are going to be disappointed when they finally see the distant places."

"He knew that. But meanwhile he had to think of more distractions. He even created an arson squad to go to remote parts of the city and start fires. He started rumors of hidden enemies. He urged the workers to greater and greater efforts to complete the city walls, and made the army drill day and night. That's why he became so foul-tempered at the end— he'd become completely obsessed. I think he would even have welcomed an attack by the spiders."

The captain, who had been following all this as he loped gently alongside, asked: "Did he never think of attacking first?"

Typhon nodded. "In effect, that's what he did." And although he did not add: "And look where it got him," Niall knew that was what he meant.

It made him deeply thoughtful. As Typhon was speaking, Niall had been reflecting that the karvasids were one of the most remarkable dynasties in human history. And they had encountered the same problem as most other great rulers in history: how to keep their people contented. The strange fate that had made the women infertile had spelled the end of the dynasty.

But at least the globe Niall was carrying in his pocket guaranteed their place in the history books.

Meanwhile, they were passing the lake with the grilweed, which made Niall aware that it had been three hours since breakfast and that he was hungry. He opened the bag of cinnamon cakes, and found them excellent—so excellent that he was struck by an excuse to bring Umaya to Korsh: giving her a job in the palace kitchen.

During the remainder of the journey to the northern exit, he and Typhon ate their way through a dozen cakes, and agreed she deserved a wider field for the exercise of her talents.

The point had come where they had to leave the cart. They dismounted on level ground, so the gelbs could find their way back to the city, and at Typhon's command, they turned and trotted off. Then began the long climb uphill, to the cave guarded by the headless moog.

This reminded Niall of something else he had intended to ask Typhon: whether moogs could be transported to Korsh to perform heavy labor, such as the rebuilding of the harbor. But there was, it seemed, a problem. The moogs' digestive system was almost nonexistent, so they could not eat normal food. They lived on the Magician's blue elixir, and unless Niall could learn to reproduce the strange machine that made it, and find a kalinda tree to collect it, they would quickly lose their energy and decay like any corpse.

During the long climb to the top meadow, Niall studied the path carefully, calculating where it might be turned into a road suitable for wheeled vehicles. He decided this could not be done without blasting, or possibly the use of Reapers, and that he would have to bring Doggins on his next trip to Shadowland, to give him professional advice. According to Typhon, the Reapers in the Shadowland arsenal were virtually useless, being low on their radioactive fuel; one alternative might be to persuade the master of the bombardier beetles to grant permission to use those he was holding in the city armory.

When they arrived at the top meadow shortly before one o'clock, Niall was glad to see that it was a sunny day, with a vigorous north wind that drove the high white clouds like sailboats on a choppy sea. The vale itself was warm, being sheltered from the wind, and Niall flung himself down on the thick grass and gave himself up to the pleasure of feeling sunlight on his face.

The spider balloons came into sight half an hour later. The captain, who was standing on the top of the south peak, guided them in telepathically. The first landed within a dozen feet of where Niall was standing, and he was amused to note that the nauseating smell of the porifids actually brought a flash of nostalgia.

These balloons were twice the normal size—it was Niall himself who had suggested that they should be constructed to carry passengers. The mass of legs and fur that disentangled itself from the undercarriage was Grel, son of Asmak, and again Niall wished that it was physically possible to embrace a spider.

It seemed that Asmak had given in to his son's pleas to be allowed to go and meet Niall, since the other two pilots were skilled veterans of the aerial survey who could rescue him in the event of trouble. But they had not expected the strength of the north wind, and had almost come to grief over the Valley of the Dead.

A quarter of an hour later they were airborne again, Niall sharing the double compartment with Grel, whose soft, glossy fur somehow aroused an amused and protective feeling. The compartment below the balloon was made of a flexible, transparent material, exuded by the black rupa worm of the Delta, and smelled oily and oddly like a geranium.

The balloon carrying Typhon was a hundred feet away, so they were able to wave to one another as the Vale of Thanksgiving dropped away below them. Niall's balloon rocked heavily as it was caught by the full force of the wind, then steadied as it entered a current as swift and eddy-less as a deep river. At a height of about two thousand feet the wind ceased to be audible, and only the clouds they passed betrayed that they were moving.

It was at this point that Niall stared intently at a bird flying power-fully alongside the balloon, and startled Grel by exclaiming aloud. It was the raven. Curious about how it felt to be exposed to the gale, Niall transferred his consciousness to the bird, which, since it was moving several times faster than it had ever traveled in its life, was not even aware of Niall's intrusion inside its head.

Instantly, Niall was plunged into one of the most remarkable experiences of his life. His consciousness had divided into two: half in the soundproof and insulated world of the undercarriage, half in the roaring chaos outside.

He had, in effect, become two persons. In an exhilarating surge of freedom, he understood suddenly how every human being spends a lifetime trapped in a narrow room behind his eyes, becoming so accustomed to the prison that he is not even aware of his captivity.

And this, he realized, was the root of the human dilemma. Every one of us is so accustomed to seeing the world from a single point of view that it is almost impossible to believe that other people are as real as we are.

That also explained the Magician's ruthlessness. He was a double prisoner: inside his palace, and inside his head. With no one to love, no close confidants, he had been sentenced to a lifetime in solitary confinement.

One single moment of Niall's double consciousness—inside his own head and inside the raven's—would have given him back his freedom and changed his life. As it was, he continued to believe he was alone in a universe of illusions until the moment he died.

In that same dazzling bird's-eye view, Niall could also see the answer to another question that had puzzled him: why the Magician was so cruel. His prison had convinced him that the whole world was his enemy, and that safety lay in power. He believed that only cruelty and ruthlessness could ensure his survival.

But the karvasid was merely suffering from a more intense form of the negativity that afflicted the human race. Why had the spiders felt it necessary to enslave human beings? Because they recognized this element of cruelty and impatience as a human characteristic. Man felt they were necessary if he was to survive.

The chameleon men knew better. Close to the living soul of nature, they knew that every rock, every tree root, every vein of quartz, embodies the force of life. And this force could afford to be benevolent, for it was infinitely powerful.

But unless Niall's fellow men could grasp that secret, they were doomed to remain trapped in this attitude that had brought the human race so much misery.

Could man ever realize that he was the chief cause of his own misery and misfortune, that a mere habit of negative-seeing, and a lack of the courage to dare to abandon it, had trapped him in a destiny of conflict and self-mistrust? Could he ever grasp, as Niall could now grasp so clearly, that an enormous optimism was justified?

It seemed strange to be flying through space at sixty miles an hour, and to know that he had just seen the answer to the most basic problem of human existence.

It had been half an hour since they had flown over the Valley of the Dead, and Niall had caught sight of the tower of Sephardus. Now they were approaching the domain of the chameleon men. Soon they would be back in the spider city, where Niall would escort Typhon into the presence of the Death Lord and the ruling council, and explain that this human was the first of thousands of new subjects of the spider empire.

The spiders, of course, would accept Typhon, for they trusted Niall, knowing him to be the representative of the goddess. But to make sure their trust was not misplaced, Niall had to find some way of making his fellow men understand the secret he had just grasped. And at the moment he could not even imagine how to begin.

The answer came a few minutes later, when he caught his first glimpse of the spider city on the horizon, and the dark blue line of the October sea beyond it. Niall waved to attract Typhon's attention, but Typhon was looking down at the landscape below. Then Niall sent a telepathic signal, and when Typhon looked across at him, pointed and said: "Korsh."

Typhon waved back. "Wonderful!" His pleasure was communicated as clearly as a handshake.

It was then that Niall recalled that there are more direct ways of conveying insights than through words, and realized that communicating the secret might be less difficult than he had thought.

Eight hours later, in the early hours of the morning, Niall awoke from a vivid dream about the Magician.

He was back in the laboratory in Shadowland. It no longer smelled of blood because the walls and ceiling had been washed, and were still wet. The room was full of ghosts, including troglas and four-legged graddiks. The Magician was not among them, but when he suddenly spoke, his voice was clearly recognizable. It said: "Help me."

"Where are you?"

"I don't know. The boca took away my life body, and now I am lost."

The word "lost" filled Niall with a wholly unexpected sense of compassion. It conjured up emptiness and loneliness.

"What can I do?"

"Ask Typhon to perform the ceremony to lay me to rest."

"Does he know what to do?"

"Yes. He did it for my father."

Niall said: "I promise I will give him your message."

"Tell him twenty-one days. It must be within twenty-one days, or I shall die the second death."

Then Niall woke up. The room was full of moonlight, for it was the night before the full Moon. Outside, the city was so silent that he could hear the loud ticking of the new town clock on the other side of the square.

Ever since the events of two days ago, Niall had thought about the death of the Magician, and his own part in it, with a certain satisfaction. That was quite simply because he thought of him as a monster who deserved to be punished for his ruthlessness.

But now, suddenly, he could see that being in a state of eternal forgetfulness was not punishment, since the Magician would have no idea why he was being punished.

No longer sleepy, Niall lay on his back and thought about the dream. Was it really a plea for help? Or was it inspired by all their talk about the karvasid just before Niall had said good night and come to bed?

Twenty-one days . . . What if Typhon did not want to return within twenty-one days? He certainly seemed to be enjoying himself.

Then Niall noticed that the Magician's crystal globe was now lying on the carpet. When he had climbed into bed, it had been on the circular table by the open window. Yet there was not even the faintest breeze.

At that point, Niall decided that a promise, even one made to a ghost in a dream, should be honored, and resolved to tell Typhon about his dream over breakfast.

He immediately experienced a curious sense of peace, and sank into a dreamless sleep.

About the Author

Colin Wilson is the author of more than eighty books, including *The Outsider* and *From Atlantis to the Sphinx*. His work ranges from existential philosophy, psychology, and criminology to the paranormal, fiction, and plays. He resides in Cornwall, England, with his wife, Joy.

Hampton Roads Publishing Company

. . . for the evolving human spirit

Hampton Roads Publishing Company
publishes books on a variety of subjects,
including metaphysics, health, integrative medicine,
visionary fiction, and other related topics.

For a copy of our latest catalog, call toll-free
(800) 766-8009, or send your name and address to:

Hampton Roads Publishing Company, Inc.
1125 Stoney Ridge Road
Charlottesville, VA 22902

e-mail: hrpc@hrpub.com
www.hrpub.com